PRAISE FOR ZOM-B:

"Horror with a social conscience...This compelling page-turner builds steadily to the climax then throws the reader off the cliff with a twist that is impossible to see coming." —*VOYA*

"Shan packs in the bites, and he rips out enough entrails for even the most jaded zombie fan; the cliffhanger ending...closes on just the right note to leave the audience gnawing for more." —*Kirkus Reviews*

"A raw and deeply observant tale of a morally questionable kid trying, and usually failing, to move beyond the ingrained racism instilled by B's father. It is a brave move by Shan to posit such a bigoted hooligan as our protagonist." —*Booklist*

"Character development is impressive...and Shan executes the transition from normalcy to wholesale terror masterfully." —*Publishers Weekly*

THE
ZOM-B

CHRONICLES II

ZOM-B ANGELS

ZOM-B BABY

ZOM-B GLADIATOR

DARREN SHAN

Ⓛ Ⓑ LITTLE, BROWN AND COMPANY   NEW YORK   BOSTON

Collected edition copyright © 2015 by HOME OF THE DAMNED LIMITED
Zom-B Angels and *Zom-B Baby* text copyright © 2013 by HOME OF THE DAMNED LIMITED
Zom-B Gladiator text copyright © 2014 by HOME OF THE DAMNED LIMITED
Zom-B Angels and *Zom-B Baby* illustrations copyright © 2013 by Warren Pleece
Zom-B Gladiator illustrations copyright © 2014 by Warren Pleece
Excerpt text from *Zom-B Mission* copyright © 2014 by HOME OF THE DAMNED LIMITED
Zom-B Mission illustrations copyright © 2014 by Warren Pleece

Little, Brown and Company

Hachette Book Group
1290 Avenue of the Americas, New York, NY 10104
Visit us at lb-teens.com

Little, Brown and Company is a division of Hachette Book Group, Inc.
The Little, Brown name and logo are trademarks of Hachette Book Group, Inc.

The publisher is not responsible for websites (or their content) that are not owned by the publisher.

First Collected Edition Printing: September 2015
Zom-B Angels first published in the U.S. in July 2013 by Little, Brown and Company
Zom-B Baby first published in the U.S. in October 2013 by Little, Brown and Company
Zom-B Angels and *Zom-B Baby* first printed in Great Britain by Simon & Schuster in 2013
Zom-B Gladiator first published in the U.S. in January 2014 by Little, Brown and Company
Zom-B Gladiator first printed in Great Britain by Simon & Schuster in 2014

ISBN 978-0-316-30073-5

10 9 8 7 6 5 4 3 2 1

RRD-C

Printed in the United States of America

For:

She's slim and trim,
And she's not my mother,
It's Rosie Brock,
Could be no other!

my best men and ushers—thanks for accompanying
me into the deadliest arena in the world!

OBE (Order of the Bloody Entrails) to:
Phil Earle—gone, but only half-forgotten!!
Hallie Patterson, for nursing me
through a top-notch tour
"Lady" Jade Westwood

Dead good editors — Venetia GoZling
and Kate Zullivan

my heart goes out, as always, to the
ChriZtopher Little brainiacs

BY DARREN SHAN

THE THIN EXECUTIONER

ZOM-B SERIES

ZOM-B

ZOM-B UNDERGROUND

ZOM-B CITY

ZOM-B ANGELS

ZOM-B BABY

ZOM-B GLADIATOR

ZOM-B CIRCUS—A ZOM-B ENOVELLA

ZOM-B MISSION

ZOM-B CLANS

ZOM-B FAMILY

ZOM-B BRIDE

ZOM-B FUGITIVE

THE SAGA OF LARTEN CREPSLEY

BIRTH OF A KILLER

OCEAN OF BLOOD

PALACE OF THE DAMNED

BROTHERS TO THE DEATH

THE DEMONATA SERIES

LORD LOSS

DEMON THIEF

SLAWTER

BEC

BLOOD BEAST

DEMON APOCALYPSE

DEATH'S SHADOW

WOLF ISLAND

DARK CALLING

HELL'S HEROES

THE CIRQUE DU FREAK SERIES

A LIVING NIGHTMARE

THE VAMPIRE'S ASSISTANT

TUNNELS OF BLOOD

VAMPIRE MOUNTAIN

TRIALS OF DEATH

THE VAMPIRE PRINCE

HUNTERS OF THE DUSK

ALLIES OF THE NIGHT

KILLERS OF THE DAWN

THE LAKE OF SOULS

LORD OF THE SHADOWS

SONS OF DESTINY

CONTENTS

Zom-B Angels
1

Zom-B Baby
191

Zom-B Gladiator
355

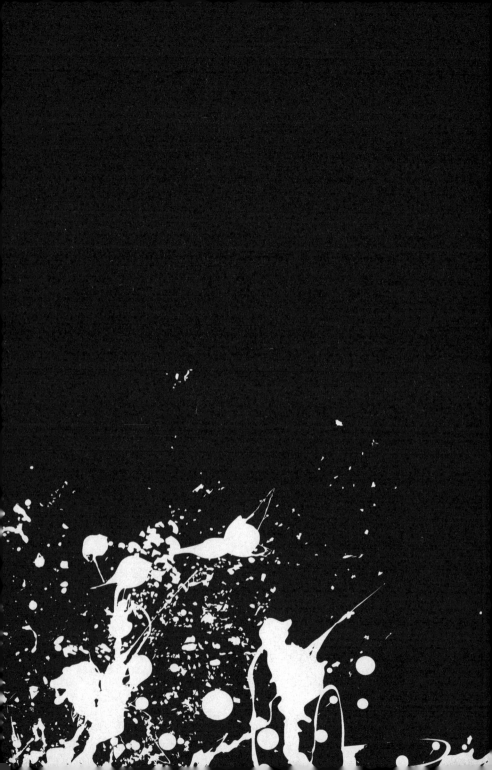

BOOK 4:

ZOM-B

ANGELS

THEN...

Becky Smith was at school the day the dead came back to life and took over the world. She tried to escape with a group of friends, but it wasn't meant to be. Her heart was torn from her chest and she became a zombie.

Several months later B recovered her senses in an underground military complex. The soldiers lumped her in with the zom heads, a pack of revitalized teenagers like her who had somehow regained their minds. They were told by their captors that they had to eat brains to stay conscious, and had a life expectancy of just a couple of years.

B would probably have remained a prisoner for the rest of her days, if not for the intervention of a monstrous clown called Mr. Dowling. He invaded with a team of mutants, set the zombies free and killed many of the staff. B didn't think he did it because he was pro-zombie—it looked to her like he did it for kicks.

Most of the zom heads were executed while trying to escape, but B made it out. She thought Rage might have gotten away as well. He was a self-serving bully who turned on his guards and proved just as clinical and merciless as they had been, casually killing one of the scientists before setting off on his own and warning his fellow zom heads not to follow him.

B roamed the streets of London for a while, mourning the loss of the normal world. It was a city of the dead, dotted with just a handful of living survivors. Some had chosen to stay, but others were trapped and desperately searching for a way out.

When B heard that the army was mounting a rescue operation, she went to offer herself to them, figuring they might be able to use her DNA to help other zombies recover their minds. But the soldiers saw her as a threat and tried to kill her. Once again the killer clown saved her. He slaughtered the humans, then asked her if she wanted to join him. B could think of nothing worse than teaming up with Mr. Dowling, his creepy mutants and an eerie guy with owl-like eyes who had shown an interest in her even before the zombies attacked. She told him to stick his offer.

Wounded, bewildered and alone, B wandered across the river and staggered into an old building, County Hall, once the home of local government, now a deserted shell. At least that was what it looked like. But as B stared out of a window at the river, a man called to her by name and said he had been waiting for her.

ONE

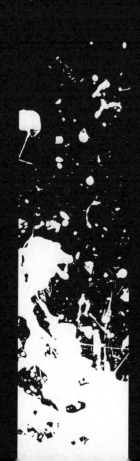

NOW...

I whirl away from the window that over-
looks the Thames. A man has entered the
room through a door that I didn't notice on
my way in. He's standing in the middle of
the open doorway, arms crossed, smiling.

My survival instinct kicks in. With a
roar, I hurl myself at the stranger, ignoring
the flare of pain in my bruised, broken
body. I curl my fingers into a fist and raise
my hand over my head as I close in on
him.

The man doesn't react. He doesn't even
uncross his arms. All he does is cock his
head, to gaze with interest at my raised
fist. His smile never slips.

I come to a stop less than a meter from the man, eyeing him beadily as my fist quivers above my head. If he'd tried to defend himself, I would have torn into him, figuring he was an enemy, as almost everybody else in this city seems to be. But he leaves himself open to attack and continues to smile.

"Who the hell are you?" I snap. He's dressed in a light gray suit, a white shirt and purple tie, and expensive-looking leather shoes. He has thin hair, neatly combed back, brown but streaked with gray. Calm brown eyes. Looks like he's in his forties.

"I am Dr. Oystein," he introduces himself.

"That supposed to mean something to me?" I grunt.

"I would be astonished if it did," he says, then extends his right hand.

"You don't want to shake hands with me," I sneer. "Not unless you want to end up with a taste for brains."

"I was an adventurous diner in my youth," Dr. Oystein says, his smile widening. "I often boasted that I would eat the flesh or innards of just about any creature, except for humans. Alas, ironically, I can now eat nothing else."

I frown and focus on his fingers. Bones don't stick out of them the way they poke out of every other zombie's, but now that I look closely, I see that the flesh at the tips is broken, a small white mound of filed-down bone at the center of each pink whorl.

"Yes," he says in answer to my unvoiced question. "I am undead like you."

I still don't take his hand. Instead I focus on his mouth. His teeth are nowhere near as jagged or as long as mine, but they're not the same as a normal person's either.

Dr. Oystein laughs. "You are wondering how I keep my teeth in such good shape, but there is no magic involved. I have been in this lifeless state a lot longer than you. One develops a knack for these things over time. I was brought up to believe that a gentleman should be neatly groomed and I have found myself as fastidious in death as I once was in life.

"Please take my hand, Becky. I will feel very foolish if you do not."

"I don't give a damn how you feel," I snort, and instead of shaking his hand, I listen closely for his heartbeat. When I don't detect one, I relax slightly.

"How do you know my name?" I growl. "How could you have been expecting me? I didn't know that I was coming to County Hall. I wandered in randomly."

Dr. Oystein shakes his head. "I have come to believe that nothing in life is truly random. In this instance it definitely was no coincidence that you wound up here. You were guided by the signs, as others were before you."

I think back and recall a series of spray-painted, z-shaped symbols with arrows underneath. I've been following the arrows since I left the East End, sometimes because they happened to be pointing the way that I was traveling, but other times deliberately.

"*Z* for zombie," Dr. Oystein says as he sees my brain click. "The signs mean nothing to reviveds, but what curious revitalized could turn a blind eye to such an intriguing mystery?"

"You know about reviveds and revitalizeds?"

"Of course." He coughs lightly. "In fact I was the one who coined the terms."

"Who are you?" I whisper. "*What* are you?"

Dr. Oystein sighs. "I am a scientist and teacher. A sinner and gentleman. A killer and would-be savior. And, if you will do me the great honor, I would like to be your friend."

The mysterious doctor waves his extended arm, once again inviting me to accept his hand. And this time, after a brief hesitation, even though I'm still suspicious, I lower my fist, uncurl my fingers and shake hands with the politely spoken zombie.

TWO

"You have a strange accent," I remark as Dr. Oystein releases my hand. "Where are you from?"

"Many places," he says, slowly circling me, examining my wounds. "My father was English but my mother was Norwegian. I was born in Norway and lived there for a while. Then my parents moved around Europe – my father had itchy feet – and I, of course, traveled with them."

I try not to jitter as the doctor slips behind me. If he's been concealing a weapon, he'll be able to whip it out and strike. My shoulders tense as I imagine him driving a long knife between them. But he doesn't attack, just continues to circle, and soon he's facing me again.

"I heard that your heart had been ripped out," he says. "May I see?"

"How do you know that?" I scowl.

"I had contacts in the complex where you were previously incarcerated. I know much about you, but I hope to learn more. Please?" He nods towards my top.

With a sigh, I grab the hem of my T-shirt and lift it high, exposing my chest. Dr. Oystein stares at the cavity on the left, where my heart once beat. Now there's just a jagged hole, rimmed by congealed blood and a light green moss.

"Fascinating," the doctor murmurs. "We zombies are all freaks of nature, each a walking medical marvel, but one tends to forget that. This is a reminder of our ability to defy established laws. You are a remarkable individual, Becky Smith, and you should be proud of the great wound which you bear."

"Stop it," I grunt. "You'll make me blush."

Dr. Oystein sniffs. "Not unless you are even more remarkable than the rest of us. Without a heart, how would your body pump blood to your pale, pretty cheeks?"

Dr. Oystein makes a gesture, inviting me to lower my T-shirt. As I do so, he steps across to the window where I was standing when he first addressed me. County Hall boasts one of the best views in the city. He looks out at the river, the London Eye, the Houses of Parliament and all the other deserted buildings.

"Such devastation," he mumbles. "You must have encountered

horrors beyond your worst nightmares on your way to us. Am I correct?"

I think about all of the corpses and zombies I've seen... Mr. Dowling and the people he tormented and killed in Trafalgar Square... his army of mutants and his bizarre sidekick, Owl Man... the hunters who almost killed me... Sister Clare of the Order of the Shnax, the way she transformed when I bit her...

"You're not bloody wrong," I wheeze.

"The world teeters on the brink," Dr. Oystein continues. "It has been dealt a savage blow and I am sure that most of those who survived believe that there is no way back, regardless of what the puppets of the military might say in their radio broadcasts."

"You've heard those too?"

"Oh yes. I tune in whenever I am in need of bittersweet amusement." He looks back at me. "There are many fools in this world, and it is no crime to be one of them. But to try and carry on as normal when all around you has descended into chaos... to try to convince others that you can restore order by operating as you did before... That goes beyond mere foolishness. That is madness and it will prove the true downfall of this world if we leave these people to their sad, petty, all-too-human devices.

"There *is* hope for civilization as we once knew it. But if the living are to rise again, they will need our help, since only the conscious undead stand any sort of chance against the brain-hungry legions of the damned."

Dr. Oystein beckons me forward. I shuffle towards him slowly, not just because of the pain, but because I've almost been mesmerized by his words. He speaks like a hypnotist, slow, assured, serious.

When I join him at the window, Dr. Oystein points to the London Eye, turning as smoothly and steadily as it did when thousands of tourists flocked there every day.

"I consider that a symbol of all that has been lost but which might one day be restored," the doctor says. "We keep it going, day and night, a beacon of living hope in this city of the dead. But no ordinary human could operate the Eye—they would be sniffed out and besieged by zombies. We, on the other hand, can. The dead will not bother us, since we are of no interest to them. That lack of interest is our strength and humanity's only hope of once again taking control of this planet.

"You are not the first revitalized to find your way here," Dr. Oystein goes on. "There are others – weary, battered warriors – who have crawled through the streets of bloodshed and nightmares in search of sanctuary and hope, following the signs as you did."

"Are you talking about zom heads?" I ask.

"Yes," he says. "But we do not use that term here. If you choose to stay with us and work for the forces of justice and mercy, you will come to think of yourself as we do, not as a zom head but an *Angel*."

I snort. "With wings and a harp? Pull the other one!"

"No wings," Dr. Oystein smiles. "No harp either. But an Angel nonetheless." He moves away from the window, towards the door. "I have much to show you, Becky. You do not have to accompany me – you are free to leave anytime that you wish, and always will be – but, if you are willing, I will take you on a tour and reveal some of the many secrets of the newly redefined County Hall."

I stare at the open doorway. It's shadowy in the corridor outside. There could be soldiers waiting to jump me and stick me in a cell again.

"Why should I trust you?" I ask.

Dr. Oystein shrugs. "I could tell you to listen to your heart, but…"

The grisly joke eases my fears. Besides, there's no way I could turn back now. He's got me curious and, like a cat, I have to follow my nose and hope it doesn't lead me astray.

"All right, doc," I grunt, limping over to him and grinning, as if I haven't a care in the world. "You can be my guide. Just don't expect a tip at the end."

"I will ask for no tip," he says softly. "But I *will* ask for your soul." He smiles warmly as I stiffen. "There's no need to be afraid. When the time comes, I believe you will give it to me gladly."

And with that cryptic remark, he leads me out of the room of light and into the vast, dark warren beyond.

THREE

"This is an amazing building," Dr. Oystein says as we wander through a series of long corridors, popping into massive, ornately decorated rooms along the way. "Four thousand people worked here at its zenith. To think that it is now home to no more than a few dozen…" He makes a sighing sound.

"I came here a few times when I was younger," I tell him. "I went on the Eye, visited the aquarium and the London Dungeon, hung out in the arcade, ate at some of the restaurants. My dad brought us up one New Year's Eve for the fireworks. We were in line for ages to get a drink from a shop nearby. Worth it though—it was a cool show."

Dr. Oystein pushes open a door to

reveal a room with a handful of beds. They haven't been made up and I get the sense that nobody is using them.

"I had no idea how many revitalizeds would find their way to us," he says. "I hoped for many, feared for few, but we prepared for an influx to be on the safe side. There are many rooms like this, waiting for teenagers like you who will in all likelihood never come."

I frown. "Why just teenagers? Don't you accept adults too?"

"We would if any came, but adult revitalizeds are rare."

"Why?" I ask.

"I will explain later," he promises.

He closes the door and pushes on. After a while the style of the corridors and rooms changes and I realize we've crossed into one of the hotels that were part of County Hall before the zombie uprising.

"Oh, for the simple comforts of life," Dr. Oystein says drily as we check out a suite that's bigger than my family's old flat in the East End. "Did you ever stay in a hotel like this, Becky?"

"No. And it's B," I tell him. "That's what everybody calls me."

"Is that what you prefer?"

"Yeah."

He nods. "As you wish. We all have the right to choose our own name."

"How about you?" I counter. "Dr. Oystein's a mouthful. What's your first name?"

He smiles. "Oystein *is* my first name. It has been so long since I used my surname that I have almost forgotten what it is."

We double back on ourselves but take a different route. This place is a maze. My head is spinning as I try to chart all the twists and turns, in case I need to make a quick getaway. The doctor seems like a nice old bloke, but I'm taking nothing for granted.

"How many rooms are there?" I ask.

"Far too many to count," Dr. Oystein says. "We use very few of them. It's a pity we cannot make more use of the space, but we do not have the numbers at the moment. Maybe one day we can bring it fully back to life, but for the time being we must rattle around in it."

"Why don't you move somewhere smaller?"

Dr. Oystein coughs as if embarrassed. "To be honest, I always had a fondness for County Hall. When I was casting around for a base, this was my first choice. The Angels seem to share my love for the building. I hope that it will come to feel like home for you over time, as it has for us."

"So who lives here with you?" I ask. "You haven't told me about the setup yet, how you came to be here, who your Angels are, how you plan to save the world."

"Those questions will all be answered," he assures me. "We do not keep secrets from one another. We are open in all that we do. But there is no need to rush. As you adjust and settle in, we will reveal more of our work and background to you, until you know as much about us as I do."

I don't like being told to wait, but this is his gig. Besides, I'm exhausted and my brain hurts, so I don't think I could take in much more anyway. There's one thing that does disturb me though, and I want to bring it up before pushing on any farther.

"How come there are no regular zombies here? Every other big, dark building that I've seen has been packed with them."

"I had already recruited a small team of Angels before I established a permanent base," he says. "We drove out the reviveds before we moved in."

"That must have been messy."

"It was actually the easiest thing in the world," he replies. "With their sharp sense of hearing, reviveds – like revitalizeds – are vulnerable to high-pitched noises. So we simply installed a few speakers and played a string of high notes through them, which proved unbearable for those who had taken up residence. They moved out without any protest, then we slid in after them and shored up the entrances."

"I got in without any hassle," I remind him.

"We saw you coming on our security cameras," he says. "We switched off the speakers – we repositioned them around the building once we had moved in, and normally play the noises on a constant loop, to keep stray reviveds at bay – and made sure a door was open when you arrived."

We come to a huge room and I catch my first glimpse of what I assume are some of Dr. Oystein's Angels. There's a small group of them at the center of the room, in a boxing ring, sparring. They're my sort of age, no more than a year or two older or younger than me.

"They spend most of their days training," Dr. Oystein says.

"For what?"

"War."

I swivel to look at him, but he doesn't return my gaze.

"The years ahead will be hard," he says quietly. "We will be tested severely, and I am sure at times we will be found wanting. We face many battles, some of which we are certain to lose. But if we prepare as best we can, and have faith in ourselves and the justness of our cause, we will triumph in the end."

I snort. "I hate to burst your bubble, doc, but if those Angels are like me, you'd better tell them to get their arses in gear. In another year or two we'll be pushing up daisies. You can't win a war if all your troops are rotting in the grave."

Dr. Oystein frowns. "What are you talking about?"

"Our limited lifespan. We've only got a year and a half, two years max. Then our senses will dissolve, our brains will melt and we'll be dead meat. If you've got a war you want to win, you'd better crack on and –"

"You were told many things when you were a prisoner," Dr. Oystein interrupts. "Some were true. Some, you must surely know, were not. Your captors wanted to bend you to their will. They told you lies to dampen your spirit, to break it, to make you theirs."

23

I stare at him, hardly daring to believe what he's telling me. "You mean it was bullshit about me only having a year or two to live?"

"Of the highest grade," he smiles.

"I'm not going to die soon?" I cry.

"You are already dead," he says.

"You know what I mean," I groan. "My brain's not going to pop and leave me truly dead?"

"Far from it."

I clench my fingers tight and give the air a victory punch. "Bloody *YES*, mate! You've made my day, doc. I was ready to accept an early end, but as crap as my excuse for a life is, I'd rather this than no life at all."

"Most of us share your view," he chuckles, then grows serious. "But they did not tell you a total lie. We do not age the same way that humans do. Our lifespan, for want of a better term, is not what an average human might expect."

"So it was half true," I growl. "Those are the best sort of lies, I guess. Go on then, doc, hit me with the bad news. I can take it. How long do I have? Twenty years? Ten? Five?"

"We cannot be absolutely certain," he says. "I have run many tests and made a series of predictions. But we have no long-term data to analyze, and will not have for many decades to come. There are all sorts of genetic kinks of which I might be ignorant."

"Your guess is better than mine," I smile. "I won't blame you if you're off by a few years."

25

"Very well. I won't tease you with a dramatic buildup. As I said, this is a rough estimate, but based on the results of my tests to date, I think we probably have a life expectancy of between two and three thousand years.

"And no," he adds before I can say anything, "I'm not joking." He leans in close, his eyes wide as I stare at him, stunned and numb. "So, B Smith, what do you think of this *crap life* now?"

FOUR

I'm in shock for ages. To go from thinking you have only months to live, to being told you might be hanging around for a couple of millennia…it's a cataclysmic leap and my mind whirls as we continue the tour.

We visit a kitchen where a good-looking, stylishly dressed woman with a big smile is scraping brains from inside severed human heads and dumping them in a mixing bowl. Dr. Oystein introduces us, but I forget the woman's name even before we leave the room.

"Some of the heads are delivered to us from people who die of natural causes in human compounds," he says. "We have contacts among the living who view us as allies, and they give us what they can. But

most come from fresh corpses that we found in morgues or dug up not long after the first zombie attacks. I knew brains would be a pressing issue, so I made them my number-one priority. For a couple of weeks, grave-robbing was practically our full-time occupation."

He tells me how he's trying to create a synthetic substitute that will give us the nutrients we need, so that we don't have to rely on reaping brains from dead humans in the future, but I'm barely listening.

More bedrooms, another training center – again, I only spot teenagers – and the impressive council chamber. Dr. Oystein starts waffling on about the history of County Hall, but I can't focus. I keep thinking about the centuries stretching out ahead of me, the incredibly long life that has been dropped on me without any warning.

Halfway down another of the building's long corridors, I stop and shake my head. "This is crazy," I shout. "You're telling me I'm gonna live at least twenty times longer than any human?"

"Yes," Dr. Oystein says calmly.

"How the hell can anyone last that long?"

He shrugs. "A living person could not. But we are dead. We do not age as we used to. If we take care of our bodies, and sustain ourselves by eating brains, we can defy the laws of living flesh."

"Then what's to say we won't live forever?" I challenge him. "Where did you pull two or three thousand years from? If we don't age –"

"We *do* age," he cuts in smoothly. "I said that we do not age as we used to, but we definitely age, only at a much slower rate. Our external appearance will not change much, except for scarring, wrinkling and discoloring. Our internal organs are to all intents and purposes irrelevant, so even if they crumble away, it won't really matter.

"Only our brains are susceptible to the ravages of time. From what my tests have revealed, they are slowly deteriorating. If they continue to fail at the rate I have noted in the subjects that I have been able to assess, we should manage to hold ourselves together for two or three thousand years. But it could be less, it could be more. Only time will tell."

I shake my head again, still struggling to come to terms with the revelation.

"Try not to think about it too much," Dr. Oystein says kindly. "I know it is a terrifying prospect—a long life seems enviable until one is presented with the reality of it and has to think of all those days and nights to come, how hard it will be to fill them, to keep oneself amused for thousands of years. And it is even harder since we do not sleep and thus have more time to deal with than the living.

"But as with everything in life, you will learn to cope. I'm not saying it will be easy or that you won't have moments of doubt, but I suggest you turn a blind eye to your longevity for now. You can brood about it later." He sighs. "There will be plenty of time for brooding."

"Why tell me about it at all if that's the case?" I snap.

Dr. Oystein shrugs. "It is important that you know. It is one of the first things that I tell my Angels. Our approach to life – or our semblance of it – differs greatly depending on how much time we have to play with."

"Come again?" I frown.

"If you think you have only a year to live, you might behave recklessly, risking life and limb, figuring you have little to lose. Most people treat their bodies with respect when they realize that they may need them for longer."

"I suppose," I grumble.

Dr. Oystein smiles. "You will see the brighter side of your circumstances once you recover from the shock. But if it still troubles you, at least you have the comfort of knowing that you will not have to go through this alone. We are all in the same boat. We will support one another over the long decades to come."

"All right," I mutter, and we start walking again. My mind's still whirling, but I try to put thoughts of my long future on hold and focus on the tour again. It's hard – I have a sick feeling in my stomach, like I get if I go too long without eating brains – but the doctor's right. I can obsess about this later. If I try to deal with it now, I'll go mad thinking about it. And madness is the last thing I want to face in my state. I mean, who fancies spending a couple of thousand years as a slack-jawed, drooling nutter!

FIVE

The tour draws to its conclusion shortly after our conversation in the corridor. We pass through one of the large courtyards of County Hall – I remember seeing them from up high when I went on the Eye in the past – and into a room that has been converted into a lab, lots of test tubes and vials, some odd-looking machines beeping away quietly in various places, pickled brains and other internal organs that have been set up for dissection and examination.

"This is not my main place of work," Dr. Oystein says. "I maintain another laboratory elsewhere in the city. I had a string of similar establishments in different countries around the world, but I do not know what has become of them since the downfall."

He looks at me seriously. "I told you that we keep no secrets from one another here, and that is the truth, with one key exception. The other laboratory is where I conduct the majority of my experiments and tests, and where I keep the records of all that I have discovered over the years."

"You mean you haven't just started researching zombies since the attacks?"

"No. I am over a hundred years old and have been studying the undead since the mid-1940s." As I gape at him, he continues as if what he's told me is no big deal. "I have a team of scientists who have been working with me for many years. They are based at my main research center. I lost a lot of good men and women when the city fell, but enough survived to assist me in my efforts going forward.

"I dare not reveal the location of that laboratory to anyone. It is not an issue of trust but of fear. There are dark forces stacked against us. You are aware of the one who calls himself Mr. Dowling?"

"You know about the clown?" I gasp.

Dr. Oystein nods somberly. "I will tell you more about him later. For now, know only that he is our enemy, the most dangerous foe we will ever face. He yearns for the complete destruction of mankind. I guard the secrets of deadly formulas that Mr. Dowling could use to wipe out the living. If I told you where my laboratory was, and if he captured you and forced the information from you…"

I smile shakily. "That's all right, doc. I know what a bastard he is. You don't need to feel bad about not sharing."

"Yet I do," he mutters glumly, then grimaces. "Well, as limited as this laboratory is, it does feature one of my more refreshing inventions, a device which is literally going to blow your mind. Come and see."

Dr. Oystein quickens his pace and leads me to four tall, glass-fronted cylinders near the rear of the lab. Each is about three meters high and one meter in diameter. One is filled with a dark gray liquid that looks like thick, gloopy soup.

"I have a complicated technical name for these," Dr. Oystein says. "But one of my American Angels nicknamed them Groove Tubes some years ago and it stuck."

"What are they for?" I ask.

"Recovery and recuperation." The doctor pokes one of the deep gashes on my left arm and I wince. "As you will have noticed, our bodies do not generate new cells to repair cuts and other wounds. Our only natural defense mechanism is the green moss which sprouts on open gashes. The moss prevents significant blood loss and holds strands of shredded flesh together, but it is not a curative aid. Broken bones don't mend. Cuts never properly close. Pain, once inflicted, must be endured indefinitely."

"Tell me about it," I huff, having been hunched over and limping since Trafalgar Square.

"We can endure the pain when we have to," Dr. Oystein continues, "but it is a barrier. It is hard to focus when you are racked with agony. Like you, I have suffered much in my time. I realized long ago that I needed to find some way to combat the pain, to ensure it did not distract me from my work. I conducted many experiments and eventually came up with the Groove Tube. In the fledgling world of zombie chemistry, this probably ranks as the most significant invention to date. If the undead awarded Nobel Prizes..."

He smiles at the absurdity of the suggestion, then clears his throat. "Although the technology is complicated, the results are easy to explain. The liquid inside a Groove Tube is a specially formulated solution that uses modified brain cells as its core ingredient. If you are undead and you immerse yourself, the solution stimulates some of the healing functions of your body.

"Your lesser wounds will heal inside the Tube. The cuts on your elbows and head will scab over, as they would have when you were alive. It won't have much of a visible effect on the hole in your chest, but it will patch up the worst damage and you will not bleed so freely.

"There are other benefits. Broken bones will mesh. Your eyesight will improve and your eyes will sting less. You will not need to use drops so often. You might get a few of your taste buds back, but that sensation won't last for long. You will come out feeling energetic and the pain will be far less than it currently is."

"Sounds like a miracle cure," I mutter, suspicious, as I always am, of anything that sounds too good to be true.

"A miracle, perhaps," he says, "but not a full-blown cure. The effects are not permanent. If a bone has broken, the gel holding the two parts together will start to fail after a few years. All wounds will reopen in time. But you can immerse yourself again when that happens and be healed afresh. It is too soon to know if we can use the Tubes indefinitely, but so far I have not noticed any limit on the number of times that they can work their wonders on a given body."

"Fair enough, doc. You've sold me." I start to strip.

"One moment," he stops me. "I want you to be fully aware of what you are getting yourself into."

"I knew it," I scowl. "What's the catch?"

"We cannot sleep," Dr. Oystein says. "Wakefulness is a curse of the undead and I have been unable to find a cure for it. But when we enter a Groove Tube, we hallucinate."

"Go on," I growl.

"It is like getting high," the doctor murmurs, staring longingly at the gray gloop inside the cylinder. "As the solution fills your lungs — you cannot drown, so it will not harm you, although we'll have to pump you dry when we pull you out — you will start to experience a sense of deep, overwhelming bliss. You will have visions and your brain will tune out the world beyond the Tube, as you enter a dreamlike state."

"Sounds good to me," I beam.

"It *is* good," he nods. "But there are dangers which you should be aware of. One is the addictive nature of the experience. You will not want to leave. I could let my Angels soak in the Tubes regularly, but I do not. They are reserved for the treatment of serious wounds. The main reason I insist on that is to help them avoid becoming addicted. You may wish to reenter the Tube at the end of the process, but I will not permit it. They are for medicinal – not recreational – purposes only."

"Understood. And the real kicker?"

Dr. Oystein nods. "You are sharper than most of my Angels, B. Yes, I have held back the real kicker, as you call it, until the end." He pauses. "It will take two or three weeks for your wounds to fully heal. During that time you will be unaware of all that is happening around you. It would be a simple thing for me or anyone else to attack you while you are in that suspended state. You will have no way of defending yourself. If someone wanted to cut your head open and pulp your brain, it would be child's play. Or we could just leave you inside the Tube and never pull you out—if we did not haul you clear, you would bob up and down inside the solution for the rest of your existence, never fully waking. Once you succumb to the allure of the Groove Tube, you will be at our mercy."

I stare at the doctor long and hard. "That's a pretty big ask, doc."

"Yes," he says.

"Can I wait to make my decision?"

"Of course."

"Will anything bad happen to me if I choose not to enter the Tube?" I watch him warily for his answer, ready to bolt for freedom if I get the feeling that he's spinning me a lie.

"If you mean will your wounds worsen, no. You will have to endure the pain, but that is all."

I nod slowly, thinking it over. Then I decide to hell with it. Maybe I'm a fool, but I want to trust this guy. I *need* to trust him. I've felt so alone since I came back from the dead, even when I've been surrounded by others. Without someone to believe in, what's the point of going on?

"All right, doc," I sigh as I take off the rest of my clothes. "I can't be bothered waiting. I'm hopping in. You might have to adjust the temperature for me though—I like my bathwater *hot*."

SIX

GggggggggROOOOOOOOveeeeeeeeee!!!!!!!

SEVEN

Next thing I know, I'm flopping about on the floor of the lab like a dying fish, vomiting up liquid. The room seems extraordinarily bright. I moan and start to shield my eyes with a hand. Before I can, someone tosses a towel over my head and says something. I can't hear them clearly, so I slide my hand in under the towel to stick a finger in my ear and clear it out.

"No!" comes a roar loud enough to penetrate even my clogged ear canals. "You might damage your ear with the bone sticking out of your finger."

I'd forgotten about the bones. Lowering the hand, I try to ask the person their name, but my throat and mouth are full of the solution from the Tube.

"Keep as still as you can," a boy says. "We know what we're doing."

Someone lifts the towel and gently runs a cotton bud round the inside of my left ear, then my right. A plastic tube slides up under my chin and I'm instructed to feed it down my throat.

"I know it's gross," a girl says, "but we have to pump your stomach dry, otherwise you won't be able to talk."

With a grimace, I stick the tube into my mouth — it's tricky because my teeth sprouted while I was blissed out — and force it down. When it can't play out anymore, I hold it in place while a machine is switched on, and keep my lips open wide while liquid is pumped out of my stomach.

After several minutes there's nothing left to come up. The machine is turned off and I'm handed a pair of sunglasses.

"Put them on," the girl tells me. "The room will still seem brighter than normal, but you'll soon adjust."

I slip on the shades and tug the towel from my head. Squinting against the light, I spot the boy and girl, both a bit younger than me.

"*Groo gar goo?*" I gurgle.

"Take it easy," the boy says, picking up a smaller hooked tube. "Your lungs are still full. We have to slide this down into them. Are you ready?"

"*Ghursh.*"

"I'll take that as a yes," he smirks, and carefully slides the tube into my mouth. He has a flashlight attached to a headband, the sort

44

that surgeons use, and he shines it between my teeth as he searches for the correct opening. When he finds it, he begins to poke the tube down my windpipe. It's a horrible feeling and my instinct is to grind my teeth together and snap through the tube. But I know these guys are trying to help, so I fight the urges of my body.

The boy switches on the machine again and pumps my lungs dry. When he turns it off and withdraws the tube, I cough and scowl at the pair.

"Ish that iht?" I mumble, words still coming out garbled because of my oversized teeth, but a lot clearer than before.

"Just about," the girl giggles. "But the pump doesn't force out every last drop. The liquid will have made its way through your digestive system. We need to give you an enema."

"What'sh that?" I ask.

She holds up a third tube. "We need to insert this up your..." She nods at my bum.

"Ihf you try to shtick that fhing ihn me, I'll ram iht up *your* hole!" I bark, slapping the tube from her hands.

"Fine," she shrugs. "You can wear a nappy for the next week instead."

I swear and glare at the grinning pair. "Mahke him turn his bahck," I growl.

"Like it's something I *want* to see," the boy snorts, and turns away, focusing his attention elsewhere.

45

I've never had an enema before, and I don't ever want one again, and that's all I'm saying about that!

When the girl has cleared me out, she leads me to a shower and I hose myself down, washing off the gray gunk from the Groove Tube. When I step out, she hands me a robe. I pull it on gratefully. Even though I'm cleaner than I've ever been, I feel strangely soiled.

"No need to be ashamed," the girl says as I towel my hair dry. "We all have to suffer this when we come out of the Groove Tubes. It's a small price to pay. Look at your arms."

I roll up the sleeves of the robe and study my elbows. When I slid into the Tube, the flesh around them had been ripped to pieces, the bone exposed in places. Now they look almost as good as new. Scarred, pink flesh, but whole and healthy-looking.

I part the front of my robe and examine the hole in the left side of my chest. It's still an ugly, gaping wound, but it doesn't look as messy as it did. Some of the green moss has come away in the tank, and it's not as foresty as it was.

I close my robe again and stare at the glass-fronted cylinder. The liquid is being drained from it, but slowly. It's murkier than before, having absorbed dead cells, blood and all sorts of gunk from my body while I was bobbing up and down inside. I showered thoroughly before getting in, however many weeks ago it was, but there was still a lot of dirt to come out.

"Where'sh Docktohr Oyshteeen?" I ask.

"He's not here," the boy says. "He's been gone the last week or

more, at his other laboratory. He told us to apologize on his behalf. He would have liked to be here to welcome you back into the world, but his work called him away."

"It often does," the girl says, "so don't take it personally."

"I whon't. Who are yhou?"

"I'm Cian," the boy says.

"And I'm Awnya," the girl adds. "We're twins."

"The only twin revitalizeds in London as far as we know," Cian says proudly.

"Probably the world," Awnya beams.

"Congrachulayshuns," I mutter sarcastically.

"We're in charge of clothing, bedding, furniture and so on," Cian tells me. "If there's anything you need that you can't be bothered going to look for yourself, let us know and we'll do our best to get it for you, whether it's designer clothes, a certain brand of shoe or a specific type of hat."

"We got rid of your old clothes," Awnya says, "but we held on to the slouch hat in case it had sentimental value. You'll find it on a shelf in your bedroom."

"Thanksh."

My gaze returns to the Groove Tube, longingly this time. I don't remember much after Dr. Oystein helped me climb inside. I recall the feeling of the liquid oozing down my throat – surprisingly not as unpleasant as when I had to force it back up – but then I drifted off into a blissful state where everything seemed warm and right. It was like I used to feel when I'd lie in bed on a Sunday morning, having stayed up late to watch horror movies the night before, not asleep but not yet fully awake. The feeling of being somewhere comfortable and safe, the world not totally real, still part dreamy.

I smoked a bit of weed back in the day – Mum would have killed me if she'd known! – but I didn't try anything more exotic. Based on what friends of mine who had done harder drugs told me, the feeling I had inside the Groove Tube must have been a lot like going on a head trip. Part of me wants to crawl back inside and bliss out again, return to the land of dreams and stay there forever, escape this world of the living dead. But I recall what Dr. Oystein told me about only using the Tubes to cure injuries. Besides, that would be like committing suicide. This is a bad, mad world, but running away from it isn't the answer. Well, it's not *my* answer.

I'm about to ask the twins to show me to my room when I glance at the other Groove Tubes and come to a halt. One of the Tubes is occupied by a large teenager. He has a big head, hair cut close, small ears, beady eyes. Fat, rosy cheeks, a chunk bitten out of the left one. He looks like a real bruiser, and I know that in this case looks are definitely *not* deceptive.

The last time I saw this guy was in a corridor deep underground. He'd just killed a scientist and scooped the still-warm brain from the dead man's skull. He was a zom head like me and the others, but he took off solo, leaving the rest of us to rot. He cared only for himself and was prepared to kill his guardians and betray his friends as long as it suited his own selfish purposes.

He looks comical, floating in the Tube, naked, eyes open as they are on all zombies, but expression distant. He's unaware of everything, defenseless, at the mercy of Dr. Oystein and his Angels.

And me.

But I'm not prepared to show him mercy, just as he didn't show any to me, Mark or the other zom heads. This bastard deserves execution more than most, and I'm just the girl to do the world that small favor.

"*Rhage!*" I snarl, pressing my face up close to the glass of the Groove Tube. Then I step back and look around eagerly for a weapon to kill him.

EIGHT

"No, B," Cian snaps, and tries to pull me back.

I wrestle with the boy and throw him to the floor. Awnya rushes me, but I grab her by the throat, then slam her to the ground beside her brother. Good to see the old fighting touch hasn't deserted me.

The twins quickly and easily dealt with, I turn back towards the Groove Tube, fingers flexing, snarling viciously. But before I can focus, someone says, "Take one more step towards him and I'll fry you."

I pause and peer around the lab. At first I can't see anyone. Then he moves and I spot him, standing close to the door that opens onto the courtyard. He takes several strides towards me and his face swims into view. A burly man with brown hair and stubble, wearing a dark blue outfit that wouldn't look out of place on a security guard. The last time I saw him, he was in military fatigues.

"*Rheilly?*" I gape.

The soldier smiles tightly. "None other."

"What the hell are yhou doing here?"

"The same as usual—guarding those who don't deserve guarding."

Reilly stops a couple of meters from me. He's holding some sort of a gun, but it doesn't look like any I've seen before.

"Step away from the Tube, B."

"Shkroo yhou, arsh hohl," I snap.

His smile broadens. "That was one of the first things you said when we originally filed your teeth down, back when you revitalized. It's like we've come full circle. I feel nostalgic."

"Fhunny guy," I sneer, than tap the glass of the Groove Tube. "He killed Docktohr Sherverus."

"I know."

"Pohked his eye out, cut his head open and tuhcked in."

"I'm not a goldfish," Reilly sniffs. "I was there. I remember."

"Sho I'm gonna kill him. Retchribooshun."

"Don't make me laugh," Reilly snorts. "You hated Dr. Cerveris. His death didn't matter to you in the slightest."

I shake my head. "Yesh, I hated him. But I didn't whant to kill him. Rhage ish a shavage. Becaush ohf him, Mark and the othersh are dead."

52

"I know," Reilly says, softly this time. "That sucks, the way they slaughtered the revitalizeds. It's one of the reasons I cut my ties with Josh and the rest after they'd regained control of the complex. But Dr. Oystein offered Rage a home when he came here, wounded like you were, in need of sanctuary, even though he wouldn't admit it. Rage was dubious, especially when he saw you. He wanted to kill you, like you want to kill him. But Dr. Oystein protected you and promised to do the same for Rage while he was incapable of defending himself."

"Don't care," I growl. "Gonna kill him anywhay."

Reilly raises his gun.

"Don't tell me it'sh me ohr him," I groan.

"No," Reilly says. "I'm not going to kill you. This is a stun gun. It fires spiked electrodes into your flesh, then fries you with a burst of electricity that would bring down an elephant. You're tough, B, but this will floor you for at least half an hour. Trust me, you do *not* want to put yourself through that. However bad your enema felt, it's nothing in comparison with this."

"Yhou were whatching that?" I snarl.

"Don't worry," he grins. "I averted my gaze during the more sensitive moments. I've visited the great pyramids, Petra, the temples of Angkor Wat. Your bunghole doesn't rank high on my list of must-sees."

I laugh despite myself. "Yhou're a bashtard, Rheilly."

54

"Takes one to know one," he retorts. "Now step away from the Tube and let the twins escort you to your quarters."

"What ihf I shay shkroo the quahrters? What ihf I don't whant anything to do with idiotsh who give shelter to a monshter like him?"

Reilly shrugs. "You need the Angels a lot more than they need you. Dr. Oystein will be sad if you reject his offer of hospitality, but as for the rest of us, nobody will miss you."

I come close to leaving. I'm on the verge of telling Reilly that he can marry Rage if he loves him that much. Then Awnya steps up beside me and shakes her head.

"Don't do it, B. It's horrible out there. Cian and I were lucky—we had each other. But we were lonely until we came here. And scared."

"We saw terrible things," Cian murmurs. "We *did* terrible things." He pulls his sweater aside to reveal a deep, moss-encrusted bite mark on his shoulder. "We became monsters when we turned. Dr. Oystein doesn't care. He gave us a home, and he'll give you one too if you let him."

"But thish guy ish a bruhte!" I yell. "He'sh not like ush. He killed when he didn't need to and kept the brain for himshelf."

"Are you pissed because he didn't share Dr. Cerveris's brain with you?" Reilly chuckles.

"No," I sneer. "I'm pisshed becaush Mark was killed. Ihf Rhage had let the resht of ush eat, the othersh wouldn't have needed to kill Mark. Maybe Josh would have shpared them too."

55

"I doubt it," Reilly says. "I wasn't privy to the decisions that were made that day, but I think all of the zom heads were scheduled for execution once it became clear that we had to evacuate. They didn't dare let you guys run wild. I don't know why Josh let you go, but the others would have been eliminated no matter what."

"Maybe," I concede. "That doeshn't change the fact that Rhage did whrong."

"No," Reilly agrees. "It doesn't. But it's part of my job now to look after those who need help, regardless of anything they did or didn't do in the past. I might not like it – in fact forget about *might*, I *don't* – but we're playing by Dr. Oystein's rules here. Maybe he sees potential for good in Rage that you or I missed. Or maybe he's taking a gamble and will come to view him as the sly, turncoat killer that we both know and loathe. If he does, and he asks me to handle the situation, I'll be only too delighted to pay back Rage for what he did to Cerveris and the others, but –"

"Othersh?" I interrupt.

"Cerveris wasn't the only one he killed while he was breaking out," Reilly says. "I didn't have many friends in that place, but he murdered a couple of guys I knew who were good men, just trying to do their job. I've no sympathy for him."

"Then why don't you help me shettle the shcore?" I whine.

"Because I trust Dr. Oystein," Reilly says simply. "I trust his judgment even more than my own. I've only known him for a month and a bit, so maybe that's a crazy claim, but it's how I feel. I went along with orders underground because that was what I'd always done. Everything had gone to hell and I thought the only way to deal with the madness was to carry on as if it was business as usual.

"But I'm cooperating with Dr. Oystein because I truly believe that he can lead the living out of this mess, that he can help those of us who survived to find a better way forward. If he says that Rage has the same rights as the rest of the revitalizeds, who am I to question him?"

I swear bitterly, knowing I can't win this argument. My choice is clear—walk away and return to the chaos and loneliness of the undead city beyond these walls, or play along and see what Dr. Oystein has to say for himself when he returns.

"Thish ishn't ohver," I tell Reilly. "Rhage and I have unfhinished bishness."

"Sure you do," Reilly laughs. "Just don't try to sort it out while I'm guarding him—if we got into a fight and you scratched me, you'd turn me into a revived, and I don't think either of us wants that, do we?"

"Don't be sho shure about that," I jeer, showing him my fangs, but it's an idle threat. I'd hate to have his blood on my hands.

I give Reilly a long, slow stare. Then Cian and Awnya drag me out of the lab. I leave reluctantly, finding it hard to tear my gaze away from Reilly and the devious, deceitful creep bobbing up and down inside the gray, clammy solution of the Groove Tube.

NINE

I scowl and mutter to myself as I stomp through the courtyard. Cian and Awnya have to jog to keep up.

"You really like that guy then?" Cian jokes.

"He abahndhoned me and my fhriends," I growl. "Lehft ush to be killed. Called ush a bunch of looshers. He'sh shkum."

"Dr. Oystein will be able to help him," Awnya says confidently.

"He doeshn't need help," I sneer. "He needsh execyooshun."

I shake my head, sigh and slow down. We're still in the courtyard. I look up at the sky. It's a cloudy, gray day, I'm guessing late morning or early afternoon.

"Here," Cian says, handing me a small

metal file. I think it's one of the ones I was carrying when I arrived. "I was going to give you this in your room, but maybe you'd prefer it now."

"Thanksh." I set to work on my teeth – it's tricky without a mirror – and grind away at those that have sprouted the most. The twins wait patiently, saying nothing as bits of enamel go flying across the yard. When I feel halfway normal, I lower the file, run my tongue around my teeth and say my name and old address out loud. I'm still not perfect, but a lot better than I was before.

"How long was I in the Groove Tube?" I ask.

"Just over three weeks," Awnya says.

"Twenty-four days," Cian elaborates.

"*Twenty-four Days Later*," I say somberly, deepening my voice to sound like a movie announcer. The twins stare at me blankly. "You know, like *Twenty-eight Days Later*?" They haven't a clue what I'm talking about. "Didn't you watch zombie movies before all this happened?"

"No," Awnya says. "They scared me."

"And we always watched movies together," Cian says. "So if one of us didn't like a certain type of film, the other couldn't watch it either."

"That's why I never got to see any chick flicks," Awnya says, shooting her twin a dark look.

"Life's too short," Cian snorts. "Even if we live to be three thousand, it will still be too short as far as chick flicks are concerned."

"Well, I won't let you watch any zombie movies either," Awnya pouts.

"Like I want to watch any now," Cian laughs.

I study the twins. They're about the same height. Both have blond hair and fair skin. They look similar and are dressed in matching, cream-colored clothes. A chunk has been bitten out of Awnya's left hand, just above her little finger. I see bone shining through the green, wispy moss. In the daylight they look even younger than they did in the lab, no more than twelve or thirteen.

"Were you guys attacked at the same time?" I ask.

"Yeah," Cian says.

"But I got bitten first," Awnya says. "He could have escaped but he came back for me. The idiot."

"I wouldn't have bothered if I'd known you were going to tuck into me," Cian sniffs, rubbing his shoulder through the fabric of his sweater.

"She turned on you?" I smirk wickedly.

"It wasn't her fault," Cian says, quick to defend his sister. "She didn't know what she was doing. None of us did when we were in that state. At least she didn't rip my skull open, or that would have been the real end of me."

"Your nasty brain would have turned my stomach," Awnya says, and the twins beam at each other.

"Nice to see you don't bear a grudge," I note.

Cian shrugs. "What's done is done. Besides, this way we can

61

carry on together. I wouldn't have wanted to escape and live normally if it meant leaving Awnya behind. I'd rather be a zombie with her than a human on my own."

"Pass me the barf bag," I groan, but grin to let them know I'm only joking.

It starts to rain, so we step inside and the twins lead me to my bedroom.

"How long have you guys been here?" I ask.

"Ages," Awnya yawns. "We revitalized quickly, less than a week after we were turned."

"We were among the first to recover their senses," Cian boasts. "Dr. Oystein says we're two of his most incredible Angels."

I frown. "This place was open for business that soon after the attacks?"

"No," Awnya says. "We wandered for a couple of weeks before we noticed the arrows."

"That was a scary time," Cian says softly, and the pair link hands.

"Dr. Oystein was based in Hyde Park when we found him," Awnya continues. "He put up a tent in the middle of the park and that's where his first Angels joined him and sheltered. He was already working on modifying this place, but it was another few weeks before we were able to move in."

"Did he have Groove Tubes in Hyde Park?"

"He had one," Cian says, "but it was no good. There was a generator to power it, but the noise attracted reviveds. They kept attacking and knocking it out—they didn't like the sound. He wasn't able to mount a proper guard, so in the end he left it until we moved here."

"A couple of revitalizeds died because of that," Awnya says sadly. "They were so badly wounded, in so much pain, that they killed themselves."

"I've never seen Dr. Oystein look so miserable," Cian croaks. "If he could cry, I think he'd still be weeping now."

There's a long silence, broken only by the sound of our footsteps.

"How did you end up doing this?" I ask. "Taking people round and getting stuff for them?"

"We're good at it," Awnya smiles. "Dr. Oystein says we're like jackdaws—we can find a pearl anywhere."

"Our mum was a shopaholic," Cian says. "She dragged us everywhere with her. We got to be pretty good at finding our way around stores and tracking down items that she was interested in. When Dr. Oystein saw how quickly we could secure materials, he put us in charge of supplies. It didn't matter that we're two of the youngest Angels. He said we were the best people for the job."

"Of course he was probably concerned about us too," Awnya says. "Being so young, I think he was worried that we might not be as capable as the others, and he wanted to find something to keep us busy, so we didn't feel out of place."

"No way," Cian barks. "I keep telling you that's not the case. We train with the other guys and hold our own. Dr. Oystein could send us on missions if he wanted. We just happen to be better than anyone else at doing this."

Awnya catches my eye and we share a secret smile. Boys always want to think that they're able to do anything. We usually let them enjoy their fantasies. They're happier that way and do less whining.

"What sort of missions do the others go on?" I ask.

"Dull stuff mostly," Cian huffs, and I decide to leave it there for the time being, as it's obviously a sore point for him.

We come to a closed door and Cian pushes it open. We step into one of County Hall's many huge rooms. There are six single beds arranged in a circle in the center. The sheets and pillows on four of them have the crumpled look that shows they've been used recently. The other two have perfectly folded sheets and crease-free pillowcases.

There are three wardrobes, lots of shelving and two long dressing tables, one on either side of the room, with mirrors hanging on the walls above them, chairs set underneath.

A girl is sitting on one of the chairs, my age if not a bit older. She looks like an Arab, light brown skin, a plain blue robe and white headscarf. She's working on a model of the Houses of Parliament, made out of matchsticks. It looks pretty damn cool.

"Oh, hi, Ashtat," Awnya says. "We didn't know you were here."

The girl half waves at us without looking round.

"This is Becky, but she prefers B," Awnya presses on.

"Hush," Ashtat murmurs.

"What's your problem?" I growl.

Ashtat scowls at me. "I do not like being interrupted when I'm working on my models. You cannot know that, never having met me before, but the twins do. They should not have admitted you until I was finished."

"Like Awnya said, we didn't know you were here," Cian protests. "We thought you'd still be training with the others."

"I came away early today," Ashtat sniffs.

"Well, I'm here, so you'll have to live with it," I tell her, determined to make my mark from the start. If I let her treat me like a dog now, I'll have to put up with that all the way down the line.

Ashtat raises an eyebrow but says nothing and returns to her model, carefully gluing another matchstick into place.

"She's okay when she's not working on a model," Awnya whispers. "Let's come back later."

"No," I say out loud. "I'm staying. If she doesn't like that, tough. Which bed is mine?"

Awnya shows me to one of the spare beds. There's a bedside cabinet next to it. A few files for my teeth rest on top of the cabinet, along with the watches I was wearing, one of which was smashed to pieces in Trafalgar Square.

"Your hat's over there," Cian says, pointing to a shelf. The shelf is blue, and so are the two shelves above it. "The blue shelves are yours. You can stick anything you want on them, clothes, books, CDs, whatever. Half of that wardrobe" – he points to my left – "is yours too. You're sharing with a guy called Jakob. He doesn't have much, so you should have plenty of room."

"What about a bedroom of my own?" I ask.

Cian and Awnya shake their heads at the same time, the exact same way.

"Dr. Oystein says it's important for us to share," Cian says.

"It's the same for every Angel," Awnya says. "Nobody gets their own room."

I frown. "That's weird, isn't it?"

"It's meant to bring us closer together," Awnya says.

"Plus it stops people arguing about who gets the rooms with the best views and most space," Cian says.

"All right," I sniff. "I don't suppose I'll be using it much anyway. It's not like we need to sleep, is it?"

"No," Cian says hesitantly. "But Dr. Oystein prefers it if we keep regular hours. We act as we did when we were alive. Most of us get up about seven every morning, do our chores, train, hang out, eat, whatever. Then we come to bed at midnight and lie in the dark for seven hours, resting."

"It's good to have a routine," Awnya says. "It's comforting. You don't have to use your bed – nobody's going to force you – but if you want to fit in with the rest of us..."

"Sounds worse than prison," I grumble, but I'm complaining

just for the sake of it. Sinking on to the bed, I pick at my robe. "What about clothes?"

"We thought you might want to choose your own," Awnya says. "We can get gear for you if you have specific requests. Otherwise we'll take you out later and show you round some of our favorite shops."

"That sounds good," I smile. "I like to pick my own stuff."

"We figured as much," Awnya says smugly. "We'll come and collect you in an hour or so."

"What will I do until then?" I ask.

The twins shrug in unison.

"Get the feel of the place," Cian says.

"Relax," Awnya suggests.

"Keep quiet," Ashtat lobs in.

I give her the finger, even though she can't see me, and slip on the watch that works, an ultra-expensive model that I picked up in the course of my travels. As the twins leave, I start to ask them for the correct time, in case the watch is wrong, but they're gone before I can.

I sigh and stare around the room, at the bed, the furniture, the silent girl and her matchstick model. Then, because I've nothing better to do, and because I'm a wicked sod, I start filing my teeth again, as loudly as I can, treating myself to a mischievous grin every time Ashtat twitches and shoots me a dirty look.

TEN

The twins take me over the river and into the Covent Garden area. True to their word, they know all the best shops, not just those with the coolest gear, but those with the least zombies. The living dead don't bother us much once they realize we're like them, but it's still easier to browse in places where they aren't packed in like sardines.

I choose several pairs of black jeans, a variety of dark T-shirts, a few sweaters and a couple of jackets. New sunglasses too, and a baseball cap with a skull design that I spot in a window, for those days when I don't feel like the Australian hat that has served me well so far.

When it comes to shoes, the twins have a neat little device that screws into

the material, making holes for the bones sticking out of my toes to jut through. They measure my feet and bore the holes with all the care of professional cobblers.

"I like it," I grunt, admiring my new sneakers.

"Dr. Oystein invented that years ago," Cian tells me, pocketing the gadget. "He's like one of those crazy inventors you read about in comics."

"Only not actually crazy," Awnya adds.

"I don't know about –" I start to say, but a rapping sound on the shop window stops me.

We all instantly drop to our knees. There's another rap, a loud, clattering sound, but I can't see anyone.

"Do you think it's a revived?" I whisper.

"I don't know," Cian says.

"I hope so," Awnya croaks.

There's a long silence. I look around for another way out. Then there are two more raps on the glass. I spot a hand, low down and to the left, close to the open door. Another two raps. Then a series of short raps.

I roll my eyes and stand. "Very funny," I shout.

"Careful, B," Awnya moans. "We don't know who it is."

"But we know they have lousy taste in movies," I snort. "I recognize those raps. It's the theme from *Jaws*."

"And what's wrong with that?" a girl challenges me, stepping into view outside. "*Jaws* is a classic."

"Like hell it is," I reply. "A boring old film with lousy special effects, and hardly anyone gets killed."

"You don't know what you're talking about," the girl says, stepping into the shop. Four teenage boys appear and follow her in. The girl smiles at the twins. "Hey, guys, sorry if we frightened you."

"We weren't frightened," Cian says with a dismissive shake of his head, as if the very idea is offensive to him. "We were excited. Thought we were going to see some action at last."

"This is Ingrid," Awnya introduces the girl. "She's one of us."

"I figured as much." I cast an eye over the tall, blond, athletic-looking girl. She's dressed in leathers, a bit like those the zom heads used to wear when they were tormenting revived.

"You must be B," Ingrid says.

"Word travels fast," I smile.

"Not that fast," Ingrid says. "You were in a Groove Tube for almost a month."

My smile vanishes.

"What are you doing over here?" Cian asks. "Are you on a mission?"

"Yeah," Ingrid says.

"What sort of a mission?" I ask.

"The usual," she shrugs. "Looking for survivors. Searching for brains. Keeping an eye out for Mr. Dowling or any other intruders."

"We do this a lot," one of the boys says. "Not the most interesting of jobs, but it gets us out of County Hall."

"Sounds like fun," I lie, eager to see what they get up to. "Can I come with you?"

"Absolutely not," Ingrid says. "You haven't been cleared for action by Master Zhang."

"Aw, go on, Ingrid," Cian pleads. "If it's a normal mission, where's the harm? We can tag along too. We won't tell."

"I don't know," Ingrid says. "This is serious business. If anything happened to you..."

"It won't," Awnya says, as keen as her brother to get involved.

Ingrid checks with the rest of her pack. "What do you guys think?"

They shrug. "Doesn't matter to us," one of them says.

"Three mugs to throw to Mr. Dowling and his mutants if they turn up," another guy smiles. "Might buy us enough time to slip away."

"Bite me," I snap, and they all laugh.

"Okay," Ingrid decides. "You can keep us company for a while. The experience will be good for you. But don't get in our way, do what we tell you and run like hell if we get into trouble."

"How will we know?" Awnya asks nervously.

"Oh, trouble's easy to spot," Ingrid says with an icy smile. "It'll be when people start dying."

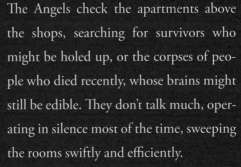

ELEVEN

The Angels check the apartments above the shops, searching for survivors who might be holed up, or the corpses of people who died recently, whose brains might still be edible. They don't talk much, operating in silence most of the time, sweeping the rooms swiftly and efficiently.

One of the guys opens all of the doors. He has a set of skeleton keys and can deal with just about any lock that he encounters.

"That's Ivor Bolton," Awnya whispers.

"Was he a thief when he was alive?" I ask.

"No. Master Zhang taught him."

"Who's that?"

"Our mentor," Awnya says. "He trains every Angel. You'll meet him soon."

"Do you all learn how to open locks?" I ask.

"Only those who show a natural talent for it," Cian says.

I stare at Ivor enviously. I hope I show that sort of promise. I'd love to be able to crack open locks and gain entrance to anywhere I wanted.

We explore more rooms, Ingrid and her team taking it slowly, carefully, searching for hiding places in wardrobes and under beds, tapping the walls for secret panels.

"Do you ever find people?" I ask as we exit a building and move on.

"Living people?" Ingrid shrugs. "Rarely, around here. Most of the survivors in this area moved on or died ages ago. We dig up the occasional fresh corpse, but mainly we're checking that the buildings are clear, that potential enemies aren't setting up base close to County Hall."

"What do you do if you find someone alive?" I ask.

She shrugs again. "It depends on whether they want to come with us or not. Many don't trust us and leg it. If they stop and listen, we tell them about County Hall and offer to take them to it, and from there to somewhere safe."

"That's one of the main things the Angels do," Awnya chips in. "We lead survivors out of London to secure camps in the countryside."

"It's not as easy as it sounds," Cian says.

"I bet not," I grunt, thinking of all the difficulties I faced simply getting from the East End to here. "Have you been on any of those missions yet?" I ask Ingrid.

"No," she sighs. "It's all been local scouting missions for us so far."

"Long may they continue," one of the boys mutters.

Cian scowls. "You don't want to tackle the harder challenges?"

"We're not suicidal," the boy snorts.

"Do you feel the same way?" I ask Ingrid.

She looks uncertain. "Part of me wants to be a hero. But some of the Angels who go on the more dangerous missions don't make it back."

We enter another building, a block of flats set behind a row of shops. We start up the stairs, the plan being to work our way down from the top. We're coming to the top of the fourth flight when Ingrid stops abruptly and presses herself against the wall.

"What's wrong?" I ask as she makes some gestures to the boys in her team.

"I think I heard something," she whispers.

"What?"

"I'm not sure. But we were here just a week ago. The place was deserted then." She points to Ivor and another of the boys and sends them forward to check.

We wait in silence for the pair to return. I feel out of my depth. I want a weapon, something to defend myself with. Although, looking round at the others, I see that they don't have any weapons either. I want to ask them why they came out without knives or guns, but I don't want to be the one to break the silence.

There's no sign of Ivor and his partner. Ingrid gives it a few minutes, then signals to the other two boys to go and look for them.

"This is bad," Cian groans quietly.

Ingrid fries him with a heated look and presses a finger to her lips.

The seconds tick away slowly. I keep checking the time on my watch. I want to push forward to find out what's happening, but I'm a novice here. I don't have the right to take control.

Ingrid waits a full five minutes, then swears mutely, just mouthing the word. She looks at me and the twins. Makes a gulping motion and licks her lips. Nods at us to backtrack and follows us down to the third floor.

"I don't know what's going on, but it can't be anything good," she says quietly. "Wait here for me, but no more than a couple of minutes. If I don't come back or shout to let you know that it's safe, return to County Hall and send others after us. *Do not* follow me up there, no matter what, OK?"

"I'm scared," Awnya whimpers.

Cian hugs her, but he looks even more worried than his sister.

Ingrid casts a questioning glance at me.

"I'll take care of them," I tell her.

She nods, then pads up the stairs.

I fix my gaze on my watch, willing the hands to move faster, wanting Ingrid and her crew to appear and give us the all-clear. But when that doesn't happen, and the time limit passes, I look up at the twins.

"We're leaving?" Cian asks.

I shake my head. "I can't. I've got to help them if I can. You guys go. Don't wait for me. Go now."

"No," Awnya says, horrified. "Come with us, B. You can't go up there by yourself."

"I have to. Don't argue. Get the hell out of here and tell the others what has happened."

"But…" She looks like she wants to cry, but being undead, she can't.

I start up as the twins start down. They go slowly, hesitantly, unable to believe that I'm following Ingrid and her team. I can barely believe it either. I must be mad. I hardly know them. I don't owe them anything. I should beat it with the twins.

But I don't. Maybe it's because I want to be a dumb hero. Or maybe it's because I don't think anything can be as scary as Mr. Dowling and his mutants. Or maybe it's the memory of Tyler Bayor, and what I did to him, that drives me on. Whatever the reason, I climb the steps, readying myself for battle, wondering what can have taken the Angels so swiftly and silently. I didn't even hear one of them squeak.

As I get to the top step and turn into the corridor, there's a sudden, piercing scream. It's Ingrid. I can't see her, but I hear her racing footsteps as she roars at me, "Run, B, run!"

"Bloody hell!" I yell, and I'm off, tearing down the stairs like a rabbit, running for my life, panting as if I had lungs that worked.

I catch up with the twins. They're making sobbing sounds.

"What –" Awnya starts to ask.

"No questions," I shout. "Just run!"

We hit the ground floor in a frightened huddle and spill out onto the street. Our legs get tangled up and all three of us sprawl across the road. I curse loudly and push myself to my feet. I grab Awnya and pull her up. I'm reaching for Cian, to help him, when I hear...

...laughter overhead.

I pause, a familiar sickening feeling flooding my guts, and look up.

Ingrid and the boys are spread across the third-floor landing, and they're all laughing their heads off.

"Suckers!" Ivor bellows.

"Run, fools, run," another of the boys cackles.

"Those sons of bitches," I snarl.

"What's going on?" Cian asks, bewildered. "Was it a joke?"

"Yeah," I snap. "And we fell for it."

"Oh, thank God," Awnya sighs. "I thought they'd been killed."

"Arseholes!" I roar at the five Angels on the landing, and give them the finger.

"You've got to be alert when you're out on a mission, B," Ingrid cries. "Wait. What's that behind us? No! Help us, B. Save us. There's a monster coming to..." She screams again, high-pitched and false.

"Yeah, laugh it up," I shout. "You won't be laughing when I stick my foot so far up your arse that..."

I shake my head, disgusted. But I'm disgusted at myself for falling for the trick, not at the Angels for pulling it. I should have known better.

"Come on," I grunt at the twins. "Let's leave them to their precious mission. We've better things to be doing back at County Hall."

"That wasn't nice, Ingrid," Awnya shouts.

"It was horrible," Cian agrees.

"I know," Ingrid says, looking contrite. Then she cackles again. "But it was *fun!*"

We head off, pointedly ignoring those who made fools of us, but I stop when Ingrid calls to me.

"B!"

I turn stiffly, expecting another insult.

"All joking aside, we respect that you came back to try and help."

"Yeah," Ivor says. "That took guts."

"We'll be seeing you again soon on a mission, I think," Ingrid says. "But next time you'll be one of us, in on the joke, not the butt of it."

"Whatever," I sniff.

I carry on back towards County Hall with the twins, as if what Ingrid and Ivor said meant nothing to me, but it's a struggle to maintain my scowl and not smile with stupid pride all the way.

TWELVE

We head back over the river. We can laugh about what happened in the building by the time we've crossed the bridge.

"We've got to play a joke on them now," Cian says. "Not straightaway, but within the next day or two. I'll think of something good. Maybe make them believe we're being attacked in the middle of the night, so that they panic and rush outside."

There's a strange buzzing in the air as we step off the bridge and start towards County Hall. "What's that?" I ask, grimacing as I draw to a halt.

"The speakers," Awnya says. "There are lots of them positioned around the area, to stop reviveds coming too close. They play this high-pitched noise all the time."

"We'll slip past them as we get closer to the building," Cian says. "The speakers all point away from it, so we'll be fine once we're through."

"How come I didn't hear it before?" I ask.

"Most of them have a small button that you can press to temporarily disable them," Awnya says. "I did that as we were leaving."

"I didn't notice."

Awnya shrugs. "No reason why you should have."

The twins show me the speakers as we get closer, and show me how to turn them off if I'm ever passing by myself. Then we head on into the building. They take me to my bedroom – I'm still not sure of the layout of the building, and where everything is – and I lay my gear on the shelves. There's no sign of Ashtat or any of the others.

The twins go off on their own for a while, leaving me to sort through my stuff and rest. Then they return and guide me to a dining room, close to the kitchen that I passed through earlier. Circular tables dot the room and groups of teenagers are clustered round them, chatting noisily. I do a quick count—there are just over thirty Angels.

"That's yours," Awnya says, pointing at a table of three boys and Ashtat.

"Are those my roommates?"

"Yes."

"What are they like?"

Awnya shrugs. "Ashtat can be moody, like you saw, but she's not so bad. Carl and Shane are OK. Jakob doesn't say much."

"Which one's he?" I ask.

"The thin, bald one."

"Carl's the dark-haired one," Cian adds. "Shane's the ginger."

I wince, recalling the fate of the last redhead zom head I knew, poor Tiberius.

"Go on over," Awnya says. "You don't want to eat with us. It'll look strange if you avoid them."

I nod. "Thanks for showing me around today."

"That's our job," Cian smirks.

"All part of the service," Awnya grins.

They slip away to their own table and I stare at the teenagers seated at mine. Carl's dressed in designer gear, real flash. Shane's wearing a tracksuit, but with a gold chain dangling from his neck, like a wannabe rapper. Jakob is wearing a white shirt and dark pants that look about two sizes too big for him. He's one of the unhealthiest-looking people I've ever seen, even by zombie standards. If I didn't know he was already dead, I'd swear he was at death's door.

And then there's Ashtat, dressed as she was when I saw her earlier. She spots me and says something to the others. They look at me curiously. I feel nervous, like I did on my first day of school.

"Sod it," I mutter. "They've got more reason to be scared of me than I have to be scared of them. I'm badass B Smith, and don't you forget it!"

With a scowl and a disinterested sniff, I cross the great expanse of the dining room, walking big, trying to act as if I belong.

"All right?" I grunt as I take a seat at the table.

Everyone nods but nobody says anything.

"I'm B."

"We know," Carl says, checking out my clothes. He nods again. I think I have his approval on the fashion front.

"Have the twins been taking care of you?" Shane asks.

"Yeah."

"They're good at that."

"Yeah." There's an uncomfortable silence. Then I decide to wade straight in. "Look, I don't like being told who my friends are. If it was up to me, I'd mix with the others, chat with different people, make up my own mind who I like and who I don't. I've already met Ingrid and her team, and I'd be happy to hang out with them. But I've been stuck with you lot for the time being, so we're just going to have to live with it."

Carl laughs. "You were never taught how to make a good first impression, were you?"

I shrug. "This is me. I won't pretend to be something I'm not."

"And what are you exactly?" Ashtat asks quietly.

"That's for you to work out," I tell her, meeting her gaze and not looking away.

"We've got a live one here," Shane chuckles.

"So to speak," Carl adds, then sticks out a hand. "Carl Clay. Kensington born and bred."

"I was wondering about the posh accent," I say as we shake hands.

"You should hear it when I'm trying to impress," he grins.

I haven't had much contact with people like Carl. Kids from Kensington didn't wander over east too much in my day, unless to see some grungy art gallery or to go shopping in Canary Wharf. I don't like his accent, and I don't want to like him either, but his smile seems genuine. I'll give him a chance—just not much of one.

"Shane Fitz," the ginger introduces himself. Shane doesn't offer to shake hands, just nods at me. I nod back. The chain-wearing Shane's the sort of bloke I'd have kicked the crap out of if our paths had crossed in the past. But times have changed. We're in the same boat now. As with Carl, I'll wait to pass judgment, see what he's made of.

"Ashtat Kiarostami," the girl says softly, tilting her head. "I would like to apologize if I was rude to you earlier. I don't like to be disturbed when I'm working on my models and sometimes I react more sharply than intended."

"Don't worry about it," I sniff, and look to the last of the four, the thin, bald kid with dark circles under his eyes.

"Jakob Pegg," he wheezes, and that's all I get out of him.

"So what's your story?" Carl asks, settling back in his chair. "Where are you from? How were you killed? When did you revitalize?"

I tell them a bit about myself, the East End, the attack on my school, regaining consciousness in the underground complex. They're intrigued by that and pump me for more information. They haven't heard of anything like it before.

"I bet Dr. Oystein was furious when you told him about that place," Shane remarks.

"He knew about it already," I reply. "He said he had contacts there."

Shane frowns. "It can't have been anything to do with Dr. Oystein. He wouldn't approve of revitalizeds being imprisoned and experimented on."

"Dr. Oystein's approval doesn't mean much to the army," Carl snorts. "They do what they like. He has to keep them on his side or they'll target us."

"Bring 'em on," Shane growls.

"Don't be stupid," Ashtat chides him. "They could level this place from the air. We would not even see who killed us."

"So how'd you get out of there?" Carl asks as Shane seethes at the injustice of the world.

"Ever hear of a guy called Mr. Dowling?"

Carl's eyes widen and Ashtat shivers. Shane pulls back from me, while Jakob leans forward, looking interested for the first time.

"I'll take that as a yes," I say drily.

"We have heard rumors," Ashtat murmurs, shivering again. "Terrible rumors. If we could sleep, we would all have nightmares about him."

"Speak for yourself," Shane snorts, but he looks uneasy.

I tell them how the crazed clown and his mutants invaded the complex and slaughtered many of the staff. But they didn't harm me or any of the other zom heads. Mr. Dowling freaked me out – I wince as I recount how he opened his mouth and spat a stream of live spiders into my face – but he set me free once he'd made me tremble and shriek.

"I don't get it," Shane frowns. "Why did he free you? I thought Mr. Dowling was our enemy."

"He is," Ashtat says. "But he must have use for the living dead too. His mutants are clearly not enough for him. He wishes to recruit our kind also."

"He should be so lucky," Shane says witheringly. "If he ever tries to sign me up for *Team Dowling*, I'll shove those spiders where the sun don't shine."

"I'm sure that will make him quake in his boots," Carl sneers.

"Do you know anything about Mr. Dowling?" I ask before a fight breaks out between them.

"Not much," Ashtat answers. "And it is not our place to tell you what we know. Dr. Oystein will do that when he returns."

"You're all in love with that bloody doctor, aren't you?"

"He has given us a home," Ashtat says. "He has given our lives meaning. He has rescued us from an unliving hell and made us feel almost human. Of course we love him. You will too when you realize how fortunate you are to have been taken in by someone as accepting and forgiving as Dr. Oystein."

"I don't need his forgiveness," I snort.

"No?" Ashtat asks quietly, eyeing me seriously.

I think about Tyler Bayor. Sister Clare of the Shnax. How I wasn't able to save Mark.

I go quiet.

"Grub's up!" someone calls out brightly. Looking up, I spot a smiling lady in a flowery apron entering the room, pushing a trolley loaded with bowls. It's the woman I noticed when Dr. Oystein was first showing me around, the one who was scooping brains out of heads.

The Angels around me cheer loudly, as do all the others. The elegantly dressed dinner lady beams and takes a bow, then starts handing out the bowls.

"This is Ciara," Ashtat says as she approaches our table. "Ciara, this is Becky Smith, but she likes to be called B."

"Pleasure to meet you, B," Ciara says cheerfully. She looks more like a model than any dinner lady I ever met, with high cheekbones, carefully maintained hair, and clothes you'd only find in exclusive boutiques. Even the apron, white cap and green plastic gloves look more suited to a catwalk than a kitchen. But there's one thing about her that's far more extraordinary than her glamorous appearance.

She has a heartbeat.

"You're alive!" I gasp, the beat of her heart like a drum to my sensitive ears.

"Just about," Ciara grins. "But don't go thinking that means you can eat my brain. There should be more than enough for you there."

She hands me a bowl filled with a familiar gray, gloopy substance. It's what the zom heads were fed in the underground complex, human brains mixed up in a semi-appetizing way.

"For afters," Ciara says, slamming a bucket down in the middle of the table. She winks at me. "Don't be offended if I don't stick around, but I can't stand all the vomiting. Come and have a chat with me later if you want. I used to work in Bow long ago, which – if I'm any judge of an accent – isn't too far from your neck of the woods. I'm sure we'll find plenty to talk about."

Ciara sticks out a hand and pretends to ruffle my hair, only she doesn't quite touch me. Can't, since she's human and I'm not. I'd probably contaminate her if one of my hairs pierced her glove and stabbed into her flesh. I'm pretty sure that every cell of my body is toxic.

"I didn't expect to find living people here," I remark as Ciara leaves.

"There aren't many," Carl says, "but we get a few passing through, and Ciara is a permanent fixture."

"She was here when we first moved in," Ashtat explains. "She worked in one of the hotel restaurants. Dr. Oystein calls her the queen of the dinner ladies. She's so stylish, isn't she? I asked her once why she chose to follow such a career. She said because she liked it, and we should all do what we like in life."

"Isn't she afraid of being turned into one of us?" I ask.

"That cannot happen," Ashtat says. "If she was infected, she would become a revived. But no, she is not afraid. She feels safe around us. She knows we would not deliberately turn her. Of course it could happen accidentally if she fell against one of us and got scratched, but she is happy to take that risk. She says there are no guarantees of safety anywhere in this world now."

"But if she is ever turned, God help the bugger who does it to her," Shane growls. "I don't care if it's an accident—if anyone hurts Ciara, I'll come after them with everything I have."

"You're my hero," Carl simpers. "Now shut up and eat."

Shane scowls but digs in as ordered.

I tuck into the gruel, not bothering with the spoon that Ciara supplied, just tipping it straight into my mouth from the bowl. I used to think it was disgusting, but having had to scoop brains out of skulls to survive since leaving the underground complex, I'm less fussy now.

Jakob is first to finish – he doesn't eat all of his gruel – and he reaches for the bucket and turns aside, sticking a couple of fingers down his throat. The rest of us follow his example when we're ready and the room comes alive with the sound of a few dozen zombies throwing up.

The children of the night—what sweet music we make!

THIRTEEN

Nobody says much for a while after we've finished eating and puking. We all look a bit sheepish. It's not easy doing this in public, even for those who've been living together as Angels for months. It feels like taking a dump in front of your friends. I've done a lot of crazy things over the years, but I drew the line at that! Yet here we are, all thirty plus of us, looking like we've been caught with our pants down around our ankles.

Ashtat pulls something out of a pocket, closes her hands over it and starts to pray silently. I roll my eyes at the boys and make a gagging motion, but they don't laugh. When Ashtat finishes and unclasps her hands, I see that the object is a crucifix.

"What are you doing with that?" I ask.

"Praying."

"With a cross? Don't you guys use...I don't know...but not a cross. Those are for us lot."

"Us lot?" Ashtat repeats icily.

"Christians."

"What makes you think I'm not a Christian?"

I snort. "You're an Arab. There aren't any Christians in the Middle East."

"Actually there are," Ashtat says tightly. "Quite a few, for your information."

"I'm not talking about people who go there on pilgrimage," I sniff.

"Nor am I," she says. "I'm talking about Arab Christians."

"Pull the other one," I laugh.

Ashtat raises an eyebrow. "You don't think you can be both an Arab and a Christian?"

"Of course not. You're one or the other."

"Really?" she jeers. "So you think that all Arabs are Muslims?"

"Yeah," I mutter, although I'm getting a sinking feeling in my stomach. "You all worship Allah."

"And who is Allah?" she presses.

"Your god."

"No," she barks. *"Our* god. God and Allah are one and the same. Assuming you believe in God."

"Well, I'm not religious, but if I did believe, it would be in God, not Allah."

"As I just told you," she says, "Allah *is* God. Our religions have the same roots. Muslims believe in the Old Testament and they revere Christ, Mary and all the saints that Christians do."

I scratch my head and stare at her, lost for words.

"You don't know anything about Islam, do you?" she says.

"Not really, no," I admit grudgingly.

Ashtat starts to laugh, then grimaces. "I'm sorry. I should not mock you for being ignorant. In my experience, most of your people knew nothing about mine. We were just potential terrorists in your eyes."

I want to protest but I can't, because it's the truth.

"I'm not going to give you a history lesson," Ashtat goes on. "If you are truly interested, you can look up the facts yourself. But Muslims and Christians – Jews too – all started out in the same place and believe in the same God. We branched along the way, but at our core we are the same.

"I'm Muslim," she continues, "but one of my grandmothers was Christian. She converted when she came to this country and married my grandfather, but she told her children and grandchildren about her old beliefs and encouraged us to respect Christianity. The Virgin Mary was her favorite and I often say a prayer to her, thinking of my grandmother, especially in these troubled times."

Ashtat stops and waits for me to respond. I can only gape at her.

It's like I've been told that the Earth actually is flat or the moon truly is made of cheese.

"Why did your people hate us if that's the case?" Shane asks. This is obviously news to him too.

"Why did *your* people hate *us*?" Ashtat retorts.

"Because of September the tenth and all the other crap," Shane says.

"You mean September eleventh," Carl sighs, rolling his eyes.

"What about the Crusades?" Ashtat counters. "Western Christians tried to wipe out my people, to steal our land and treasures. Later, in the twentieth century, you divided up our nations as it suited you, to govern us as you saw fit. You..." She shakes her head. "We could argue about this forever, but it would not do any good. I don't hate anyone or blame anyone or see myself as being part of any army except the army of the Angels. The old grudges seem ridiculous now that the world has changed so much."

"You're the one who started the argument," I pout.

"I was not arguing," she contradicts me. "I was simply pointing out a matter of fact, in response to your assertion that Arabs could not also be Christians."

"All right. I stand corrected. Happy now?"

"Yes," Ashtat says, putting away her crucifix.

"I didn't mean any harm," I add softly.

She smiles. "I know. Forget about it."

"My dad..." I consider telling them how I was raised, about my

98

racist father, what happened with Tyler, how I'm trying to be different. But before I can decide how to start, a Chinese guy enters the dining room and claps loudly.

All conversation comes to an immediate halt. Everyone rises and bows. The newcomer waits a moment, then bows smoothly in return. When he straightens, he looks around, spots me and comes across.

He's a bit taller than me, although not a lot older, maybe five or six years my senior, dressed in jeans and a white T-shirt. No shoes. Bones jut out of his toes and fingers. They've been carefully trimmed into daggerlike tips.

He stops in front of me. I'm the only person still sitting. I glance at the others but they don't look at me. Their gazes are fixed dead ahead.

"I am Master Zhang," he says softly. "In the future you will stand and bow when you see me."

"Why?" I snap.

His right hand flickers and before I can react, his fingers are tightening round my throat. I slap at his arm and try to pull free, but he holds firm.

"Because I will kill you if you do not," he says without changing tone.

"Don't … need … breath," I growl. "You … can't … choke … me."

"No. But I can rip your head from your neck and dig into your brain. I could do it now. I would not even need to alter my grip. Do you doubt that?"

I stare into his dark brown eyes – one of them is badly blood-shot – and shake my head stiffly.

"Good," he says, releasing me. "That is a start. Now you will stand, bow and say my name."

I want to tell him to get lost, but I've a feeling my head would be sent rolling across the floor before I got to the end of the insult. I don't think this guy plays games, that he's someone you can push to a certain point. You show him respect or he rips you apart, simple as that.

Pushing my chair back, I stand, bow and mutter as politely as I can, "Master Zhang."

"Good," he says again, then turns to face Carl. "You will bring her to me when you are finished here. I will test her."

"Yes, Master Zhang," Carl says, bowing again.

Zhang leaves without saying anything else. Once he's gone, the Angels sit and conversation resumes as if we were never interrupted.

I rub my throat and glare at the others. "You could have warned me," I snarl.

Carl waves away my accusation. "We all have to go through that. Master Zhang likes to make his own introductions."

"Do you really think he would have ripped my head off?" I ask.

"If you were dumb enough to assume he was joking, yes," Carl says. "But so far nobody's made that mistake. Even Shane knew better than to give Master Zhang any grief."

"I'd like to see him tear someone's head off though," Shane says. He shoots me a quick look. "I was hoping *you* might talk back to him, just to see what he'd do."

"Good to know you have my back if things ever get ugly," I snarl. For a few seconds I consider walking out the door and leaving—in some ways this place is just as bad as the underground complex where I was held prisoner. But where would I go? Who could I turn to? Grumbling darkly, I sit down like the rest of them. "So that guy's your mentor?" I ask, recalling what Awnya said when she mentioned him.

"Yes," Ashtat says. "He teaches us how to fight and fend for ourselves, so that we are ready for the missions on which we are sent."

"Just him?"

"Yes. He is the only tutor we need."

"And the test he mentioned?"

Ashtat snickers. "Every Angel trains with Master Zhang, but some are deemed more worthy of his attention than others. He will take your measure when you spar with him. If he is impressed, you will train to join the likes of us on life-or-death missions."

"If you disappoint him," Carl says, "you'll end up rooting through shops for supplies with the twins."

"Or mixing up brains with Ciara to put in the gruel," Shane giggles.

"It's time to find out if you're a lion or a lamb," Ashtat says.

"I'm no bloody lamb," I growl.

She purses her lips. "No, I do not think that you are." Then her expression softens and she adds hauntingly, "Although if you are cleared to come on missions with us, you might end up wishing that you were."

FOURTEEN

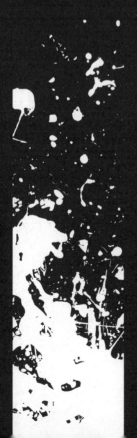

When everyone's had their fill, they stack up the bowls and leave them on the tables, then file out of the dining room. Carl tells me to accompany him to the gym for my test with Master Zhang. I expect the others to come with us, but they head off to do their own thing.

"This won't be the gladiatorial showdown of the year," Carl smirks, noting my disappointment.

"What do you mean?"

"It's not going to be some amazing duel, with you pushing Master Zhang all the way. The test for newbies is pretty boring. That's why no one's interested."

"Maybe I'll surprise you," I grunt.

"No," he says. "You won't."

Carl takes me by the swimming pool

on our way. A couple of Angels are doing laps, moving faster than any Olympic swimmer, like a pair of sharks following a trail of blood.

"Can you swim?" Carl asks.

"Yeah."

"You're free to train here whenever you want," he says. "But make sure you plug up your nostrils and ears—water will lodge if you don't. And keep your mouth firmly shut. Liquids slip down our throats easily enough, but they're a real pain to get rid of. Trust me, unless you like wearing diapers, you don't want to go sloshing around with a few liters of water inside you."

"I'll bear that in mind."

The gym is fairly standard, cross trainers, rowing machines, weights and so on. Several Angels are working out, some under the gaze of Master Zhang, others by themselves.

Master Zhang ignores me for a few minutes, studying a girl as she performs a series of gymnastic routines in front of a dummy that must have been brought here from a shop. Each spin or twirl ends with a flick of a hand or foot to the dummy's head or torso. She's already chipped away at a lot of it, and keeps on tearing in, cracking it, knocking chunks loose, ignoring the cuts and nicks she's picking up.

"Keep going until there is nothing left to destroy," Master Zhang says to the girl, then strides for the door, nodding at Carl and me to follow.

He leads us to a bare room that looks like it was once a conference room for high-flying businessmen. Any chairs and tables have been removed, though there are still some whiteboards on the walls.

"Each revitalized is different," Master Zhang says, wasting no time on chitchat. "Our bodies react uniquely when we return to life. There are similarities common to all – extra strength and speed – but nobody can judge the extent of their abilities until they test themselves. Physical build is not a factor. Some of us have great potential. Others do not.

"We can fine-tune whatever skills we possess, but if you are found lacking at this stage, you will forever be limited by the restraints of your body. When you died, you lost the capacity to improve on what nature provided you with. In short, your response to today's test will decide your role within the Angels for the next few thousand years. So I suggest you apply yourself as best you can."

Master Zhang marches me to one end of the room, then tells me to make a standing jump. I crouch, tense the muscles in my legs, then spring forward like a frog. I hurtle almost two-thirds of the way across the room, much farther than any human could have ever jumped. I'm delighted with myself, but when I look at Master Zhang, he makes a so-so gesture.

"Carl," he says, and Carl copies what I did, only he sails past me and bounces off the wall ahead of us.

"Does that mean I've failed?" I ask bitterly.

"No," Master Zhang said. "It simply means that if someone is required to leap across a great distance – for instance, from the roof of one building to another – we will choose Carl or another like him."

Next we step out into the corridor and I perform a running jump. I do better this time, although still nowhere near what Carl can do. Then Master Zhang times me racing up and down. He's pleased with my speed. "Not the fastest by any means, but quicker than many."

We step back into the room and Master Zhang tests my sense of balance by having me stand in a variety of uncomfortable positions and hold the pose as long as I can. Then he tests my reflexes by lobbing small, hard balls at me. Again he's happy with my response, but far from overwhelmed.

We return to the gym and he tries me out with weights. I come up short on this one. Others are lifting weights around me and I can see that I don't match up. I lift far more than I could have when I was alive, but ultimately I fall low down the pecking order.

"Do not look so upset," Master Zhang says as I step away from the weights, feeling defeated. "I am by no means the strongest person here, but that has never worked against me. I taught myself how to deal with stronger opponents many years ago and my foes have yet to get the better of me."

"Have a lot of foes, do you?" I laugh.

"Yes," he says simply, not bothering to elaborate.

Then it's back to the conference room, where Master Zhang has me face him. Carl watches from a spot near the door, grinning eagerly.

"This is the part you have probably been looking forward to," Master Zhang says. "I am going to test your sharpness and wit. I want you to try to hit me, first with your fists, then with your feet. You can use any move you wish, a punch, chop, slap, whatever."

"Shouldn't we be in karate or boxing gear for this sort of thing?" I ask.

"No. We do not wear special clothes when we fight in the world outside, so why should we wear them here? I want to see how you will perform on the streets, where it matters."

With a shrug, I size up Master Zhang, then jab a fist at his nose. He shimmies and my fist whistles through thin air. I expected as much, and also guessed the way he would move, so even while he's ducking, I'm bringing up my other fist to hit him from the opposite side.

Master Zhang grabs my arm and stops my fist short of its target.

"Good," he says, releasing me. "Again."

I spend the next ten minutes trying to strike him with my fists, then ten trying to hit him with my feet. I fare better with my feet than fists, connecting with his shoulders and midriff a number of times, and once – sweetly – with the side of his face. I don't cause any damage but I can tell he's impressed.

"Rest awhile," he says, taking a step back.

"I didn't think zombies needed rest."

"Even the living dead need rest," he says. "We are more enduring than we were in life, but our bodies do have limits. If we demand too much of ourselves, it affects our performance. We can struggle on indefinitely, sluggishly, but our battles need to be fought on our terms. It is not enough to be dogged. We must be incisive."

"Who do we fight?" I ask. "Mr. Dowling and his mutants? Reviveds? The army?"

"Dr. Oystein will answer your questions," Master Zhang says. "I am here merely to determine how useful you might be to us and to help you make the most of your talents."

Master Zhang spends the next ten minutes throwing punches and kicks at me. I manage to duck or block many of them, but plenty penetrate and by the end of the session I'm stinging all over. But it's a good kind of pain and I don't mind.

After opening up a small cut beneath my right eye, Master Zhang says, "That will be enough. Return tomorrow. I want to see how your cuts moss over."

"What do you mean?" I ask.

"We cannot heal as we could when we were alive," he explains. "Moss grows in places where we are cut, but it sprouts more thickly in some than in others. If the moss grows thinly over your cuts, you will continue to lose blood when you fight, which will affect your performance, making you of little use to us."

"Nothing wrong with my moss," I say confidently. "Look, it's already stitching the wound closed, I can feel it." I tilt my head backwards, so that he can see.

Master Zhang smiles thinly. "I believe that it is. But as I said, come back to see me tomorrow, and we will test it then."

"Assuming the moss grows thickly," I call after him as he turns to leave, "how did I do on the rest of the tests? Am I good enough to be a proper Angel with Carl and the others?"

Master Zhang pauses and casts a slow look over me with his bloodshot left eye. I feel like I'm being X-rayed.

"Physically, yes, my feeling is that you are, although there are a few more tests that you must complete before we can say for certain. Mentally?" He looks unsure. "Most living people fear death more than anything else, but our kind need not, since we have already died. So tell me, Becky Smith, what do you fear more than anything else now?"

I think about telling him that I don't fear anything, but that wouldn't be the truth. And I think about saying that I fear Mr. Dowling, Owl Man and the mutants, but while I'm certainly scared of the killer clown and his strange associates, they're not the ones who gnaw away at my nerves deep down. I'm sure that if I'm not totally honest with Master Zhang, he'll pick up on the deception and it will go against me. So, even though I hate having to admit it, I tell him.

"I'm afraid of myself," I croak, lowering my gaze to hide my shame. "I've done some bad things in the past, and I'm afraid, if I don't keep a close watch on myself every single day, that I might do even worse."

There's a long silence. Then Master Zhang makes a small clucking sound. "I think you will fit in here," he says.

And that marks the end of the first round of tests.

FIFTEEN

"I told you it wouldn't be exciting," Carl says as we head back to our room.

I grunt.

"You'll have to get used to the boredom," he continues. "We spend most of our time training. It sounds like it will be great, learning how to fight, and there *are* times when I learn a new move and it feels amazing. But for the most part it's pretty dull."

There's no one in our room when we get there. Carl changes his shirt – there wasn't anything wrong with the old one, he just wants to try something new – and we head to the front of the building, out onto a large terrace overlooking the river. Carl doesn't stop to admire the view, but hurries down the stairs and along the path.

"Are we going to the London Dungeon?" I ask, spotting a sign for it.

Carl gives me an odd look. "Isn't the world grisly enough for you as it is?"

"But the Dungeon's fun," I laugh.

"It used to be," he agrees. "Not so much now that there aren't any actors to bring the place to life. We sometimes train down there, but we don't really make use of it otherwise. It's not a fun place to hang out."

"Do the rides still work?" I ask.

"Yes," he says.

"Come on. Let's try them."

"Maybe later," he says, then heads for the old arcade center. I could go and explore the Dungeon by myself, but I don't want to be alone so, with a scowl, I follow him.

Most of the video games in the arcade still seem to be operational, but although a handful of Angels are hanging around, nobody's playing. That seems strange to me until I recall my advanced sense of hearing and the way bright lights hurt my eyes. I guess half an hour on a video game in my current state would be about as much fun as sticking my hand in a blender.

Our lot are bowling. They have the lanes to themselves. Jakob is taking his turn as we approach. He knocks down the four standing pins and gets a spare.

"Nice one," Shane says.

Jakob only shrugs. I've never seen anyone who looks as miserable as this guy. I wonder what it would take to make him smile.

"How did the test go?" Ashtat asks as we slip in beside her.

"I aced it. Master Zhang said I was the best student he'd ever seen."

"Sure," she drawls. "I bet he got down on his knees and worshipped you."

We grin at each other. We got off on the wrong foot, but I'm starting to warm to the Muslim girl, which is something I never thought I'd hear myself admit.

Shane hits the gutter and swears.

"You're lucky Master Zhang wasn't here to see that," Carl tuts.

"Why?" I ask. "Don't tell me he's a master bowler too."

"It's part of our training," Shane sighs, waiting for his ball to return. "He says bowling is good for concentration. Our eyes aren't as sharp as they were, and no amount of drops will ever change that. We have to keep working on our hand-to-eye coordination."

"Eye to hand," Carl corrects him.

"Whatever," Shane mutters, and throws again. This time he knocks down seven pins but he's not happy. He flexes his fingers and glares at them as if they're to blame.

Ashtat throws and gets a strike. Jakob steps up next, then pauses and offers me the ball.

"Don't you want to finish the game?" I ask.

"No," he whispers. "It doesn't matter."

I take the ball from him and test the holes. They're too small for my fingers – I cast a quick glance at Jakob and note how unnaturally thin he is – so I put it back and find one that fits. I take aim, step up and let the ball rip.

It shoots down the lane faster than I would have thought possible and smashes into the pins, sending them scattering in every direction. A few of them shatter and go flying across the adjacent lanes.

"Bloody hell!" I gasp, shocked and dismayed. "I'm sorry. I didn't mean to..."

I stop. The others are laughing. Even Jakob is smiling slightly. Shane high-fives the thin, bald kid, then slaps my back. "Don't worry. That happens to most of us the first time."

"We're stronger than we look," Ashtat says. "We have to learn to control our strength. That's another of the reasons we practice here."

"You could have told me that before I threw," I say sourly.

"It wouldn't have been as funny then," Carl giggles.

"No," I smile. "I guess it wouldn't."

We move to another lane while Jakob clears up the mess and replaces the pins. It takes me a while to get the balance right – I throw the first few balls too softly, then hit the gutters when I lob more forcefully – but eventually I find my groove. It's tricky to be accurate because of my weak eyesight, but I can compensate for that by throwing a bit harder than I did when alive.

After a couple of games – I finish last the first time, but fourth

in the next game, ahead of a disgusted Shane – we spill out of the arcade. Night has fallen and dark clouds drift across the sky. I suggest the Dungeon again, but the others say they want to go on the London Eye. I'm curious to see what the city looks like now from up high, so I don't argue.

We step into one of the pods and rise. I turn slowly as we ascend, taking in the three-hundred-and-sixty-degree view. As I'm turning, I spot an Angel sitting on the bench in the middle of a pod on the opposite side of the big wheel, staring solemnly out over the river.

"What's up with that guy?" I ask.

"He's a lookout," Carl says. "There's always an Angel on duty in the Eye, in touch with a guard inside County Hall, in case we get attacked by Mr. Dowling and his mutant army. They use walkie-talkies—mobile phones don't work anymore."

"I noticed that," I frown. "Any idea why not?"

"It's the end of the world," Carl says. "Lots of things don't work."

"I know, but I thought mobiles would be all right, since they operate through satellites."

"You thought wrong," Carl sniffs. "That's why we rely on the walkie-talkies. You'll be posted to a pod once you settle in. We all have to take our turn, even the twins and those who don't come on missions."

"Except for One-eyed Pete," Ashtat says.

"Obviously," Carl replies.

I whistle, impressed. "There's really an Angel called One-eyed Pete?"

Carl and Ashtat gaze at me serenely and I realize I've taken the bait, hook, line and sinker.

"All right," I growl as they burst out laughing. "I'm an idiot. I admit it. Just throw me off this thing when we get to the top and have done with me."

We chat away as the pod glides upwards, admiring the view over County Hall, looking down on the roof and into the courtyards. I try to spot the room where the Groove Tubes are, but it's hard to be sure.

"I came up here a few times with my mum and dad when I was younger," I mumble, remembering happier days when the world wasn't a nightmarish place.

"What happened to them?" Ashtat asks quietly.

"I don't know. I think Dad might have made it out. Mum…" I shake my head, wondering again about her, hoping she's alive, but not able to believe that she is. And Dad? Well, it's kind of the opposite with him. I'm pretty sure he slipped away, but part of me hopes he didn't, that he paid for what he made me do to Tyler. But I don't *want* to feel that way. He's my dad, and as much as I hate him for what he is – what he always was – I love him too.

"How about the rest of you?" I ask. "Did you all lose family?"

"Yes," Ashtat says. "Parents, brothers, sisters…"

"A girlfriend," Shane adds morosely.

119

"A boyfriend," Carl sighs, then winks at a startled Shane. "Only joking."

"You'd better be," Shane huffs. "I'm not sharing a room with you if you're not."

Carl fakes a gasp. "Hark at the homophobe! Just for that, I'm going to convert. Come here, you big sap, and give me a kiss."

They wrestle and stumble around the pod, Carl laughing, Shane cursing. The rest of us look on wearily.

"Boys never change, do they?" I note.

"Sadly, no," Ashtat murmurs. "They might have lost their carnal appetites, but that won't stop them being bothersome little pests."

"Lost their...? Oh yeah, I forgot about that."

Apparently zombies can't get down and dirty—none of the necessary equipment is in working order. Apart from snogging – which probably isn't much fun with a dry tongue and cold lips – there's not much we can do.

Shane and Carl break apart. Both are grinning. Then Carl's expression darkens as he recalls what we were talking about.

"I went to the offices where my father used to work once I'd revitalized. I found him there. He's a revived now. I thought about killing him but I didn't dare, just in case anyone ever discovered a cure for them."

"You know that won't happen," Ashtat says sympathetically.

"Yeah, but still..."

"Your dad might revitalize," I say, trying to cheer him up.

120

Carl squints at me. "What are you talking about?"

"Well, we recovered our senses, so maybe he will too."

"He can't," Carl says. "He wasn't vaccinated."

"What?" I frown.

"Leave it." Ashtat stops Carl before he can continue. "Dr. Oystein will explain it when he returns."

"I'm getting sick of hearing that," I growl. "What is he, the bloody keeper of all secrets? Are you afraid the world will go up in flames if you tell me something behind his back?"

"It's just simpler if he tells you," Ashtat says calmly. "He's used to explaining. If we tried, we might confuse you."

"At least you admit that you don't know what the hell you're talking about," I mutter, then cast an eye over Jakob who, as usual, is standing silently by the rest of us. "What about you, skeleton boy? Did zombies eat your nearest and dearest, or did they leave Ma and Pa Addams alone?"

Jakob stares at me uncertainly, then gets the reference. "Oh. I see. I look like one of the Addams Family. Very funny."

"You bitch," Ashtat snarls.

"What?" I snap. "Aren't we allowed to have a go at skinheads anymore?"

"You don't think he shaved himself, do you?" she asks.

"Well, yeah, of course. I mean why else...?"

I stop and wince. How dumb am I? Pale skin. Bald. Dark circles under his eyes. Skinny in an unhealthy way.

"You've got cancer, haven't you?" I groan.

"Yes," Jakob says softly. "It was terminal. I was close to the end. I had maybe a few weeks left to live. Then I was bitten. Now I'm going to be like this forever."

"Is the cancer still active?" I ask. "Will it carry on eating you up?"

"No," he sighs. "But it hasn't gone away. It still hurts. I can ignore the pain and function normally when I focus, which is why I'm allowed to go on missions, but the rest of the time I feel weak, tired and disoriented. It's why I often seem spaced out."

"I'm sorry. Really. I wouldn't have had a go at you if I'd known."

He waves away my apology. "It doesn't matter. Nothing that you said could hurt me. Nobody could. Not after..."

He stops and I think he's going to clam up again. But then he continues, his voice the barest of whispers, so that even with my sharp ears I have to strain to catch every word.

"I'd come to London with my parents and younger sister. One last visit. Nobody phrased it that way but we all knew. Our final day out together. Mum and Dad took time off work, even though they couldn't afford to—they were struggling to make ends meet, having spent so much on me over the last few years.

"We got delayed on our way down, so we had to cut out some of the things we'd planned to do. In the end we went to Trafalgar Square first. I loved the lions, the fountains, looking up at the National Gallery."

I consider telling him what happened the last time I was in Trafalgar Square, but I don't dare interrupt him in case he goes silent again.

"We had lunch in the crypt in St. Martin-in-the-Fields. I had a Scotch egg. I knew it would make me sick – my stomach couldn't handle rich food – but I didn't care. It was sort of my last supper. I wanted it to be special." He smiles fleetingly. "That's how bad things get when you're that close to death. A Scotch egg becomes something special."

Jakob retreats from the window and sits on the bench. Rests his hands on his knees and carries on talking. No one else makes a sound. If we could hold our breath – if we had breath to hold – we would.

"I was one of the first to be attacked when zombies spilled into the crypt. In a way that was a mercy. I didn't have to witness the madness and terror which must have surely followed.

"I was still in the crypt when I regained my senses weeks later. I'd made a base there, along with dozens of others. I'd fashioned a cot out of a few of the corpses. I suppose it was a bed-cum-larder, as I'd eaten from them too. I know that because I was eating when I revitalized, digging my fingers into a skull, scraping out a few dry, tasteless scraps of brain.

"It was my sister's skull," he says, and the most horrible thing about it is that his tone doesn't change. It's like he's telling us the time. "My mum and dad were there too. Well, in my dad's case it was just his head. I couldn't find his body. I did search for it but…"

Jakob pauses, then decides to stop. He lowers his head and starts to massage his neck. Nobody says anything.

Without discussing it, we spread out around the pod, giving Jakob some privacy. We stare at the river and the buildings, smoke rising into the air from a number of places, corpses strewn everywhere, abandoned boats and cars, paths and roads stained with blood, black in the dim night light.

I think about asking Ashtat if I can borrow her cross. But I don't. And it's not because I don't want to be a hypocrite and say a prayer to a God I barely believe in. It's because I figure what's the point in saying any prayers for this broken, bloodied city of the ungodly dead?

SIXTEEN

Carl wasn't joking about training being boring. Over the next three days I perform the same routines over and over—swim (having carefully plugged up my nose and ears), work out in the gym and get thrown around the hollow conference room by the stone-faced Master Zhang.

"It is important that you learn how to fall correctly," he says when I complain after being slammed down hard on the floorboards for the hundredth time. "In a fight, you will often be thrown or knocked over. If you can cushion your landing, you will be in a better position to carry on."

"How long will I have to do this?" I grumble, rubbing my bruised shoulders. I'm beginning to wish he'd ruled me unfit for active service.

"Until I am satisfied," he says and hurls me over his shoulder again.

I'm keen to learn all sorts of cool moves, and disgusted by what I consider a waste of my time, so I leave the sessions with a face like thunder, but Ashtat tells me I have to be patient. They all had to endure this to begin with.

"Master Zhang wants to turn you into a fighting machine," she explains. "That isn't a simple task. You should be thankful he's spending so much time on you, even if it is only to throw you around. If he didn't consider you worthy, he would not be proceeding so diligently with you."

I know she's right, but it's hard to maintain my interest and temper. I was never the most patient of girls. Maybe that's why I didn't have a boyfriend—I couldn't be bothered putting in all the time and effort required.

If I'd come to Master Zhang when I was human, I doubt I'd have stuck with him more than a day. I definitely wouldn't have made it past the second. But things are different now. It's not like I have more attractive options. If I don't play ball here, I can go off by myself, regress and become a shambling revived, or maybe hook up with Mr. Dowling and his merry band of mutants. Hardly the sort of career prospects that young girls around the world dream about.

At least I get on pretty well with my roommates. They're not the sort I would have been friends with in my previous life, but they're not a bad bunch. They do their best to help me find my feet, show

126

me round County Hall, give me tips like how to groom the bones sticking out of my fingers and toes.

I haven't spoken to many of the other Angels. I've picked up names here and there, and I know a few to nod to in the gym and pool – such as Ingrid and her crew – but I haven't tried to bond with any of them. I'm still not sure if this place is for me, and won't know for certain until I've had a chance to chat with Dr. Oystein again. If I don't like what I hear, and decide that I'm better off out of it, I don't want the added aggro of having to leave friends behind.

On the afternoon of the fourth day, after lunch, when I have free time on my hands, I head down to the lab with the Groove Tubes to catch up with Reilly, something I've been meaning to do since our first reunion.

The soldier isn't in the lab, nor is Rage, who must have been fished out not long after I was. I get an angry feeling in my gut when I spot the empty Tube, recalling the way Rage threw the rest of the zom heads to the lions, how he killed Dr. Cerveris. I'm uneasy too—I don't trust Rage. It wouldn't surprise me if he popped up behind me and dug a knife into the back of my skull.

I ask around and track down Reilly in the kitchen where Ciara works. Reilly and the dinner lady are talking while she washes up. As far as I'm aware, they're the only two humans here, so I guess they feel closer to one another than to the cannibalistic zombies they serve.

"Hey," Reilly says when he spots me. "I was wondering when you'd come looking for me."

"What made you think I would?" I snort.

"I've always known you had a crush on me," he grins.

"Not if you were the last guy in the world," I jeer, hopping up onto a table across from the pair and letting my legs dangle. "Isn't there a dishwasher for that?" I ask Ciara as she scrubs another plate.

"I prefer washing by hand," she says cheerfully. "It passes the time and it keeps my mind off... other matters."

Her shoulders shudder slightly and I don't ask any more questions. I'm sure, like any other survivor in this post-apocalyptic city, that she has memories she'd rather not dwell on.

"Go on then," I say to Reilly. "Tell me how you came to be here."

He shrugs. "There's no big story. Josh and the others who hadn't been killed by the clown and his mutants pulled out of the underground complex in the wake of the assault. I'd had doubts about the place from the beginning. What I saw that day – the way the reviveds and revitalizeds were executed like rabid animals – helped make up my mind. I wanted out, so I walked away while they were evacuating. I doubt if anyone missed me. If they did, they probably assumed I was killed or converted by a stray zombie."

"Took you long enough to see them for what they were," I sniff.

Reilly sighs. "Things aren't black and white anymore. They never were, I suppose, but there used to be law and order, right and wrong. Now it's all chaos. I don't think Josh or Dr. Cerveris were bad guys. They were trying to uncover answers, to figure out a way to put the world back on track. I didn't approve of how they went about it, but if they'd cracked the zombie gene and come up with a way to rid the world of the living dead..."

"They'd have been your heroes?" I sneer.

"Yeah," he says. "You've got to remember, *you're* the enemy. Dr. Oystein is doing an incredible job, and I admire how his Angels have dedicated themselves to helping the living. But you're all part of the problem. Dr. Oystein acknowledges that, so it's not like I'm being disrespectful. The world has been torn apart by a war between the living and the dead, and even though you guys are on my side, I can't trust you. One scrape of those bones, if I stumbled and you instinctively reached out to grab me, and I'm history."

I frown. "So why swap Josh for Dr. Oystein?"

"I think he can do more than Josh could," Reilly says. "He knows more about what makes you lot tick. He's working from within to solve the problem and that gives him an edge over everybody else. I also like the fact that he goes about his business humanely, but I won't kid you, that's just a bonus. If I believed that we could sort out this mess by slicing you up in agonizing, brutal ways, you wouldn't get any sympathy from me. I'd feel bad about it, but that wouldn't stop me forging ahead."

"He says such nasty things sometimes, doesn't he?" Ciara tuts.

"He's no saint, that's for sure," I mutter.

"Then again, this is hardly a time for saints, is it?" Reilly notes.

"True," I nod. "So how'd you find your way here? Did you follow the arrows?"

"No." Reilly scratches the back of his neck. "I was on my way out of the city. I wanted to join a compound in the countryside or head for one of the zombie-free islands and try to gain entry. Then I ran into a pack of Angels on a mission. I would have avoided them, except I recognized someone with them. I tracked the pack until he parted company with the zombies, then revealed myself and asked what he was up to. When he explained what was going on here, I decided I wanted to be part of it. I offered my services. They were accepted. So here I am."

"Who was the guy you recognized?" I ask.

"You'll find out soon," Reilly says. "Dr. Oystein returned earlier today and my contact was with him. I'm guessing the pair of them will want to see you."

I get a prickle of excitement when I hear that the mysterious doctor is back. I was starting to think that I'd only dreamt about him. It seems like months since he introduced himself to me and took me on my first tour of the building.

"One last question. Do you know where Rage is?"

Reilly grimaces. "We hauled him out of the Tube a couple of days ago. I've been watching my back since then."

I bare my teeth in a vicious grin. "I thought you trusted him."

"I never said that," Reilly corrects me. "I said that Dr. Oystein

130

trusts him, and I trust Dr. Oystein. I protected Rage because the doctor asked me to. That doesn't mean I liked it. And it doesn't mean I feel safe now that he's out on the prowl."

Reilly looks around nervously and touches the handle of the stun gun that he has strapped to his side. "Truth be told, I'm crapping myself."

I laugh harshly. "You should become one of us, Reilly. We don't crap, we just vomit."

With that, I hop down and head back to the gym, treading carefully, judging the shadows as I pass, on the lookout for a cherubic monster.

SEVENTEEN

Now that Dr. Oystein is back, I expect him to summon me for a meeting, but there's no sign of him that evening or night, and I head to bed at the usual time, surprised and frustrated.

When I mention the doctor's return to the others, they're not that bothered. Shane and Jakob say that they already knew. Ashtat and Carl didn't, but it's not a big deal for them, since they're accustomed to him coming and going.

"I never thought to tell you," Shane shrugs when I ask why he didn't let me know. "It's not like we announce it with bugles every time he returns."

In the morning I report for training again with Master Zhang. He lobs me around and slams me down hard on my back, time after time, studying the way I land, making suggestions, urging me to twist an arm this way, a leg that way.

After one particularly vicious slam dunk that makes me cry out loud, someone gasps theatrically and says, "I hope that's as painful as it looks from here."

I glance around, spirits rising, thinking it must be Dr. Oystein, even though that would be a strange thing for him to say. But it's not the doctor. It's Rage, standing by the wall and smirking.

"Nice to see you again, Becky," Rage says with fake sweetness. "Last time I saw you, you were hanging naked in the Groove Tube."

"Same here," I sneer. "Sorry for your little problem."

"What do you mean?"

I cock the smallest finger on my right hand and flex it a couple of times.

Rage laughs. "I don't worry about those sorts of things anymore. You'll have to do better than that to wind me up."

"I'll do my best," I snarl.

"Do you get the feeling she doesn't like me?" Rage asks Master Zhang.

"I have no interest in your petty squabbles," Zhang says as I stand and grimace, still aching from when he threw me. "In my company, you will treat one another with respect, as all of my students must."

"You've been training Rage too?" I ask.

"For the last couple of days, yes," Zhang nods.

"Be careful what you teach him," I growl. "He might use it against you."

"Now, now, Becky," Rage smiles. "Remember what Master Zhang told you. It's all about *respect*."

"Respect this," I spit, giving him the finger.

"Enough," Zhang says quietly. "I will not tolerate disobedience."

"Hear that?" Rage beams. "You're gonna have a hard time –"

"That applies to you as well," Zhang stops him. "Both of you will be silent."

I expect Rage to challenge Master Zhang, but he shuts up immediately and bows politely. I glare at him but hold my tongue.

"Oystein told me of your feud," Zhang says, "but that is not why I have kept you apart. I prefer to train new recruits by themselves for the first few days, so that I can evaluate them independently."

"I bet I'm doing better than you," Rage murmurs to me.

I ignore him, as does Master Zhang.

"There is a test that I subject my students to, usually after a couple of weeks," Zhang continues. "But Oystein wishes to speak with both of you later today, to explain more about our history and goals. I have decided to give you the test ahead of that meeting."

"Why?" Rage asks.

"It is an important test," Zhang says. "If you fail, it will be an indication that you are not cut out for life as a fully active Angel. If

136

Oystein knows that you will not be taking part in our more serious missions, it might affect what he chooses to share with you."

"You mean, if we turn out to be a pair of losers, he won't want to waste too much time on us," I grunt.

"Precisely," Zhang says smoothly, then heads to the door and nods for us to follow him.

"You're not giving us the test here?" Rage asks as we turn into the corridor.

"No," he says. "We need reviveds for the test." He looks back at us and his eyes glitter. "*Lots* of reviveds."

Rage and I share a worried glance, then trail Master Zhang through the building. He stops off at a small storage room to pick up a couple of rucksacks, then leads us outside and over to Waterloo Station. We pass one of the speakers along the way, but he doesn't bother to turn it off.

"What's that noise?" Rage winces.

"I'll tell you about it sometime, if you pass this test," I grin, delighted to know something he doesn't.

Zhang leads us up to the station concourse. This used to be one of the busiest train stations in London, but now it's home to hundreds of resting reviveds. The mindless zombies are scattered around the concourse, squatting, sitting, lying down, or just standing, waiting for night to fall. It's strange to think that so many of them are on our doorstep. I haven't seen any since I came to County Hall.

I stare at the old ticket machines, the shops and restaurants, trying to recall what it would have been like back in the day, wanting to feel nostalgic. But it's getting harder to remember what the world was like, to treat the memories as if they're real, rather than fragments of some crazy dream I once had.

"This is a very straightforward task," Zhang says. He points towards the far end of the concourse, to an open doorway at the rear of the station. "I want you to race to that exit. If you make it out in one piece, you pass the test."

"That's all?" Rage frowns. "But that's too easy. The zombies won't attack us. They know we're the same as them. Unless these are different than the ones I've seen elsewhere?"

"They are no different," Zhang says. "I did not arrange for them to be present, or interfere with them in any way. These are the usual residents, revivals who have chosen to base themselves here."

"Then what's the catch?" Rage asks.

"The rucksacks of course," I tell him.

"Correct," Zhang says. He passes one of the rucksacks to me, the other to Rage, and gestures at us to put them on.

"I still don't get it," Rage growls. "They're not heavy. They won't slow us down."

"They are not meant to slow you down," Master Zhang tuts, then drives the fingers of his right hand into the rucksack on Rage's back, making five holes in it, before doing the same thing to mine.

The scent of fresh brains instantly fills the air and my lips tighten.

"This isn't good," Rage mutters as the heads of the zombies closest to us start to lift.

"If you stood still, they would come and examine you," Zhang says. "When they realized that the brains are stored in your rucksacks, they'd let you be – reviveds do not fight with one another – and stand nearby, waiting, hoping to finish off any scraps that you might leave behind."

"But we're not going to stand still, are we?" I sigh.

"No," Zhang says. "You are going to run." He pokes some more holes in our rucksacks. "*Now.*"

Rage swears under his breath and shoots a dirty look at Master Zhang. Then, since he has no other choice, he runs towards the zombies, who are stirring and getting to their feet. And since I have no choice either, I race after him, closing in quickly on the growing, undead wall of snarling, hungry reviveds.

EIGHTEEN

Rage barrels into several of the zombies, sending them flying. They howl with anger and excitement, more of them becoming alert, catching the scent of brains, closing in on us, fangs bared, finger bones twitching.

I take advantage of the confusion Rage has caused and angle to the right, hoping to slip by unnoticed. But other zombies who were sheltering on the platforms have heard the noises and come to investigate. When they spot me tearing by, they clamber over the ticket barriers and surge towards me in a mob, forcing me back into the center of the concourse.

Rage is surrounded and is lashing out with his fists, trying to shove past those who block his way. It looks impossible, but he's kept up his momentum, like a burly rugby player forcing back a scrum.

I take a different approach. As zombies clutch at me and throw themselves in my path, I duck and shimmy and veer around them. I've been in a situation like this before, in Liverpool Street, when I was trying to escape with Sister Clare of the Shnax, so I put that experience to good use.

A sprawling zombie – he looks like he was a construction worker when he was alive – grabs my left leg just above my ankle and pulls me down. I kick out at him as I fall and he slides away from me. I realize he has no legs – they look like they were torn from him at the knees when he was turned – which is why he's lying on the floor.

Taking advantage of my unexpected fall, I slip through the legs of a couple of zombies ahead of me. One is a woman in a miniskirt. I grab hold of the skirt and spin her around, so that she clatters into several other zombies and knocks them over. As the skirt rips, I let her go, propel myself to my feet and carry on.

Rage has found a way through the press of zombies around him and has picked up speed. He calls cheerfully to me, "This is the life, isn't it?"

I ignore him and stay focused on the reviveds, ducking their grasping fingers, kicking out at them, looking for open channels that I can exploit.

Master Zhang is trailing us, slowly, as if out for a Sunday stroll.

He watches calmly, but not too curiously. I guess he's seen all this lots of times before.

A girl sort of my own age grabs the rucksack on my back and tries to wrestle it from me, either realizing that the smell is coming from there, or simply seeing it as the best way to slow me down. I turn sharply and slam the flat of my palm up into her chin, snapping her head back and knocking her loose.

"An interesting move," Master Zhang says. "Most people in your position would have simply punched her."

I don't reply. There's no time. Before the girl staggers away from me, I grab her and force her to her knees. Then I step onto her back and launch myself forward, flying over the heads of a pack of zombies who were closing in on me.

"Oh, now even I've got to applaud that one," Rage booms, clapping loudly. He's been forced to a standstill close to where I land. "How about we do this as a team?" he bellows, offering me his hand.

"Get stuffed," I snap, and look for another small zombie that I can use as a springboard.

This time, as I'm hurling myself into the air, one of the reviveds catches hold of my left foot and hauls me to the floor. A cluster of them press in around me, fingers clawing at my face, trying to rip my head open, to get to the juicy brain that they think is the source of the smell.

"No!" I scream, pushing them back and struggling to my feet. I look around desperately, hoping that Master Zhang will help. But he just stands there, gazing at me, challenging me with his expression to figure my own way out of this mess.

Rage is moving forward again. He's snapped an arm off one of the zombies and is using it as a club, lashing out at anyone within range. Many of the zombies who get knocked back by him shake their heads, then refocus on me, figuring I offer easier pickings. A huge crowd of them starts to close in around me.

"Sod this," I pant, knowing my number's up if I don't act swiftly.

Wriggling free of the rucksack, I rip it open and start throwing slivers of brain around, as if it was some weird kind of confetti. When the zombies spot the gray chunks, they go wild, but now they're concentrating on the bits of brain, trying to catch them as I toss them about, emptying the rucksack as quickly as I can.

When the rucksack is clean, I let it drop and fall still, letting the zombies see that I'm not trying to escape, that I have no need to run, that I'm the same as them.

A few of the reviveds sniff me suspiciously, growling like dogs, but then they leave me be and tear the remains of the rucksack to shreds, trying to squeeze out any last morsels of brain that might be hidden in the folds.

I look up at Master Zhang, shamefully, as the zombies part around me, but he's following Rage, no longer interested in me. I think about heading back to County Hall, or maybe just slipping away completely, figuring that's the end of my career as an Angel. But I want to see what happens to Rage. I'm hoping he'll brick it like I did and cast his rucksack aside.

But Rage is like a wrecking ball. The zombies slow him down, but they can't stop him. He slaps them back with the arm, punches and kicks them when the arm is no longer any good, sticks his head down and forces his way forward, refusing to accept defeat. I almost cheer on the rampaging brute, but then I recall how he killed Dr. Cerveris and deserted the rest of the zom heads, and I hold my tongue.

He finally makes it to the end of the concourse and squeezes through the exit. As soon as he's out, he tears off the rucksack and lobs it back inside the station. The reviveds scurry after it, quickly losing interest in him, as they lost it in me.

"Now *that* was fun," Rage grins as we join him outside. He wipes blood – not his own – from his face. "I guess some of us have what it takes, Becky, and some of us don't."

"Bite me," I snarl, then cast a miserable look at Master Zhang. "I guess this means I've had it."

"Not at all," he says, surprising both of us.

"What are you talking about?" Rage snaps. "She failed."

"No," Zhang says. "The test is designed to measure one's bravery, ingenuity and strength, but also one's level of common sense. Almost no novice Angel has made it all the way across the concourse. In fact you are only the third, and the other two made it with cunning and speed, not sheer muscle power."

"Sweet!" Rage beams, thrilled with himself.

"So...I didn't fail?" I frown.

"No. You showed that you were willing to face adversity, and you handled yourself well. In fact you made it farther than most. But just as important, when you realized you could go no farther, you were sensible enough to rid yourself of the beacon which was attracting the reviveds. Those who fail are those who break too early with fear, or those who lack the wit to throw away the rucksack."

"Then I did better than Rage, in a way," I joke.

"In your dreams," Rage grunts.

"There is no better or worse in my eyes," Master Zhang says. "You both passed. That is the end of the matter."

With that, he heads back to County Hall, but circles round the rear of the station this time, rather than return through the concourse. Rage slides up beside me as we trail our mentor. He points to himself and says, "One of three." Then he points to me and says, "One of *who cares?*"

He laughs and moves on before I can reply, leaving me to scowl angrily at his back with a mixture of hatred, jealousy and grudging respect.

NINETEEN

Master Zhang leads Rage and me back to the room in County Hall where I was training earlier. He says that since he has both of us with him, he will train with the pair of us for the rest of the session.

I get excited when I hear that. After passing our Waterloo-based test, I assume that we're ready to move on, that he'll start teaching us complicated moves. But it's business as usual, the only change being that he now takes turns to throw us to the floor. I'm pleased to see that Rage is treated the same way I am, but disappointed that Master Zhang isn't taking us a few stages farther forward.

We've been back about an hour when the door opens and Dr. Oystein steps into the room. He's not alone. Ashtat, Carl,

Shane and Jakob are with him, as well as a man I recognize but didn't expect to see here.

"Mr. Burke?" I gasp.

"Hello again, B," my ex-teacher says as our training draws to a halt. "We seem to keep meeting in the strangest of places, don't we?"

As I gape at my old teacher, I recall what Reilly said about seeing someone he knew with a pack of Angels after he'd deserted the army following the riots in the underground complex, and it starts to make sense.

Billy Burke had worked in the complex with Reilly, but he'd never seemed to fit in with the soldiers and scientists. Of them all, only he truly cared about the welfare of the zom heads. That was why they'd recruited him, to help them with the sometimes rebellious teenagers.

I should have figured this out before. Having severed his ties with the army, Reilly wouldn't have wanted to approach any of his old crew. Burke was different. Reilly wouldn't have considered him the same as the others. He'd have felt he could trust the compassionate counselor.

"Josh told me he'd released you," Burke says as I stand, staring at him silently. "I was hoping you'd find your way here. That's why I passed on your description to Dr. Oystein."

I frown. "*You* told the doc about me?"

"Yes," Dr. Oystein answers. "That is how I knew your name when you first came here, and some of your background."

I scratch an ear. "I thought Reilly spotted me on the cameras and told you."

The doctor shakes his head. "No. It was Billy."

"Well... thanks... I guess," I mutter, lowering my hand.

"It is good to see you again, B," Dr. Oystein says. "You have settled in nicely, I hear."

"I'm doing all right," I sniff.

"Zhang," Dr. Oystein says, bowing towards our mentor.

Master Zhang bows in return.

"How did our pair of fledgling Angels fare with their test earlier?" Dr. Oystein asks.

"They passed," Zhang says simply, giving us no more credit than that.

"I told you they would," Burke smiles. "They're a rare pair, those two."

"Some of us are rarer than others," Rage says, cocking an eyebrow at me.

"Why don't you shut up for once?" I snarl.

"Who's gonna make me?" Rage growls, squaring up to me.

"I would rather you did not fight," Dr. Oystein says quietly, and Rage immediately goes all sheepish and shuffles his feet.

"Sorry," he mutters.

"Oh, isn't he a good boy," I coo, then spit with contempt, which isn't easy with my dry mouth. "Don't trust him, Dr. Oystein. He's only buttering you up to make you like him, the same way he did with Dr. Cerveris."

"Why should I?" Rage counters. "Dr. Oystein hasn't tried to cage me up like those other buggers did. I'm free to leave whenever I please."

"And you will," I snort. "When it suits you. And you'll probably kill a few of us along the way, just for the hell of it."

Rage shrugs and turns to Dr. Oystein. "I told you, when I saw her in the lab, that she'd have nothing good to say about me."

"Yes, you did," the doctor nods. "And B has warned us to be wary of you. I have chosen to ignore both of your opinions, so please save your bickering for another time. You are going to be roommates, so you will have plenty of –"

"You're not sticking him in with us!" I shout.

"Please, B, there is no need to raise your voice."

"But –"

"Please," Dr. Oystein says again. The fact that he sounds as if he is actually asking, rather than issuing an order, slows me in my tracks. I grumble something beneath my breath but otherwise hold my tongue.

Carl and the others are watching our exchange with interest, eyeing up Rage.

"This is Michael Jarman," Dr. Oystein says to them. "But he prefers –"

"*Michael Jarman?*" I laugh.

"You didn't think I was christened Rage, did you?" he says.

"I brought you here to meet him, because Rage will be sharing your room if nobody has any objections," Dr. Oystein continues, then smiles fleetingly at me. "With the noted exception of Miss Smith."

"If he moves in, I'm moving out," I say stiffly.

Dr. Oystein sighs. "That would be regrettable. I let everyone decide where they want to room once they have adjusted to life here, but I prefer to assign places to begin with. If you choose not to respect my decision, I will take that as a sign that you do not trust my judgment."

"No, it's not that...I mean I don't..." I growl with frustration. "He's a killer. He betrayed me and the other zom heads."

"I know."

"But you want to stick him in with me anyway?"

"Yes."

Dr. Oystein's expression never alters.

"Fine," I grunt. "Whatever."

"Thank you," he says, and seeks the approval of the others. They shrug, knowing nothing about Rage or my beef with him. "In that case, thank you for your time, and feel free to return to your usual duties. B and Rage, would you please accompany Mr. Burke and me

154

on a short walk? There are certain matters I wish to discuss with the pair of you."

"Sure," I say, shooting Rage an evil look. He only smirks in return.

We file out, Dr. Oystein and Burke in front, Rage and I a few steps behind, keeping as far apart from one another as we can.

TWENTY

We wind our way through the corridors of County Hall, Dr. Oystein taking his time. Burke looks back at me. "I was so relieved when Josh said that he'd spared you."

"Yeah, well, I was the only one he did spare," I say bitterly, recalling how he torched the other zom heads.

Burke looks contrite. "If I'd been there, I would have tried to stop him."

"Really?" I challenge him. "You seemed to be fine with what he was doing the rest of the time."

My old teacher sighs heavily. "I'm sorry for all of the deception and lies. They thought I was on their side. They knew I didn't approve of everything they were doing, but they had no idea I was in league with Dr. Oystein. I had to play ball or they might have become suspicious."

"You were a spy?" I frown.

"Yes."

"I do not trust the military," Dr. Oystein says without pausing or turning. "They wish to restore order to the world, which is my wish too, but they want to do so on their own terms. We must be wary of them. They include me in some of their plans and experiments, since they respect my specialist knowledge of the undead, but I like to keep track of all that I am excluded from too. Billy agreed to act as my inside man, as he had already earned their trust before our paths crossed."

"You mean you were working for the army before you met Dr. Oystein?"

Burke nods.

"Not especially loyal, are you?" I snort.

"I'm loyal to those I deem deserving of loyalty," he says sharply.

Silence falls again. We exit the building onto the riverbank. I think for a second that Dr. Oystein plans to take us bowling, but then I see that he's heading for the aquarium. "Was the story about you convincing Josh and the others to feed me and keep me revitalized the truth?" I ask Burke.

"Yes," he says.

"Thanks," I mutter.

"No need. You would have done the same for me." I raise an

eyebrow and Burke chuckles wryly. "Well, I like to tell myself that you would."

We share a quick grin, then we're stepping off the path into the dim, silent world of the aquarium. I came here in the past, but not since I rocked up at County Hall as a zombie. I hadn't even thought about this place. Fish have been among the last things on my mind recently.

I find, to my surprise, that most of the tanks are still in working order, teeming with underwater life as they were before.

"Do zombies eat fish brains?" I ask.

"Only those of a certain size," Dr. Oystein says. "We thrive primarily on human brains, but those of larger animals and fish are nourishing too. Fortunately a small band of people managed to drive back the zombies on the day of the attack and barricade themselves in here. Ciara was one of them. They survived and hung on until we set up camp in County Hall. All except Ciara chose to be relocated to compounds beyond the city once we gave them that option. She had grown fond of the place, and of my Angels, so she decided to stay."

We move in silence from one tank to another, studying an array of fish, turtles, squid and all sorts of weird species. Many are beautifully colored and strangely shaped, and I'm reminded of how exotic this place seemed when I came here as a child. I never saw the appeal of aquariums before I visited. I thought they were dull places for nerds who loved goldfish.

We come to a glass tunnel through a huge tank of sharks. There are other things in there with them, but who takes notice of anything else when you spot a shark?

Dr. Oystein draws to a halt in the middle of the tunnel and gazes around. "I did not know much about the maintenance of aquariums when I first moved in, but I have made it my business to learn. Some of my Angels share my passion and tend to the tanks in my absence. Perhaps one of you will wish to help too."

Rage shakes his head. "I only like fish when it's in batter and served up with chips."

"Philistine," I sneer.

"Up yours," he says. "They don't do anything for me. I'd rather go on a safari than deep-sea diving."

"I doubt if anyone will be going on a safari anytime in the near future," Dr. Oystein murmurs. "And the zoos have been picked clean of their stock by now—I sent teams to check, in case we could harvest more brains. But at least this small part of our natural heritage survives."

Dr. Oystein sits down and nods for us to join him on the floor. He says nothing for a moment, relishing the underwater world that we've become a temporary part of. Then he makes a happy sighing sound.

"For many decades I have found God in the creatures of the sea," he says. "The sheer diversity of life, the crazy shapes and colors, the way they can adapt and flourish...I defy anyone to stroll

through an aquarium and tell me our world could throw forth such wonders without the guiding hand of a higher power."

"You're not a fan of Darwin then?" Rage snickers.

"Oh, I believe in evolution," Dr. Oystein says. "But you do not have to exclude one at the expense of the other. All creatures – ourselves included – are servants of nature and the changing forces of the world in which we live. But how can such a world have come into being by accident? If evolution was the only force at work, large, dull, powerful beasts would have prevailed and stamped their mark on this planet long ago. Only a curious, playful God would have populated our shores and seas with such a glittering, spellbinding array of specimens."

Dr. Oystein turns his gaze away from the sharks to look us in the eye, one after the other, as he speaks.

"I did not bring you here by chance. As I said, I find God in places like this, and God is what I wish to discuss. I was not always a believer, so I will not be dismayed if you do not share my beliefs. I am not looking to convert either of you, merely to explain how and why I came to put together my team of Angels.

"I was born shortly after the turn of the twentieth century. It might seem odd, but I no longer recall the exact date. It is even possible that I was born in the late nineteenth century, though I do not think I am quite that old.

"For the first thirty-five or forty years of my life, I was an atheist. I hurled the works of Darwin and other scientists at those who clung to the ways of what I thought was a ridiculous, outdated past. Then, in the 1930s, in the lead-up to the Second World War, God found me and I realized what a fool I had been." Dr. Oystein lowers his gaze and sighs again, sadly this time.

"God found me," he repeats in a cracked voice, "but not before the Nazis found me first…"

TWENTY-ONE

Dr. Oystein traveled around Europe with his parents when he was a child. As a man, he continued to tour the world, but ended up settling in Poland, where his wife was from and where his elder brother – also a doctor – had set up home.

They were happy years, he tells us, the brothers working together, raising their families, enjoying the lull between the wars. Dr. Oystein and his brother were noted geneticists who could have lived anywhere – they had offers from across the globe – but they were happy in Poland.

Then the Nazis invaded. Dr. Oystein's instincts told him to flee, but his wife and children didn't want to leave their home and his brother refused to go too. With an uneasy feeling, he agreed to remain and hoped that he would be allowed to carry on his work in peace and quiet, since he had no strong political ties and wasn't a member of any of the religions or races that the Nazis despised.

Unfortunately for the doctor, the Nazis were almost as interested in genetics as they were in killing Jews and gypsies. They were intent on improving the human form and creating a master race. They saw Dr. Oystein and his brother as key allies in their quest to overcome the weaknesses of nature.

When Dr. Oystein rejected their advances, he was imprisoned in a concentration camp along with his brother and their families. The camps weren't as hellish as the death camps that were built later in the war, but the chances of survival were slim all the same.

"If the guards disliked you," Dr. Oystein says quietly, "they worked you until you could work no more, then executed you for failing to complete your tasks. Or they tortured you until you confessed to whatever crime they wished to charge you with. They might make you stand still for hours on end, under the threat of death if you moved, then shoot you when you collapsed from sheer exhaustion."

Dr. Oystein had three children. His brother had four. The Nazis killed one of Dr. Oystein's children and two of his brother's, and made it clear that their wives and the surviving children would be executed as well if the brothers didn't do as they were told. When they saw what they were up against, they agreed to be shipped off to a secret unit to work for their monstrous new masters.

The Nazis yearned to unravel the secrets of life and death, to bring the dead back from beyond the grave. There were two reasons. One was to create an army of undead soldiers, to give them an advantage in the war. The other was so that they could survive forever, to indefinitely enjoy the pleasures of the new society that they were hell-bent on creating.

Dr. Oystein and his brother were part of an elite team, some of the greatest minds in the world, all working towards the same warped goal. Some were there by force, some by choice. It didn't matter. They all had to slave away as hard as they could. Nazis were not known for their tolerance of failure.

"We made huge strides forward," Dr. Oystein says without any hint of pride. "We unlocked secrets that are still beyond the knowledge of geneticists today. If we had been allowed to share our findings with the world, we would have been hailed as wonders and people of your generation would be benefiting from our discoveries. But the Nazis were selfish. Records of our advances were buried away in mounds of paperwork, far from prying eyes."

Dr. Oystein created the first revived. He brought a woman back to life after she had died of malnutrition in a concentration camp. (He says that most of their cadavers were drawn from the camps.)

"It should have been a wondrous moment," he whispers. "I had done what only God had previously achieved. Mankind's potential skyrocketed. The future opened up to us as it never had before. Immortality – or at least a vastly extended life – became ours for the taking."

But instead he felt wretched, partly because he knew the Nazis would take his discovery and do terrible things with it, but also because he felt that he had broken the laws of the universe, and he was sure that nothing good could come of that.

The Nazis rejoiced. The revived was a mindless, howling, savage beast, of no practical use to them, but they were confident that the doctor and his team would build on this breakthrough and find a way to restore the mind as well as the body. But they couldn't. No matter how many corpses they brought back to life, they couldn't get the brains to work. Every zombie was a drooling, senseless wreck.

"The Nazis discussed dropping the living dead behind enemy lines," Dr. Oystein says, "but as vicious as they were, they were not fools. They knew they could not manage the spread of the reviveds once they released them, and they had no wish to inherit a world of deadly, infectious zombies."

Dr. Oystein was sure that they had pushed the project as far as they could. He didn't share that view with the Nazis, but all of his results suggested to him that they had come to a dead end. He didn't think the brain of a corpse could ever be restored.

While all this was happening, the Nazis kept presenting the brothers with regular reports of their wives and children, photographs and letters to prove that they were alive and well. One day that stopped. They were told that the information was being withheld until they created a revitalized specimen, but the doctors were afraid that something terrible had happened.

"And we were right," Dr. Oystein mutters. "I found out much later that both of my remaining children had died. My wife went wild and attacked those who had imprisoned her. My brother's wife tried to pull her away, to calm her down.

"The women were shot by an overeager guard. That left only my brother's daughter and son. The girl died a couple of years later, but the boy survived." Dr. Oystein coughs and looks away. "I thought of my nephew often over the decades but never sought him out. I didn't want him to see what I had become."

With no news of their loved ones, and fearing the worst, the brothers made up their minds to escape. They hated working for the Nazis, and if their families had been executed, they had nothing to lose—their own lives didn't matter to them. They put a lot of time and thought into their plan, and almost pulled it off. But their laboratory was one of the most highly guarded prisons in the world. Luck went against them on the night of their escape. They were caught and tortured.

Under interrogation, Dr. Oystein told the Nazis that he thought it was impossible to revitalize a subject, that the vacant zombies in their holding cells were as good as it was ever going to get. The Nazis were furious. They decided to teach the brothers a vicious lesson, to serve as an example. They infected the pair with the undead gene and turned them into zombies.

"That should have been the end of us," Dr. Oystein says, eyes distant as he remembers that dark, long-ago day. "But there was something nobody had counted on. Like every other revived, I could not be brought back to consciousness by the hand of man. But there was another at work, a doctor of sorts, whose power was far greater than mine or anyone else's.

"Mock me if you wish – many others have before you, and for all I know they are right – but I am certain that my mind and soul were restored by a force of ultimate good, a force I choose to call *God*."

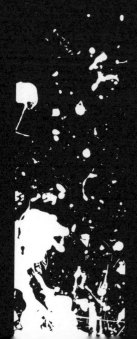

TWENTY-TWO

Dr. Oystein pauses to study the sharks. I glance around at the others, disturbed by what I've been told. Burke returns my gaze calmly, giving no sign whether he buys this or not. Rage is more direct. He puts a finger to the side of his head and twirls it around—*cuckoo!* But I can tell by the way he peeks guiltily at Dr. Oystein as he lowers his arm that the story has troubled him too.

"God spoke to me when He saved me," Dr. Oystein continues. "He told me what had happened, why I had been spared, what I must do."

The reviveds were kept in holding pens, secure but not foolproof. Plenty of security measures were in place, but all had been designed with the limitations of brainless subjects in mind. The Nazis hadn't considered the threat of a conscious, intelligent zombie.

Dr. Oystein freed the reviveds and set them on the soldiers and scientists, who were taken by surprise. Nobody was spared. The zombies ran riot, killing or converting everyone, helped by the doctor, who opened doors and sought out hiding places.

When all of the humans had been disposed of, Dr. Oystein destroyed every last scrap of paperwork and evidence of what had been going on. He knew that reports had been sent to officials elsewhere, but he did what he could to limit the damage. After that, with a heavy heart, he killed all of the zombies one by one, ripping out their brains to ensure they were never brought back to life again.

Dr. Oystein doesn't mention his brother, but I'm sure he must have killed him too. I'm not surprised that he doesn't go into specifics. It's not the sort of thing I imagine you want to spend a lot of time thinking about.

His work finished, Dr. Oystein slipped away into the night, to set about the mission that he had been given by the voice inside his head.

God told Dr. Oystein that the human race had become too violent and destructive. Bringing the dead back to life was the final straw. There had to be a reckoning, like when the Bible said that He flooded the world. A thinning of the ranks. A cleansing.

The voice told Dr. Oystein that there would be a plague of zombies in the near future. On a day of divine destiny, a war would break out between mankind and the living dead.

"Are you saying God unleashed the zombies?" I ask incredulously, unable to keep quiet any longer.

"Of course not," Dr. Oystein replies. "But God saw that scientists would conduct fresh experiments and create new strains of the zombie gene. And one day one of them would accidentally or deliberately release an airborne strain that would sweep the globe and convert millions of humans into undead monsters. He could have spared us the agony if He had wished, but honestly, B, can you think of any good reason why He should have intervened?"

"Lots of innocent people died," I mutter.

Dr. Oystein nods. "They always do. That is the nature of our world. But do you think it was a perfect society, that our leaders were just and good, that as a race we were not guilty of unimaginable, unpardonable crimes?"

"You can't punish everyone for the sins of a few," Rage growls.

"Of course you can," Dr. Oystein says. "Just step outside and look around if you do not believe that. As a people, we offended our creator and turned on our own like jackals. We soiled this world. Was the plague of zombies a harsh judgment? Perhaps. But unfair? I think not."

Dr. Oystein shakes his head when nobody says anything else, then continues.

He crisscrossed the world in the years to come, building up contacts among all sorts of officials. His first priority was to crack down on undead outbreaks, and to contain them when they happened. With the help of his contacts, he kept the existence of zombies a secret. Rumors trickled out every so often, but nobody in their right mind paid any attention to them. Hollywood filmmakers were paid to weave wild tales about the living dead, to turn them into movie monsters, like Dracula or the Mummy.

But no matter how hard he worked, the experiments continued. Nazi scientists in hiding created their own small zombie armies in the hope of launching a bid to control the world again. Some sold their secrets to rich men or leaders in countries where power struggles were a way of life.

Dr. Oystein experimented too. God had told him that he would need to fight fire with fire if he was to have any chance of redeeming the human race. The doctor was the first of what could be a highly effective force of revitalizeds. If he could find a way to restore others, the world might regain a sliver of hope.

"Although it repulsed me, I returned to my work," he says, hanging his head with shame. "If there was any other way, I would have seized it gladly, but there wasn't."

"What makes you think you're any better than the rest of the creeps then?" I sneer. "Maybe the airborne gene was created by one of *your* associates, using technology that *you* pioneered."

"Perhaps," Dr. Oystein nods. "But I do not think that is the case. I have learnt much about the gene over the decades, but the airborne strain was new to me. It is a destructive strain, while my work has been focused on the positive possibilities, on the human mind and its restoration.

"I finally figured out a way to create revitalizeds," he goes on. "I hoped to perfect a vaccine that would stop people returning to life when they were infected—if zombies could only kill, not convert, they would be far easier to deal with. Failing that, I hoped to provide the undead with the ability to recover their wits, so that they could be reasoned with.

"Until that point I had experimented solely on corpses or on those who had been revived. But if prevention was to serve as the key to our survival, it meant I would have to –"

"– experiment on living people," Rage cuts in, beating Dr. Oystein to the punch. He doesn't look outraged, simply fascinated.

"You're sick," I snarl, but for once I'm not insulting Rage. My comment is directed at Dr. Oystein. I rise and glare at him. "You're just like the Nazis and the scientists who were experimenting on the zom heads."

"I do not claim to be any nobler than them," Dr. Oystein says softly. "I have done many dreadful things and you have every right to vilify me."

"Then why shouldn't I?" I snap. "You said I was an Angel. You offered protection and told me we could do good. Why should I accept the word of a man who experimented on living people and probably killed more than a few in the process?"

"Many have died at my hands over the years," he admits. "I see their faces every night, even though I don't dream."

"So why should I pledge myself to you?" I press. "Why shouldn't I storm out of here and never look back?"

Dr. Oystein shrugs. "Because I was successful," he whispers. "I found a way to revitalize zombies."

Now it's my turn to shrug. "So? Does that mean we should forgive you?"

Dr. Oystein looks up at last. There's no anger in his gaze, only misery. "I am not worthy of forgiveness, but I do think that I am worthy of your support."

"Why?" I ask again, barking the question this time.

"Because I created you," Dr. Oystein says. And as I stare at him, trying to figure out what he means, he says, "Tell me, B, do you have a little *c*-shaped scar on your upper right thigh?"

In the silence that follows, all I can do is stare at him, then through the glass walls of the tunnel at the sharks circling patiently, their wide mouths lifting at the corners, almost in wicked, mocking smiles.

TWENTY-THREE

I've had the *c*-shaped scar since I was two or three years old. I was injected with an experimental flu vaccine. It worked like a charm and I've never had so much as a sniffle since. I sometimes thought it was odd that the vaccine hadn't taken off—nobody else I knew had been vaccinated with it. I figured there must have been side effects, which I'd been lucky enough to avoid.

"Haven't you wondered why virtually all of the revitalizeds are teenagers?" Burke asks softly.

I stare at him, thinking back. In the underground complex I never saw any adult revitalizeds. I assumed they were being held in a different section, that we'd been grouped together by age.

Apart from Dr. Oystein and Master

Zhang, they're all teenagers or younger here in County Hall too. Dr. Oystein told me that adult revitalizeds were rare, but I never pushed it any further than that. I've gotten so used to being around others my own age that it didn't seem strange.

"I developed the vaccine about forty years ago," Dr. Oystein says. "It is unpredictable and does not work in everyone. Many who have been vaccinated do not recover their senses when infected. Those who revitalize do so at different rates. The fastest has been eighteen hours. At six months, you are one of the slowest."

"See?" Rage smiles. "You're slow. It's official."

I ignore him and stay focused on Dr. Oystein.

"My intention was to have teams vaccinate every living person before the wave of reviveds broke across the world. But the vaccine was unstable. It could not be held in check indefinitely. If a person was not bitten by a zombie, after fifteen or so years it turned on its host. The body broke down. The bones and flesh liquefied. It was swift – from start to finish, no more than half a day – and incredibly painful."

"You're telling me that if I hadn't been attacked by zombies, I'd have ended up as a puddle of goo in another year or two?" I gasp.

The doctor nods and I laugh bitterly.

"You're some piece of work, doc. The Nazis had nothing on you."

He flinches at the insult.

"But now that we've been infected..." Rage says.

"The vaccine will not harm us while it is fighting with the zombie gene," Dr. Oystein says. "We are safe now that we have revitalized.

"If I had known when the day of reckoning was due, I could have vaccinated as many people as possible," he continues. "But God never revealed the date to me. If I had miscalculated, I could have wiped out the entire race by myself, no zombies required."

Rage whistles softly. "That's some crazy power. Were you ever tempted to...you know...just for the hell of it?"

We all stare at him.

"Come on," he protests. "You guys were thinking the same thing. If you had the world in the palm of your hand, and all you had to do was squeeze..."

"You're a sick, twisted bastard," I sneer.

"No," Dr. Oystein says. "Rage is right. I *was* tempted. But not in the way he thinks. I had no interest in crushing nations. I was tempted because I was afraid. I knew the terrors and hardships we must face, and I did not want to embrace such a future. It would have been easier to condemn mankind to a swift, certain end, to accept defeat and ensure that nobody need suffer the agonies of a long, drawn-out war of nightmarish proportions. Death by vaccine would have been simpler, the coward's way out.

"I am various low, despicable things," Dr. Oystein whispers, "but I do not think I am a coward. I am guilty of many foul crimes, but I have always accepted my responsibilities. I ignored the pleas of my weaker self and remained true to my calling. If mankind is to perish, it will not be because I was found wanting."

Dr. Oystein rises and starts walking. The rest of us head after him. He moves faster than before, striding through the aquarium, leading us out into the open. On the riverbank he hurries to the wall overlooking the Thames and bends over it as if about to throw up.

"I'm sorry," he moans, but it's unclear whether he's apologizing to us or the souls of the people he experimented on and killed over the course of his long and dreadful life.

TWENTY-FOUR

Dr. Oystein stays facing the river for a couple of minutes while the rest of us stand back, waiting for him to recover.

"This guy needs to see a shrink," Rage murmurs.

I turn to rip into him for being an insensitive pig, but I see by his expression that he wasn't having a dig. The big, ugly lump looks about as pitying as he ever could.

"I doubt if any ordinary professional could help him," Burke says softly. "This isn't a normal complaint. To have endured all that he has... I'm stunned he's not a gibbering wreck."

"Do you believe everything he told us?" I ask. "About Nazis, God, all that..." I was about to say *crap* but decide that's not the right word. "...stuff?"

"We'll discuss that later," Burke says, and nods at Dr. Oystein, who is turning from the river at last. He looks embarrassed.

"My apologies. Sometimes the guilt overwhelms me. I know that I have done what was asked of me, but there are days when that does not seem like a justifiable excuse. God did not authorize the experiments, the tests that went awry, the lives that I have sacrificed. I see no other way that I could have proceeded, but still I wonder... and fear."

He sighs and glances up at the London Eye, turning as smoothly as ever, the pods shining brightly against the backdrop of the cloudy sky.

"So why are all of your Angels teenagers?" I ask to draw him back to what he was talking about earlier. "Why didn't you vaccinate adults too?"

"I felt that children would be more appropriate," Dr. Oystein says. "They are, generally speaking, more innocent and pure of heart than adults."

"You wouldn't think like that if you'd gone to my school," I mutter, and share a grin with Mr. Burke.

Dr. Oystein smiles ruefully. "That was not the only factor. There were practical reasons too. Children were easier to vaccinate than adults—they received so many jabs that nobody took notice of one more. And since their bodies were undergoing natural changes during growth, they were better equipped to contain the vaccine—children generally held out a few years longer than grown-ups before succumbing to the side effects.

182

"Also, I distrusted adults. They were set in their ways, less open to fresh ideas and change. I needed soldiers who would think nothing of their own lives, who would dedicate themselves entirely to the cause. I decided that children were more likely to answer such a demanding call.

"Every year my team vaccinated a selection from newborns to teenagers in cities, towns and villages across the world. Every time I looked at the files – and I made a point of acknowledging each and every subject – I suffered a conflict of interests. I found myself hoping that the plague would strike soon, to spare the vaccinated children the painful death they would have to endure if it did not, yet also wishing that it wouldn't, because that would mean so many more people dying."

Dr. Oystein falls silent again, remembering some of the faces of the damned.

"How many did you vaccinate each year?" I ask.

"Several thousand," he says. "Always in a different area, with a fresh team under a different guise, to avert people's suspicions."

"What do you mean?" Rage frowns.

"One year we offered a cure for the flu," Dr. Oystein explains. "The next year we promoted a measles vaccine. The year after something to help prevent AIDS. Each time we hid behind a fake company or charity."

"So if you've been doing this for decades…" I try to do the math.

"Hundreds of thousands," Dr. Oystein says softly.

"How the hell do you cover up that many deaths?" I explode. "Especially if they melted down into muck. I never read about anything like that in the Sunday papers."

"As I already explained, I had contacts in high places," Dr. Oystein says. "They clamped down on any talk that might have compromised our position."

"Still," I mutter, "*somebody* must have leaked word of what was going on."

"They did," Burke says. "It was all over the place, in self-published books and on the Internet. I remember coming across articles back when I knew nothing about Dr. Oystein or his work. Like any sane person, I dismissed them. Who could believe stories of a drug that made people melt?"

"Truth is stranger than fiction," Rage says smugly, as if he's just come out with an incredibly original, witty line.

"All right," I mutter. "I'm getting it. You vaccinated thousands of kids every year to create an army of revitalizeds when the Apocalypse hit. So there must be, what, a few hundred thousand of us, ranging in age from adults down to babies?"

"Less," Dr. Oystein says. "Many failed to revitalize, particularly those who had matured. Others were slaughtered during the assaults and their brains were eaten. Young children who revitalized either failed to follow the signs to my safe houses or reverted due to not being able to feed.

"We cannot be sure, but we think there are maybe a couple of thousand Angels worldwide, possibly less."

"You didn't get a great return for all those sacrifices, did you, doc?" Rage asks quietly.

"No," the doctor says, even quieter.

"And are there centers like this in different countries, full of Angels?" I ask.

"Yes," Dr. Oystein says hesitantly.

"Something wrong with the others?" I press.

"No. But they are not as important as the Angels in London."

I laugh shortly. "I bet your people say that to all the Angels."

He shakes his head. "We are in a unique position. Several of the revitalizeds who came to us here asked to be relocated once I revealed what I am about to reveal to you."

"That sounds ominous," Rage growls, but his face is alight with curiosity. I bet mine is too. I haven't a clue what's coming next or how it can be any worse than what he's told us already.

"This is a universe of good and evil," Dr. Oystein says. "I am sure you know from your lessons in school that for every action there is an equal and opposite reaction."

"Quit with the dramatic buildup, doc," Rage huffs. "Give it to us straight."

"Very well," the doctor says as a rare angry spark flashes across his eyes. "Just as there is an ultimate force of good in this universe, there is also one of evil. To put it into the terms I find easiest to understand, God is real but so is Satan."

Rage's smirk fades. I get a sick feeling in my stomach. Burke looks away.

"When God revitalized me, it was an act of love," Dr. Oystein says. "He did it because He wished to hand mankind a lifeline. He was obliged to punish us, but He wanted to give us a fighting chance in the war to come.

"If God had left me to my own devices, I would have remained a mindless revived. Other scientists would have continued their experiments and the airborne strain of the disease would have been developed. When the ferocious undead arose, humanity would have lacked champions. The living need us. We can go where they can't, fight in ways they cannot.

"But there are laws which even God abides by. They are laws of His making, but if He ignores them, what use are they? A law which does not apply to all is no real sort of law.

"The forces of good and evil do not engage one another directly," Dr. Oystein continues. "Their followers clash all the time, humanity forever swaying between the extremes of right and wrong, taking a positive step forward here, a negative step backwards there. But God told me that if He or Satan ever takes a direct role in the affairs of man – if they interfere in any way – then the other has the right to counteract that."

"Tit for tat," I whisper, and Dr. Oystein nods somberly.

"That is why God so rarely reaches out to us. He might often wish to, when He looks down and sees us in pain, but He does not dare, because if He extends a hand of love, Satan can stretch forth a claw of hate."

"This is bullshit," I croak. "It's madness." I seek out Burke's gaze. "Isn't it?" I shout.

Burke only shrugs uncomfortably.

"When God restored my consciousness," Dr. Oystein says, raising his voice ever so slightly, "it allowed Satan to create his own mockery of the human form, a being of pure viciousness and spite who could wreak as much damage as I had the power to repair.

"I have sought long and hard for my demonic counterpart over the decades, but our paths never crossed. There were many occasions when I came close – and when he came close to tracking me down and striking at me, for he loathes me as much as I fear him – but something always kept us apart. Until now."

Dr. Oystein crosses his arms and trains his sights on me. "You know evil's true name, don't you, B?"

"Get stuffed," I whimper.

"Don't deny the truth. I can see the awareness in your eyes. Say it and spare me the unpleasant task. Please."

"What the hell is he –" Rage starts to ask, but I blurt out the answer before he can finish.

"*Mr. Dowling!*" I shout.

"Yes," Dr. Oystein says, shuddering. "The clown with the smile

187

of death. The creator of mutants and executioner of innocents. A creature of immense power and darkness, who relishes chaos and devastation, just like his grim master.

"Mr. Dowling is the earthly representative of the force of ultimate evil. With the sinister clown's malevolent help, the Devil, as I call him, hopes to lead the zombies to victory and plunge our world into eternal, tormented night.

"The war between the living and the dead rages across the globe, but this is where it will be decided. London has been chosen as the key battleground. I set up base here for reasons I cannot define, and Mr. Dowling has done likewise. The war we wage in this city of the damned will be the most instrumental of the conflict.

"We must take the fight to Mr. Dowling," Dr. Oystein says, and his face betrays the terror he feels. "He is our most direct and deadly nemesis. We will engage in a brutal, bloody battle to the death. If we triumph, peace and justice will reign and mankind can resume its quest to win heavenly favor.

"If we lose," he concludes, and he doesn't need to drop his voice to make his sickening, dizzying point, "every single one of us is damned and this world will become an outpost of Hell."

To be continued...

BOOK 5:

ZOM-B

BABY

ONE

The London Dungeon used to be one of the city's top tourist attractions. It was a fun but grisly place, a cross between a museum and a horror house. It recreated some of London's darker historical moments, bringing back to life the world of people like Jack the Ripper and Sweeney Todd. It featured sinister, imposing models of buildings from the past, props like hanging skeletons and snarling rats, nerve-tingling videos and light shows, and actors to play the various infamous figures. There were even some stomach-churning rides. I visited it quite a few times when I was alive, and always had a brilliant time.

I haven't been in the Dungeon since returning to County Hall as a revitalized, but right now it feels like the most natural part of the complex to head for.

I wander through the deserted rooms, enjoying the isolation and the gloominess. The actors are gone, and someone must have done the rounds and turned off all the projectors and video clips, but most of the lights work, and the sets and props haven't been disturbed. It's still the coolest damn place in London.

I also think, looking back, that it served as a taste of what was to come. The London Dungeon painted a picture of a blood-drenched city full of terror and murder, and the people who built it were right—this *is* a realm of madness and death. We were never more than one sharp twist away from total chaos, from demonic clowns prancing through the streets and tenderhearted but loopy scientists setting themselves up as spokesmen for God.

I thought I'd escaped the craziness when I came to County Hall. London had been destroyed, zombies had taken over, life as we knew it had come to an end. But Dr. Oystein seemed to offer sanctuary from the grim bedlam of the streets. I thought I could rest easy, make friends, learn from the good doctor, start to build a new life (or should that be *un*life?) for myself.

That was before the doctor told me that God speaks to him.

I creep along a street that looks like it's been transported to the present day from Victorian London. I pause, imagining banks of swirling fog, waiting for Jack the Ripper to leap out and claim me for his own. That's not very likely, I know, but it wouldn't surprise me. I reckon just about anything could happen in this crazy, messed-up world.

That's what's so weird and scary about the story Dr. Oystein fed us. There was a time when I would have written him off as a kook, but given what I've seen and experienced recently, I can't say for sure that he *is* barking mad. He told me he was forced by Nazis to create the zombie gene—that's probably fact. It's clear that he's an expert on the living dead, having studied them for decades. He's the one who gave me the ability to revitalize.

If all that and more is true, then why not the rest of it? The world has always been full of people claiming to be in contact with God. Surely they can't *all* have been nutters. If some of them were the genuine article, maybe Dr. Oystein is too. The trouble is, how's an ordinary girl like me to supposed to be able to tell the difference between a prophet and a madman?

I curse loudly and slam a fist into one of the fake walls, punching a large hole through it. Someone chuckles behind me.

"Now *there's* a cliché if ever I saw one."

I turn and glare at Rage, who has followed me in from the riverbank. Mr. Burke is with him. Rage is sneering. Burke just looks uncomfortable.

"Why don't you go drown yourself?" I snarl at Rage.

"I would if I could," he smirks, then pokes his chest. "I'm the same as you. My lungs don't work."

195

I had left Rage, Burke and Dr. Oystein abruptly, without saying anything, once the doctor had hit us with the revelation that he was God's envoy, locked in battle with Mr. Dowling, aka the literal spawn of Satan. I couldn't take any more. My head was bursting.

"I haven't been in this part of the building before," Burke says, looking around.

"This was the London Dungeon," I tell him.

My ex-teacher nods. "I often meant to check it out, but I never got around to it."

"I came here lots," I sniff. "My mum hated the place, but Dad was like me, he thought it was great. He'd bring me here, just the two of us, and we'd have a wicked time."

"I bet," Burke says.

"What's that supposed to mean?" I shout, thinking he's having a dig at my racist dad, implying that he liked the horrors of the Dungeon because he was horrific himself.

Burke blinks, startled by my tone. "Nothing. It looks like it must have been a lot of fun back in the day. That's all I was saying."

Rage snorts. "Always thought the Dungeon was rubbish myself."

I laugh shortly. "That's because you're a moron with no taste."

"Yeah," he says. "That must be why I fancy you."

I give him the finger, but chuckle despite myself.

"So what do you think of old Oystein's story?" Rage asks.

I shrug and look away.

"He's off his head, isn't he?" Rage pushes.

"I suppose…"

"Do you think any of it was real? Being imprisoned by the Nazis, inventing the zombie gene, working with governments and armies all these years to suppress breakouts?"

"Those are undeniable facts," Burke says quietly. "I discussed Dr. Oystein with my military contacts when I was leading a double life. Everything he told us today checked out."

"What about his direct line to God?" Rage jeers.

Burke sighs. "That's where we hit a gray area."

"Nothing gray about it," Rage says cheerfully. "The doc's a lunatic. I don't believe in God, the Devil, reincarnation, nothing like that. Even if I did, his story doesn't ring true. The all-powerful creator of the universe teaming up with a brain-hungry zombie? Get real!"

"Many prophets were outcasts of their time," Burke murmurs. "They were mistrusted and feared by their contemporaries, mocked, abused, driven from their homes. Christ was crucified, John the Baptist's head was chopped off, Joan of Arc was burned at the stake."

"Yeah," Rage says, "but they were human, weren't they? They were alive."

"Lazarus," I say softly, the memory coming to me out of nowhere. "Jesus raised him from the dead. The first zombie."

Rage starts to laugh, then considers what I've said and frowns. "You think the doc's telling the truth?"

I pull a face. "How the hell do I know? It sounds crazy, but…"

"I don't do *buts*," Rage says. "It's a simple world as long as you don't let others complicate it for you. The doc's a genius, no one's denying that, but he's mad too. I respect him for the Groove Tubes, bringing the Angels together and all the rest, but I'm not gonna pretend there wasn't steam coming out of his ears when he started telling us about his cozy chats with God."

"So what are you gonna do?" I ask.

"About what?"

"This war he wants us to fight. The Angels versus Mr. Dowling and his army of mutants. If you don't believe God's on our side, or that we're fighting the forces of darkness, where does that leave you?"

"Right where I want to be," Rage smirks. "In the thick of it all."

He walks up to the plasterboard wall I punched and studies the hole I made.

"We're built to fight," he whispers, rubbing together the bones sticking out of his fingers. "We were reborn as perfect killing machines. I always wanted to join an army. I had it all planned. I was gonna give myself a couple of years after school to see the world, have some laughs, sow my wild seeds."

"Oats," Burke corrects him.

"Whatever. Then I was gonna join the French Foreign Legion or something like that. Go where the battles were, test myself on the field of combat, maybe become a mercenary further down the line, hire myself out to whoever paid me the most."

"You don't believe in loyalty to a cause?" Burke asks diplomatically.

"Loyalty's for mugs," Rage says.

Burke looks disappointed. "Then you're not going to stay with Dr. Oystein?"

Rage frowns. "Weren't you listening? I want to be where the action is. Dr. Oystein's five cans short of a six-pack, but if he's gonna start a war with the clown and his mutants, I want to be there when they clash. So, yeah, I'm his man if he'll have me."

"You're going to stay even though you think Dr. Oystein is mad?" I gape.

"Of course," Rage says calmly. "War's in my blood. I want to be a warrior and Oystein's offering me the best fight in town. Why would I turn my back on the chance to go toe-to-toe with an army of mutants and their diabolical leader? Hell, if we win, I might end up saving the world from the Devil—how ironic would that be, given that I don't even believe in the bugger?"

Rage turns to leave.

"And what if the Devil makes you a better offer?" Burke asks.

Rage looks back uncertainly.

"What if Mr. Dowling asks you to join him somewhere down the line?" Burke presses. "Would you consider a proposal from our enemy?"

"Might do," Rage nods. "Offhand I can't think of anything he could offer to tempt me, since money doesn't mean anything these days. But never say never, right?"

"You'd sell us out?" I shout.

"In a heartbeat," Rage says, then flashes his teeth in a merciless grin. "God, the Devil, forces in between... It makes no difference to me. I'll go where the going's good. Right now I'm best off sticking with Dr. Oystein. But I'm not in this game to save the world or what's left of mankind. I'm just a guy in search of some kicks to pass the time before my tired old bones give up the ghost."

Rage cocks his head and grunts. "If the doc's right about us being able to survive for thousands of years, that's a lot of time to play with. I'll need a lot of kicks. Maybe spend a century working for the good guys, then a century for the villains. Or take on the whole lot of you together—Rage against the world. Wherever the opportunity for the most excitement lies, that's where you'll find me.

"Take care, folks. And watch your backs."

Then, with a laugh, he's gone, leaving Burke and me to stare at each other in openmouthed disbelief.

TWO

"Maybe you were right," Burke mutters. "We might have been better off if we'd killed him when he was in the Groove Tube."

I chuckle. "You don't really mean that."

"No," he smiles. "I suppose I don't. But I'll have to keep a close watch on him. I hadn't realized he was this dangerous."

"The clue was in the name," I note drily.

Burke winces. "It's always a dark day when the student becomes the teacher. Especially a student as limited as you were. No offense."

"Get stuffed."

We laugh, and for a while it's like we're back in school, just a cool teacher and a teenage girl sharing a joke.

"So what do *you* think of the whole Dr. Oystein and God thing?" I ask.

Burke sighs. "Does it matter?"

"Of course it does."

"Why?" he challenges me. "Isn't faith a personal choice? Don't we all listen to our hearts and choose to believe – or not – based on what we feel rather than on what other people tell us?"

"No," I snort. "We believe whatever our parents tell us, until we're old enough to decide for ourselves. Then most of us go along with what we grew up with because it's easier than trying to learn something new."

Burke claps enthusiastically. "My star student. Why did you never come up with airtight reasoning like that in class?"

"Because school was boring," I tell him.

"Ouch," he says, then sighs again. "You're right, of course. But whether we choose to believe or just stick with the faith we've grown up with, the truth is that nobody can ever say for sure if there's a God or not. Dr. Oystein is convinced that there is, and for all I know he's right."

"But if he's not?" I press.

"I don't think it matters." Burke grimaces. "I mean, under different circumstances I'd be wary of him. Lots of wars have been fought by people who used religion as an excuse. Kings, politicians and generals twisted the beliefs of their followers as they saw fit, playing the religious card to justify their crusades over land, oil, gold or whatever it was they were really fighting for."

"Isn't that what Dr. Oystein is doing?" I ask.

"I don't think so. He's asking us only to have faith in him, not in his God, to accept that he's working in the name of good, to overcome the forces of darkness that are stacked against us. Whatever you think about God, nobody can deny that we're facing dark times. The zombies, Mr. Dowling and his mutants... These are forces we can't ignore, enemies that have to be faced. Every so often a war that *must* be fought comes along, and I think this is one of them."

"Yeah, fair enough," I mumble. "But is a nutjob the best man to lead the fight against the bad guys?"

"If not Dr. Oystein, then who?" Burke asks. "You?"

"Hell, no. I'm not a leader."

"Nor am I," Burke says. "It takes a certain breed of person to command. Dr. Oystein is a rarity, a man with the ability to lead but not the desire—he's told me that he's only doing this because it's him or nobody, and I believe him. The alternative is someone who craves power—the likes of Josh Massoglia or Dr. Cerveris. Do you really want to pledge yourself to someone like that?"

"No, but..." I shift uncomfortably. "I didn't like Josh or Dr. Cerveris, but they ran a tight ship."

"Until Mr. Dowling penetrated their defenses," Burke says, then leads me from the Victorian chamber, through the rest of the Dungeon, and out towards the front of the building. When we're in the fresh air, beneath the shadow of the London Eye, he continues.

"This is a chance to start afresh," he says softly. "Whether it was divine retribution or a mess of our own making, the world *has* fallen, the old order *has* crashed and burned. If we can find a way to deal with the zombies, this is an incredible opportunity to begin again and try to improve upon the mistakes of the past.

"If you believe the stories of the Old Testament in the Bible, this isn't the first time this has happened. The Flood wiped the slate clean and people had to start over. Things didn't work out too well that time, but who's to say we can't do better now? The zombies and mutants are clear-cut enemies. Everyone can recognize them as a threat and join against them—Jew, Christian, Muslim, Hindu, white and black, all fighting together, differences set aside.

"If we win this war, power-hungry people will immediately start thinking about how to establish control over the remnants of mankind. They'll look for new foes and threats, and work the survivors up into an agitated state. Hatred and domination are the ways of the past and will in all likelihood be the ways of the future too. Unless Dr. Oystein and his Angels can help us change."

Burke makes a face. "I know I'm being a crazy optimist, but I can't help myself. The best that the old leaders can offer is a return to the status quo. I think, based on what I've seen of him, that Dr. Oystein holds the promise of true redemption. He's what a leader should be—a man who is reluctant to tell others how they should behave and what they should believe."

"I don't know if I agree with you," I say miserably. "I want to, but I can't get over the fact that this is a guy who claims to be in touch with God. It's hard for me to go along with someone like that."

Burke nods. "I understand. I won't try to pressure you, just as Dr. Oystein won't. If you can reconcile yourself to working with us, we'll welcome your support and you can help us take the fight to Mr. Dowling, rescue survivors, work with those who've established compounds beyond the confines of the city, search for a way to suppress the zombies. There's going to be so much to do, so many wars to be waged. We'll need all the help we can get.

"But if you can't trust the doctor, we'll respect your decision. You're free to leave any time you want. I doubt you'll find a more secure home anywhere else in this ruin of a country, but if you need to search for one, you'll depart with our best wishes."

I growl uncertainly. "I want to stay with you, but I'm gonna need more time to think about it."

"That's fine," Burke says. "We're in no rush. Take all the time you want." He turns to leave, then looks back at me with a wicked twinkle in his eyes. "You know what might help?"

"What?" I ask suspiciously.

Burke points to the sky. "You could pray," he says, then skips along with a laugh as I hurl a most unholy curse after him.

opposite him. He's sitting cross-legged on the floor, but I just plop down on my bum and draw my knees up to my chest.

There's a sweet smell in the air. Some kind of flavored tea. It's coming from a pot to the master's right. There's a kettle of water boiling on a small stove to his left.

"I miss the taste of tea more than anything," he says softly, lifting the lid of the pot to stir the contents. "It was one of the great pleasures of my life. I did not realize how important it was to me until I was denied it."

Zhang sniffs the fumes then pours some more water into the pot. He turns off the stove and leaves the kettle to cool. There are some cups stacked behind him. He reaches back slowly, picks up two, passes one to me and sets the other down in front of him.

"Is this a tea ceremony?" I ask.

"You know of such things?" He sounds surprised.

"I saw it on a few travel programs. Looked like a lot of hassle for a simple cup of tea."

"The tea ceremony is an ancient Japanese ritual," Zhang says, pouring a cup of tea for me and one for himself. "It has much more to do with etiquette and tradition than tea. It is a purification process for the soul, a way to honor your guests and bond with them.

"This is not a tea ceremony," he says, picking up his cup and inhaling. "I just enjoy the smell and the memory of the taste."

Zhang sips from the cup, swishes the liquid round his mouth, then picks up a bowl that had been standing next to the cups and spits into it. He passes me the bowl and I follow suit, smelling the fumes, sipping the tea and spitting it out.

"Didn't get much of a kick from it," I note.

"No," he says sadly. "This is a delicate blend. The flavors are subtle and difficult to detect even with an appreciative tongue. With our useless taste buds, we might as well be sipping water."

"Then why bother?" I frown.

"We might not be able to dream," Zhang says, "but we can use our imaginations. With the aid of the scent and the texture of the tea, I can sometimes trick myself into believing that I still taste."

He takes another sip, swishes, spits it out and makes a sighing sound. "This is not one of those days."

We take a few more sips, pretending there's a point to this. The smell grows on me after a while, and sets me thinking about something.

"Why do you suppose we can smell when we can't taste?"

I'm not really expecting an answer, but Zhang surprises me.

"It is for practical reasons," he says. "Zombies need to smell, in order to be able to sniff out brains. But since brains are all we eat, we can function without our taste buds."

I scratch my head, thinking it over. "Yeah, that makes sense. I should have figured it out before."

"Yes," Zhang says. "You should have."

I scowl, then laugh. "You're Chinese, aren't you?" I ask, changing the subject.

"Yes."

"But the tea ceremony is Japanese...."

"I have traveled widely," he says. "I like to think of myself as a citizen of the world. Besides, the Chinese introduced tea to Japan, so I feel that I have a natural entitlement to engage in the ceremony."

"What's the situation like in China now?" I ask.

"Not good," he says quietly. "We had the largest population in the world. That means we now have the largest number of zombies. Life is grim everywhere for those who have survived, but it is particularly difficult in China and India."

We finish off the tea in silence. When we're done, Zhang stands and moves to the center of the room, beckoning me to follow. I stand opposite him, ready to be hurled to the floor. But this time he throws a punch at my face.

With a yelp, I knock his hand aside and step back. He follows, throwing another punch. Again I block it and move away from him. Zhang sweeps his leg beneath both of mine and I fall in a heap.

"What the hell!" I snap, rolling away from him.

"You blocked admirably," he says calmly. "And your first defensive step was well judged. Your second, on the other hand..." He tuts.

I stand and dust myself off. "Is this the start of my real training?" I ask.

"No," he says. "The real training started the first time I threw you."

He chops at me and forces me back again. This time I repel four of his attacks before he sweeps my feet from under me.

"You know what I mean," I mutter, rising again. "Are you going to teach me to fight now, to strike and defend myself, the way you teach the others?"

"Yes," he says, and comes forward a third time, lifting his left foot high to kick my chest. I grab the leg and try to twist it. Zhang rolls with the twist, brings his right leg up and kicks the side of my head, knocking me to the ground.

"That was ambitious," he says. "Ambition is good. Caution is better, at least to begin with."

"You're telling me to walk before I try to run?" I ask, getting up again.

"No," he says. "We have no time for walking here. You must learn swiftly and take shortcuts. I do not have time to train you in all the ways of the martial arts. So, when in doubt, go for the simplest solution."

Zhang kicks at me with his left foot again. This time I chop at his ankle then step back out of reach.

"Good," he grunts, and closes in, kicking, punching, chopping, forcing me back, testing my reflexes.

Zhang spars with me for half an hour before telling me to go and rest. "You did well," he says. "We will focus on specific moves next time. This was a useful first workout."

I bow to Master Zhang and turn to leave. But something's niggling me. I stop and face him again. He raises the eyebrow of his bloodshot eye – it must have been bloodshot when he was turned into a zombie, and since we don't heal properly, I'm guessing it will be like that forever – then nods to let me know I can speak.

"Did Dr. Oystein tell you to do this?" I ask. "To step up my training and stop just throwing me about?"

"Why would you think that?" he replies.

"Dr. Oystein told me about his conversations with God."

Zhang's expression doesn't change. He waits for me to continue.

"I think it's a load of nonsense. I'm not sure if I believe in God. Even if I do, I don't think He talks to zombies and asks them to save the world."

"You must be a wise young lady to be able to dismiss the teachings and beliefs of your elders so easily," Zhang says.

"Of course I'm not," I say sourly. "I know my limits. But my nose works as well as yours. I recognize bullshit when I smell it."

"Really?" Zhang smiles thinly. "Did you eat cheese when you were alive?"

I look at him as if he's crazy. "What sort of a question is that?"

"A simple one. I enjoyed cheese very much and tried many varieties over the years. They all tasted good to me, but the smell... Some smelled as good as they tasted. Others stank of old socks, fresh vomit, even, yes, *bullshit*."

"Is this one of those famous Chinese riddles?" I ask when he doesn't continue.

"No," he says. "I am merely pointing out the fact that sometimes one cannot judge by smell alone. Oystein said nothing to me of his meeting with you. I decided to vary your routine because I thought the time was right. I will be doing the same with Rage when he next comes to me. There is nothing more to it than that, no matter what your nose might tell you."

"Fair enough," I grunt.

"You believe me?" he asks.

"Yeah."

"Then why don't you believe Oystein?"

"Because you're not telling me that you can talk with God." I pause. "You're not, are you?"

213

Zhang shakes his head. "I do not believe in God. Or reincarnation. Or any kind of supernatural realm." He makes a small sighing sound, looking his age for once—he can only have been in his early twenties when he was turned into a zombie. "My lack of faith was a source of grave concern for my parents."

"Then what the hell are you doing here?" I growl.

He shrugs. "I believe in the doctor. He rescued me years ago. I was living in a small village but had moved there from a large city. I had been vaccinated against the zombie gene. Oystein kept track of me, the way he tried to keep track of all his children—and that is how he thinks of us.

"When there was an outbreak of zombies in my village, troops moved in to contain it. We were sealed off from the world and those who had been infected were executed. Oystein made sure that I was not killed. He had me isolated and fed. My guardians were issued with strict instructions not to harm me.

"I took almost five months to revitalize. Most people would have given up on me. Not Oystein. He hates abandoning any of us."

"But it's got to be a problem for you," I mutter. "How can you believe in him if you don't believe he really speaks with God?"

"It is not an issue," Zhang insists. "He has never asked me to accept his beliefs. He has only asked me to fight, which is all he is asking of you too."

Zhang returns to his cups and bowls and begins to tidy them away. "It is very straightforward in my view," he says. "A war to

214

decide the future of this planet is being fought. We must choose sides or pretend it is not happening. Assuming you do not go down the road of blind ignorance, and are not on the side of evil, you must back Oystein, regardless of whatever flaws you perceive in him, or look for another leader to support."

"Do you think there are others out there?"

"I am sure there are. But they will have flaws too. You must ask yourself which is worse—a leader firmly rooted in reality who thirsts for power and control, or a truly good-hearted man who might be a touch delusional.

"I do not think that God exists," Zhang says, heading for the door. "But there are certainly godly people on this planet, and I am honored that one of them has deemed me worthy of his friendship and support. You should be too, as I doubt there are many pure people in this world who would see goodness within *you*." He looks at me with a probing expression. "Do you even see it within yourself?"

I think of the bad things I have done. Of my racist past. Of Tyler Bayor.

And I can't say a word.

"I will see you tomorrow for training," Zhang says softly, and shuts the door with a heel, leaving me even more confused and unsure than I was when I came in.

I head back to my room, taking my time, creeping through the deserted corridors of County Hall, thinking about all that I've been told. As I'm passing one of the building's many chambers, I hear a strange moaning noise. I slow down and the noise comes again. It sounds like someone in pain. Worried, I open the door. The room is pitch-black.

"Hello?" I call out nervously, wary of a trap.

"Who's that?" a girl snaps.

"B," I reply, relaxing now that I've placed the voice.

There's a pause. Then the girl says, "Come in and close the door."

Shutting the door behind me, I shuffle forward into darkness. I'm about to ask for directions when a dim light is switched on. I spot the twins, Awnya and Cian, in a corner. Awnya is sitting against a wall. Cian is lying on the floor, his head buried in his sister's lap. He's trembling and moaning into his hands, which are covering his face. Awnya is stroking the back of her brother's head with one hand, holding a small flashlight with the other.

I cross the room and squat beside Awnya. "What's going on?" I whisper as Cian makes a low-pitched weeping noise, his body shaking violently. "Is he sick?"

"Only sick of this world," Awnya says quietly. She looks at me with a pained expression. "We often come to a quiet place like this. We feel so lonely and we've seen so many horrors... Sometimes it gets too much for us and we have to break down and cry."

"Zombies can't cry," I remind her.

"Not the normal way," she agrees, "but we can cry in our own fashion." She strokes Cian's head again. "We take it in turns to comfort one another. We can't both break down at the same time or we might never recover. One of us always looks out for the other."

Cian starts to gibber nonsense sentences, then he curses and whimpers. Awnya lays down her flashlight, massages his shoulders with both hands and sings to him, an old ballad that I vaguely recognize. It should be laughable but it's strangely touching.

"Do you want me to leave?" I whisper between verses.

"Not unless you feel awkward," Awnya says, and carries on singing.

I lay my head against the wall and listen to the song. I'd like to close my eyes but I can't. Instead I study the shadows thrown across the room by the flashlight. There are cobwebs running along the top of the skirting board opposite us. The world has gone to hell, but life goes on as usual for these spiders. They know nothing of zombies, mutants, God. They just spin their webs and wait for dinner. Lucky sods.

Cian eventually stops sniveling and sits up. He rubs his cheeks and smiles shakily at me, embarrassed but not mortified.

"We're lucky," Awnya says, brushing Cian's blond hair out of his eyes. "We have each other. I don't know how the rest of you cope."

I shrug. "You learn to deal with it."

"It's because we're the youngest," Cian mutters. "Dr. Oystein says that a year or two makes a big difference. He says we can go to him anytime we want, for comfort or anything else, but he thinks it's better if we can support ourselves."

"This is a hard world for the weak," Awnya notes.

"We're not *weak*," Cian snaps.

Awnya rolls her eyes, then squints at me. "Did Dr. Oystein tell you everything?"

"Yeah."

"It's brilliant, isn't it?" Cian says. "Being on the side of God and all."

"I think it's scary," Awnya murmurs.

"That's because you're a girl. Girls are soft," Cian sniffs, apparently

220

forgetting that moments earlier he was whining like a baby. "I'm not afraid of the Devil, Mr. Dowling or anyone else."

"Of course you are," Awnya says. "We all are. And we're right to be afraid, aren't we, B? You met the clown. He's as scary as Dr. Oystein says, isn't he?"

I nod slowly. "He's a terrifying bugger, there's no doubt about that. But as for him working for the Devil, don't make me laugh."

"What do you mean?" Awnya asks.

"You don't really believe that, do you, about God and the Devil?"

"Of course we do," Cian says stiffly. "Dr. Oystein told us."

"And you buy everything he says?" I sneer.

"Yes, actually," Awnya growls, pushing herself away from me.

"Dr. Oystein saved us," Cian says.

"He gave us a home," Awnya says.

"He's a saint," Cian says.

"Our only hope for the future," Awnya says.

"Yeah, yeah," I rumble. "He's doing a fantastic job and he's a first-rate geezer, but that doesn't change the fact that he's crazy. If God is real, He doesn't get involved in our affairs. This is all about what our stupid scientists and armies have done to the world, not about a war between God and Satan."

"Hmm," Awnya says, pretending to think hard. "Who should I trust? A genius who's been working for decades to try to save mankind, or a girl with a chip on her shoulder?"

"What chip?" I grunt.

221

"I don't know," Awnya says. "But you must have one, otherwise why are you saying nasty things about Dr. Oystein? You've only been here five minutes, yet you're telling us we're stupid, that we should listen to you instead of the man who loves and protects us."

"I'm just saying it's madness," I whisper.

"Dr. Oystein's maybe the only person in this world who *isn't* mad," Cian huffs. "God spoke to him, touched him, changed him. He's the best of us all."

"You really believe that?"

"Yes," Cian says.

"Absolutely," Awnya says.

"One hundred percent," Cian adds, in case there's any doubt.

"Fine," I shrug, and get to my feet. "I wish I could believe it too. I'm not trying to stir things up. I just can't see it. I want to but I can't."

"Then you're in an even worse state than us," Awnya says, and there's genuine sympathy in her tone.

"Yeah," I say hollowly. "I guess I am."

I start for the door but Awnya stops me. "B?" I look back at her questioningly. "If it's any comfort, we're jealous of you."

"Why?" I frown.

"Dr. Oystein and Master Zhang chose you to fight," she says.

"They didn't pick us," Cian says glumly.

"Dr. Oystein loves us all," Awnya says, "but even though I'm sure he'd deny it, he's got to love his warriors more than the likes of

Cian and me. You're the ones who are going to defeat Mr. Dowling and save the world."

"We're just the guys who find things for the rest of you," Cian says.

"If we could swap places with you, we would," Awnya says.

I scratch my head while I think that over. "You two are a couple of freaks," I finally mumble. We all laugh—they know I meant it in a nice way. Cian and Awnya wave politely at me. I flip them a friendly finger then let myself out.

FIVE

All of my roommates are present when I get to my bedroom, including Rage, who's studying Ashtat's model of the Houses of Parliament.

"It's all matchsticks?" he's asking.

"Yes," Ashtat says.

"There isn't a ready-made frame underneath that you've stuck them onto?"

"No, it is all my own work."

"Cool."

Ashtat smiles sappily and tugs shyly at her white headscarf.

"You want to be careful," I call to her, "or he'll burn the bugger down."

Rage grins. "Don't say such nasty things about me, Becky. I want to make a good impression on my new friends."

"You don't have any friends here," I snort.

"Isn't that for us to decide?" Ashtat snaps.

"She's got a point," Carl says. "We know you don't like this guy, but that doesn't mean the rest of us have to hate him."

"Yeah," Shane grunts. "He seems all right to me."

"He's a killer," I growl. "I saw him murder a man."

"She's got me dead to rights," Rage says chirpily as the others stare at him. "I can't deny it. Guilty as charged, officer."

Rage swaggers over to his bed and sits on it, testing the springs.

"What Miss Smith *might* have failed to mention," he adds, "was that I'd been kept captive and denied brains for several days, which meant I was close to reverting and becoming a mindless revived. The man I killed had imprisoned and starved me. In my eyes that made him fair game."

"The rest of us had been starved too," I snarl. "We didn't turn into killers."

"As I recall, you were quite keen to tuck into Dr. Cerveris's brain once I'd cut open his skull," Rage notes. "If I hadn't stopped you, you'd have torn in like a pig at feeding time."

"Maybe," I concede. "But I didn't kill him. You were the only one of us who killed."

"Really?" Rage starts looking around as if searching for something. He even bends and peers under the bed. "Where's Mark?" he finally asks.

"Bastard," I sneer.

"Reilly told me what happened," Rage chuckles. "Your lot found out Mark was alive and you tore the poor sod apart. True or false?"

"The others did. Not me."

"You abstained?"

"Yeah."

"Then you have my respect," Rage says quietly, his smile fading. "You were able to control yourself. You're a better person than I am. Better than any of the zom heads were. But will you look down your nose at those of us who are made of weaker material?"

I stare at Rage uncomfortably. I didn't expect the argument to go like this. He was supposed to fight his corner, not praise me and make me feel bad for insulting him.

"I'm not proud of what I did in that hellhole," Rage says. "But I was in bad shape. I needed brains. If it hadn't been Dr. Cerveris, if it had been someone good and decent, would I have killed them anyway? I like to think not, but I can't say for sure."

I gulp – old habits die hard – and try to think of something to say, but I can't.

"All this honesty," Rage says, grinning again. "I never knew how invigorating it would make me feel to tell the truth all the time. You should try it, Becky. A bit of honesty's good for the soul."

"I can be as honest as anyone," I shout. "I hate your guts and always will, no matter what you say or do. How honest is that?"

"Good enough for me," Rage laughs, cocking his head swiftly to the side, the closest any of us living dead can get to a wink.

I stomp to my bed, throw myself down and glare at the ceiling. A few minutes later, Carl comes and sits beside me. He's changed his clothes again, choosing an old-fashioned suit that looks plain wrong on a guy his age. He's brushed his dark hair back too, gelling it flat the way businessmen used to in old movies that I sometimes watched with my dad on a lazy Sunday. All he needs is a bowler hat and a fancy umbrella and he could be a fresh-faced banker from fifty or sixty years ago.

"How are you feeling?" he asks softly.

"Sick to my stomach at having to share a room with *him*," I snap.

"I meant about the rest of it, what Dr. Oystein told you."

I prop myself on one elbow and squint at Carl, who looks a bit sheepish.

"It can be hard to take it all in when he first tells you," Carl continues. "I was in shock for a few days. There's so much to think about and process."

"You don't believe either," I whisper. "You think he's mad."

"Who's that?" Rage pipes up. "The doc? You can bet your sorry excuse for a life that he is. Mad as a hatter."

"You shouldn't say things like that," Shane barks.

"Why not?" Rage shrugs. "It's what I think, how I feel. The doc won't mind. He has bigger things to worry about than whether or not the likes of us think he's the Messiah or a howling maniac." He looks around at everyone. "Come on, how many of you really believe that he speaks with God?"

Ashtat and Shane stick up their hands immediately. Jakob starts to raise his, wincing at the pain as he lifts his thin, skeletal arm, but then he stops and shakes his head. "I don't know," he croaks.

Carl keeps his hands on his knees. He looks troubled.

"Three against three," Rage beams. "Sounds about right to me. This world has always split down the middle when it comes to gurus. One man's prophet is another man's crackpot."

"The difference here," I mutter, "is that those who doubt don't usually throw themselves behind the lunatics."

"Of course they do," Rage says. "People pick their religion for all sorts of selfish, unspiritual reasons. We don't choose our holy men just because we think they'll sort us out when we die and our souls move on—we like to get some benefit from them in this life too."

"I can see now why B doesn't like you," Carl sniffs. "You're a real cynic."

"It's my best quality," Rage smirks. "But you're the same. Why are you trailing around after the doc if you don't believe he speaks with God? No need to answer. I know already. He's good for you. He set you up in this swanky spot, provides you with brains, trains you to fight. You'd have to be crazy to walk away from a cushy number like this. If the only downside of that is having to swallow his *I am the Right Hand of God* rubbish, well, that's an easy enough sacrifice to make. Am I right or am I right?"

"You think you're clever, don't you?" Carl growls.

"I do, actually, yeah," Rage chuckles, then gets up and walks

over to the foot of my bed. He stares down at me as I glare up at him. "What's your problem?" Rage asks, and he sounds genuinely curious. "You've a face like a slapped arse. Why can't you just take the doc's out-there beliefs with a grain of salt and go along for the ride like everyone else?"

"It's not that simple," I mumble.

"Of course it is," Rage says. "All you have to do is hold your tongue when the doc's warbling on about heavenly missions. How hard can that be? In fact I bet he doesn't mention it that often. Am I right, Clay?"

Carl nods. "He's barely mentioned religion to me since that first time. In fact he even apologizes on the rare occasions when he name-drops God, since he knows that makes some people feel uncomfortable."

"See?" Rage beams. "Simple, like I told you."

"It's not!" I shout, pushing Carl away and getting to my feet. I think about picking a fight with Rage but I don't. And it's not just because I know he'd wipe the floor with me. He's trying to help. He deserves an answer, not an angry retort.

"It's because of my dad," I say sadly, sinking back onto my bed. "He wasn't a nice guy. He used to beat me and my mum, and he was a racist. He made me do something even worse than what Rage and the other zom heads did underground…"

I spill my guts, telling them everything, about Dad, how he campaigned to keep England white, the way he pressured me to copy his lead, how I went along with him for the sake of a quiet life. I end with what happened to Tyler Bayor, Dad screaming at me to throw him to the zombies, obeying because it was what I'd become accustomed to.

I choke up towards the end. I'd cry if I could, but of course the tears aren't there and never will be again. Still, my chest heaves and my voice shakes. I even let rip with a few involuntary moans, like Cian a while earlier.

There's a long silence when I finish. Everyone's looking at me, but I don't glance up to check whether they're staring with sympathy or loathing.

"I knew my dad for what he was," I moan. "A nasty sod, a bully, a manipulator. In the end, a monster. But I loved him anyway. I still do. If he walked in now, I'd hug him and tell him how much I've missed him, and it would be true. He was my father, whatever his faults."

I get up and wander across the room to the model of the Houses of Parliament that Ashtat has been working on. I stare at it, gathering my thoughts.

"People complained about politicians in the old days, called them self-serving, greedy, power-hungry gits. But hardly anyone tried to change the system. They were our elected leaders and we felt like we had to go along with them because there was no other way.

"I did that with my dad and it was wrong, just as people were wrong to put up with the political creeps. There's *always* another way. If it's not clear-cut, we have to work hard to find it. We shouldn't trudge along, putting our faith in people who don't deserve it, accepting things because we're afraid of what will happen if we break ranks and try to build something better.

"Dad was a good man in certain ways. He was loyal to his friends. I don't think he ever cheated on Mum. He was brave—he risked his life to try to save me when the zombies attacked. But he thought that whites were superior to other races. It was a huge flaw in him. I could see it, but I put up with it because I didn't dare confront him."

I turn away from the model and face the others. "Dr. Oystein's like my dad. A good man in many ways, but too sure of himself and the way the world should be ordered. I can't believe that God spoke to him. That doesn't seem to be an issue for Rage and Carl, but it is for me. Because I've seen what happens when you put your trust in people like that. They break your heart." I tug at the material of my T-shirt and grimace. "Some of the buggers even rip it from your chest."

Then I go and lie down and stare at the ceiling and don't say anything else for the rest of the night.

SIX

I train hard for the next week. Now that Master Zhang has started practicing proper moves with me, I learn new things every day. It's a real mix—karate, judo, boxing. We also focus a lot on fighting with knives, steel bars, hammers, screwdrivers, things like that.

"This is all about practical application," he tells me. "Apart from some knives, we will not send you out armed. You will fight mostly with your hands, but if you ever need a weapon, you must know how to make use of whatever you can find."

I ask him why we don't use guns. "The zombies don't have any. Surely we could just go out with rifles and mow them down."

"There would be no honor in that," he replies.

"But isn't this all about winning?" I press.

"Not at any cost," he says. "Oystein is adamant about that. If we are to build a better world, we cannot do so by relying on the barbaric ways of the past."

"Reilly has a taser," I note.

"Reilly is human," Zhang says calmly. "We are not. We have a choice—we can be less than we were or we can try to be more."

"It would be a lot easier if we had guns," I mutter.

"The easy way is not always the better way," he says. "If we wish to rise above our foul situation, we must work harder to be honorable in death than we ever had to in life."

Zhang shows me how to most effectively sharpen the bones sticking out of my fingers and toes. He says they're our best weapons and he teaches me how to incorporate them into the moves, how to dig and slice and gouge.

He also trains me to file my teeth in a different way. "You never know when you might have to rip out someone's throat or chew through to their brain in a hurry."

"Is there honor in biting open a person's throat?" I ask innocently.

"Less of your back talk," he growls, but I know he's smirking inside. We get along all right. We're similar in many ways. Tough nuts.

I don't discuss Dr. Oystein with the other Angels. In fact I don't talk to them much at all. I've been brooding ever since that day in

236

the aquarium. No matter which way I look at it, I can't accept what the doc told me. And being unable to accept that he's on a mission from God, I find it hard to accept anything else about him, his offer of refuge or a role in the war he's waging. Rage and Carl are able to sweep their misgivings under the carpet. I can't.

Rage is fitting in better than me. He's in his element, training hard with Master Zhang, messing about with our roommates, getting to know other Angels. He's taken to this with ease.

That pisses me off. I was sure that Rage would be the outcast here, the one that the others would be wary of. I was almost looking forward to the day when he betrayed us, so I could say, "Told you so!" But, as things stand, I'm the one who doesn't belong, who's falling adrift a little further every day. It's not that the others aren't trying to be nice to me. They are. But I see them as stooges who are playing along with Dr. Oystein for all the wrong reasons, so I feel awkward around them and keep pushing them away.

The worst thing is, there's no one for me to confide in. I've seen Dr. Oystein a few times over the week, in corridors, the dining room and gym. He's always smiled at me, made small talk a few times. I'm sure he'd be happy to discuss my concerns if I approached him, but what could I say? "Sorry, doc, I think you're crazy and dangerous. Other than that you're OK."

Mr. Burke is the only person I'd feel comfortable chatting about this with, but he's gone off again on a mission, to infiltrate another complex like the one where I was held captive, or to spy on Mr. Dowling, or…

Actually, I don't know what Burke, Dr. Oystein and the others get up to. There hasn't been much talk of how we're supposed to take the fight to Mr. Dowling and his mutants. Things seem to operate on a need-to-know basis around here. Or maybe it's on an *if-we-can-trust-her* basis. Perhaps they're withholding information from me because they sense that I'm not fully committed.

I suppose that's logical. You don't want to share all your secrets with someone who might walk out the door at any given moment. In their position I wouldn't be too forthcoming with someone like me either. Still, that doesn't make life any easier, just increases my belief that it's me against the rest of them. Roll on, full-blown paranoia!

"Oh, this is ridiculous," I snap, and push myself away from the table.

I'm in the dining room, having just tucked into a bowl of Ciara's latest batch of cranial stew. The others are still chewing. They stare at me uncertainly, surprised by my outburst.

"What's wrong?" Ciara asks, having stayed to chat with Reilly, who's munching a hamburger that I'd give my left ear to be able to taste. "Is it too hot? Too cold? Lumpy?"

"I wasn't talking about the food." I force a smile, not wanting to offend the sweet, fashionably dressed dinner lady. "The food's great. Honest. I just... I can't deal with this anymore. I've got to get some air. I'm going for a walk. I'll be back later."

I storm away. I don't know why things should have come to a

head here, now, but they have. Something inside me snapped when I was sitting at the table, thinking about Dr. Oystein and his claim to have a link to a higher power, and how everyone is happy to go along with whatever the doc says. I've been playing the good little girl, saying nothing, but I can't do it anymore.

I'm tramping down a corridor, not sure where I'm going or what my plans are, when someone rushes up behind me. Before I can react, arms snake across my stomach and grab me. I'm hauled into the air and twirled round. I catch a glimpse of Rage's face as I'm whirling.

"Let me go!" I shout.

"Your wish is my command," he says, and instantly releases me.

I stagger across the floor, slam into a wall and fall. My head is spinning badly. I lean forward and dry heave. There are white flashes in front of my eyes.

"Are you all right?" Rage asks.

"No," I gasp, then sit back against the wall and wait for my head to clear. When it finally does and the heaving stops, I glare at him. "What did you do that for?"

"Just trying to cheer you up. Did you get dizzy?"

"What does it look like, numbnuts?"

"Did that used to happen when you were spun around in the past?" he asks.

"Yeah. Not as bad as this, but my ears were never the best. They used to pop like mad when I flew. If I went on a spinning ride at a carnival, I'd have a headache for hours."

239

"Oh. I thought it might be something to do with being dead. I was worried for a minute."

"No need to be," I snarl, getting to my feet. "You can still go on merry-go-rounds anytime you like."

"I preferred you when you were suffering," Rage sniffs, and reaches out to grab me again.

"You'll lose both hands if you try it," I snap, then squint at him. "Why the hell are you trying to cheer me up anyway? What does it matter to you how I feel?"

"It doesn't," he says. "But the others thought someone should come after you. They were concerned, thought you might do something stupid, maybe off yourself. I figured I'd look like a caring, sensitive guy if I volunteered to help you, especially as they all know that you hate me. So here I am."

"You're too sweet for this world," I jeer. "Head on back to those muppets and tell them I'm fine."

"Not yet," Rage says. "It's too soon. It wouldn't look like I'd tried very hard. I'll tag along with you for a while."

"What if I don't want you to?"

"Tough." He flashes me a grin. "If you do want to off yourself, I know a place where you can get some great power drills. I'll even help you choose the best bit for it. I'd love to see someone drill through their own skull."

"There's the Rage I know and loathe," I chuckle.

"*Honest Rage*," he smirks. "That's how I define myself these days. Telling the truth is what I'm all about."

"It must be a nice change," I sneer.

"It is." There's a long silence while we eye each other. "But seriously," Rage says, breaking it, "if you *do* want me to recommend a good drill…"

SEVEN

We exit County Hall and walk to the corner of the building. We can see part of Waterloo Station from here, and the London Eye.

"Have you been back into the station since Zhang tested us?" Rage asks.

I look at him oddly. "No. Why the hell would I?"

"I have," he says. "I've gone in there with a rucksack seeded with brains, done the run through the zombies again, trying to improve my time."

"Why?" I frown.

"I want to be top dog. You've got to push yourself if you want to get ahead."

"You'd better be careful," I say drily, "or you'll wear yourself out."

"Nah," Rage grins. "It's not just all about the training. I make time for fun stuff too. For instance, I walked up to the IMAX theater the other day. Wanted to see if I could screen a film."

"Could you?" I ask.

"Wasn't able to try. The place was packed with zombies. I forced my way through to the projectionist's booth, but the buggers had beaten me to it. Some of them had made it their home and it was a mess, equipment smashed to pieces. A shame. I was hoping to screen *Night of the Living Dead* there."

It's hard to tell if he's joking or not.

"The noise would have been awful anyway," I note. "The IMAX had the best sound system in London, great for a living person with normal hearing, but with ears like ours it would have been deafening."

"Yeah," Rage says. "But fun. The reviveds would have hated it. They'd have howled like wolves." He stretches, looks at the sky and grimaces. It's a cloudy day but still way too bright for the likes of us. "Where were you headed before I stopped you?"

"Nowhere."

"Really? You were marching like a girl with a purpose."

"I just wanted to get away."

Rage scratches an armpit and grunts. Must be force of habit—we don't sweat, so he can't have itchy pits.

"It's boring here, isn't it?" he says. "That's why I keep looking for

244

things to do. I hate the silence. A city should be buzzing, not quiet like this. It's like the God-awful countryside these days."

"Nothing wrong with the countryside," I sniff. "I used to enjoy days out."

"No, you didn't," Rage argues. "It was hell out there, nothing but fields, trees and Mother bloody Nature. If people loved that so much, they wouldn't have built cities and moved to them. The countryside's boring and so's London now."

He turns in a circle, looking for something to amuse himself. He pauses when he spots the London Eye, then nods at me. "Come on."

"I'm not going on the Eye. I've been up a few times since I moved into County Hall. It always leaves me feeling down, seeing how much of the city has been ruined."

"Just follow me," he insists.

At the Eye, instead of hopping aboard one of the pods, he heads for the control booth. There's always an Angel on watch in a pod, as well as one in the booth to monitor the big wheel. Today the person on duty is Ivor, a guy I know pretty well, although I wouldn't claim to be a close friend. I first ran into him when he was on a mission with his team, and we've had a few conversations since then, when our paths have crossed.

Ivor has brought a load of locks with him, and is fiddling with them to while away the time. He's able to pick just about any lock.

I'd love to be able to do that, but although I've tried a few times, I'm not a natural.

"Don't you ever stop practicing?" Rage shouts, startling Ivor, who was focused on the locks and didn't see us approach. He almost drops the lock that he's working on, but catches it just in time.

"It's good to keep your hand in," Ivor says, smiling at us. "My fingers are like a lock—they get rusty if I don't keep using them."

Ivor spends a few minutes showing us how to pick the lock. He makes it look so easy, but I get nowhere with it. Rage doesn't even try.

"These fingers weren't made for work like that," he says, giving them a wiggle.

"They're like sausages," I laugh.

"Yeah," he says. "Perfect for smashing, not picking."

We chat with Ivor for a while, then Rage asks if he can stop the Eye.

"Stop it?" Ivor frowns.

"Just for ten or fifteen minutes. You don't mind, do you?"

"I'm not supposed to," Ivor says. "Dr. Oystein likes us to keep it going all the time."

"I know. But we'll pretend that someone in a wheelchair was boarding and they got stuck."

Ivor laughs. Rage works on him a bit more and finally he agrees to the odd request.

"But no more than a quarter of an hour," he insists. "And if the doc or Master Zhang asks, I'll tell them it was for you."

"Cheers," Rage says, hurrying out of the booth.

"What are you up to?" I ask suspiciously as I follow him.

"You'll see in a sec," he promises, and trots to the nearest pod.

There are small handles running around the pod. Rage grabs hold and climbs quickly until he's standing on the roof. I still don't know what he's planning, but I'm curious, so I climb up after him.

"They must be the biggest spokes in the world," Rage says, staring at the mesh of links above us. "Imagine if you had another wheel the size of this and you could make a bike out of them."

"You're crazy," I laugh.

"Yeah," he grins, then jumps and grabs hold of one of the bars. He pulls himself up then slides across until he's hugging the rim of the wheel. "Race you."

"What?"

"Race you," he beams. "Come on, up you get."

I stare at him uncertainly.

"Are you chicken?" he growls.

"Sod you," I snap. "I just don't know what you're talking about."

"A race," he says. "Along the inside of the rim, all the way to the top."

I frown, then study the metal rim. I follow it with my gaze as it curves outwards and upwards, before arcing back in on itself past the halfway mark and coming full circle at the top.

"You *are* bloody crazy!" I gasp, seeing now what he wants to do.

"I might be crazy but I'm no coward," Rage chuckles. "Come on, I dare you—a race. We're stronger than we were. We've got these neat bones sticking out of our fingers and toes to help us grip. I'm sure we can do it."

"Even if we could, why the hell would we want to?"

"Now who's the crazy one?" he jeers. "I'm challenging you to a race up the London Eye. Nobody could have done that in the past, not without equipment. How cool will it be to be the first pair in the world to free-climb this baby?"

"It's impossible," I mumble. "If we made it past the halfway point, we'd have to hang upside down." I point to the bar running up the center of the Eye, linking the two rims of the wheel. Smaller bars from the rims connect with it at regular intervals. We could use them for support. "What about that way? It would be safer and easier."

"This isn't about safe and easy," Rage says. "I think we'll be all right even if we fall – we're hard to kill – but if not, what of it? We've all got to go eventually. How would you prefer to leave this world— as a decaying, decrepit old fart, or trying to climb the London Eye in your prime?"

"Dr. Oystein won't like it if a couple of his precious Angels risk their lives on something this pointless," I murmur with a wicked smirk.

"I don't think either one of us is that bothered about keeping Dr. Oystein happy," Rage snorts. "Last one up's a rotten zombie!"

And off he shoots.

For a few seconds I shake my head and tut loudly. Then, with a whoop, I leap, grab hold of a bar, pull myself up, steady myself on the rim and off I tear.

EIGHT

This is crazy. I know that even before I start. But hell, there's no denying it's fun! I haven't had an adrenaline rush like this since I returned to consciousness. Well, OK, it's not an actual adrenaline rush, since I doubt my body produces that anymore. But it damn sure feels like it.

The rim of the wheel is thicker than I expected. A cable runs along the inside, good for gripping, but on the outside it's pure steel, which isn't so accommodating.

At first it's easy. I scuttle along, no problem with my toughened flesh and bones. I laugh with delight, not bothered by the sunlight or what might happen to me if I fall, the gloom of the last week forgotten, focusing on nothing except my ascent.

Then it starts to get tricky. The higher I climb, the more gravity drags at me. From the ground the incline didn't look too steep, but when you're up here and following it, you get a fresh perspective. From about the quarter mark it's like climbing at ninety degrees. I start to slip and sway in the breeze, which seems much stronger than it did a few minutes ago.

I struggle on, teeth gritted, refusing to look at the ground. Cuts open on both hands as the steel and cable slice into them when I slip. Thankfully my blood doesn't flow as swiftly as it once did – it just seeps out slowly – or I'd have to stop. As it is, I can push on, pausing every so often to wipe the congealed blood from my palms.

I'm almost halfway up the wheel when I lose my grip completely. I fall with a cry that's cut short when I slam into one of the support poles that connects with the central bar. I cling on desperately as my legs swing freely beneath me. I hear Rage whooping with glee—he must have paused at the perfect time to catch my big slip. I'd love to shoot him the finger but I don't dare loosen my grip.

If I was human, I'd be done for. The wind would have been knocked from my sails, my muscles would be aching from the climb. Not being a Hollywood movie star, I doubt I'd be able to pull myself to safety. It would be the long drop for me.

But being dead has its advantages. I don't breathe, and my body isn't as confined by the laws of physics as it used to be. After dangling for a while, I haul myself up until I'm hanging across the bar.

I wipe my hands dry, steady myself, grip the rim and start climbing again.

I'm just past the halfway mark when Rage shouts to me. "Oi! Smith!" His voice is tinny, coming from so far away, but the wind carries it and my supersharp ears pick it up.

I take a firm hold and look across to where he's hanging opposite me. My eyes are less effective than my ears, so he's only a vague blob in the distance. "What?" I roar.

"What are we gonna do now?" he yells. "It would be easier if we shifted to the outside of the rim. If we stick to the inside, we'll be hanging upside down the rest of the way."

I'd been thinking about that myself. I was going to suggest we move to the other side, so we could crawl on top of the rim instead of dangle from its underside. But now that he's getting cold feet, I don't want to ease up. He was the dope who suggested this crazy challenge. I want to make him go through with it, even though that means me suffering as well.

"If you want to back down, let me know," I roar cheerfully. "I won't tell anyone you chickened out. Well, except for everyone we know."

"Screw you!" he bellows. "I'm game if you are."

"Then what are you waiting for?" I laugh, and start climbing again.

It soon becomes clear that we really *are* mad to attempt this. As hard as it was before, it's ten times more difficult now. I'm hanging from the rim like a squirrel, but squirrels have tails, padded paws and the benefit of countless generations of instinct to draw upon. Humans were never meant to climb like this, not even undead buggers like me.

The hardest parts are where the bars to the inner circle connect. The rim bulges out in those spots and I have to ease around the protuberances. That was easy on the lower sections, but not when I'm hanging upside down and every muscle in my arms is stretched to a snapping point.

I keep my feet hooked over the rim for as much of the climb as I can, dragging them along, feeling the steel and cable slice deeply into my flesh. Pain doesn't hit you as much as it used to when you're a zombie, but we're not immune to it and I'm starting to really sting. I haven't felt this rough since I staggered away from Trafalgar Square after my last encounter with Mr. Dowling.

My feet keep slipping. Eventually, when I move into the last quarter of the climb, I unhook them and hang at full stretch, supported solely by my hands. I was good on the monkey bars in playgrounds when I was a kid. I could swing across as often as I pleased, laughing at the others who couldn't match me. Time to find out if I still have the old magic.

I inch forward, moving my hands one at a time, concentrating as I never have before. I don't want to slip, and it's got nothing to do with the threat of smashing my skull open or the possibility that Rage will beat me to the top. I need to prove to myself that I can do this. As ludicrous as it is, this has become important to me. I figure if I can do this, I can attempt just about anything. Maybe this is what I need to clear my head and haul me out of the miserable, indecisive pit that I've been rotting in this past week.

It feels like the climb is never going to end. I want to shut my eyes but I can't. I want to take the strain from my arms but I can't. I want to rest for a while but... You get the picture.

I spy Rage across from me. He hasn't made it as far as I have. He's struggling. He's stronger than me but a hell of a lot heavier too. In a situation like this, where weight comes into play, it's good to be a slim snip of a girl.

I get a second wind (relatively speaking) when I see that I'm doing better than Rage. With something between a triumphant shout and a despondent groan, I force myself on, finding fresh strength somewhere deep inside me, ignoring the pain, physics, gravity, the whole damn lot.

Finally, when I'm sure I can't go any farther, I reach the highest point. I hang there for several long seconds, staring down at my feet and the drop beneath. I feel strangely peaceful. The pain in my arms seems to fade. If I fell right now and split my head open on a spoke, I could go happy into the great beyond.

But this isn't a day for bidding my final farewell to the world. With a determined moan, I pull myself up, hook a leg over the rim, pause to let my arms recover, then search for the handles on the uppermost pod. Finding them, I haul myself up, almost scurrying compared to the slow pace of my previous progress, and moments later, I'm lying on top of the pod, staring at the clouds in the sky, a BIG smile on my face, waiting for the slow, shamed Rage to join me.

Bloody *yes*, mate!

Rage crawls onto the roof of the pod about a minute later. He's not huffing or puffing – with our redundant lungs we don't do that anymore – but his limbs are shaking, especially his arms, the same way mine are.

"Sod me!" he gasps, collapsing onto his back and covering his eyes with a weary, trembling arm.

"No thanks," I smirk, then dig him in the ribs with my knuckles. "Who's the queen of the castle and who's a dirty rascal?"

"Get stuffed," he barks.

"Come on, you set the challenge. Don't be a sore loser, just tell me who's the queen and –"

"Enough already," he growls. "You beat me fair and square. Happy?"

"Ecstatic," I beam.

"I don't know how I made it," Rage mutters. "Those last few meters were hell. I just wanted to drop and end the agony."

"You're too big for climbing," I chuckle. "Size matters but sometimes it's better to be small."

"Yeah," he says. "I guess."

We lie there a while longer, relaxing, ignoring the glare of the daylight and the itching it causes. Then the Eye starts slowly revolving again. Ivor either saw us make it to the top or else he decided enough was enough.

I get to my feet to have a good look around. It's hard to see clearly without sunglasses to protect my eyes, but I force myself to turn and peer. Everything's blurred to begin with, but things start to swim into focus (well, as much as they're ever going to) as my eyes slowly adjust.

Rage stands up beside me. He doesn't bother with the sights, just rolls his arms around, working out the kinks and stretching his muscles.

"I bet we'll ache like hell later," I note. "We might even have to go back into the Groove Tubes."

"Dr. Oystein won't let us," Rage says. "He'll make us endure the pain. The Groove Tubes are for Angels who really need them, who get injured in the line of duty, not for thrill seekers like us."

"Oh well," I smile, "I don't care. It was worth it. I never thought I could have done something this amazing. You're still a murderous git, but you made a good call."

"That's what I'm all about," Rage says smugly. "Making good

calls and helping people realize their ambitions. The Good Samaritan had nothing on me."

"He was bit more modest though."

"Screw modesty," Rage sniffs, then takes a step closer to me. "Now, speaking of making good calls, here's another. B?"

I was looking off in the direction of Vauxhall, trying to see if there were any signs of life over there. When Rage calls my name, I turn to face him. My back's to the river.

"Enjoy your flight," Rage says.

And he pushes me off.

My arms flail. I open my mouth to scream. Gravity grabs hold. I fall from the pod and plummet towards the river like a stone.

TEN

I hit the water hard. It feels like slamming into concrete. The lights temporarily blink out inside my head and everything goes dark.

When consciousness flickers on again, I think for a few seconds that I'm properly dead, adrift in a realm of ghosts. There are sinuous shadows all around, encircling and breaking over me. I assume that my brain was terminally damaged in the fall. I turn slowly, at peace, glad in a way to be done with life and all semblance of it. I spot a glimmering zone overhead—the legendary ball of light that summons the spirits of the departed?

No, of course not. After a brief moment of awe, I realize the truth. I'm still in the land of the living and the living dead. The shadows are nothing more than the eddies in the water. And the light is coming from the sun shining on the Thames.

I howl mutely, water rushing down my throat, cursing Rage and this world that refuses to relinquish its hold on me. Then, with disgust, I kick for the surface.

I haven't drifted far from the London Eye. I can still see it gleaming above me, turning smoothly. No sign of Rage but I hurl a watery insult his way regardless. Then I swim towards the bank and pull myself ashore close to a bridge. I lie on the pebbly, rubbish-strewn bank, next to the remains of a bloated corpse, and make myself throw up. Then I get to my legs – understandably shaky – and stagger to a set of steps, then up to the South Bank.

I slump to the ground in front of what used to be the Royal Festival Hall. There are some restaurants and shops at this level, all closed for business now. There's also an open, ramped section where teenagers used to practice on their rollerblades and skateboards. To my surprise and bewilderment, judging by the rumble of small, hard wheels, people are still using it.

I look up, wondering where the teenagers have come from, and how they dare take to the outdoors like this, when the area must be riddled with zombies. Then I realize they have nothing to fear from the zombies because they're undead too.

There are at least five or six of them, maybe a few more. They have the blank expressions common to all reviveds, but some spark of instinct is urging them to act as they did when they were alive, and they trundle around the gloomy space on their skateboards, rolling down ramps, grinding along bars, slamming into the graffiti-covered walls.

The skateboarding zombies are nowhere near as graceful as they must have been in life. They fall often, clumsily, their hands and faces covered in scars, and they don't try any sophisticated jumps or moves. But it's still a strangely uplifting sight, and I start to clap stiffly, feeling somebody should applaud their efforts.

When they hear me clapping, the zombies instantly lose interest in their boards. The teenagers growl with hungry excitement and dart towards me, flexing their fingers, sniffing the air, thinking supper has come early.

They can't see the hole in my chest, and I'm too tired to push myself upright, so I wave a weary hand in the air and they spot the bones sticking out of my fingertips. With some disappointed grunting sounds, they return to their patch, pick up the skateboards and start listlessly rolling around again, killing time until it's night and they can set out in search of brains.

I watch the show for a few minutes, then make myself puke again and more water comes up. For once I'm glad I don't have functioning taste buds—the water of the Thames was never the most inviting, but it's worse than ever these days, stained with the juices and rotting remains of the bodies you often see bobbing along.

I'm still trembling with shock. My head is throbbing. I think

265

several of my ribs are broken. My left eyelid is almost fully shut now and won't respond to my commands. The fingers of both hands began to shake wildly when I stopped clapping and are spasming out of control.

I want to find Rage and rip his throat open, but in my sorry state I can't go anywhere at the moment. I just have to sit here, suffer pitifully and hope that I recover.

After a while, the clouds part. The sunlight stings my flesh and hurts my eyes, but helps dry me off. The warmth revives me slightly and the shakes begin to subside. When my hands are my own again, I roll onto my front, groaning, wishing the fall had put me out of my misery. I lie on the pavement like a dead fish, steam rising from my clothes, feeling sorry for myself, plotting my revenge on Rage.

A shadow falls across me. I look up through my right eye and spot a familiar face. Speak of the Devil...

"Have you checked out that lot?" Rage mutters, staring at the skateboarding teenagers.

"You're dead," I gurgle.

"Aren't we all?" he laughs, squatting beside me. "I half-hoped the fall would knock your brains out."

"Only half?" I wheeze.

"Yeah. Despite what you think, I don't enjoy killing. I do it when necessary and don't worry about it, but I never wanted to become a serial killer. I'm not out to break any records on that front."

"So why did you push me off?" I snarl, sitting up and shaking my head to get rid of the water in my ears.

"Making a point," he says. "I got sick of watching you mope around. Decided you needed a good, hard kick up the arse." Rage stands and starts rolling his arms again, still aching from the climb. "Dr. Oystein would have done all he could to save you up there. If I'd told him what I was planning, he would have thrown himself between us and stood up for you. He's not like me. He doesn't think you're worthless scum."

"That's your opinion of me?" I bristle.

Rage shrugs. "It's my opinion of us all. I never thought people were anything special. A grim, brutal, boring lot. You got the occasional interesting person, like those skateboarders over there—still cool, even in death. But most of us were only good for breeding, fighting and screwing up the planet."

"You're some piece of work," I snort.

"Just being honest," he smiles. "I'm a lot of bad things but I'm not a hypocrite. I always saw people for what they were, and I never thought that was very much. Dr. Oystein, on the other hand, sees the good stuff where I see the bad. He wants to make heroes out of me, you, Ivor and all the rest. I don't think he's gonna get very far with that, but I respect the mad old bugger for trying."

"I'm sure he'd be delighted to hear that," I sneer, getting up to face Rage.

"You need to accept the doc for what he is, or get the hell out of here," Rage says softly. "What I liked about you when we first met was that you stood up for your beliefs. You didn't like the way we were experimenting on the reviveds, so you refused to play ball. If you really don't trust Dr. Oystein, you need to do that again. I hate seeing you mope around. You're better than that. Stronger than that."

I stare at Rage, confused. He sounds like he's genuinely trying to help me. Or maybe he just wants me out of the way because I can see through him, because I know he's a threat.

"Listen up," Rage says. "These are your options: You can come back with me to County Hall, quit moaning and be a good little Angel like the rest of us. Or you can bugger off and look for a home elsewhere. Choose."

"Screw you!" I roar, finding my fiery temper again. "I don't have to do what you tell me!"

Rage grins. "Are you gonna tell me I'm not the boss of you?"

I laugh despite myself. "Bastard," I mutter, shaking my head.

"B," Rage says calmly, "I'm saying all this because I think of you as an equal. I wouldn't bother with most of the others. They're mindless sheep, like the zom heads were. You need to get with the program or get lost. If you're not happy here, go look for happiness somewhere else. You know the setup with Dr. Oystein. If you can't buy into it, get out now before you drive yourself mental."

"And go where?" I mumble. "Who'll look out for me apart from the doc and Mr. Burke?"

"That doesn't matter," Rage says. "You're not a child, so don't act like one."

"I'm more of a child than an adult," I argue.

"Nah," he says. "We've all had to grow up since we died. You can look after yourself. You survived on your own before you came to County Hall. You can survive on your own again."

"But I don't want to," I whisper.

"Tough. You're acting like a sulky little girl. Nobody else will tell you to your face. I don't know if they're being diplomatic or if they're afraid of losing you, given how few of us there are. But you're not doing anyone any good like this. Be honest with me—does part of you wish you'd cracked your head open when I pushed you off the Eye? Were you tempted to not crawl out of the river, to just let it wash you away and dump you somewhere nobody could ever find you?"

I nod slowly, hating him for knowing me so well, hating myself for it being true.

"It's a big world," Rage says. "I'm sure there's a place in it, even for a moody cow like you."

He turns to leave.

"Will you tell the others I said good-bye?" I call after him.

"No," he grunts without looking back.

I treat myself to a grim smirk. Then, accepting the decision that

270

Rage has helped me make, I push to my feet and cast one last long-ing glance in the direction of the London Eye and County Hall. Snorting water from my nose, I turn my back on them both and head off into the wilderness, abandoning the promise of friendship and redemption, becoming just another of the city's many lost, lonely, godforsaken souls.

ELEVEN

I limp along like a sodden rat, making my way past Waterloo before turning onto the Cut, once home to theaters, pubs and restaurants, now home only to the legions of the damned.

I don't look up much, just trudge along, head low, spirits even lower, cursing myself for being such a fool. Am I really going to turn my back on Dr. Oystein, the Angels, Mr. Burke and maybe the only sanctuary in the city that would ever accept someone like me? Can I really be that dumb?

Looks like it.

I make slow progress, hampered by my injuries and lack of direction. With nowhere to aim for, there's no need to rush. I'm itching like mad from the daylight but that doesn't deter me. I figure it's no more than a loser like me deserves. I don't even stop to pick up a pair of sunglasses or a hat.

I only pause when I reach Borough High Street. Borough Market is just up the road. That was one of London's most famous food markets. Mum dragged me round it once, to check it out. She decided it wasn't any better than our local markets, and a lot more expensive, so she never came back.

I'm sure the food stocks have long since rotted, and even if they haven't, food is of no interest to me these days. But most of Borough Market was a dark, dingy place, built beneath railway viaducts. I bet the area is packed with zombies.

Ever since I revitalized, I've looked for a home among the conscious. Maybe that's where I've gone wrong. I might fit in better with the spaced-out walking dead.

I turn left and shuffle along. As I guessed, the old market is thronged with zombies, resting up to avoid the irritating light of the day world. I nudge in among them, drawing sharp, hungry stares. I rip a hole in the front of my T-shirt to expose the gaping cavity where my heart used to be. When they realize I'm one of their own, they leave me be.

All of the shops are occupied but I find a vacant spot in a street stall. There are a few rips in its canvas roof, through which old rainwater drips, but it's dry and shaded enough for me. There are even some sacks nearby that I shake out and fashion into a rough bed.

When I'm as comfortable as I can get, I take off my clothes and toss them away. No point leaving them out to dry—I can easily pick up replacements later. It doesn't matter to me that I'm lying here naked. The zombies aren't watching and there's nobody else around. Hell, maybe I won't bother with clothes again. I don't really need them in my current state, except to protect me from the sun when I go out in the daytime. But if I stick to the night world as my new comrades do…

Dusk falls and the zombies stir. I head out with them to explore the city, interested to see where they go, how much ground they cover. I hunted with reviveds when I first left the shelter of the underground complex, but I never spent a huge amount of time in their company. I'd follow a pack until we found brains or, if they didn't seem to know what they were doing, I abandoned them and searched for another group.

Some of the zombies peel off on their own, but most stay in packs, usually no more than seven or eight per cluster. Hard to tell if they're grouped randomly or if these are old friends or family members, united in death as they were in life. They don't take much notice of one another – no hugging or fond looks – unless they communicate in ways that I'm not able to understand.

There's a woman in a wheelchair in one of the packs. Curious to see how she fares, I pick that one and stick with it for the whole night, trailing them round the streets of Borough and the surrounding area.

The zombie in the wheelchair has no problem keeping up with the others. Like the skateboarding teenagers, she remembers on some deep, subconscious level how she operated when alive.

They don't seem to be moving in any specific direction though, taking corners without pausing to think, circling back on themselves without realizing it, covering the same ground again. Their heads are constantly twitching as they stare into the shadows, sniff the air and listen for shuffling sounds that might signify life.

Rats are all over the place, foraging for food. They clearly don't consider the zombies much of a threat. And from what I see, they're right not to. One member of the pack catches a couple of rodents that were rooting around inside the carcass of a dog. He bites the head off each and chews them with relish. But those are the only successes of the night. The other zombies spend a lot of time stumbling after rats – the disabled woman launches herself from her wheelchair when she senses a kill, then sullenly drags herself back into it afterwards – but the fanged little beasts are too swift for them.

I know from chatting with the Angels that some zombies hole up in a particular place and stay there. Jakob did that when he was a revived, made his base in the crypt of St. Martin-in-the-Fields. But these guys don't have that inclination, and rather than head back to the market when dawn breaks, they nudge into a house just off the New Kent Road and make a nest for the day.

The disabled woman struggles to mount the step into the house. She moans softly but the others don't help her. Finally she throws herself forward, leaving the chair to rest outside until she reemerges when it's night again.

I stand by the wheelchair, scratching my head and scowling. I'd

hoped to make a connection with the zombies of Borough Market, slot in with them, find a place to call my own. As deranged as they are, many still function as they did in the past, driven by instinct and habit to behave as they did when they were alive. I thought the locals of the market might grow used to me, nod at me when they saw me, invite me to hunt and eat with them.

Doesn't look like that's the case, not if this pack is anything to go by. They hunt together for some unknown reason, but they have no real sense of kinship. It's every zombie for him or herself.

I could go back and try again, follow another group when night falls and see if they prove any brighter or more welcoming. But what's the point? I'm not the same as these poor, lost souls, and there's nothing to be gained by pretending that I am. Why the hell would they bother about an outsider like me when they don't even truly care about their own?

"You're a mug, B," I mutter. "And getting muggier every day."

With a sigh, I turn my back on the house of zombies and head off on my own again. If a home exists for me in this city, it isn't among the reviveds. Not unless I choose to go without brains for a week or two. I'd revert if I didn't eat, lose my mind, become one of them.

It doesn't sound like much of an option, but I consider it seriously as I hobble away. After all, what's worse, having company as a brain-dead savage, or remaining in control of your senses but feeling lonely as hell all the time?

TWELVE

I can't tolerate the daylight without clothes. My skin itches like mad and my eyes feel as if they're being burnt from the inside out. So I make for the shopping center in the Elephant and Castle. It's hardly a shopping mecca, but I find jeans, a T-shirt, a hoodie, a baseball cap and a jacket with a high collar. I pull on gloves and a few pairs of socks, finish up by tracking down some sunglasses.

I pick up a bottle of eye drops in a pharmacy, and squirt in some of the contents while there. My eyes would dry out without regular treatment. I wouldn't go blind, but my vision would worsen.

I'm also going to need heavy-duty files for my fast-growing teeth and bones, since I left all mine at County Hall, but I can sort those out later. It will be a few days before my teeth start to bother me. Hell, maybe I'll just let the buggers grow. I mean, if I don't have anyone to chat with, what difference does it make?

Loaded up with supplies, and having ripped a hole in the front of the hoodie and T-shirt to reveal my chest cavity, I head back up the New Kent Road. I'm still in a lot of pain from the fall off the Eye, but I can cope with it as long as I don't rush. I've dealt with worse in the not-too-distant past.

I come to a roundabout and swing left onto Tower Bridge Road. I take my time, checking out the windows of old shops, acting like a tourist. I pause sadly when I come to Manze's, an old-style pie-and-mash shop, where they soak the pies and mashed potatoes in a sickly green sauce, known as liquor. I wasn't into that sort of grub, but Dad loved it and he often talked about this place. He worked here for a while when he was a teenager. The stories he told were almost enough to turn me vegetarian. But as much as he'd spin wild tales about what went into the pies and liquor, he always swore this was the best pie-and-mash shop in London.

They used to do jellied eels too, and that reminds me of a guy I haven't thought about since finding my way to County Hall. Pursing my lips, I nod and carry on, a girl with a purpose, having made up my mind to go in pursuit of an actual target rather than just wander aimlessly.

As I'm coming to the junction of Tower Bridge Road and

Tooley Street, I draw to a surprised halt and do a double take. Then I remove my sunglasses, just to be absolutely sure.

There's a sheepdog in the middle of the road.

The dog is lying down, clear of all the buildings, keeping a careful watch on the area around it, though it must be hard with all that hair over its eyes. It has a beautiful white chest, running to gray farther back. Its hair is encrusted with dirt and old bloodstains. It pants softly and its tail swishes gently behind it.

I watch the dog for several minutes without moving. Finally, as if hypnotized, I start forward again, taking slow, cautious steps. The dog spots me and growls, getting to its feet immediately.

"It's all right," I murmur. "I'm not gonna hurt you. You're gorgeous. How have you survived this long? Are you lonely like me? I'm sure you are."

The dog scrapes the road with its claws and growls again, but doesn't bark. It must have figured out that barking attracts unwanted attention. Zombies don't like the daylight, but they'll come out if tempted. There aren't many large animals left in this city—most of them were long ago hunted down and torn apart by brain-hungry reviveds. This dog knows that it has to be silent if it wants to survive.

I stop a safe distance from the dog and smile at it. I want it to trust me and come to me. I picture the pair of us teaming up, keeping each other company, me looking out for the dog and protecting

it from zombies, while in return it helps me find fresh brains. This could be the start of a beautiful friendship.

"You and me aren't that different," I tell the dog. "Survivors in a place where we aren't wanted. Alone, wary, weary. You should have headed out to the countryside. You'd be safer there. The pickings might be richer here but the dangers are much greater. Why haven't you left?"

The dog stares at me with an indecipherable expression. I don't know if it sees me as a threat or a possible mistress. Hell, maybe it sees me as lunch! I doubt a dog like this could be much of a threat, but maybe it's tougher than it looks. It might have survived by preying on zombies, ripping their throats open, using the element of surprise to attack and bring them down.

I spread my arms and chuckle at the thought of being taken out by a sheepdog. "I'm all yours if you want me. I've no idea what zombies taste like, but anything must be better than rat."

The dog shakes its head. I know it's just coincidence, that it can't understand what I'm saying, but I laugh with delight anyway.

"Stay here," I tell it. "I'll fetch a bone for you to chew and a ball to play with."

I start to turn, to go and search the shops of Tower Bridge Road. As soon as I move, the dog takes off, tearing down the street to my right, headed east.

"Wait!" I yell after it. "Don't go. I won't hurt you. Come back. Please..."

But the dog isn't listening. I don't blame it. I wouldn't trust a zombie either, even one who can speak. It won't have lasted this long by taking chances. A creature in that position will have learnt to treat every possible threat as a very real challenge to its existence. Better to run and live than gamble and die.

I stay where I am for a while, reliving my encounter with the dog, smiling at the memory, hoping it will come back to sniff me out if I don't move. But in the end I have to accept that the dog has gone. I stare one last time at the spot where it was lying, then push on over the bridge, alone but not quite as lonely as I felt a few minutes before.

THIRTEEN

I glance at the HMS *Belfast* as I'm crossing the bridge, remembering the last time I wandered past. There were people on board then, heavily armed, and they opened fire as soon as they saw me. I'm too far away to see if they're still there, but I've no wish to go check. Hostile hotheads with guns are best left to their own devices.

As I draw close to the Tower of London, I recall the Beefeater who tackled me when I tried to sneak past. I wonder if he's still guarding the entrance, demanding a ticket from anyone who wants to enter. I bet he is. In an odd way I feel sorry for him. I'd like to take him some brains, a little surprise gift. I examine the corpses littered across the bridge, but their skulls have been scraped clean. Oh well, maybe another time.

I slowly make my way towards Whitechapel, then up Brick Lane. It feels like years since I was last here, even though it can't be more than...what? Two months or so, and I spent a good deal of that in the Groove Tube. I blame my skewed perception on not being able to sleep. Time moves much more sluggishly when you can't drop off at night.

I come to the Old Truman Brewery. The steel door is locked and there's no sign of life inside. But then there wouldn't be. Its artist-in-residence might be a God-obsessed nutter like Dr. Oystein, but he's smart enough to keep a low profile when at home. If he was in – which he probably isn't, since the sun's been up for quite a while and he's an early starter – I wouldn't know it from out here.

I don't knock on the door or bellow the artist's name. I could attract company if I did. Instead I lower myself to the ground, sit by the door and wait, patient as a spider. It might be a waste of time – a zombie might have snagged him ages ago – but I've nothing better to be doing.

The day passes slowly. I miss Master Zhang – time flew by when I was training with him – and the Angels. Even a sneering match with Rage was preferable to sitting on my own on a deserted street all day.

I don't see any other living or undead creatures, except for some rats who give me a wide berth. And insects of course. Lots and lots of insects. The streets are awash with them. Zombies have no interest in ant or cockroach brains, so they don't hunt them. They're not creeped out by insects either – it takes a lot to startle a walking corpse – so they don't bother stamping on them or doing anything else to keep them in check.

I pass the hours counting the different types of insects that I see. I lose track a few times, until eventually I give up altogether. Then, late in the afternoon, I spot a man walking along, lugging an easel and whistling softly. I bet he doesn't know that he's whistling. He must be doing it subconsciously, unaware of the noise he's making. Even a soft whistle like that could bring a pack of zombies down on him, daylight or not.

He's almost at the door before he spots me. As soon as he does, he yelps, drops the easel and turns to flee.

"It's all right, Timothy," I call. "It's me, B."

He pauses and looks back uncertainly. "Mee-bee?"

"No, you dope." I stand, groaning as fresh pain flares in my battered bones. "It's me—B. Becky Smith. Remember?"

Timothy's expression clears. "Of course. B Smith, the talking zombie. I'm so delighted that you're still going strong. How are you? What have you been up to?"

Timothy bounds forward, smiling widely, hand outstretched. He's wearing the same sort of clothes as before, yellow trousers, a purple shirt, a tweed jacket. His brown hair is even longer than when I last saw him, shot through with streaks of paint. His eyes are still swamped by terribly dark circles in his long, thin face.

"You don't want to shake hands with me," I tut. "I'm not safe."

He comes to an immediate stop. "Oh, that's right. I was so excited to see you, I forgot. Silly me." He lowers his hand and chuckles. "As you can probably tell, I haven't spoken to anyone since we last met. I'm desperate for company. The painting keeps me going, but there's nothing like a good old bit of gossip to really stir the senses."

Timothy retrieves his easel and checks to make sure it hasn't been broken.

"I had hoped to see you sooner than this," he says, trying to phrase it lightly. "I thought you might come and visit me. When you didn't, I assumed you had either been welcomed with open arms by the soldiers you went off in pursuit of, or had been mown down by them."

"The latter," I grimace. "They opened fire when they realized I was undead, even shot a missile at me from a helicopter."

"But you survived and escaped?" Timothy claps enthusiastically. "Top-drawer! Where have you been since then? Why didn't you come back? I've painted some marvelous images. I'd love to share them with you."

"I've been busy," I mutter. "Things took a strange turn. Have you been over to County Hall since you started painting?"

"A few times," he nods. "I sketched it from the north bank of the river."

"You should wander south. You'd find a whole lot of interesting stuff to paint."

"That sounds intriguing," he purrs. "I look forward to hearing all about it. You are staying, aren't you? For a while at least?"

"If I'm welcome, yeah."

"Of course you're welcome," Timothy booms, bouncing to the door and getting out his key. "And you aren't the only one with news to share. I've played host to a most unique visitor since our paths last crossed. I'll have to introduce you, see what your opinion is, if you can make any more sense of it than I have."

I squint at him. "I thought you said you hadn't been talking to anyone since I left you."

"I haven't," he smirks. "This guest isn't much of a one for talking. But I think you'll be fascinated nevertheless. And who knows, maybe you'll manage to draw a response of some sort. I believe you might have more in common with the strange little dear than I have."

He laughs at my confused expression, then throws open the door and ushers me inside, politely asking me to wipe my feet on the way.

Timothy Jackson is an artist who survived the zombie attacks. Rather than lie low afterwards or flee the city as so many others did, he decided to make paintings of the downfall of London. Like Dr. Oystein, he thinks he has been handpicked by God, except in his case the Almighty only wants him to record images of the mayhem, not put a stop to it.

Once Timothy has stowed his equipment, he leads me upstairs, through a room of mostly blank canvases, to one crowded with finished works. It's even more jam-packed than it was the last time I was here. There's barely space to move.

"You've been busy," I note.

"Yes," he says with passion. "I feel like I've really hit my stride these last few weeks. I'm getting faster, without having to compromise my style. Here, look at this."

He shows me a large painting of a mound of bodies stacked in a heap, St. Paul's Cathedral rising behind them in the distance. Many of the faces are vague blobs and splashes of paint, but he's paid close attention to detail on a few of them, and also to the cathedral.

"Two days to complete," he says proudly. "That would have been at least a week's work just a couple of months ago, and I doubt I could have captured the expressions as clearly as I did. I'm improving all the time. Another year and who knows what I might be capable of?"

"How did the bodies end up in a pile like that?" I ask, staring at the morbid painting. "Did you gather them together?"

"Certainly not," Timothy huffs. "I paint only what I find. I never stage a scene. That would be cheating."

"Then how...?" I ask again.

"They were zombies," Timothy says softly. "They'd been shot, I assume by soldiers or hunters. If by soldiers, I imagine they stacked the bodies that way in order to come back and incinerate them at some point in the future. If by hunters, I suppose they did it so that they could pose for photos in front of their kills."

"Sometimes I think that your kind are worse than mine," I growl, recalling my own brush with the American hunter, Barnes, and his posse. "I've no problem with survivors killing zombies because of the threat we pose, but doing it for sport is sick."

"I agree," Timothy says. "Humans are far more dangerous than the

undead. I keep my head down when I hear gunfire. I know where I stand with zombies, but I never know what to expect from the living."

Timothy heads for the larder, washing his hands along the way, and prepares a simple meal for himself, cold beans on bread, some tinned carrots and a glass of red wine to wash it all down.

"Why don't you heat the food?" I ask.

"Zombies might pick up the smell," he explains. "I avoid cooking when I can. On those days when I simply *must* have a hot meal, I set up a barbecue in a park or public square and cook a big lunch. I tried cooking in a restaurant's kitchen once and was almost caught. I only barely got out alive."

Timothy has a mouthful of wine after he tosses away the tins, before tucking into his meager meal. He closes his eyes dreamily, savoring the taste, then cocks an eyebrow at me. "Are you sure you won't share a glass?"

"Apart from brains, I can't process anything," I tell him. "Liquids run clean through me. If I had any of that, I'd be sitting in a puddle by the end of the night."

Timothy clears his throat. "Ah. That might explain...I don't wish to be rude, but you might want to..." He wags a finger at me.

"What are you talking about?"

"When I was coming up the stairs behind you, I couldn't help but notice that the back of your trousers seemed rather damp."

My right eyelid flies wide open. (The left lid still doesn't work properly.) I feel behind and, sure enough, my fingers come away soaking.

294

"Damn it! I fell into the Thames yesterday and swallowed a load of water. I puked up most of it but obviously not all. Sorry about this."

"No need to apologize," Timothy says. "We all have our crosses to bear. Can I be of any assistance? There are plenty of towels and sheets here. If you wish, I could fashion you a..."

"...diaper?" I growl.

Timothy gulps and smiles sheepishly.

"Don't worry about it," I chuckle. "A wet bum is the least of my worries. I'll be happy with a towel to sit on, if that's all right with you."

"Absolutely." Timothy hurries off and comes back with two thick towels that he carefully places on a plastic chair. He waits for me to sit and give him the OK before taking his own seat and tucking into his food with a plastic knife and fork that he probably picked up from a takeout restaurant.

We chat as Timothy eats. He asks me where I went when I left him and I talk him through my trip to the West End, my run-in with Barnes and the other hunters, Sister Clare and her mad Order of the Shnax, their gruesome finale at the Liverpool Street Station, all the rest. I hesitate when I get to the Trafalgar Square part of the story, finding it hard to talk about even now.

"The soldiers drove you away?" Timothy asks sympathetically.

"No. They tried to kill me. They would have too – they had me pegged – except for Mr. Dowling and his mutants."

I expect Timothy to look blank, but to my surprise he knows

what I'm talking about. He was working on his last slice of bread, but now he lays it down and stares at me. "You've seen the mutants?"

"Yeah."

His voice drops. "And the clown?"

"Oh yeah. That's Mr. Dowling."

"You know his name?" Timothy sounds amazed.

"Of course. There's a big badge on his chest with his name on it."

"Really? I never got that close to him. And the man with the eyes? Do you know him too?"

I make a growling noise. "Him especially. He paid me a home visit back before all the madness started. I call him Owl Man. You've seen him too?"

Timothy nods, then stands and scurries away from the table, beckoning for me to follow. He leads me back to the room of finished canvases and roots through a pile stacked against one of the walls. I'd find it hard to distinguish between them since it's so dark — the windows are boarded over — but his eyes must have adjusted to the gloom over the months he's spent living and working here.

"I hung this up when I finished it," he mumbles as he searches, "but it gave me the shivers, so I took it down again. Those eyes followed me every time I passed, and not in a good way."

He produces a medium-size canvas and carries it to one of the rooms with no windows, the only places in the building where he dares turn on lights at night. He sets the painting down and stands back to study it, then slides aside to make space for me.

I don't recognize any of the buildings, just plain office blocks that could be anywhere in London. But there's no mistaking the horrific clown at the center of the painting, Mr. Dowling in all his dreadful finery. I'm familiar with the mutants surrounding him too, in their standard hoodies, with their rotting skin and yellow eyes.

And there's Owl Man, tall and thin, except for a ridiculously round potbelly. He has white hair and pale skin, but doesn't appear to be deformed in any other way. Except for his eyes, the largest I've ever seen, at least twice the size of mine. They're almost totally white, but with an incredibly dark, tiny pupil at the heart of each.

"If I hadn't seen him in the flesh, I wouldn't have believed his eyes could have been that big," I whisper.

"I know," Timothy says. "I almost made them smaller, to make them appear more in keeping with the size of his face, but I try not to distort reality when I paint."

"What were they doing?" I ask.

"Just talking. At least the man with the eyes was talking. The clown didn't seem to say much."

"He can't speak. He communicates with his mutants by making squeaking noises that they can interpret."

Timothy stares at me. "You seem to know a lot about them."

"Our paths have crossed a few times."

I study Mr. Dowling and Owl Man. The clown is the more frightening of the two, but Owl Man's eyes are unsettling—as Timothy said, they seem to follow me when I move. I wouldn't want to

297

run into either of those eerie men on a dark night. Or a sunny day, come to that.

"Where did you see them?" I ask, turning away from the painting and trying to put it from my thoughts.

"Somewhere in the City," Timothy says. "I was wandering as normal, saw them in the distance and decided after one look that they weren't the sort of people I'd like to get better acquainted with. I managed to sneak close enough to sketch them. They didn't hang around for very long. As soon as they left, I hurried back here and worked up the painting. I didn't want to forget any of the finer details."

"When was this?"

He has to think. "Not long after you left. Maybe a week or so after."

"Have you seen them since?"

He shakes his head. "I haven't been looking either. There are some things that even I shy away from. I'm determined to capture this city in all its nightmarish glory, but I've a feeling I wouldn't last long if that clown and his crew were aware of me. I doubt they'd be as easy to shake off as the zombies if they gave chase."

"You've got that right," I sigh. "They let me go for some reason, but if they'd wanted to stop me, I don't think I could have done a hell of a lot about it."

"Do you know anything else about them?" Timothy asks. "Where they came from, what they are, what they might be planning?"

"No." I chuckle sickly. "But I know a man who does. At least he thinks he does. You're not the only guy working for God in London. And if this other prophet is to be believed, that clown is your direct opposite. If you were sent by God to paint the city as you find it, that nasty bugger was sent by the Devil to paint it black."

Timothy gapes at me, lost for words. I laugh at his expression and shake my head. "Come on, let's go back to the kitchen. I'll tell you all about it while you finish your food. Those creeps aren't worth missing a meal over."

FIFTEEN

I tell Timothy about my weird encounters with Mr. Dowling and his merry mutants, how we first met in the underground complex, and how he later spared my life in Trafalgar Square.

"I don't know why he didn't kill me. Although, having said that, I haven't seen him harm any zombies. Maybe he only kills living people."

"That's a great comfort to me," Timothy sniffs.

"Don't worry," I grin. "You must have the luck of the Devil to have survived this long and, according to Dr. Oystein, Mr. Dowling is the Devil's spawn, so you're both in the same boat. He'd probably look upon you as a long-lost cousin."

"Why do you keep talking about the Devil?" Timothy frowns. "And who is this doctor you've referred to?"

"I'm coming to it," I tut. "What's the rush? We've got all night."

"You might have," Timothy says, "but I have to sleep, or had you forgotten?"

"Do you know," I say softly, "I had. It's been so long since I've slept that I've forgotten that it wasn't always this way, that there are people out there who don't have to sit up all night counting the circles on their fingers."

"Those are called whorls," Timothy informs me.

"Whorls my arse," I snort, then tell Timothy what happened after the battle between the soldiers and Mr. Dowling, finding the Angels in County Hall, training with them, Dr. Oystein's revelation about God's plans for him.

Timothy's last piece of bread remains uneaten, the beans soaking into it until it's a soggy mess. He's too engrossed in my story to focus on food. He hardly even sips his wine.

"Incredible," he murmurs when I finish. "What a load to take upon oneself. To bear responsibility for the future of the world... He has my admiration whether his story is true or not."

"Of course it's not true," I snap. "He's a nutter like Sister Clare and..."

I pause pointedly, waiting for Timothy to say wryly, "...and *me*?" But he only stares at me blankly. He's so sure of his calling that he finds it impossible to think that anyone might question him.

"Anyway," I chuckle, not wanting to burst poor Timothy's bubble, "I tried to overlook his God complex and fit in with the others, but in the end I couldn't stomach it, so I left."

Timothy nods slowly, then stares into his glass of wine, swirling the liquid around. He purses his lips, looks at the bread and beans, then picks up the plate and takes it to the sink to clean.

"Do you think Dr. Oystein is a liar or a madman?" Timothy asks while washing the plate in a bucket of cold water.

"Mad," I reply instantly. "He believes everything he says."

"You don't think he is trying to con you?"

"No."

Timothy stands the plate on a rack to dry, then turns and looks at me seriously.

"In that case, maybe he's right. Maybe he *is* a servant of God."

"Nah."

"How can you be so sure?" Timothy challenges me.

"Because..." I scowl. "Look, I don't want to piss you off, but it's rubbish, isn't it? God, the Devil, Heaven and Hell, reincarnation. I mean, I dunno, maybe there's some truth to some of it, but nobody can be sure. There have been so many different religions over the years, so many *truths*. How can one be right and all the others wrong?"

"I don't think it's about being absolutely right," Timothy says. "The main message of most religions is the same—be kind to other people, lead an honorable life, don't cause trouble. I've always seen

God as a massive diamond with thousands – maybe millions – of faces. We get a different view of the diamond, depending on which angle we look at it from. But there must be *something* there, otherwise what are we all looking at?"

"Maybe you're right," I huff. "I'm no expert, far from it. But there's more to why I left than the religious angle. It's the whole…" I grimace, not sure how to put my thoughts into words.

"Look," I try, "I've never seen ghosts, vampires or anything like that. This isn't a supernatural world. I believe in evolution. I'm sure there's life spread around the universe, more aliens out there than we can imagine. But I bet they're the same as us in that they just roll along wherever the universe pushes them, bound by the laws of nature as we are."

"My mother swore that she often saw the ghosts of her parents," Timothy murmurs. "They died when she was a girl, yet she never missed them because she saw so much of them as she grew up."

"Did she see fairies too?" I sneer.

"No," Timothy says calmly. "She was a mathematician. She had a doctorate from Cambridge. One of the sharpest minds in her field according to those who knew about such things. She wasn't especially religious. But she saw ghosts and accepted them as real. She even developed a mathematical equation to explain their relationship to the material world, though obviously I couldn't make head or tail of that."

"All right," I nod. "Sorry for poking fun at her. But that kind of proves my point. You say she came up with a formula to describe how ghosts work. I can accept that. There are all sorts of weird things in the world, but they can be explained with math and science. There's nothing miraculous about them."

"I disagree," Timothy says. "This *is* a world of miracles, of things that defy explanation, maybe even understanding. You're proof of that, a reanimated corpse, a girl whose soul has been restored. You might not believe in ghosts or vampires, but surely you believe in zombies?"

"Very clever," I growl as he smirks at me. "But there's nothing God-inspired about us. We're the result of an experiment gone wrong. I wasn't created by God, just as Dr. Oystein wasn't given heavenly orders to save the world from the Devil's henchman. This mess is our own fault, and if we're gonna fix it and put the world back together, we have to do it ourselves."

Timothy thinks about that. He finishes his wine and pours another glass. Takes a long, pleasing sip.

"What if you're wrong?" he asks quietly.

"I'm not."

"You can't be sure of that," he presses. "Using your own logic, no one can truly know the workings of the universe, or how much of a role God might play in our day-to-day lives. What if the creator *did* choose Dr. Oystein? There's no way of proving it, it's purely a matter of faith. But surely we all have to put our faith in someone. If you choose not to believe this particular prophet, fine, maybe you're right to doubt him. But why are you so set against even the possibility that he might be telling the truth?"

"Because it would stink if it was true!" I shout, then swiftly lower my voice, not wanting to alert any zombies that might be passing by outside.

"According to Dr. Oystein, God knew this was going to happen. He had decades of warning, and what did He do in all that time? Nothing, except give one guy the power to try and light the flames of a revival once the world had gone to hell. What sort of a God could do something like that to us?"

"A God who isn't the same as we are," Timothy says. "A God who has more to worry about than just our fate. A God who maybe has an eye on billions of worlds, who can't afford to spend His entire time trying to steer one particular species in the right direction. We can't understand the mind of God and, from what you say, Dr. Oystein doesn't claim to. He's simply doing what was asked of him. I can buy into that, a God who doesn't govern directly, but who tries to lend a helping hand. In a way I'd prefer that to a God who ruled by divine decree."

"The only person who lent Dr. Oystein a helping hand is himself," I jeer. "The voice in his head is his own. It has to be."

"It doesn't," Timothy insists. "This is a world of marvels and wonders. A world of miracles, if you wish to put it that way. In such a world, why can't God speak to Dr. Oystein or anyone else?"

"Because it's *not* a world of marvels," I snarl. "It's a world of science, math and nature."

"*And* miracles," Timothy says stubbornly. "There are things that science can't explain, wonders that confirm there is more to this universe than we know."

He downs the remains of his wine and sighs with contentment. Then he stands, a sparkle to his eyes.

"It's time I let you see my other visitor," he says. "Perhaps then you will be more inclined to accept the reality of the miraculous."

"If it's not Elvis Presley or Michael Jackson, I'll be very disappointed," I joke.

"It's neither of those fine men," he says. "But you'll be impressed regardless, I guarantee it."

Then he leads me from the room and up the stairs of the echoing old brewery in search of wonder.

SIXTEEN

Timothy guides me to a small room just off the massive area where most of his paintings are stacked. I recall spotting this door the last time we came through. I thought it was a storage room or something like that. And maybe it was once. But not any longer. Now it's been turned into a bizarre nursery.

There's a crib in the middle of the room. Several mobiles hang from the ceiling. Lots of dolls and cuddly toys are stacked neatly in the corners. There's a large, inflatable dinosaur. Soft balls. A couple of activity gyms. A mix of blue and pink curtains draped around the walls.

"It's overkill, I know," Timothy says with a sheepish chuckle. "I just couldn't help myself. I had to have anything that

I thought my guest might enjoy. It's not like there are limits anymore. The shops are full of toys that will never be used. Why not spoil the poor creature? Although, having said that, I don't know if the little dear notices any of this."

"What are you talking about?" I start towards the crib, then stop dead. "Don't tell me it's a zombie baby. It is, isn't it? You've adopted a bloody undead baby!"

"B..." he starts to defend himself.

"What the hell were you thinking?" I shout. "I don't care how cute it might look—if it's a zombie, it's deadly. One scratch or nip and you're history. I can't believe you'd risk everything just so you can play daddy."

"It's not a zombie," Timothy says without losing his temper.

I stare at the crib suspiciously. "Are you telling me it's a real baby?"

"I wouldn't describe it that way either."

"You're not making sense," I scowl.

"That's why you have to go and look," he smiles.

I don't want to. Something about this feels wrong. I want to back out and get far away from here and whatever's in the crib. But fascination propels me.

I edge forward cautiously, ready to turn and run if I sense a threat. Then I come within sight of the baby and I freeze. My right eye widens and even my injured left eyelid lifts a bit. I feel the walls of reality crumbling around me, the world tilting on its axis, the fingers of a nightmare reaching out to grab me.

The baby is dressed in a long, white christening gown. Its tiny

310

hands are crossed on its chest. Its nails are sharper and more jagged than a normal baby's, but no bones jut out of the fingertips. Its feet are hidden by the folds of the gown.

Its face is a stiff mask, like a cross between a human's and a doll's, but there's nothing human about its mouth and eyes. The small mouth is open, full of tiny, sharp teeth. Its eyes are pure white balls, no pupils. Its eyelids don't flicker, though its lips twitch regularly and an occasional tremor runs through its cheeks.

A metal spike has been stuck through the baby's head. The spike enters the skull above the left eyebrow and the tip pokes out just behind the baby's left ear.

"Have you ever seen anything like that?" Timothy whispers.

"It's not real," I croak.

"I thought that too at first," he says. "I was sure it was a doll or a zombie. But it has a heartbeat. And if you watch closely, you'll see its chest rise and fall—it's breathing, just very slowly."

"It can't be real," I whisper. Then I add numbly, in answer to his question, "Yes. I've seen babies like that before."

"Where?" Timothy frowns.

"In my dreams."

I used to have a recurring nightmare when I was alive. I'd be on a plane and it would fill with babies that looked just like this one. In the dream they'd call me their mummy and clamber over me, ask me to join them, tear at me, bite, rip me apart, tell me I was one of them now.

311

That dream terrified me all of my life. I thought I'd finally escaped it when I stopped sleeping. But now it's somehow followed me out of the realm of the unreal and into the wide-awake world.

"You can't have dreamed of anything like this grisly beauty," Timothy says, dismissing my claim with a wave of his hand. "I took off its clothes when I brought it back. I wanted to see if it had been infected—I assumed it had to be a zombie, even with its heartbeat.

"It's not. No marks anywhere. No bites, scratches, nothing. Except for the spike through its head of course. I thought there might be undead germs on the metal, that the reason the child showed signs of life was because the zombie virus had first attacked its brain and then been inhibited by the position of the spike. And maybe there's something to that theory. But it doesn't explain..."

Timothy takes hold of the hem of the baby's gown and lifts it, exposing the child's feet, legs and more.

"Bloody hell!" I shout.

"...*this*," Timothy exhales softly.

The baby doesn't have any genitals. There's nothing but smooth flesh between its thighs.

"It doesn't have an anus either," Timothy says, and for some reason that makes me laugh hysterically. Timothy blinks with surprise and adds, "I can turn it over if you want to check."

I stop laughing abruptly. Then I moan, "Do me a favor and lower the gown. I've seen enough."

Timothy lays the gown back in place and smooths down the hem.

"What is it?" I hiss.

"I don't know," Timothy says. He waits a few beats, then grins wickedly. "It's a *miracle*."

"No," I choke. "There's nothing miraculous about a freak like that. Diabolical, maybe."

"Don't say such things," Timothy frowns. "It's only a baby. It can't help the way it's been put together."

"But who created it?" I ask, voice rising again. "Where did it come from? How can it live with a spike through its head?"

"I don't know," Timothy says, smiling lovingly at the white-eyed baby. "But that's not the only remarkable thing. I found the child maybe three weeks ago. It was lying in the road close to the Aldgate East Tube entrance, near Whitechapel Art Gallery. That was one of my favorite galleries. Did you ever visit it?"

I shake my head, unable to glance away from the unnatural child.

"The baby hasn't eaten in all that time," Timothy continues. "I tried to feed it milk and biscuits when I first rescued it, but it wouldn't swallow. I was going to poke a tube down its mouth and force-feed it, but I decided there was no point keeping the poor creature alive in such a pitiable condition. So I sat back and left it to nature, waiting for it to die.

"As you can see, it hasn't. It's in the same condition today as it was when I found it."

"But how?" I ask again. "What is it? Where did it come from?"

"Like you, I've been asking those questions over and over,"

314

Timothy says. "No answers have presented themselves. For the first few days I didn't leave its side. I stood watch, waiting for it to die, putting my work on hold. When I saw that it wasn't going to pass away, I returned to my normal routine, though I spend most of my nights in here now. I've started reading stories to it. I don't know if it can hear me or understand what I'm saying, but I like reading out loud."

Timothy looks around at everything that he's gathered and sighs. "Like I said, I know it's overkill, but I can't stop bringing back presents. I guess I was lonelier than I realized."

"Has it ever said anything?" I ask, moving closer to the baby, staring at its teeth – *fangs* – and pale white lips.

"No. Its mouth moves but always silently. What age do you think it is? When do babies start to speak?"

I can't answer those questions. I don't really care.

"The babies in my dreams could speak," I whisper. "I need to know if this one can, if it says the same sort of things that they used to."

"How could it?" Timothy scoffs. "This isn't from your dreams. It's real."

"Still..." I reach towards the baby.

"What are you doing?" Timothy snaps.

"I'm going to pull out the spike."

"The hell you are!" he shouts, pushing me away.

"Easy," I say, putting my hands behind my back, wary of accidentally scratching and infecting him. "I don't want to hurt it. But I have to find out."

"You're not going anywhere near that spike," Timothy growls. "It holds the poor thing's brain in place. If you pull out the spike, you'll kill it."

"I wouldn't be so sure of that," I mutter. "But even if I do, so what? Look at it, Timothy. That's no normal baby. Whatever it is, wherever it came from, it's not one of us. One of *you*," I correct myself.

"Even so, it's alive and defenseless and I've sworn to protect it," Timothy says grandly.

"The damn thing has a spike through its head," I remind him. "It's a bit too late for protection."

"Spike or no spike, it's still alive," Timothy argues.

"But what sort of a future does it have?" I press. "For all we know it's in agony and is silently begging for someone to end its pain. Maybe it will recover if we remove the spike. Who knows how a thing like this might function? For all we know, it doesn't even have a brain.

"It has no quality of life," I say, taking a step towards the crib. Timothy doesn't try to stop me this time. "If we leave it as it is, it will definitely die in the end, whether it needs food or not. This way it has a chance. We might save it."

"Do you really believe that?" Timothy whispers.

"Yeah," I lie.

"I only want what's best for the little darling," he sighs.

"This is the way forward," I assure him. "We can cover the hole with a bandage if we need to, maybe even stick the spike back in. It's risky, I won't deny it, but what choice do we have?"

316

"We could stand by and not interfere," Timothy says, then shakes his head. "No. You're right. That would be selfish of me. This way it has a chance. Go on, B. I'll support you. I won't blame you if it goes wrong."

I stretch out a trembling hand and grip the spike above the baby's eye. I stare again at that pure white orb, remembering the babies in my dreams, how their eyes turned red when they attacked me. I gulp. Tighten my grip. And pull.

The spike comes out with very little resistance. There's a small sucking sound as it clears the clammy flesh. Blood oozes out of the hole, but slowly, not in huge amounts. A few bits of brain trickle from the spike.

Timothy and I stare at the baby. Neither of us says a word.

Nothing happens.

Then, maybe a full minute after I've withdrawn the spike from the baby's head, it shudders. Its arms uncross and its fingers claw at the blankets beneath it. As I watch with disbelief and horror, its eyes turn red, as if filling with blood, and it starts to scream in a terrifyingly familiar, tinny voice. "*mummy. mummy. mummy. mum-meeeeeEEEEEEE.*"

SEVENTEEN

The baby keeps squealing, the same word repeated without even a pause for breath, calling for its *mummy*. The high-pitched noise cuts through me, making me wince and grind my teeth. Timothy is staring slack-jawed at the whining, red-eyed child.

"Make it stop," I bark, covering my ears with my hands.

"How?" Timothy asks.

"Stick the spike back in its head."

"No," he says, face turning a shade paler at the thought. "We can't do that. Let's find it a pacifier."

He lurches to a shelf stacked with baby stuff. He roots through the neat pile until he finds one. He hurries back and leans over the crib, cooing to the hellish baby, "There, there. It's all right. We'll take care of you. No need to cry. Does it hurt? We'll make the pain go away. You're our little baby, aren't you?"

"Less of that crap," I snort, shuddering at the thought of being mother to such an unearthly creature. "Just shut the damn thing up."

"Be nice, B," Timothy tuts, then yelps and takes a quick step away from the crib. "It tried to bite me!"

"Oh, give it to me," I snap, nudging him aside and taking the pacifier from him. I bend over, fingers of my left hand extended to widen the baby's mouth if necessary. Before I can touch its lips, the tiny creature's head shoots forward and its fangs snap shut on the bones sticking out of my middle and index fingers.

"Let go!" I roar with fright, and try to pull my hand free. The baby rises with my arm, dangling from the bones, fangs locked into them, chewing furiously, head jerking left and right.

I wheel away from the crib, shaking my arm, trying to dislodge the monstrous infant. Timothy is yelling at me to be careful, not to drop the child. I swear loudly and try to hurl the baby loose.

I lose my balance, crash into the inflatable dinosaur and stumble to my knees. As I push myself to my feet again, the baby chews through the bones, drops to the floor and collapses on its back. It immediately resumes screaming for its mummy.

"Bloody hell!" I pant, retreating swiftly. My hand is trembling.

"I told you it wasn't a good idea," Timothy says smugly. "It obviously doesn't want a pacifier, and with teeth like that, who are we to argue?"

"Sod what it wants," I snarl. "We have to shut it up."

"You can try again if you wish," Timothy chuckles. "Personally I like my fingers the way they are. Those teeth are amazing. I wonder what they're made of?"

"You go on wondering," I growl, crossing the room to pick up the spike. "I'm putting a stop to this."

"No," Timothy says sternly. "You can't do that."

"I bloody well can," I huff, advancing on the wailing baby.

Timothy steps in my way and crosses his arms.

"Move it, painter boy. I'm not playing games."

"Neither am I," he says. "You're not sticking that into the baby's head. You might kill it."

"Do I look like I care?"

"No. That's why I can't let you proceed. You're not thinking clearly. You're upset and alarmed, understandably so. But when you calm down, you'll see that I'm right. This is a living baby, calling for its mother. It's afraid and lonely, probably in pain and shock. We have to comfort it, not treat it like a rabid animal that needs to be exterminated."

"Didn't you see what it did with those teeth?" I roar, waving my gnawed fingerbones at him.

"Yes, but to be fair, you were attacking it. I would have bitten in self-defense too if you'd come at me like that."

"But you wouldn't have been able to chew through my bones," I note angrily.

321

"Perhaps," Timothy grins, understanding from my expression that I can't follow through on my threat. "But we have to take that chance. Now let's see what we can do to help this poor lamb. Maybe it will stop screaming if we put it back in its crib, tend to its wound and show that we mean no harm. I'm sure that with a little TLC it will respond to our ministrations and –"

Timothy stops. He had started to bend to pick up the baby, but now he turns and stares at the doorway, into the gloom of the large room beyond. He cocks his head and frowns.

"Do you hear that?" he whispers.

"What?"

I step up beside him, trying to focus. The screams of the baby – "*mummy. mummy. mummy.*" – fill my head and I find it hard to tune them out.

Timothy moves through the doorway as if sleepwalking, eyes wide, a slight tic in his left cheek. I follow and close the door behind me, muffling the sounds of the baby.

I zone in on the new noises. They're coming from outside the building. Loud, scratching sounds, similar to a nail being dragged across a blackboard, only much sharper, and not one nail but dozens at the same time.

"What is it?" I ask softly, although part of me has already guessed. I'm not stupid. As I've stated proudly on more than one occasion in the past, I can put two and two together.

"Zombies," Timothy says, and his expression never alters.

"They've heard the baby. They're climbing the walls." He points to the boarded-over windows with a surprisingly steady finger. Unlike the thick boards nailed over the windows on the ground floor, those up here were designed primarily to keep in the light, not keep out the ranks of the living dead. With all the oversized windows in this place, that would be impossible. This is a gallery, not a fortress. Anonymity was its only real defense.

"They know that we're here," Timothy says. "They're going to break in."

And with those few calm words he pronounces his death sentence.

EIGHTEEN

"We have to get out of here!" I roar. "Where are the exits?"

Timothy shakes his head wordlessly. He's staring at the boards covering the windows. He looks more thoughtful than scared.

"Timothy!" I scream, wanting to grab and shake him, but afraid of piercing his skin with my bones.

"The roof," he murmurs.

"No good," I grunt. "They're climbing the walls. They can get to us in seconds on the roof. We have to go down to the ground floor, escape out the back, try to lose them on the streets."

The first zombies start pounding on the glass and it shatters. They tear into the boards, ripping them loose. I catch glimpses of bones, fingers, faces, fangs.

Windows run the whole length of this room. The boards on pretty much all of them begin to crack and snap beneath the strain. There must be dozens of zombies out there, maybe more.

"Come on," I shout, heading for the stairs.

"The baby," Timothy says.

"You've got to be bloody joking!"

"The baby," he says, stubbornly this time. "I won't leave it to them."

"You can't save it," I growl. "Its cries are what's drawing them. If we take it with us, they'll follow the noise."

"But it's a baby…" he says miserably.

"No baby of our world," I snort, then run with a wild idea. "Maybe one of the zombies is its mother. That might explain why it looks so strange. She might have been pregnant when she was turned. Maybe it was born after she died."

"That sounds feasible," Timothy nods.

"If that's the case, they might accept it as their own. It might find a home with them."

"Or they might rip it to shreds," Timothy notes glumly. "Maybe zombies stuck the spike through its head in the first place."

I roll my eyes. "Either way, the baby's going to be theirs in a minute. We can't stop them. We can put up a pointless fight and get torn apart or focus on our own necks and maybe make it out of here. Your choice, Timothy. I already died once. If they kill me again, it's not that big a deal."

I wait for him to make up his mind. I'll stick by him no matter what he decides. He's my friend and I want to do whatever I can to protect him, even though I know I can't.

Timothy licks his lips, torn between wanting to be a hero and knowing his limits. There's a loud snapping noise and the first of the zombies tumbles through the broken boards.

"God forgive us!" Timothy cries and races for the stairs, leaving the screeching baby to whatever fate has in store for it.

We pound down the stairs, taking them two or three at a time. I'm in agony, my broken ribs digging into my flesh and organs with every lurching movement. I ignore the pain as best I can, trying to focus on Timothy and getting him out of here before the zombies catch up.

We race through the room of blank canvases and supplies, the sound of the snapping boards above following us like the beat of tom-toms.

"Almost there," Timothy pants, overtaking me as I stumble. "There's a door at the rear of the building which I earmarked for an eventuality such as this. It opens quickly and quietly. If we can get outside, there's a good chance we can –"

He stops.

"Keep going," I snap. "This is no time to –"

I stop too.

We've come to a short set of steps. They lead to the main down-stairs room, a huge, open space. The windows at this level were boarded over professionally to keep out zombies. This should be the safest room in the entire building.

It's not.

The boards have held. So has the front door. But there are other doors. I'm sure that Timothy and the people who occupied this building before he came here did all that they could to secure those entrances. But there must have been a weak link somewhere, a chain that snapped, a lock that broke, hinges that crumbled.

Because the room is thick with zombies.

They stand silently, an army of them, motionless, faces raised to the ceiling, as if trying to determine exactly where the shriek of the baby is coming from.

Timothy trembles, losing his cool at last.

"Easy," I whisper. "They're not moving. They look like they're in some kind of a trance. We might be able to slip through them."

I take a step down.

No response.

Another step.

Not a single zombie moves.

A couple more, then I stretch out my right foot to take the final step.

As soon as my toes touch the ground, the neck of every zombie snaps down as they lower their heads in perfect timing. They bare their teeth and snarl, then surge towards us without breaking ranks.

"Bugger!" I scream, turning to start back up the stairs. "Come on!" I roar at Timothy. "We've got to try for the roof."

"We'll never make it," he sobs, but tears along after me.

We hurry through the room of supplies. Timothy is praying

aloud, his words coming fast and furious, sounding like gibberish. We reach the stairs to the main gallery. They're clear. No sign of any zombies. I silently thank God and ask Him for another minute, sixty seconds, that's all we need. If we can make it to the roof, Timothy can cling to my back and I can either leap to another roof or all the way to the ground. My legs should be able to take a drop like that. I might break a few bones but it won't scramble my brain. Even if I can't carry on, Timothy can escape by himself. The zombies won't harm me once he's gone. He can return for me later. A minute. That's all we need. That's not too much to ask for, is it?

Apparently it is.

We're not even halfway up the stairs when the zombies from the upper floor come spilling towards us. They've made it through the windows and boards. They stagger down the steps, arms outstretched, leering hungrily.

Timothy screams and turns to flee, but more zombies are coming up the steps, having tracked us from the room below.

We're screwed.

I reach out to grab Timothy and pull him in tight, meaning to bite his neck, figuring the best I can do for him now is to end it quickly and maybe give him a chance of revitalizing. I was injected with Dr. Oystein's vaccine when I was a child. That's why I recovered my wits when I was turned into a zombie. Maybe I can pass some of my revitalizing genes on to Timothy. I doubt he stands much of a chance but it's better than none at all.

But I'm too late. A zombie tackles me before I can strike and I fall to the steps, driven down by the weight of my assailant. Others throw themselves on top of me, burying me at the bottom of a pile of bodies.

"Timothy!" I shriek.

"Good-bye, B," he says sadly as the first of the zombies pins him to the wall and scrapes at his stomach. Others swarm around him, digging into the flesh of his arms and legs with their bony fingers. Timothy screams, a cry of pure agony and loss. He screams again as zombies rip chunks of flesh from his body with their teeth. They're not concerned about converting him—they want to finish him off.

Madness fills Timothy's eyes, but with a supreme effort he shrugs it off for one last instant and locks gazes with me as I stare at him helplessly from my position on the floor.

"Take care of my paintings," he wheezes pleadingly.

Then a zombie digs its fingers through Timothy's eyes. He has time to scream once more before the zombie breaks through to his brain and starts scraping it out and cramming pieces into its foul, eager mouth.

There's no more screaming after that. Timothy Jackson is dead and gone. And all I can do is wait for the zombies to rip me apart and maybe send my soul to join Timothy's in the peaceful, welcome realms beyond.

NINETEEN

The zombies piled on top of me poke and maul me, unable to strike cleanly because so many are pressed in around me. Then, as the others retreat from Timothy's bloody, shredded remains, those holding me down fall still. I hear them sniffing and I sense them cocking their heads, listening for a heartbeat. When they realize I'm dead, they go slack and start pushing themselves off me, no longer viewing me as either a threat or a tasty treat.

I rise with a groan, prop myself against the wall and stare miserably at all that is left of my artistic, eccentric friend. He was a crazy but sweet guy. He deserved better than this. But then so did billions of others. In this world of savagery and death, there's only what you get. *Deserve* doesn't come into it anymore.

The zombies don't budge. Those with nothing to eat aren't moving at all, just standing on the steps, faces raised again, looking towards the top of the stairs. They're all silent, motionless, eyes fixed on the same spot. It's eerie.

I think about trying to slip away, but they reacted aggressively the last time I did that. I figure it's safer to give it some time, see what happens.

I don't have to wait long. After about a minute, the zombies part, moving to both sides of the stairs, forming a bizarre guard of honor. They don't lower their heads as they shuffle over, gazes fixed on that same spot at the top of the stairs.

This is really freaking me out. I ready myself to run, sod the consequences. I'd rather be torn apart than remain among this lot. There's something sinister going down and I don't want to be here when it hits.

But I'm too late. Even as I'm stretching out my foot to take my first tentative step, a pack of zombies appears at the top of the stairs. They march three abreast. They're holding their arms above their heads, linked together. Those at the front are children, then women, then men, arranged according to height, the way they would be if marching in a parade.

The children pass me, two rows of them. Then the women, three rows. Then the men start to come past. The first half-dozen have their arms linked over their heads, the same as the women and children. So have the men in the last two rows. But those between are holding something up high, as if it was a holy relic. Except this is no religious artifact.

It's the crib from the baby's room.

As they draw level with me, the procession comes to a stop. I'm staring at the side of the crib. As I watch, the baby crawls to the bars, then pulls itself up until it's standing. It looks calmer than it did before, a slight smile in place. It's stopped screaming. Its unblinking eyes are white again, the red sheen having receded.

The baby is looking at me.

"What the hell are you?" I moan.

"*mummy*," the baby says softly.

"No," I wheeze, shaking my head, denying the claim. "I'm not your mother. I'm nothing to you."

The baby's expression doesn't alter, but its hands move and it pulls the bars farther apart, as if they were made of rubber. When the space is wide enough, the baby gently pokes its head through the gap. Its smile spreads.

"*join us mummy*," it says in its tinny, unnatural voice.

"No," I say again. My throat has tightened. If I could cry, I'd be weeping now.

The baby frowns. "*don't be frightened mummy. you're one of us. come with us mummy.*"

"I'm not one of you!" I scream. "I don't even know what the hell you are."

The baby giggles. "*yummy mummy. come.*"

"I'm not coming anywhere," I snarl. "You're a bloody freak. I wouldn't spit on you if you were on fire."

The baby seems to consider that. After a long pause, it draws its head inside the crib and bends the bars back into place. It looks disappointed.

The zombies start to move again, down the stairs. The baby turns its face away and I think it's over. Then they stop. The baby's neck swivels and its nightmarish features swim back into view. Remembering the dreams I used to have, I expect it to tell me that I have to die now. I brace myself, waiting for the baby to climb the bars and hurl itself at me from the top of the crib.

But this baby doesn't appear to have murder on its mind. Its eyes don't redden and its mouth doesn't split into a vicious sneer. In fact it looks sad, maybe even lonely. And when it addresses me again, it's not to threaten or scare me. Instead it whispers something that makes me gape at it with bewilderment.

"we love you mummy."

With that, the macabre infant faces forward. It looks like a tiny prince or princess on a very grand throne, borne along by a team of devoted courtiers. It giggles, then the zombies resume their march. At the bottom of the stairs they process through the room of supplies, then down the small set of stairs to the ground-floor room and the exit.

The zombies around me hold their position until the retinue

passes from sight. Then they fall in behind and follow the crib and its carriers out of the building. A minute later, every single one of them has gone, and all that's left behind are the paintings, Timothy's scattered remains and the most incredulous, slack-jawed girl the world has ever seen.

TWENTY

For a long time I don't move. I don't even slump to the floor to take the weight from my weary legs. I'm frozen in place, replaying the scene in an endless loop inside my head, remembering everything about the baby, its face, what it said, how the zombies around it reacted.

It was controlling them. It called for them when I removed the spike. They came in their hundreds, rescued it, took it wherever it told them to take it. Like the mutants who work for Mr. Dowling, the baby somehow has the power to make zombies do what it wants.

But it didn't have the power to bend *me* to its will. I was able to resist its call to follow it back to its lair.

Or was I? Maybe it simply let me go.

It called me its mummy. It said it loved me. Maybe it thinks I really am its mother. It might have the potential to control me, but chose not to exercise it because of the bond it believes we share.

This is insane.

This is impossible.

This is terrifying.

Eventually I force myself to move. I struggle back up the stairs, taking them one slow step at a time. I shuffle into the nursery and gaze at the toys, the mobiles, the space where the crib stood. I spot the spike on the floor and seriously think about picking it up and driving it through my own skull. Escape from this world of horrors tempts me more than ever before. How can I witness something like this and carry on as if all is well or can ever be made well again?

Ultimately I reject suicide, fearful that it might not achieve anything. The baby and its clones originally tormented me in my dreams. Now they've chased me into this world. Who's to say they couldn't follow me into the afterlife too?

I limp back down the stairs to the room of supplies and search for a bag. I find a suitable one without too much difficulty, empty it of its contents, then retrace my steps and gather up the remains of poor Timothy. I hate having to do this – it would be much simpler to just leave – but I feel like I owe him. I brought the zombies down upon him. If I hadn't come here, he might never have tried to pull the spike from the baby's head. He could have gone on living and painting for months, maybe years, until his luck ran out. He's dead because of me. The least I can do is tend to his remains and give him some sort of a halfway decent burial.

I pick up every last scrap of Timothy, clothes as well as bones, skin and organs. I bag them all. After a while, I realize I'm making a low moaning noise, the closest I can get to crying. I don't make myself stop.

Job complete, I start to drag the bag down the stairs. I pause when I spot the trail of blood that I'm leaving behind. The bag isn't blood-proof. The bits inside are leaking.

I find another couple of bags, more resistant to liquids than the first, and triple-bag the corpse. That does the trick. There are no stains now.

I lug the grisly package to the front door, then climb the stairs once more, get a bucket of water and a mop and go to work on washing away the blood. Timothy's last request was that I looked after his paintings. The blood would attract flies and insects, maybe larger creatures like rats, which might attack the canvases. If I survive long enough, I plan to come back here every month or so, dust and clean, take care of the paintings, do all that I can to maintain the legacy of Timothy Jackson. That probably won't prove much of a comfort to him where he's gone, but it's all I can do to honor his memory.

When I'm finished cleaning, I return to the bag by the door and sit beside it. I don't want to go out until night has passed and day has dawned. Too many zombies at large in the darkness. Too many shadows in which the living dead and killer babies can hide.

I spend the night silently thinking, reexamining the world, my life, the very nature of the universe.

I thought I had it figured out. I told Burke, Rage and Timothy that this wasn't a world of miracles. If God existed, He didn't get involved in what was happening to us. I couldn't see His hand at work anywhere. We were on our own, I was sure of it.

The baby suggests to me that I was wrong. For years I dreamed of babies just like this one. They looked the same, wore the same clothes, had the same eyes and fangs, even said the same things.

"join us mummy."

"don't be frightened mummy."

"you're one of us."

How could I have dreamed about them, never having seen such a demonic baby until tonight? How could my nightmares have been so accurate, correct down to the tiniest detail? Did God send me visions of the future, to prepare me for what was to come, so that I would realize He was real and put my faith in others that He had chosen? Does He want me for His team?

I don't know. I want to believe – it would be so wonderful to think that I understood everything, and had been handpicked by such a powerful being – but I can't, not a hundred percent. What I can do, however, after my run-in with the baby, is doubt. Not Dr. Oystein but myself. There are enough questions in my mind now to

344

make me far less sure that the doctor is deluded. I'm not saying I'm taking him at his word about God speaking to him. But I'm willing to listen to him now, to give him a chance, to put my faith in him.

Hell, from where I'm standing after my experiences tonight, it makes as much sense as anything else in this wickedly warped world.

TWENTY-ONE

The sun rises and I haul Timothy's remains outside. I shut the door behind me and hide the keys in the yard of the old brewery. I only remember the other door – the one the zombies used to get into the building – on my way down Brick Lane. I wince and think about retrieving the keys, going back inside and searching for the other entrance, to seal it.

"Sod it," I mutter. "Life's too short."

I'll do my best for Timothy's paintings, but I'm not going to go overboard. Right now I'm exhausted. I'm not in my worst-ever physical state – that was after Trafalgar Square – but mentally I'm beat. I reckon I need to spend at least a month in a Groove Tube to recover. I can't face even the minor challenge of searching for an open door.

I'll do it the next time I come. If zombies or other intruders beat me to the punch, sneak in before I return and wreak havoc, tough.

I know where I want to take Timothy. I can't be sure but I think he'd like it. Too bad if he doesn't because he can't complain now.

I lug the bag through the streets, shivering and straining, itching beneath the sun—I have my hoodie pulled up but I forgot the hat and jacket. It should be a short walk – no more than five or ten minutes any normal time – but it takes me half an hour. I don't mind. I'm not in a rush.

Finally I reach my destination. Christ Church Spitalfields, one of London's most famous churches, always popping up in films and TV shows about Jack the Ripper. It's a creepy place, but beautiful in a stark way, and I think Timothy would have appreciated it. He loved the East End. I don't recall him mentioning Christ Church, but I'm confident he would have raved about it if the subject had come up.

There's a small, grassy area in front of the church, some headstones dotted about. I find a nice spot for Timothy, somewhere that looks like it gets a lot of sun, then go in search of a shovel. I find one in a shop in Spitalfields Market, a colorful designer spade for ladies who wanted to look chic in their garden. There are no zombies in any of the shops or restaurants. I suppose they abandoned their resting places in response to the baby's call.

It takes me longer than I thought to dig the hole, and not just because I'm so drained. Digging a grave is hard work. I wouldn't have liked to do this for a living in the old days.

I go down a couple of meters, not wanting to take chances and come back this way to find the grave dug up and raided by wild animals or zombies. When I'm happy with the depth, I haul myself out and lie on the grass for a while, an arm thrown across my face to shield my eyes from the sunlight.

Rising, I consider removing Timothy's remains from the bags, but why bother? Let them serve as his coffin. Probably not the way he would have liked to be buried, but better than nothing.

I lower the bags into the grave, then stand over it hesitantly, trying to think of the proper prayers to say.

"Ashes to ashes, dust to dust," I murmur, but I can't remember the rest, and that doesn't seem like enough. In the end I recite a few Hail Marys and an Our Father.

"I hope you can carry on painting in the next world," I conclude weakly, then fill in the grave, silently bid Timothy one last farewell and glance at the spire of Christ Church. Shivering, I wonder if there really is a God or if I'm just grasping at straws, if the babies of my nightmares actually were a sign or just some freakily incredible coincidence. Am I right to trust Dr. Oystein, or am I making the worst mistake of my life?

With no way to know for sure, I shiver again, then turn my back on the church and shuffle along. I've spent enough time on the dead. Time to return to the business of the living and those caught in-between.

TWENTY-TWO

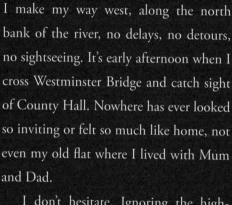

I make my way west, along the north bank of the river, no delays, no detours, no sightseeing. It's early afternoon when I cross Westminster Bridge and catch sight of County Hall. Nowhere has ever looked so inviting or felt so much like home, not even my old flat where I lived with Mum and Dad.

I don't hesitate. Ignoring the high-pitched noises coming out of the speakers dotted around the place – they deter normal zombies, but not a girl on a mission like me – I hobble down Belvedere Road, let myself into the building and make straight for Dr. Oystein's small lab, where the Groove Tubes are housed. I have a feeling I'll find him there, and I'm right. He's working on something when

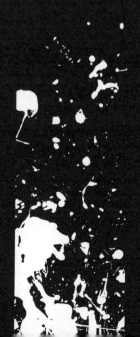

I enter without knocking, running tests, studying the contents of a test tube.

The doctor doesn't look up, unaware that his privacy has been disturbed. I don't announce myself. Instead I strip and dump my clothes on the floor, then limp to the nearest Tube, smiling warmly at the thought of immersing myself and blissing out, of emerging whole and fresh in a few weeks.

There's a ladder close to the Groove Tube. I climb up and in. I hold on to the sides of the cylinder, half submerged. I think about saying nothing, grinning as I imagine the perturbed look on Dr. Oystein's face when he turns from his work later and spots me. But I can't hold my tongue.

"Doc," I call.

The doctor looks up and his eyes widen. *"B?"* he gasps.

I smirk at him, let go of the sides and slip beneath the surface of the liquid. As I'm falling, just before I go under, I shout out playfully—"I'm in!"

To be continued...

BOOK 6:

ZOM-B

GLADIATOR

ONE

There's a tunnel beneath Waterloo Station that used to be a haven for graffiti artists. Anyone was allowed to paint whatever they wanted on the walls, floor or ceiling.

The zombies put a stop to the artists with their stencils and spray paint, but the art remains, bright, bold and colorful. It covers every inch of the tunnel. If humans ever eliminate the undead and take control of the world again, I bet a lot of people will come to this place to admire the paintings.

But I'm not here today for the graffiti.

I'm here for the zombies.

We usually keep this tunnel clear of the living dead. It's easily done. Zombies have sensitive ears. High-pitched noises cut through our skulls and make our teeth shake. When Dr. Oystein moved into County Hall, he placed speakers in hidden places around the area and played a loop of sharp noises through them, guaranteed to send any zombie within range running for cover. It keeps the drooling, brain-hungry riffraff from our door.

But we haven't been playing the loop in the tunnel for the last few nights. We wanted company and figured the dark, quiet space would draw a crowd once we cut the power to the speakers.

We figured right. There are twenty-five or thirty zombies in residence, a mix of men, women and kids, some in suits or nice dresses, others in more casual wear, a few naked or close enough. Blank expressions, long, sharp teeth, bones sticking out of their fingers and toes, wisps of green moss wherever they were bitten or cut when they were alive.

I study the zombies with a touch of nerves, but no disgust, revulsion or pity. They're my own kind. Except for the fact that my brain works, I'm no different than them.

I'm part of a group of six. The others are the same as me, revitalized Angels, soldiers in Dr. Oystein's undead army. Carl Clay stands to my left, looking impeccable in his top-of-the-range, designer gear. Ashtat Kiarostami is to my right, dressed in a blue, loose-fitting suit, with a white headscarf. The bulky Rage is on the other side of Carl, wearing the leathers that he's favored since his time as a zom head. Shane Fitz and Jakob Pegg are next to Ashtat, Shane looking like a gangster wannabe in a tracksuit and with a gold chain dangling from his neck, Jakob pale and sickly in a pair of jeans and a shirt that sags on his bony frame.

We're all unarmed.

"Do you think there are enough of them?" Carl asks, frowning as he counts the zombies.

"Five to one," Shane sniffs. "Those are good enough odds for me. How many more do you want to face?"

"There aren't many men among them," Carl notes.

"Are you suggesting that women are inferior?" Ashtat asks coldly.

Carl winces. "No. But generally speaking they're not as strong as men. It's the way of the world. You can't argue with that."

"In life, no," Ashtat says. "But death levels the playing field. I have noticed no real difference between the sexes in our battles so far. Muscles are not the factor they once were, not in reviveds. Or revitalizeds," she adds pointedly.

Carl makes a sighing sound, which isn't easy when you don't have functioning lungs. "All right. I don't want an argument. Are we all happy to press ahead? We don't want to wait another day in case more of them come to seek shelter here?" He looks around and everyone shrugs or nods. "Fair enough. We'll crack on. How about you, Reilly? Are you ready?"

The soldier is standing behind us. He's not a happy bunny.

"I can't believe I let Zhang talk me into this," he mutters. He's

359

sweating. That's something no revitalized could ever mimic. The walking dead don't sweat.

"Don't be a baby," Rage grins. "We've all got to be prepared to make sacrifices for the cause."

"Yeah?" Reilly snarls. "What have *you* sacrificed lately?"

"My sense of compassion," Rage snaps. "Now quit moaning or we'll leave you here by yourself. Are you ready or not?"

"I suppose," Reilly mutters miserably. He's really not enjoying this. I don't blame him. It can't be easy, placing your life in the hands of a surly shower of teenage zombies.

Ashtat and I nudge apart and Reilly steps through the gap. He's covered himself from the neck down in thick leathers and he's wearing a helmet with a tough glass visor. The gear won't protect him for long if a zombie gets hold of him and rips in, but it should guard him against casual swipes, spit and flying blood.

Reilly moves a couple of meters ahead of us, gulps, then calls out loudly, "I don't suppose any of you creeps have seen Banksy?"

The zombies didn't pay much attention to us when we filed in. They could tell from our moss-covered wounds and the bones jutting out of our fingertips that we were in the same boat as them.

Reilly is a whole different kettle of fish. When he shouts, they jerk to attention and lock their sights on him. They note his covered form, his shaky grin behind the visor. They clock his heartbeat. They smell his blood, fresh and pure, his sweat, the scent of the food he ate that morning on his lips and tongue, his juicy brain.

The zombies howl with glee and hunger, a penetrating, fearsome sound. Then they move as one and surge towards us, fingers flexing, teeth gnashing, primed, deadly assassins whose only purpose in this world is to attack and tear asunder.

It's killing time!

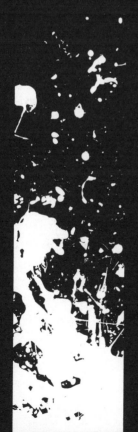

TWO

We dart ahead of Reilly and tackle the onrushing zombies. I run into a woman who is wearing a bra and knickers and nothing else. There are curlers in her hair. Looks like the living dead caught her at home when she was getting ready to go out.

I strike swiftly at the woman, a flurry of blows to her face and neck. She snarls and tries to hit back. I turn quickly, raising my leg high, and kick the back of her head as I spin. She's slammed sideways. I'm on her instantly. Making the fingers of my right hand straight and hard, I drive the bones sticking out of them down sharply into her skull, piercing the covering of bone, digging into the vulnerable brain beneath.

The woman shudders, makes a low

moaning noise, then falls still. I withdraw my hand and leave her to lie in the dust of the tunnel, truly dead now.

A man is rushing past me, hands outstretched, reaching for Reilly. I elbow him in the ribs. I can't knock the wind out of his sails – there's no wind in them to begin with – but the force of the blow sends him off course. As he staggers, I follow after him, fingers ready to crack open another head and rid the city of one more zombie.

I don't like doing this. I refused to kill reviveds when I was a prisoner in the military complex. But Dr. Oystein has convinced me that it's necessary. If we are to triumph in the war to come, we need to sharpen ourselves in combat. So, as much as I hate it, I kill as ordered, but I do it quickly and cleanly, not wanting to torment these poor lost souls.

The other Angels are busy around me. Each of us has a different ability and we've all been trained by Master Zhang to focus on our strengths. We've been told to test specific skills today, to only deviate from them if absolutely necessary. Mine is the speed with which I can strike—I have quick hands and feet, very nimble.

Ashtat is our pack's version of the Karate Kid. She whirls gracefully around the tunnel, chopping and kicking, leaping high into the air to casually swing a foot at a man's head—a second later it's been knocked clear of his neck. She lands smoothly, pounces after the head, comes down on it with a well-placed heel to squish the brain and put the zombie out of action.

Rage is a one-man wrecking machine. He's the strongest of us

all. He lets his opponents get close, then clubs them over the head or grabs them in a bear hug and squeezes until their brains seep out through their eye sockets and ear canals. He laughs and cracks jokes as he kills. He doesn't have any of the reservations that I do.

Posh Carl can jump like a grasshopper. He leaps around, landing among the reviveds, disrupting and scattering them, pushing them over or tripping them up, then springing across the tunnel to strike again. He could kill easily but he's been told not to. Today he's just here to confuse and disrupt.

Jakob isn't killing either. He's under orders to protect Reilly from any revived that gets past the rest of us. Jakob can run very fast. He's skinny and unhealthy-looking, even for a zombie, the result of the cancer he was dying from when he was turned. He's always in pain, but he can shrug it off when he has to. In the tunnel he stays focused, pulling Reilly away from stray zombies, ready to pick him up and run with him if something goes seriously wrong and the rest of us get into difficulties.

Ginger Shane's fingerbones and toe bones are tougher than anyone else's. We can all dig our bones into planks or crumbling bricks, but Shane can gouge a hole in a slab of concrete. He keeps climbing the walls and dropping on our opponents. He's laughing like Rage – the pair have become thick as thieves – until one of the zombies snags the gold chain around his neck and rips it loose.

"Not my chain!" Shane roars as it flies across the tunnel. He loses interest in the zombie and hurries after the keepsake.

366

"Shane!" Ashtat snaps. "Don't abandon your position."

"Get stuffed," he grunts, shoving a zombie out of his way, scooping to reclaim his cherished possession.

A female zombie attacks him from the side as he's brushing dirt from the chain. He goes down with a cry of surprise. The woman tears at him, digs her fingers into his stomach, bites down hard on his left shoulder.

Shane roars and slaps the revived. He shouts for help. Ashtat curses and starts towards him, but Jakob is faster. Forgetting his orders, he abandons Reilly and races to the aid of his friend, tugging the zombie away, buying Shane time to get back on his feet.

"Where's my bloody guard gone?" Reilly bellows. Then, a second later, he moans, "Oh crap."

A couple of zombies have broken through and are bearing down on him. Reilly turns to run but the living dead are faster. One, a guy, grabs his waist. The other, a woman, tries to chew through his helmet.

For a second I freeze, imagining having to break Reilly's loss to Ciara, the always stylishly dressed dinner lady who fixes our meals at County Hall. The pair of living humans have recently started dating, after the shy Reilly finally worked up the courage to ask her out. He didn't tell her he was coming with us today. Didn't want her to worry.

Snapping back into action, I throw myself in Reilly's direction, praying I'm not too late. But Carl beats me to the punch. He leaps in out of nowhere, kicks the head of the woman chewing on Reilly's helmet, grabs the ears of her partner and tugs sharply. Zombies don't feel pain as much as the living, but we can be hurt. The man screeches and loses interest in Reilly. He bats Carl away, then dives after him.

The woman is back at Reilly's helmet again, but before she can bare her fangs and chow down, Ashtat is on her, kicking furiously, short, sharp jabs, forcing her to retreat.

I attack the undead man from behind. I thrust a hand into his back and out through his chest. His heart bursts and chunks drip from my fingers. That won't stop him – zombies can survive without any organ except their brain – but it sure as hell distracts him. He writhes like a speared fish, trying to tear free.

I hold firm, wrapping my other arm round him, jamming my face in close to his back to present less of a target for his flailing arms. As he struggles, Carl makes a blade of his fingers, takes aim, then sends his left hand shooting through the revived's right eye. He goes in up to his wrist, then sneers at the zombie as he stiffens and dies.

"That'll teach you to mess with the Clay."

"Are you all right?" I shout at Reilly. He's patting himself, checking for rips in his leathers, features twisted frantically behind the visor. "Reilly! Are you okay?"

"I think so," he wheezes, starting to relax. "I don't think I've been scratched. Where the hell is Jakob?"

"Helping Shane."

Reilly growls. "My boot's gonna be helping its way up his arse when I get him back to County Hall."

"No swearing," Rage crows as he grabs the head of a boy who can't be more than eight or nine years old. "You'll set a bad example."

"A lot of use you were," I throw back at him.

Rage shrugs. "Doesn't matter to me if Reilly gets turned. Just another monster for us to kill. The more the merrier as far as I'm concerned."

I curse Rage, not for the first time, and stride towards him. "Let the kid go," I tell him, before he crushes the boy's skull.

"Why?" he laughs. "Do you want to fight me?"

"No. But you know the rules—we need to check kids out before we destroy them."

Rage scowls. "I hate rules."

"Tough. If you don't obey them, I'll tell Dr. Oystein and we'll see how welcome you are at County Hall then."

Rage mumbles something to himself, then lets the boy go. The kid immediately sets after Reilly, every bit as anxious to sink his fangs into a living human's brain as the adults are. I tackle him and easily stop his charge. I pull out the cuffs that I've brought along especially for this and slip a pair onto his wrists. Letting go, I push him to the ground, then snap another pair shut around his ankles. As the boy struggles furiously to break free, mewling miserably, I assess the situation.

Shane is back in the thick of things. He looks ashamed and so he should. A sheepish Jakob has resumed his position and is protecting Reilly again. Ashtat and Rage are picking off the last few adult reviveds. Carl has cuffed a girl even younger than the boy and is moving in on the last remaining child, another boy, this one not far from my age.

It's clear sailing now.

A minute later every zombie has been dispatched except for the three kids. As the rest of the Angels brush themselves down and give each other high fives, I examine the cuffed prisoners, searching their thighs and arms for *c*-shaped scars. Dr. Oystein spent decades injecting children with a vaccine that would help them fight the zombie gene if infected. If we find any child with the mark, we take them back to County Hall in case they revitalize farther down the line.

Sadly, none of these three bears the scar of hope. They're regular reviveds, damned from the moment they were turned. I steel myself, offer up a quick prayer, then finish them off one by one. I feel sick every time I do this. I know they're undead killers, no different than any of the adult zombies that I've put out of their misery, but it still feels wrong.

I could ask one of the others to do it – Rage has no qualms about ripping the brain from a young zombie's head – but this is a hard world and Master Zhang has warned us that each one of us needs to toughen up if we're going to thrive and be of use to Dr. Oystein.

So I grit my teeth and force myself to push through with the dirty deed. I just hope, if God is watching, that He understands and forgives me, though I'm not sure I'll ever be able to forgive myself.

"Nice work," Rage says when I'm done. He offers me his hand to high-five but I ignore him.

"I'm going to take that chain and help Reilly shove it up your arse," I bark at Shane.

"I screwed up," he winces. "I'm sorry. It won't happen again. But my dad gave me that chain. It's all I have left of either of my parents."

"Bullshit," Rage snorts. "I saw you take it from a shop last week."

The pair burst out laughing. "You shouldn't have told her," Shane giggles as I glower at him. "I had her going. She'd have melted and pardoned me."

"*I* wouldn't have," Reilly snarls, removing his helmet. "My bloody *life* was on the line. I haven't been vaccinated. There's no coming back for me if I get turned. You risked my safety over a bloody chain that you can replace any time?"

Shane's smile fades. "I really did screw up. I lost my head for a minute. I'm sorry, Reilly, honestly I am."

"You'd better be," Reilly says stiffly. "And note this, you little thug—if anything like that happens again, I'll kill you. Even if I get bitten or scratched, I'll make it my job to stab you through the brain before I turn. Understand?"

Shane nods and averts his gaze.

"Apart from that, we did brilliantly," Rage cheers, clapping loudly. "Now let's go tell Master Zhang how we fared and ask Ciara to rustle us up some delicious brain stew. I don't know about you guys, but killing always makes me hungry."

Rage licks his lips, the others laugh and cheer, then we trudge back to County Hall, experiment concluded, skills honed, one step closer to our hellish graduation.

THREE

We report back to Master Zhang, who's waiting for us in one of the rooms where he trains his recruits. He's angry when he hears what Shane and Jakob did. He's always stressing the need to focus and obey a direct order.

"No rest tonight," he snaps at them. "I want to see both of you here at lights out. I will work you through the night and it will not be a workout that you forget in a hurry."

Shane pulls a face but Jakob only nods glumly.

"What about the others?" Zhang asks Reilly. "Did they perform to your satisfaction?"

"Yeah. I don't have any complaints. They looked sharp."

Our mentor sniffs, then waves us away. Shane hesitates. "Master, I don't want to make a big deal of it, but I was injured. I think I might need a spell in a Groove Tube."

"Let me see." Zhang examines Shane's stomach and shoulder. The shoulder's no biggie, but the zombie dug quite deeply into the lining of his stomach. No guts are oozing out but it's bloody down there. "Does it hurt?" Zhang asks.

"Yes," Shane says.

"Good." Zhang pokes one of the wounds and Shane cries out and doubles over. "You will avoid the Groove Tubes. You will suffer your injuries and learn from the pain. Understand?"

"Yes . . . Master," Shane wheezes.

"Now get out of here, all of you," Zhang says. "I am expecting another group for training soon, and hopefully they will pay more attention to my instructions than you."

We bow and take our leave. Shane limps along, gingerly massaging the flesh around his stomach. "I bet the cuts get infected," he mutters.

"It will serve you right if they do," Ashtat says. "You let us down and put Reilly's life in danger."

"What about cancer boy?" Shane snaps. "Jakob screwed up too."

"Yes," Ashtat says. "But he screwed up trying to save a friend's life, not because he was worried about what would happen to an item of cheap jewelry."

Shane glares at Ashtat and starts to retort.

"Leave it, big boy," Rage chuckles, slapping Shane's back. "They're right, you're wrong. Live with it, get over it, move on. Now, who's coming with me to get some stew?"

Everyone says they'll tag along with Rage, except me.

"I'm heading back to our room," I tell them.

"Don't be a killjoy," Carl frowns. "Come with us. We did well in there apart from a couple of hiccups. Join the celebrations."

"No, it's okay, I'm fine."

"Suit yourself," Carl says, irritated. They head off in search of Ciara, a close, united pack of friends. I stare after them longingly, wishing I could belong, but at the same time knowing why I keep myself separate.

It's been a month since Dr. Oystein fished me out of the Groove Tube after my fall from the London Eye and my run-in with the inhuman baby. When I'd dried off and he'd filed down my fangs and pumped my insides clean, I told him about my adventures, the monstrous baby and the dreams I'd had when I was alive of creatures just like it.

Dr. Oystein is always hard to read, but my description of the baby didn't seem to come as a great shock. I think he already knew about the existence of such beings. My dreams, on the other hand, disturbed and intrigued him in equal measure. He made me recount them as clearly as I could.

"You are sure the babies in your nightmares were exactly the same as this one?" he asked. "You are not imagining the similarity?"

"No," I told him. "I had the dreams all of my life, as far back as I can recall, until I was killed and stopped sleeping. I'm sure this baby was the same, not just because of the way it looked, but how it spoke and what it said."

I told the doc how Owl Man had asked about my dreams when he came to visit me before the zombie uprising. That troubled him even more.

"I did not know that you had seen our owl-eyed associate before your encounter in Trafalgar Square," he murmured.

I shrugged. "I never thought to mention that. It didn't seem important. Do you know who he is?"

The doc nodded.

"What's his name?"

"That is irrelevant." He smiled. "I actually prefer Owl Man—it suits him better. That is how I will refer to him from now on."

I wanted to learn more about Owl Man and the babies, but Dr. Oystein said it was not yet time.

"Please be patient. I will share all the information that I possess with you, as I vowed when you first came here, but you must trust me to fill in the blanks as I see fit. I want to think about this first, what the nightmares might signify, how they link in with everything else."

I told him I thought that the dreams had been sent to me by some higher force, so I'd see there were hidden, inexplicable depths

376

to the world, and be more inclined to believe that the doc was telling me the truth when I came here.

"If that is the case," Dr. Oystein said softly, "there is more to you than I first suspected. None of the other Angels had such dreams when they were alive. If God shared a premonition with you, there must be a reason for it. Perhaps you have a crucial role to play in the war with Mr. Dowling."

"Is that a good thing?" I asked.

He made a low, rumbling noise. "I cannot say for sure. I know only that such responsibility is a frightening prospect. I have had to deal with it for decades. I do not wish to scare you, but I have to say that I would not wish such a burden on anyone."

Then he kissed my forehead tenderly and sent me back to my room, telling me that he would consider what I'd told him and do all that he could to help me comprehend my path and steer me along it as best he could.

FOUR

I return to my room, change clothes, then scan the books on my shelves. I don't have a lot of stuff. Spare clothes, an iPod, some video games, a few nice watches and the books. I don't feel the need to cram my share of the room with personal items. London is an open city these days. Any time I want anything, I can simply go out and find it.

The others are the same. Nobody has bothered to clutter up their shelves or store goods in the many niches of County Hall. Carl has lots of fancy gear because he's into fashion, Shane has stacks of gold chains because he thinks they're cool and Ashtat has hundreds of boxes of matches that she uses to make her brilliantly detailed models—she's currently working on one of Canary Wharf, her most ambitious project yet. Jakob has virtually nothing apart from some small photos of his family that he found in his mother's purse after she'd been killed along with his dad and sister.

My books are all about art and sculpture. If you'd told me when I was alive that I'd one day be an avid reader of such volumes, I'd have sneered. But time drags here. It's fine when we're training or on a mission, but otherwise we're stuck inside, staring at the walls.

The others play games and watch movies, but I've been keeping myself distant from my fellow Angels. Films don't hold the same appeal for me as they used to. Video games are the same. I haven't ditched them completely, but I can't spend a lot of time on them. I still listen to music, but my ears are so sensitive that I have to play the songs low, and where's the fun in that?

Art, on the other hand, has started to appeal to me. Mum was big into art and often tried to pass on her love of it to me. I resisted, in large part because I knew that Dad was scornful of it. He thought artists were pretentious wasters and I didn't want him looking down his nose at me.

My encounters with Timothy Jackson changed my view. His paintings of zombies fascinated me and I found myself thinking about them, the styles he had adopted, how they worked in different ways. I studied his paintings for a long time, then visited a few galleries to compare them with the work of other artists.

I started looking through the books in gallery shops. I wouldn't have dared go into such places in the old days. I'd have been afraid that the staff would laugh at me, or think I was just there to steal. But now there are only zombies to bear witness, and they couldn't care less about idle browsers.

I hadn't planned to read any of the books in detail, but the more I learned, the more I could appreciate the pictures in them, as well as those hanging on the walls of the galleries. I lugged a couple of art books back to flip through, and soon my shelves started to fill up. There's no problem finding new volumes—there are loads of shops in London and they're open for business twenty-four hours a day, no credit card or cash required, and only the odd zombie bookseller or two to contend with.

Dr. Oystein likes us to rest at night, to lie in our beds and act as if we're asleep. I read during that time, rather than just lie in the dark and count the seconds as they slowly tick by. No complaints from the others about my reading light—a few of them read as well, or play handheld video games.

I used to be a slow reader but I've been speeding up recently. In the beginning I tended to choose books with lots of pictures in them, but now I've moved on to thick textbooks. I don't finish everything that I start, but when a book grabs my interest, I can plow through it pretty niftily.

So what am I in the mood for today? I study the titles, pick up a few, read the blurb on the back covers, then replace them. Until I come to *The Complete Letters of Vincent Van Gogh*. I don't recall

381

bringing this back, and it's a monster, so I'm sure I would have remembered. Frowning, I slide it free of the books around it and a note falls out. It's from Carl.

I saw you reading a book about Van Gogh. My dad had a copy of this in his library and often raved about it. I thought you might like to give it a go. Let me know if it's any good and I might try it myself.

I scowl at the note. I don't like it when people do nice things for me. I never know how to react. I suppose I'll have to thank Carl now—if I don't, I'll look like a mean-spirited cow. Why couldn't he have just told me about the book and let me find it for myself? Bloody do-gooder.

I think about dumping the book in the trash, but that would make me look childish and ungrateful. Besides, Van Gogh *is* one of my favorite artists and it sounds like a good read. Grumbling softly, I head to bed and settle down for a few hours of solitary reading.

I quickly get into the letters and time flies by. Carl has picked a winner. On the one hand that annoys me, because it means I won't be able to jeer at him for giving me a piece of crap to read. But on the other hand I'm delighted to have discovered a brilliant new book, and I soon forget about Carl and having to say thank you and everything else.

A soft voice brings me back to the real world. "I never thought I'd see B Smith lost in a book."

I jump slightly – I had no idea that anyone had entered the room – and glance up. It's my old teacher, Mr. Burke, standing in the doorway, beaming at me. "I've always had a soft spot for nutters who cut their ears off," I growl, carefully closing the book and setting it aside. "Besides, this is a great read. I might have studied harder if I'd been pushed towards these sorts of books in school."

"No," Burke laughs. "You wouldn't have given it a chance. You were a busy girl, so many slacker friends, so many things not to do with them. They wouldn't have been impressed if you'd started reading books instead of hanging out with them on street corners."

Burke crosses the room, picks up the book and flips through it. He looks much older than he did in school, bags under his eyes, hair almost completely gray now. I never had a crush on Burke, but as teachers went, he was all right. Now he looks like a broken old man.

"I always meant to give this a try," Burke says.

"You'd heard about it?"

"Yes. I was never much of an art buff. Biographies were my poison. *The Seven Pillars of Wisdom*—now *that* was a book. But Van Gogh's letters were famous. I don't suppose I'll get time to read them now. I can't stay up all night like some undead people I can name."

"I could always bite you," I joke. "Get Dr. Oystein to vaccinate you first. You might turn into one of us. Then you can stay up as late as you like."

"I've already been vaccinated," Burke says, sitting on the bed next to mine, the one Jakob sleeps in.

"You have?" I sit upright and stare at him.

383

"I asked Dr. Oystein to give me the shot not long after I started working for him."

"Why?" I cry. "You know what it means, don't you? Unless you get infected, the vaccine will attack your system and melt you down. You'll be dead within the next ten or fifteen years."

Burke shrugs. "It's unlikely I'll last that long. There's a far greater probability that I'll be snagged by a zombie. If they don't eat my brain and I turn, I'd like the chance to revitalize. I know most adults don't, but still, better some hope than none at all."

I shake my head. "And what if you don't get bitten or scratched?"

Burke smiles. "Then I'll miss out on old age. I wasn't looking forward to it anyway. I'd rather go in my prime, young, virile and full of life."

"Too late," I mutter. "You missed that boat years ago."

Burke laughs out loud then leans forward. "How have you been, B? I haven't seen much of you since you returned."

It's my turn to shrug. "Fine. I've settled in. Learning lots. Training hard. Doing my bit for the cause."

"Have you been on a mission yet?"

"Only scouting or training missions close to County Hall."

The Angels do a lot of routine scouting, searching the streets and buildings of London for survivors—if we find any, we offer them a safe home at County Hall. We're also on the lookout for Mr. Dowling and his mutants, as well as any human soldiers who might be on patrol. And, of course, we hunt for brains. We need regular supplies if we're to stay in control of our senses. Certain Angels do nothing except scour hospitals, schools and public buildings in search of corpses whose skulls they can scrape clean of brains to bring back for the pot, but all of us are expected to pitch in to some extent. One of the less exciting chores that everyone has to share.

I like getting out of County Hall when we go scouting, but it's an unpleasant sensation at the same time because we never know what we're going to run into, if Mr. Dowling or his mutants will pop up, or if human hunters will set their sights on us. I crossed swords with some of them before I found my way here, the American, Barnes and his buddies. There are others, bored survivors who pass the time by notching up kills. Not that they consider it killing. I mean, zombies are already dead, so it's no big deal to them.

The others in my group have been on more serious missions, where they've escorted humans out of London, or gone into dangerous areas with orders to carry out specific tasks. But Rage and I haven't been allowed on any of those yet.

"What about in your down time?" Burke asks.

I nod at the book. "I've been making up for all those years when I never read anything other than porn stories online."

Burke blinks. "You're joking, aren't you?"

"Nothing wrong with a bit of sauce," I smirk.

"Only if you're an appropriate age," Burke huffs.

"Don't get all grown-up on me," I snap. "I had unlimited access to the Internet from the age of ten or eleven. You think I wasn't curious? You think anyone my age didn't have a look to see what all the fuss was about? It wasn't like when you were a kid. The world was our oyster. We could find out about anything."

"I suppose," he sighs, then smiles again. "*The world was our oyster.* You never used a phrase like that in the old days. All that reading must be rubbing off on you."

"Of course it is. I'm not thick."

"No," Burke agrees. "And never were. Even when you acted it."

Burke picks up the book and looks at it closely again. He's obviously come to discuss something with me. I've an idea what it is but I don't say anything. I'm not going to make things easy for him. That's not my style.

"I don't want this to come out the wrong way," Burke says hesitantly. "And I'd hate to be classed as a teacher who ever discouraged reading. But are you maybe spending a bit too much time here on your own with your head stuck in a book?"

"No," I answer shortly.

Burke chuckles, then sets the book aside and gets serious. "What's wrong, B?"

"Nothing. I'm peachy."

"No. You're not. Dr. Oystein noticed and brought it to my attention."

"Noticed what?"

"You returned to the fold after that incident with the baby,"

Burke says, "but you haven't made any effort to fit in with the other Angels. You don't socialize or hang out with your roommates."

"Maybe I don't like them," I sniff.

"I doubt that's the case," he says. "If it was, you could simply ask to move in with a different group."

"I thought that wasn't allowed. Dr. Oystein tells us where to bunk."

"When you first come here, yes. But if Ashtat and the others are still getting on your nerves after this much time, he'll be happy to let you switch. But they're not the problem, are they?"

"Rage is a pain," I mutter.

"You don't get on with him?"

"I don't trust him. Never have, never will."

"But the others?" Burke presses.

I shrug stiffly.

"If you tell me what's troubling you, I might be able to help," he says kindly. "A problem is never as bad as it seems if you share it with a friend."

"But I don't need a friend," I mumble. "I don't *want* one. I don't mind working with the Angels, but I don't want to make friends with them."

"Why not?" Burke asks, surprised.

"I'd rather be alone," I say quietly.

Burke frowns, trying to make sense of me.

"It's not that complicated," I snicker.

"It is to me," Burke says. "I'd have thought that someone in your position would give anything to find a friend."

"What's so bad about my position?" I bark.

"Well, you're undead," he says. "Living people want nothing to do with you. Regular zombies have no interest in you either. There aren't many people left who could ever be tempted to give a damn about you. If you spurn the advances of the Angels, you're unlikely to find a friend anywhere else."

"But I just told you I don't want any friends," I remind him.

"You must," Burke insists. "You can't want to be all alone in the world."

"I bloody well do," I snort.

"Why?"

"Because it's simpler that way." I reconsider my words and try again. "Because it's safer." I look down at my hands, at the bones sticking out of my fingers, remembering the blood that has stained them. "You weren't there in the school when the zombies attacked. You were off sick that day. You didn't see us as we raced for freedom. You didn't see so many of my friends die, Suze and Copper and Linzer and...

"You weren't there when Mr. Dowling invaded the underground complex either. You didn't see the zom heads tear into Mark or hear their death screams when Josh caught up with them. You didn't smell their burning flesh in the air.

"You weren't with me when all those people were killed in Trafalgar Square. Or when Sister Clare and her supporters marched into the belly of Liverpool Street Station. Or when Timothy was butchered."

"I've seen terrible things too," Burke says sadly.

"I'm sure you have. But I've *only* seen terrible things since I regained my mind. I've found death everywhere I've turned, or death has found me. I'm not saying I'm a jinx—I don't think I'm that important. But this is death's world now and I've run into the Grim Reaper every time I've turned a corner or paused for breath. Well, not actual breath, obviously, but you get the picture."

I meet Burke's gaze at last. "Pretty much everyone I've known and cared about has died or been taken from me. I'm sick of it. I don't want to endure the pain again. The Angels will be killed, I'm sure of it. Dr. Oystein will get ambushed by Mr. Dowling and his mutants. You'll be turned or slaughtered. It will all go tits up somewhere along the line.

"I don't want to feel anything when that happens. I don't want to lose friends or loved ones. I want to be able to get on with things and find somewhere else to hole up until death swings by again. I'd rather be a loner than feel lonely."

Burke's eyes fill with pity. "B..." he croaks.

"Don't," I stop him. "You came for answers and I've given them to you. Now leave me alone. It's all I ask of you. It's all I ask of anyone."

Then I pick up the book, open it and stare at the words until Burke gets up and silently slips away, leaving me by myself. Not the way I like it really. Just the way it has to be if I'm not going to go crazy and lose myself to grief and madness in this harsh, unforgiving abattoir of a world.

FIVE

Getting ready to head out on another scouting mission. I was hoping Master Zhang would give us something meatier to deal with, but no, it's just another sweep of the area, this time around Covent Garden. There are lots of streets set back from the market, crammed with flats. We've been through there before, but repetition is nothing new.

We don't take any weapons when we head out, but we dress in heavy clothes and gloves to protect our skin from the sun. We also slap on loads of suntan lotion. Our clothes have been individually prepared for us, holes cut away to reveal our wounds and the wisps of green moss that signify to other zombies that we're undead like them.

I study the hole in my chest as I twist my jacket round. I've gotten so used to it that I can't really remember what it was like before. I hated being one tit short of a full set to begin with. Now I couldn't give a toss.

"I have said it before but I will say it again," someone murmurs behind me. "You are a most remarkable example of a zombie, Becky Smith."

I turn, smiling, to face Dr. Oystein. The doc never changes much. He favors a light gray suit, neatly ironed white shirt and a snazzy tie. His thin brown hair is shot through with gray streaks and carefully combed. His deep brown eyes are as calm and warm as always.

"I bet you say that to all the girls," I chuckle.

"Only you," he vows, then reaches out to adjust my coat around the hole where my heart used to be. "There. Perfect." He cocks his head to examine my face.

"Burke told you what I said, didn't he?" I pout.

"Of course. If it is any help, I understand. You are not the first to stand alone, to avoid the complications of company. I went through such a spell myself. It lasted several years. I figured, if I could train myself to feel nothing for anyone, I could never be hurt again, the way I was hurt when my family was so savagely taken from me."

"How'd you get on with that?" I ask.

"Fine," he says. "I found it surprisingly easy to sever all emotional ties and distance myself from those I worked with."

"Then why did you start caring again?" I frown.

"Instinct compels many reviveds to stay with those they knew in life," Dr. Oystein replies. "But I do not think they truly care about those people. They have lost their souls, so they have no reason to give a damn. After a time, I realized I was behaving the same way as a revived. I came to think that God would not have restored my senses only for me to act as if I was still an unfeeling beast.

"Life was wonderful when we were alive," the doc continues. "We could love, procreate, bond. The downside was that we could be hurt too. But we endured the pain because the joy was so intense.

"I won't pretend that nothing has changed. We cannot love the way we once did. Everything now is a resemblance. But even a vague, loving forgery is better than experiencing only the emptiness of the damned."

"I'm not sure I agree with you," I say solemnly. "It'd be different if I didn't expect to lose some of you guys anytime soon. But if I was to place a bet, I wouldn't give any of you more than six months, a year tops."

"Even though I have survived more than a hundred years already?" he asks.

"Things were different then. The world made sense. It worked. Now it's just death, destruction and loss. We're all for the chop, and I don't want to care when you, Burke or anyone else gets ripped away from us."

"What about our response if *you* are taken?" the doctor asks quietly. "Will you care if nobody mourns your loss, if we wipe you from our thoughts and carry on as if nothing has happened?"

"Not in the least," I say chirpily. "When I go, I'm gone. Makes no difference to me whether you lot celebrate or wail for a week."

Dr. Oystein nods glumly. "As you wish. Like I said, I do understand. If you do not seek friendship, we will not force it on you. No Angel needs to care for their colleagues in order to fit in with them.

"But I do care, B, and I will continue to. Billy Burke cares about you too, and quite a few more. If you ever change your mind and crave a friend, we will be here for you. Always."

"Unless you're killed before me," I note.

"Touché," he smiles. Then, smile fading, he reaches out and touches my cheek, briefly but lovingly. "Be careful out there, B. Come home safely to us."

He turns and leaves. I want to call him back and accept his offer of friendship, drop my guard, have at least one person in the world that I can feel close to.

But I don't.

I can't.

I won't.

I remember my friends from school. My parents. Mark. Timothy. The pain I felt at their loss. And I make a vow to myself, not for the first time since I returned to County Hall.

Never again.

394

SIX

We patrol the streets, entering every building we come to, checking it thoroughly.
Zombies are in many of them, sheltering
from the sun. We gently edge past the resting reviveds and head up flights of stairs,
exploring the upper levels, looking for
attics or locked doors.

We haven't found any survivors while
I've been with the Angels, but lots of
humans were rescued before I joined, and
a few have been unearthed by other search
squads since. They've had to be cunning
to survive so long in a city where death is
almost a certainty.

Reviveds rely heavily on their sense
of smell and hearing. To outwit them,
the people with the smarts douse themselves in perfume or aftershave – those

smells mean nothing to a zombie, they only react to natural human scents – and wear soft shoes or slippers. The really sly ones also wrap bandages round their stomachs and chests to dull the sounds of their heartbeats and digestive systems, shave off their hair so they don't sweat as much and take other inventive, anti-detection measures.

The gutsier survivalists realized that once a zombie has given a building a once-over, it usually doesn't check again, unless it was accustomed to double-checking spaces when it was alive, for instance if it was a security guard. So some of the humans have made their bases in buildings which zombies frequent, the reasoning being that they're the safest places in London, since the inhabitants won't scour their own lair. Also, other reviveds recognize and respect a fellow zombie's home, and they almost never trespass. We're not sure why, it's just the way they're wired.

Angels on earlier missions to find survivors never bothered to check a building that was home to a nest of reviveds. Now, having been clued in by those we've rescued, we're more thorough.

"Oh what fun," Rage grumbles as we exit another block of flats with nothing to show for the time spent panning around inside.

"Patience is a virtue," Ashtat says.

"What's so special about the living anyway?" Rage sniffs. "Why should we care about them? If they find their way to County Hall, fair enough, it would be rude not to let them in. But we could be tracking down mutants, turning the tables on hunters, kicking Mr. Dowling's arse. This is a waste of our time."

"Yeah," Shane says, backing up his buddy as he normally does.

"Don't act like an infant," Carl snaps. "We're fighting this war for the sake of those who are still alive."

"Sure," Rage says, "but there are millions in camps or on islands dotted around the world. What does it matter if we rustle up a few more? It's not going to make a difference."

"It will to those we rescue," Ashtat says.

"Well, *duh!*" Rage snorts. "I'm talking about the bigger picture. That's what we're supposed to be looking at, right? The doc told us that the minor battles being fought across the globe are meaningless. The fight here, between us and the clown's forces, is the only real game in town. So why aren't we focusing on that? We should be too busy to play at being Good Samaritans."

Shane nods fiercely. "What he said."

Ashtat and Carl scowl at Rage and Shane, but don't come back with an argument because they can't think of one. I'm not bothered. It doesn't matter to me. I just do what I'm told and try not to think too much. That should be the end of the debate, a win for Rage, but then, breaking his usual moody silence, Jakob speaks up.

"I think it's to remind us that we were once human."

We stare at the thin, pale boy. He doesn't speak very often. It's easy to think of him as a mute.

"I forget sometimes," he says softly. "I find it hard to recall my life before this. It seems like I've been an undead creature for as long as I can remember."

"So what?" Rage asks when Jakob falls silent again.

"When I feel distant from my humanity," Jakob whispers, "I think about joining up with Mr. Dowling and his mutants. From all the reports, they have a grand time, going wherever they like, killing as they please, not caring about anyone except themselves. It must be liberating to be that brutal. The world has fallen. The walking dead have taken over. We don't neatly fit into one camp or the other. Why not throw in our lot with the clown and his crew, kill off the remaining humans and enjoy the party for the next few thousand years?"

"Blimey," Rage laughs. "And I thought *I* had a dark side."

Jakob shrugs, wincing at the pain that brings to his battered, cancer-ridden body. "That's just the way my mind wanders. Am I the only one who has thought such things?"

He looks around and everyone drops their gaze, except for Rage, who nods enthusiastically.

"Dr. Oystein sees through us," Jakob says. "He knows all that we imagine. He can't rely on our unwavering support, because any one of us could give in to desperation and temptation, and change sides."

"I think the searching, the rescues and escorting survivors to safe havens outside London are to keep us in contact with the memories of what it was like to be alive. Because if we lose those, or if they come to mean nothing to us, what's to hold us in place? Why should we bother to stay loyal?"

There's a long silence as we think about that. Jakob might not say much, but when he does speak, he tends to have something worth saying.

"Is that why you've been so distant recently?" Rage asks me. "Are *you* thinking about stabbing us in the back and heading over Mr. Dowling's way?"

"You're the only one I'd stab," I smirk. "I'd leave the others for the clown and his posse."

"Then you *have* been thinking about it," he challenges me, bristling.

"I think about all sorts of things," I purr, baiting him, unable to resist the opportunity to get under his skin.

"If you ever—" he starts to say, raising a finger to point at me warningly.

"Rage," Ashtat interrupts.

"Don't stick up for her," Rage barks. "We won't have *girl power* here. If this little—"

"Shut up," Ashtat says calmly, "and look to your right."

Rage glares at her but does as she commands. I see his eyes widen, so I look too.

There are a couple of people on the street, no more than ten meters ahead of us. They've come out of the remains of a shop. It's a woman and a young child. The woman is holding the child in her arms. I'm not sure if it's a boy or a girl.

But I'm sure of one thing, by the way their chests rise and fall, by the smell of the perfume they've coated themselves with, by the terror in the woman's eyes when she spots us.

They're alive.

SEVEN

For several seconds nothing happens. We stare at the woman and her child and she stares back. The child's face is turned into the woman's chest. I don't know if it's aware of us or not.

Ashtat lifts her hands over her head and calls out softly, "We're not going to hurt you."

The woman bolts the instant Ashtat moves. Not back into the shop, where we could trap her. Instead she turns and dashes along the street.

We start after her as a pack, acting instinctively. Carl stops us with a curt and commanding "Wait!"

As the rest of us pause, Carl jogs forward a couple of steps, then leaps. He lands not far behind the fleeing woman and immediately bounces into the air again, like a frog. He lands a few meters in front of her and she comes to a halt. Turns frantically, looking for an escape route. She spots an open door in a building and starts towards it.

"That's not a wise move," Carl says calmly. "There could be a dozen zombies on the other side of that door."

The woman stops and stares at Carl. Then looks back at the rest of us. We're all standing still.

"What are you?" the woman gasps, taking another step away from Carl, edging closer to the door, caught in two minds.

"That's a long story," Carl chuckles. "All you need to know right now is that we mean you no harm. We're not going to attack you. We won't even detain you. If you're suspicious of us and don't want to talk, you can carry on down this street and we won't lift a finger to stop you. I'll just say two words to you before you go. *County Hall.*"

Carl shuffles out into the middle of the road. The woman licks her lips nervously, then starts to run. She thinks this is a trick. I don't blame her.

Nobody moves, even though we'll all hate it if we lose her. I say a silent prayer that she'll stop and look back. But then she turns a corner and disappears from sight. I feel my spirits sinking. I look around and everyone is staring glumly at the spot where she vanished, even Rage.

"Hard luck, Carl," Ashtat says. "At least you tried. I thought—"

"Wait a minute," Carl hushes her. He's smiling hopefully. The fingers of his left hand are flexing slowly, as if trying to beckon the woman back. I don't think there's any chance of that, but I hold my peace along with the other Angels. I count inside my head, determined to give Carl the full minute he asked for. After that, I'll tell him to forget it, we can't win them all, maybe next time luck will be on our…

The woman edges back into view. First it's just her head, as she stares at us. Then she steps onto our street. She's still holding the child. It's looking at us now and I see that it's a boy. Just four or five years old, but well drilled, silent as a butterfly.

The woman slips closer, studying the houses on either side, eyeing us uneasily. She stops a good distance away from Carl. She's trembling.

"You could have leaped through the air again and stopped me," she says.

Carl nods.

"Why didn't you?"

"We don't want to trap you," Carl says. "If I tried to get in your way, you might run into me and scratch yourself. That would be bad."

"Then you *are* a zombie?"

"A certain kind, yes."

"Not the kind that eats brains?"

Carl laughs softly. "Oh, we definitely eat brains, we have to. But we don't take them from the living. And we don't kill. We're your friendly neighborhood kind of zombie."

The woman doesn't smile but she stops shaking so much. "And County Hall?" she asks. "What did you mean?"

"It's where we're based," Carl explains. "If you don't want to come with us, that's cool, we won't force you. But if you're ever in need of allies or shelter, or looking for a way out of the city, come to County Hall and we'll help. You'll be safe there. It's the safest place in London."

"Nowhere's truly safe," the woman says.

"Not truly," Carl concedes. "But if you seek refuge there, and anyone wants to do you harm, they'll have to cut through us first."

"What are you?" the woman asks again, frowning now.

"Like I said, that's a long story. But if you want to know *who* we are, I'm Carl Clay and these guys will be more than happy to introduce themselves if you let them."

The woman wavers, takes a step back, thinks about it some more, then makes up her mind. "I'm Emma," she says. "This is my son, Declan."

"A pleasure to meet you, Emma," Carl says, smiling broadly. "Now, do you know any place around here where we could get a decent cup of coffee?"

And when he says that, despite herself, Emma returns the smile, and as sappy as it might sound, it's one of the most heartwarming things I've ever seen. Even for an undead, heart-deprived monster like me.

EIGHT

Carl wasn't joking about the coffee. He tells us that one of his uncles ran a small espresso bar in Kensington. Carl used to work there occasionally on the weekends, learning the trade. His parents thought it would be good for him, help keep his feet on the ground—he comes from a wealthy background and I guess they didn't want him losing touch with us common folk.

We find a deserted café, Carl takes Emma's order and heads in, delighted with himself. The rest of us wait on the street. Emma stands apart from us, still unsure she made the right choice when she came back. Declan is ogling us. He seems particularly fascinated by the hole in my chest.

"I'd let you poke about in there," I smile at him, "but it's dangerous."

Declan blushes and hides his face. Emma laughs and rubs his head. "No need to be afraid," she coos. "These people aren't going to hurt us. He was always shy," she tells me. "I used to encourage him to be more outgoing, but in this climate shyness isn't a bad thing. I haven't had any trouble keeping him quiet."

I nod understandingly. "Noise attracts the zombies."

"Smells attract them too," Ashtat mutters, looking around, worried. "If any nearby reviveds get a whiff of that coffee..."

"Don't sweat it," Rage laughs. "We can handle a few dumb reviveds if we have to."

"But I'd rather not risk it," Ashtat says, and goes to see how Carl is getting on.

"Do other zombies attack you?" Emma asks me.

"Not usually," I reply. "But if we got in the way of a feed, they would."

"Then we're putting you in danger."

I shrug. "We don't mind a little danger. It's what we're here for."

Carl emerges with a mug of steaming hot coffee, beaming as if he'd delivered a newborn baby. Emma thanks him and reaches for it.

"Uh-uh," he stops her, and carefully lays the mug down on the ground for her to pick up. "Best not to take any chances."

"This is so weird," she says, pulling a face as she retrieves the

408

mug. "If anyone had told me this morning that a zombie would be serving me coffee before the day was out..."

We all laugh, but quietly, so as not to draw attention. Then we head for Leicester Square, talking softly as we progress. We tell Emma about ourselves, how we differ from reviveds, the way we try to help living survivors, Dr. Oystein and the setup at County Hall. By the time we get to the small park at the heart of the West End and make ourselves comfy on a few of the benches, Emma is shaking her head with wonder.

"I never would have dreamt this was possible. I thought you were all killers."

"Most of us are," Ashtat says. "Do not make the mistake of thinking you should give zombies a chance from now on. If you ever see one coming towards you, run. There are very few of our type around."

"What about you guys?" Shane asks. "How did you survive this long?"

"By being very careful," Emma sighs. "And with a lot of luck."

"Are there more of you?" Carl asks. "Do you want us to fetch the others and take them back to County Hall? Assuming you want to go there," he adds quickly. "No pressure. We'll understand if you'd rather stick to what you know."

"Are you kidding?" Emma says bitterly. "I hate what we've had to endure, the places we've had to stay, the loneliness. Of course we're coming with you. If I'd only known about you before..."

She starts to cry. The rest of us say nothing and look away awkwardly, waiting for the tears to pass. Declan makes a small whining sound and, when I glance at him, I see him stroking his mother's hair and kissing her cheek. I recall the monstrous babies from my dreams, and the all-too-real baby at Timothy's, and suppress a shudder.

"Sorry," Emma moans when the tears finally pass. "I've been holding those in for so long. I didn't want to cry before this. I was afraid I might not be able to stop once I'd started, that I might start howling with grief and rage."

"Howling's not good in this city," Shane notes. "It draws a crowd."

"Yes." Emma wipes tears away and grins at us, embarrassed. "Sorry," she says again.

"No need to apologize," Ashtat smiles. "We would love to cry if we could."

Emma blinks. "You mean you can't?"

"Unfortunately not. We are, in most respects, dead. There are many things the undead can no longer do—cry, sweat, breathe."

Emma shakes her head, amazed, and drains the last of her coffee. "That was so good," she says.

"I can make you some more if you'd like," Carl offers.

"Not right now," she says. "Maybe in a while. I don't like to drink too much. I'm always afraid the smell might tip off the zombies. Does it?"

"I'm not sure," Carl says. "Most reviveds aren't good at association. That's why they don't link the smell of perfume or aftershave to the living. But I've seen some react to the scent of food before. I think they remember that only a living human would bother with food, since the walking dead don't eat. Well, except for brains obviously."

"But you're safe with us," Shane brags. "You can have a barbecue if you like, here in the Square. We'll run off any nosy buggers who come sniffing round."

Emma giggles. "A barbecue! This is like a dream. I wish..." She pauses and her expression darkens. "I wish Shaun could have been here. He practically lived for barbecues. He was Australian. He grew up cooking outdoors."

"Was Shaun your husband?" Ashtat asks delicately.

"No," Emma grunts. "*He* left the picture long before the zombies struck, and good riddance to him. I hope he was one of the first to die and that it was painful and slow." She glowers, then chuckles. "I don't mean that really. But I certainly wouldn't shed any tears if I found out he was dead.

"Shaun was a friend of mine. We were together the day the zombies took over. He was a survival expert, he loved challenging himself in harsh terrains, he'd spend his holidays cheating death in hellholes around the world. I thought he was crazy, but he used to say a beach holiday was his idea of purgatory. He wasn't happy when he went away unless he staggered back bloody, bruised and exhausted.

"I was glad of his skills after the attacks," she goes on. "We wouldn't have lasted long without him. He taught us how to hide and forage. He studied the zombies, learned about them, helped us stay one step ahead. I wanted to flee the city, but Shaun said we stood a better chance here, at least to begin with. I kept urging him to take us to one of the settlements in the countryside, or to try for an island, but he was skeptical. He didn't believe all of the reports on the radio. He wanted to let things settle. I also think he was reluctant to put his life in the hands of anyone else. He liked his independence."

"Did the zombies get him?" I ask.

Emma nods. "We picked up other survivors along the way. We numbered eight at our maximum. Shaun always told me not to let myself get too attached to them. He said if we ever got backed into a corner, we had to abandon the others and look after ourselves. He said we couldn't afford the luxury of friends anymore."

"Sounds like he knew what he was doing," I mutter, thinking about my talk with Mr. Burke.

"Yes," Emma sighs. "But he couldn't follow his own advice in the end. We lost a couple of members to attacks over the months. Another couple struck out for the countryside by themselves. A few more joined up. Shaun was always in command. He was a natural leader. Nobody in the group ever challenged him.

"One of the new guys was diabetic. He needed insulin. We were in a pharmacy. Zombies were nesting on the upper floor. They chased us. The guy with diabetes got trapped. Shaun went back for him. He shouldn't have. If I'd done it, he would have yelled at me. But you could never tell Shaun anything."

Emma starts weeping again but softly this time. "That was a couple of months ago. Those of us who were left stayed together for a few weeks. Then the others decided to leave London. I hung on, remembering what Shaun had said. We've been alone since then, haven't we, Declan?"

The little boy nods stiffly. He's crying too now, but quietly, shivering in his mother's arms.

"You've done well to survive," Jakob says softly. "Shaun would be proud."

Emma nods and sniffs. Carl chews on his lower lip, wanting to say something more to comfort the pair. Then he has a brainwave.

"Does Declan have any toys?" he asks.

Both Emma and Declan stop crying and stare at Carl. "No," Emma says. "I pick up some things for him every now and then, if we're staying in one spot for a few nights, but we move around a lot and we can't carry much with us when we travel. Toys are pretty low on our list of priorities."

"I figured as much," Carl says, getting to his feet. "We're not that far from Hamleys. Why don't I pop over there and find some really cool toys for him to play with in County Hall?"

"I'm not sure," Emma says. "I've passed by Hamleys a few times. It's full of zombies. I never dared go in."

413

"They won't bother *me*," Carl laughs, and sets off, excited at the thought of exploring the different levels of the famous old toy shop.

"Do you want us to come with you?" Ashtat asks.

"No," he says. "Stay here and enjoy the sun. Emma and Declan will be safer in the open, with plenty of escape routes."

"Hold on," I stop him. "I'm coming."

"I don't need backup," he snorts.

"I'm sure you don't. Still, it can't hurt having someone to look out for you. And I can give you a hand bringing stuff back."

Carl thinks about that and shrugs. "OK, if you want. Just as long as we're clear that I'm the one who gets to choose."

"Don't worry about it," I say drily. "I know better than to come between a boy and his toys."

Carl starts to retort, then remembers that there's a young child present. He catches himself, grins sheepishly at Emma, then off we head in search of some toys that will hopefully bring a smile to the solemn boy's face.

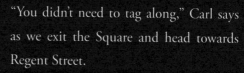

NINE

"You didn't need to tag along," Carl says as we exit the Square and head towards Regent Street.

"You shouldn't go off solo," I grunt. "Anything could happen to you."

"Would you be bothered?" Carl asks.

I shrug. "I don't want to have to explain your loss to Master Zhang."

Carl smiles. "*You* went off by yourself after you fell from the London Eye."

I haven't told them that Rage pushed me. They think I fell. I didn't even tell Dr. Oystein. I'm not a tattletale. What happened on the Eye was between Rage and me.

"I'm a special case," I mutter.

Carl looks at me sideways and smirks. "I think you fancy me."

"In your dreams."

"That's why you've come. You can't bear to be parted from me."

I fake a yawn. "Yeah, that's it." Then I tell him, "Actually it's because of the book."

He frowns. "What are you talking about?"

"The book with the Van Gogh letters. It's great. You gave it to me, so I wanted to repay you."

"It's no big deal," he says. "You could have given me a book in return."

"I couldn't be bothered looking for one."

He grins. "Or you could have just said thanks."

"Nothing says thank you better than saving a person's life," I drawl.

Carl shakes his head. "You're a strange one, Smith."

"Am I?"

"Yes. I can't figure you out. I try being nice to you, and you clearly appreciate that or you wouldn't feel compelled to repay me. But instead of just accepting me as a friend, you have to turn it into something weird."

"Nothing weird about it," I grunt. "I liked the book. This is my way of doing something nice for you in return."

"You could simply be my friend," Carl says.

"I'd rather save your neck."

"Even though you don't like me?" he presses.

"I never said I didn't like you."

"Then you do like me?"

"I never said that either."

Carl stops and squints. "Are you playing mind games with me?"

"No." I roll my eyes. "You're just a guy I work with, same as the others. I'm happy to keep things pleasant, but I don't want to do more than that. Friends aren't my thing."

"Must be lonely up there in that tower," Carl says.

"Suits me fine," I retort. "Now, are we sorting out those toys or what?"

Carl looks at me a beat longer, then shrugs and starts off again. He doesn't say anything else. I don't either. I didn't want to piss him off, but he kept asking until there was nothing else left but to hit him with the truth.

After a short, uneventful journey, we stop outside Hamleys. Anytime I passed by before, it was swarming with kids and tourists. Now it's no different than any other large building in this city, silent, no signs of life, just the occasional flickering shadow as zombies shift around inside.

"It's sad," Carl says. "It feels more like a graveyard than a toy shop now."

"Do you want to try somewhere else?" I ask.

"No. The other places will be the same. I'll go look inside, see what I can rustle up. I might be a while—I always seem to turn into a big kid in here. Do you want to come with me, or do you want to browse by yourself?"

"Actually I think I'll stay out here and keep watch," I say, not wanting to go in and be confronted with all those toys, along with the realization that no children will ever come to play with them again. "I'll give you a shout if I spot anything."

"Like what?" he laughs. "Elephants?"

"Just get on with your job, *toy boy*," I growl, and move away from the door, out of his line of sight.

As Carl goes on the hunt for the perfect present, I shuffle along, away from the windows that are still packed with displays of toys that haven't been disturbed, until I come to a stretch of wall that I can lean against. I glance around idly, then study my fingerbones, picking at them, cleaning them. I keep them in good shape, but with all the training and fighting, they get scraped and chipped. The scuffs don't really bother me, but I like to keep them neat and tidy. I guess filing down the bones is the closest I get to polishing my nails these days.

As I'm digging at a thin crack in one of the bones, trying to scrape out the dirt, I hear something rustling to my left. I look up but can't see anything. Probably just a rat. I return my attention to my bones, but then there's a shuffling sound off to my right. I frown and step away from the wall, squinting. The sun's in my eyes. I raise a hand to shade them.

Something strikes the back of my neck and a surge of electricity crackles through me. Every muscle in my body goes haywire. I collapse instantly. I try to cry out with pain, but my mouth won't work. It's like I'm filling with sparks. Lights dance across my eyes and I go temporarily blind.

As my vision starts to clear, a man rushes towards me. A gag is shoved into my mouth. My hands are jerked behind my back and tied together. Someone else binds my legs. I want to scream for help, but I'm still spasming and the gag would stop me making any noises anyway.

The guy who bound my hands starts to jam a thick sack down over my head. He pauses before he covers my eyes and waits for me to focus on him. As I do, the world swimming slowly back into place around me, I spot his dark, gray-streaked hair and brown eyes, and I think it's Dr. Oystein, that this is a test.

Then the man's features solidify and I realize it's not the doc. I don't know why I ever thought it was. The pair look nothing alike. This guy is much broader, with a menacing expression, and Dr. Oystein never went around with a bullet stuck behind his right ear.

When I spot the bullet, everything clicks and I realize what's going on. I try to scream again, to at least alert Carl, even if it's too late for me. But the hunter knows his job. He's not in the habit of making mistakes.

"Hello again, my bizarre little beauty," he whispers.

And, as he tugs the sack down over my face, thrusting me into darkness, I try screaming one last time, unsuccessfully willing myself to bellow his name out loud for all the world to hear.

"Barnes!"

TEN

My captors pick me up and hurry along the street with me. I try kicking out at them, but I'm expertly bound and my muscles are still throbbing from the shock. I've never been Tasered before. I didn't think it would hurt so much. My head is ringing and it feels like I've been sucking batteries for a week.

I'm bundled into the back of a van and the doors slam shut. The engine starts and we lurch forward. It's been so long since I was in a moving vehicle, the sensation is strange. I get a bit nauseous. I never suffered from travel sickness when I was alive. Maybe it has something to do with my altered hearing.

I've no idea what's going on. Barnes is a hunter. When I met him before, he was leading a small team, killing zombies for sport. I could understand that. But why kidnap me now instead of shoot me dead when he had the chance? Does he plan to torture me?

I wouldn't have thought he was the type. That day in the East End, when he realized I could think and speak, he let me go. He even threatened to eliminate one of his crew, Coley, a nasty piece of work who wanted to kill me despite the fact I wasn't like the other zombies.

But maybe I caught Barnes on a soft day. He might have thought about it since then and decided I was fair game. Perhaps he got tired of executing mindless zombies and wanted to experiment on one who could react to his taunts.

As I'm considering the nature of the man who now controls my fate, the sack is pulled free of my head. Barnes is squatting in front of me, grinning bleakly.

"I know you haven't forgotten me," he says quietly in his American accent. "You're in trouble and I won't pretend you're not. But I'm not figuring on killing you. If you play ball, you might get out of this alive. Now, do you want me to take out that gag?"

I nod sharply.

"If you try to bite me, I'll execute you," he says, showing me a hunting knife. "I'll dig this straight into your brain at the first snap of your teeth."

I glare at Barnes as he reaches out and removes the gag, but slide my head backwards as soon as my mouth is free, away from his

"Not this side of Hell," I snarl. "I hoped a zombie would have ripped you apart by now."

"Not this fleet-footed fox," Coley boasts.

"I'm surprised you're still together," I mutter. "I thought you'd have gone your separate ways after what happened, Barnes threatening to shoot off your kneecaps and all."

"Nothing more than a minor quarrel," Coley says, glancing over his shoulder to show me his grin. He's sporting fancy designer glasses, the same as before. His straw-colored hair is a bit longer. Both men are wearing army fatigues.

"A lovers' tiff?" I murmur, smiling back at Coley as best I can from my awkward position.

Coley's face darkens. "I say we cut out her tongue."

Barnes chuckles. "Not yet. Our lords and ladies might want her to sing for them first."

"What's going on?" I ask.

"You'll find out soon," Barnes tells me.

"You won't like it when you do," Coley cackles, and takes a bend sharply, tires squealing. Barnes almost topples onto me.

"Careful!" he barks.

"Don't worry," Coley says. "I'm in total control of this baby." We hit a bump and Barnes is jolted into the air. Again he has to steady himself before he falls within range of my infectious teeth.

"I won't warn you again," Barnes says.

"You're no fun," Coley pouts, but slows to a more reasonable speed.

Barnes scowls at the back of his partner's head, then leans in close to me. "If it's any consolation," he whispers so that only I can hear, "I hate having to do this. It won't mean much to you, I know, but for what it's worth, I'm sorry."

And the sad look he flashes me is far more worrying than any threat he might have made.

ELEVEN

We drive for what feels like twenty or thirty minutes. It involves a lot of zigzagging around crashed or abandoned vehicles, which slows us down. A few zombies hurl themselves at the vehicle every now and then, but they bounce off and are easily left behind. Coley swerves on other occasions to deliberately mow down zombies that are in his path. He whoops every time he hits one, sometimes pausing to reverse over them, trying to squash their heads.

Barnes sighs and purses his lips with disapproval, but says nothing, letting Coley have his grisly fun.

The van finally draws to a halt and Coley kills the engine. Having checked the mirrors to make sure the area is clear of the living dead, he hops out, trots round to the back and opens the doors. "Here, kitty, kitty," he purrs, and reaches in for me. He grabs my feet and starts to pull me out.

"Wait until I gag her," Barnes says.

"Don't," I ask him as he leans towards me. "I won't bite, I swear."

"I believe you but I can't take any chances," he says. "It won't be for long, just until we can set you down."

Barnes puts the gag back in place and secures it. Then he nods at Coley, who happily hauls me out of the van. I land on the ground with a thump. Coley kicks me while I'm down, hard in the ribs.

"Not such a tough girl now, are you?" he spits.

"There's no need for that," Barnes says wearily, climbing out of the van and shutting the doors.

"Don't tell me you're going to shoot me just for kicking her," Coley giggles.

Barnes frowns. "Some days I wonder why I keep you around."

"Because I'm good at what I do," Coley says smugly, kicking me again. "It's the same reason I put up with your righteous crap. We work well together. We need each other, much as it might pain either of us to admit it."

Barnes cracks his knuckles and casts an eye over me. "You take the legs," he says. "I'll take the upper body."

"You sure?" Coley asks.

"Yeah. You'd keep dropping her on her head otherwise."

Coley laughs with delight then picks up my legs. Barnes slips his hands under my shoulders and lifts. They juggle me around until they're comfortable, then start ahead. They're both strong men and they might as well be carrying a small dog for all the effort it takes them. Even so, I'm guessing they won't want to carry me too far – they're vulnerable with me in their hands, easy prey if zombies attack – and I'm proved right a minute later when they pass by the cool glass building of City Hall, head down to the bank of the Thames and take a left.

The HMS *Belfast* is docked ahead of us. I came this way when I first trekked across from the east. There were people on the deck of the famous old cruiser, armed to the teeth. They shot at me before I could ask any questions, scared me off, made it clear they didn't welcome strangers. They're still up there and look to be just as heavily armed. But they don't fire at Barnes and Coley. It seems like they're expecting us.

The hunters carry me up the gangway. They don't say anything. Once onboard, they lay me down and take a step back. The people with the rifles press closer. There are at least a dozen of them, more spread across the deck. They look like soldiers although they're dressed in suits. They don't smile, just stare at me with distaste.

"Is this one of the speaking zombies?" a man in a suit and wearing shades like Coley's asks.

"Yeah," Barnes replies.

"You finally made good and caught one," the man sniffs.

"I swore that I would."

"Took you long enough."

Barnes smiles tightly. "If you thought you could do better, you should have said so. I'd have been happy to spend my days lounging around here and let you go scour the streets instead."

The man in the suit scowls. "Think you're hot stuff, don't you, Barnes?"

Barnes shrugs. "I'm just a guy who gets the job done. Now, are the lords and ladies of the Board ready to accept their delivery?"

"Wait here," the man says. "I'll go check."

There's a short delay. Barnes and Coley stand at ease. The people with the rifles keep them trained on me, ready to blast me to hell if I show the slightest sign that I'm about to try to break free.

Eventually someone comes running towards us. "Let me see! Let me see!" a panting man cries and the guards around us part.

I spot a fat man in a sailor suit prancing across the deck. The suit is too small for him and his stomach is exposed. It's hairy and there are crumbs stuck in the hairs.

The fat man crouches next to me and stares, eyes wide, lips quivering. He notes the hole in my chest and studies my face. His smile fades. "It's a girl. I thought it would be a boy."

"I didn't know you had a preference," Barnes says. "Does it make any difference?"

The fat man purses his lips. "I suppose not. I just assumed…"
He shrugs and smiles again. "Make her talk, Barnes. Make her talk
for Dan-Dan. I want to hear her before the others. I want to be the
first."

Barnes looks at the guard in the suit and glasses, who has followed behind the guy dressed like a sailor. The guard shrugs. Barnes
carefully removes my gag and shifts out of my way.

The fat man nods at me, grinning like a lunatic. "Come on,
little girl. Talk for Dan-Dan. Let me hear you."

I look *Dan-Dan* up and down, slow as you like, then smile lazily.
"You're about three sizes too large for that ridiculous suit, fat boy."

Dan-Dan's jaw drops. Some of the guards smirk. Coley snorts
with laughter. Barnes just stares at me.

"You…you…" Dan-Dan sputters. He starts to swing a hand at
me, to slap me. Then he remembers what I am and stops. His smile
swims back into place and he blows me a kiss. "You're wonderful,"
he gurgles. "A spirited, snarling, she-snake. Everything I was hoping
for and more. We're going to have so much fun with you, little girl."

Dan-Dan lurches to his feet and claps his hands at Barnes and
Coley. "Don't stand there like fools," he barks, going from buffoon
to commander in the space of a few seconds. "Bring her through to
the Wardroom. The others are waiting and we're not renowned for
our patience."

As Barnes and Coley pick me up again – pausing only to
stick my gag back in place – Dan-Dan sets off ahead of us. He

waddles like a duck but there's nothing funny about him now. I'm in serious trouble here. And while the farcically dressed fat man is nowhere near as scary as Mr. Dowling or Owl Man, he's probably more of a threat than either of them. Both of those freaks chose to let me run free, but I've a horrible feeling that Dan-Dan wants me for keeps.

TWELVE

Barnes and Coley carry me across the deck, down a flight of stairs, then towards the rear of the cruiser, which they refer to as the aft. Dan-Dan trots ahead of us, skipping at times, singing to himself.

Dan-Dan opens a door and we enter a long room dominated by a massive table. It could easily seat a couple dozen people, but only five individuals are sitting around it. They're spread out, as if they don't want to sit too close to one another. There are ten guards in the room, standing by the walls, surrounding the table. All have handguns and are pointing them at me.

Coley chuckles uneasily. "You guys want to lower those? If you fire off a shot accidentally, you might hit Barnes or me."

"There will be no accidents here," a woman at the table says. She's in her forties or fifties. Dressed to the nines, dripping in necklaces and diamonds. If she looked any posher, she'd be a queen.

Dan-Dan takes a seat and chortles. "Lady Jemima is correct, as always. If we shoot you, it will be on purpose."

Barnes ignores the veiled threat and helps Coley set me on my feet. "Her name's Becky Smith," he tells the six people at the table. "She's one of the talking zombies."

"It's true," Dan-Dan gushes. "I heard her speak on deck. She insulted me. I didn't like that—she's a naughty little minx who must be taught the error of her ways. But she can definitely speak."

"We never doubted you, Barnes," another man says. He's smartly dressed in a purple suit. He looks young, but there are faint wrinkles around his eyes when he smiles, which make me think he's older than he appears. "We were just concerned that it was taking you so long to find one for us."

Barnes shuffles his feet and pulls a face. "I'm slow but sure." It's an act. There's nothing slow about Barnes. But he's clearly wary of these people and their armed guards.

"Remove the gag," one of the other men says. This one has an eastern European accent. He's dressed like a prince, crown and all.

"Yes, sir," Barnes murmurs and reaches up to free my mouth. "Be careful what you say to them," he whispers. "They don't have a sense of humor."

I stare silently at my regally attired captors when the gag has been removed.

"Well?" Lady Jemima asks, twisting a diamond ring as she bores into me with her gaze.

"What?" I sniff, and she stops turning the ring.

"Incredible," she sighs.

"She spoke to me first," Dan-Dan crows. "Did you hear that, Luca?" he calls to the guy in the purple suit. "I was first."

"Mother would be so proud of you," Luca purrs sarcastically. "If you hadn't thrown her to a zombie to save yourself, that is."

Dan-Dan's face drops. "I thought we weren't going to mention that again."

Luca sniffs and leans towards me. "Tell us about yourself, girl. Where are you from? How can you speak? Are there many more like you?"

I cock my head at him and don't answer. He studies me silently, then grins viciously. "The next time you refuse to answer a question, I'll have one of my men cut off the little finger on your left hand. After that, it will be your head. I only believe in a single warning. So, unless you're keen to die today, talk."

"There's not much I can tell you," I say sullenly. "I don't know how I can talk or why I'm different." That's a lie, but I'm not going to rat out Dr. Oystein to this pack of creeps. I think about saying I'm a one-off, but Barnes has seen me with other Angels. I have to be careful, lie cautiously, mix in a bit of truth.

"There are several of us that I know about. We wander around London together. We've been looking for answers but haven't found any, so we've been getting by as best we can."

"Does the girl need to eat brains?" the other woman at the table asks. She's conservatively dressed in a dark jacket and trousers. Gray hair. A pinched face. "Ask her if she needs to eat brains, Luca."

"Ask her yourself," Luca snaps.

The woman frowns. "I don't want to talk to one of *them*. She's a thing, not a person."

"But you're happy for me to talk to her?" Luca growls.

"You're more natural in situations like this," the woman simpers.

Luca barks a laugh. "You're useless, Vicky. I don't know how you got into Parliament so many times."

"By being ruthless with people who displease me," Vicky says flatly.

"Peace," the final man to speak says. He's the oldest, a white-haired, thick-limbed guy. The others quit squabbling immediately. The man rises and crosses the room to study me up close. If I leaned forward quickly, I could bite him. But it would be my final act and he knows it. I don't smell any fear on him.

"My name is Justin Bazini," he says. "If you had the right connections, you would know what that name means. I'm a man of immense wealth and power. Those are Lords Luca and Daniel Wood, not as well off as my good self, but not short of a few shillings either."

"What are shillings?" Dan-Dan asks jokingly.

Justin points at the overdressed woman. "Lady Jemima. You probably saw her picture a lot in the fashion magazines when you were alive."

"I didn't waste my time reading fashion magazines," I sniff.

He looks down at my clothes and smiles mockingly. "Evidently not. Our other good lady is Victoria Wedge. I imagine you weren't the most political of creatures, so I don't suppose you—"

"I know who Vicky Wedge is," I interrupt. "I don't recognize the face but I know the name. My dad used to talk about her. He thought the sun shone out of her backside. Not too fond of foreigners, was she?"

"There is nothing wrong with foreigners," Vicky Wedge says with an icy smile. "As long as they are invited foreigners who can be of benefit to their adopted homeland. Was your father one of my supporters?"

"Yeah. He had the real hots for you. He always had a soft spot for bigots."

I expect her to flush at the insult but she only laughs. "What a charmless little beast. The perfect example of why I campaigned for chemical castration of the more vulgar, useless proletariat."

"You surely did not campaign openly about such a controversial issue, did you?" the guy with the crown asks.

"No," Vicky scowls. "My spin doctors advised against it. They thought it might inspire some of the vile creatures to crawl to the polling stations to vote against me."

"And, finally, the gentleman with the crown is The Prince." Justin wraps up the introductions.

"No actual name?" I ask.

"I prefer not to use it," The Prince says grandly. "In this world I am one of the last of my kind. One day I will be *the* last. People might as well get used to calling me by my title."

"Not interested in being king?" I sneer.

"Oh no," The Prince says. "Nobody likes a king. But everyone loves a prince. I want to be loved. I *will* be loved."

Justin returns to his seat and rocks back and forth as he addresses me. "We are the Board. We happened to be together here in London when the world fell. Rather than flee, as so many in our position did, we stood firm and made this vessel our own, choosing it both because it's easier to defend than a landlocked building and because it's such a potent reminder of our glorious past."

"Plus I've always liked big boats," Dan-Dan giggles. "Sailors are my favorite military personnel. Their uniforms are to die for."

"We're going to run this world again one day," Luca says.

"And run it the right way this time," Vicky Wedge adds pointedly.

"From here?" I ask skeptically.

"Of course not," Justin snaps. "This is merely a temporary base. But we will maintain our position in London, you can be sure of that. Once the situation has stabilized and we've rid the streets of their zombie scum, we'll recover Downing Street and Buckingham

Palace, and run the world from the heart of the great British Empire, as it always should have been."

"Rule Britannia," Dan-Dan sings at the top of his voice.

"I think the army might have something to say about that," I mutter.

"Nonsense," The Prince chuckles. "Soldiers exist to be given orders. No military junta ever ruled for long. They will need leaders to guide them."

"And you think you guys fit the bill?"

"Who else?" Justin challenges me. "The other survivors of our stature, who might have provided competition, fled like frightened animals when the chips were down. Class will always triumph. We stood firm and that will be acknowledged."

"You're cuckoo," I sniff, ignoring Barnes's warning to be careful about what I say. "Money doesn't matter anymore. You won't be able to buy your way into power again."

"Foolish child," Lady Jemima laughs.

"Ignorant brat," Vicky Wedge adds snidely.

"Money will always be a factor," Dan-Dan says, dropping the man-child act. "Cash might not be worth what it was, but diamonds and gold hold their value no matter what."

"We have plenty of those stored away," Luca boasts.

"And we know where we can get more," The Prince beams, rubbing his hands together greedily.

"In short," Justin concludes, "we're perfectly positioned to take control of the world. It will happen, there is no question of that. It's just a matter of when. And until then we're keen to kill time." He's been drumming his fingers on the table. Now he stops and points at me. "That's where *you* come in. Tell me, Miss Smith, do you have a taste for combat? If you don't," he adds quickly before I can answer, "fret not, dear girl, because you will develop one soon, once the killing begins..."

THIRTEEN

The members of the Board file out of the Wardroom, Dan-Dan moving swiftly to make sure he's at the head of the procession. Half the guards go with them. The other half keep their weapons trained on me.

"What's going on here?" I ask Barnes.

He doesn't answer. Instead it's Coley who says, "Entertainment will always be a thriving industry. Our lords and ladies wish to be amused, and they have the funds in place to ensure those wishes are met."

"You can't care about money now," I mutter, again addressing my comments to Barnes. "Those power-hungry leeches are insane. We can never go back to the old ways."

"I'm not too sure about that," Barnes says softly. "But no, I'm not in it for the money."

"Then what?" I growl. "The kicks? Do you like seeing zombies suffer?"

Barnes only stares at me.

"He has his reasons," Coley says defensively.

"And they're mine to share or not," Barnes barks.

"Easy, big guy," Coley chuckles. "I wasn't going to say any more."

"What about you?" I sniff.

"I like the work and I like the perks," Coley grins. "There are women here who look kindly on brave soldiers like me. We have access to alcohol, drugs, anything we want. Power and wealth mean nothing to me. It's all about the fringe benefits."

A guard comes to fetch us and leads us to an even larger, longer room. Some poles run along the middle, supporting the ceiling. Thick glass panels have been set in place along one side of the room, the side with small round windows in it. Panels also cover the far end of the room, where there's an access door. The result is a sealed, self-contained, L-shaped corridor.

The half-dozen members of the Board are standing on the other side of the glass, in the corridor. The Prince and Justin Bazini are puffing fat cigars. Lady Jemima is smoking a cigarette clasped in a long, fancy holder. Lord Luca pops a few pills. Vicky Wedge is leaning against the glass, breathing heavily, her arms crossed, and Dan-Dan is close by her, tapping on the glass with his fingers, cooing at me as if I was a caged bird. At one point he leans forward and licks the glass. Then he draws a little heart in his spit and flutters his eyelashes at me.

There are bloodstains smeared across the glass on my side. Bits of flesh are stuck to it in places. Bones are scattered across the floor.

"Can you hear us, little girl?" Dan-Dan calls. "Is the sound system working? It had better be. I don't like it when that breaks down. Heads will roll if there are any technical problems today."

"We can hear you loud and clear, Lord Wood," Coley replies.

Dan-Dan smiles. "I can hear you too. That's perfect."

"Unbind her and come on round," Justin says to Barnes and Coley. "We want to share the show with you, a reward for all the hard work you've put in over the last few weeks."

Barnes faces me. "We can do this the hard way if you want. I can Taser you and release you while you're subdued. But if you give me your word not to attack us, we can just take off the cuffs and leave you be."

"No need for the Taser," I beam. "I'll be a good girl. Promise."

Barnes stares at me for a few beats, then grins tightly. "I don't believe you."

I drop the fake smile. "That's because I'm lying. If I get the chance, I'll rip your throats open and wallow in your blood before you die."

"You'd rather the Taser?"

"Bring it on."

445

Barnes sighs and gives Coley the nod. "I'm loving this," Coley says, then lets me have it. I collapse in a spasming heap. Stars fill my head again. The agony is even worse than the first time and seems to last longer.

As I start to recover, I realize that my hands and legs are free. Coley and Barnes removed the cuffs and withdrew from the room while my senses were swimming. They're on the other side of the glass now, with the guys and gals of the Board. No guards in sight.

"This used to be the dining hall," Dan-Dan tells me. He's pawing the glass, like a puppy waiting for a treat. "The Wardroom was reserved for the officers. This was for the common crew. I prefer the informal atmosphere here. How about you?"

I try to tell him where he can stuff his *informal atmosphere*, but my mouth isn't working properly yet. All that comes out is a low mumbling noise.

"You haven't broken her, have you?" Dan-Dan snaps at Barnes and Coley. "If you have, we'll kill her and send you straight out to find another one for us. I want a fully functional, talking zombie. I won't settle for second best."

"She'll be fine in a minute or two," Barnes assures him.

"She'd better be," Dan-Dan growls. "Poor thing. Did they hurt you, little girl? Don't worry, Dan-Dan will make the pain go away. I'd kiss you better if I could. Dan-Dan loves his clever zombie, yes he does."

"Heaven save us from simpletons," Lady Jemima sighs. "Maybe we should throw Daniel in there with her."

"Careful," Lord Luca snarls. "That's my brother you're talking about."

"I was only joking," Lady Jemima says quickly. "I adore him really."

As the would-be rulers of the world snipe at one another, the door to my side of the room opens and two guards step in and move to either side. They train their guns on me and tell me to take a few steps back. When I've retreated, a zombie is hustled in by another guard. There's a collar around the zombie's neck, attached to a stiff lead, giving the guard plenty of space.

Yet another guard enters, with a second captive zombie, followed by three more. Then one last guard comes in. This guy's holding a Taser like Coley's. He gives each zombie a quick burst. As they fall to the floor and writhe, their handlers set them free and slip out of the room. The pair with guns are the last to leave and they slam shut the door after themselves. While the zombies on the floor recover, I study them cautiously. Three men, a woman and a teenage boy. The men are muscular and dressed in normal clothes. The woman is wearing a chef's outfit. The boy is naked.

"I chose that one," Dan-Dan sniggers. "Nudity is so pleasing to the eye, isn't it, especially in one so young and pure?"

"You're a degenerate," Lord Luca laughs.

"Not at all," Dan-Dan tuts. "I simply like to appreciate the human form in all its natural glory."

"An interesting mix," Justin murmurs, then calls out to me. "As the street-smart young woman that you appear to be, I'm sure you've already sussed the state of play. We want you to fight to the death. We've been pitting living slaves against zombies for months now, but they've struggled to stage an engaging fight. It seems the true gladiatorial spirit died out among the human masses long ago. But we're sure you'll serve up a decent show."

I slide my jaw from side to side and wriggle my tongue about to make sure I can speak again. Then I shoot Justin the finger. "Get stuffed, grandad."

Justin shakes his head bitterly. "Why do the youth of today have to make it so hard on themselves? Vicky, would you lend me your assistance?"

"My pleasure." She moves to a small hatch that I hadn't noticed before. It's covered with a glass rectangle. She slides it open and draws a gun from a holster behind her back, kneels and aims at one of the male zombies.

"Fight or we'll kill him," Justin says.

I shrug. "You want me to kill him anyway, so what's the difference?"

"If you fight him, he stands a chance," Justin says. "And if he comes up short, at least he can die with honor."

"I couldn't care less about honor," I sniff.

"Do it," Justin yaps, and Vicky fires three times in quick succession. The man's head explodes and he slumps, truly dead now. The zombies around him snarl and dart at the hatch, angered by the attack and tempted by the scent of human brain. They slam into the glass but it barely quivers. Vicky shuts the hatch and moves to another—there are several of them set in the panels in different areas.

"Oh my God!" I scream, covering my ears with my hands. "You did it! I didn't think you'd really do it!"

"We never bluff," The Prince drawls, smiling as if he'd just won a war.

"Well, I don't either," I jeer, lowering my hands and dropping the hysterical act. "You lot are mugs. What do you think I am, zombie Spartacus or something? I don't give a toss about these walking corpses. Shoot them, fry them, chop them up into pieces if you want. I don't care."

Justin frowns. "You won't stand up to protect your own?"

"They're nothing to do with me," I tell him. "I don't have anything in common with these brain-dead abominations. Hell, I've finished off plenty of them myself over the last few months."

"Interesting," Justin murmurs. "Then I suppose we'll have to try a different tack. Daniel, will you go and fetch us one of your darlings?"

"Yes, yes, yes, yes, yes!" Dan-Dan crows. "I was hoping for this. But I want to be the one who does it if she forces our hand. They're mine. I won't let Vicky or any of the others cheat me out of my prize."

"Perish the thought," Justin says. "The honor will be all yours."

"In that case, I'll be back before you can blink." Dan-Dan shoots out of the room as if in a hurry to get to a party.

"Is this really necessary?" The Prince asks with a pained look.

"Yes," Justin says.

"It would have been so much simpler if you'd just fought when asked," The Prince admonishes me.

"What's happening?" Coley asks Justin. "Where did Lord Wood go?"

"To bring us something truly dreadful," Justin whispers, his eyes dark and sad, yet bright and excited at the same time.

FOURTEEN

Dan-Dan returns several minutes later and my heart sinks. Or would, if I had one.

He has a couple of kids with him, and both of them are alive.

"These are my darlings," Dan-Dan coos, rubbing their heads and pointing them towards me. "Say hello, my dears."

The children mumble a frightened hello. One is a boy, the other a girl. Neither is more than seven or eight years old. They're dressed in sailor suits similar to Dan-Dan's. The boy looks like he's been crying. The girl's eyes are dry but she's clearly scared. Both are trembling.

"What's going on?" Barnes asks sharply.

"Surely you must have heard the

rumors back in the day about the child-killer Daniel Wood?" Justin chuckles.

"Children had a habit of meeting with an unfortunate end whenever Daniel came to town," Vicky trills. "He was such a naughty little boy."

"My darlings," Dan-Dan beams, hugging the children. "They keep me company. I have nightmares when I'm by myself. My playmates help me keep body and soul together."

"The trouble is, Daniel plays rough," Lady Jemima notes, smiling cynically.

"He kills each child in the end, when he grows bored of them," Justin grunts.

"Allegedly," Lord Luca beams. "Nothing was ever proven in a court of law. Why, he was never even prosecuted."

Vicky Wedge winks at me. "The advantage of having an unholy amount of money, and associates like me in high places."

"You never told me any of this before," Barnes snaps.

"Why should we?" Justin yawns. "You're hired help." He turns his attention to me. "Now, Becky Smith, you might not care about the dead, but what about the living? Will you fight or does Daniel have to start squeezing?"

Dan-Dan slides his arms up and locks them round the children's throats. The girl begins to cry. Dan-Dan smiles darkly.

"It's always sad when I have to bid a darling good-bye," he

croaks. "I miss each and every one. I used to keep a list of their names, but it grew so long…"

"You won't do it," I say weakly.

"As I already told you, we never bluff," The Prince murmurs, but he sounds ashamed of his boast.

"Stop," Barnes shouts. "This is sick. I won't stand by and let you —"

"You will do what you're told!" Vicky Wedge screeches, and aims her gun at him. Lord Luca, Lady Jemima and The Prince draw weapons too. Coley curses and darts behind Barnes.

"Don't shoot!" Coley cries. "I'm on your side!"

Barnes stands firm, eyes filled with fury and contempt.

Justin gazes serenely at Barnes. "There's no need for the guns," he says to the others. "Our man Barnes is smarter than that. He knows there are guards outside. They are armed and he is not. If he threatened us, they would execute him. The children too."

"This is wrong," Barnes snarls. "You can't use innocent children this way."

"Of course we can," Justin snorts. "We make the laws. We can do anything we want."

"If it's any comfort to you, they're orphans," Lady Jemima says. "We have them delivered from camps. We only pick those who have no one to worry about them. We're not complete monsters."

"You always did have a soft heart, my lovely," Justin murmurs, and turns his back on the glaring but impotent Barnes. "We're waiting for your answer, Becky."

"He's going to kill them in the end anyway," I say softly.

"Probably," Justin nods. "But there's always a chance that he will take pity on these two. Or they might escape."

"Oh, they never escape," Dan-Dan whispers.

"There are others," Lord Luca says.

"Fourteen or fifteen the last time I checked," Vicky purrs.

"If you don't please us, he'll kill this pair and fetch replacements," The Prince adds glumly.

"He can be very petulant when he doesn't get his way," Lady Jemima concludes.

Both children are trying to tear free of Dan-Dan's grip. They're old enough to know what's going on. Dan-Dan is sweating with delight, his muscles bulging. I think he wants me to defy him, so that he can kill openly, like a disgusting, spoiled brat who wants to show off his latest vile habit.

"If I do this," I say hollowly, "I want to see the children every day, the whole group, so I can be sure that he hasn't killed any of them."

"Hold on a minute," Dan-Dan yaps. "You're in no position to make demands."

"Yes she is," Justin overrides him. "Agreed."

"No!" Dan-Dan howls. "They're mine. I'll do what I want with them."

"Not under *my* watch," Justin says, features darkening. "This isn't a democracy. The girl is something new, something different. If you have to stop killing for a few weeks or months, to entice her to play ball, so be it. You're not going to spoil things for the rest of us."

"Luca…" Dan-Dan whines, looking to his brother for support.

Lord Luca shrugs. "I'm with Justin this time. I'm bored of the same old pathetic show, humans failing miserably every time we stick them in with the undead. I crave savage duels, heated action, true drama. If the girl has a reason to battle on – if she's fighting for others, not just herself – it will be all the more interesting."

"You can have your darlings eventually," Vicky says soothingly. "We're not taking them away from you forever. You just need to be patient."

"Oh, very well," Dan-Dan pouts, releasing the children and pushing them aside. "But I won't forget this. The next time one of you asks for a favor, don't expect me to jump."

The Prince gathers the children from Dan-Dan and escorts them to the door, where he passes them to a guard who takes them back to their quarters.

"You can leave as well if you wish," Justin says to Barnes. "I won't make you watch if it offends you. This was meant to be a reward for services rendered, not a punishment."

Barnes studies the businessman, stares at the open doorway, then looks back at me and shrugs. "I was only worried about the kids. Now that we've dealt with that issue, I'm keen to stick around."

"Excellent," Justin beams. "Becky, can you agitate them by yourself or do you need some help?"

"I've got it," I mutter, flexing my fingers and preparing for battle.

I let my gaze linger on the undead men and woman for a moment, then stare glumly at the teenage boy. They're all standing with their backs to me, trying to gouge through the glass, unaware of the threat behind them. It would be easy to step up and drive my hands through their skulls, kill them all before they could react. But that wouldn't satisfy the bloodthirsty members of the Board. They want action and excitement, and it's my job to deliver that for them.

"Mum would be proud," I snort. "She always wanted me to go into showbiz." Then, to cheers of encouragement from the inhuman humans, I sweep forward and attack.

FIFTEEN

I grab the collars of the men's shirts and haul them away from the glass. I kick the boy in the chest and send him sprawling. I slap the woman's face.

The zombies snarl and regroup. They stare at me, sniffing the air. They know I'm undead, so they're not sure why I've assaulted them. Zombies don't turn on one another. They found the peaceful unity in death that is so rare in life.

"Come on," I growl, crooking my fingers at them. "I'm not as dead as I look."

They hiss and move closer, then stall and stare again. They can tell I'm not the same as them – no regular zombie can talk – but I'm more like them than the humans. They're reluctant to strike, seeing me as one of their own.

"Don't just stand there," Dan-Dan calls, banging his fist on the glass. "Make them angry."

I give him the finger, then dart forward. I kick the boy in the chest again and scratch the cheek of the nearest man. He instinctively throws a fist at me. I block it and punch him hard in the stomach.

The woman in the chef's outfit grabs my head and shakes it, pulling me away from the men. The boy leaps at me, growling like a dog. I kick him between the legs. Because he's naked, I have a clear shot. Every guy on the other side of the glass gasps and cringes. Then they cheer and clap.

I shrug off the woman and race towards a nearby pole. The men follow. I jump into the air, grab the pole and whirl around. I stick my legs out and my right foot connects with one of the men's jaws. His head snaps back and he staggers away.

"Oh, nice shot," The Prince applauds. "We never saw any of the others execute a move like that."

"It's like watching a wrestling match," Lady Jemima cackles.

"Only the result isn't fixed," Justin laughs.

I tune out the babbling members of the Board and stay focused. Any one of these zombies could slice my skull open. I can't afford to get cocky.

The boy shambles towards me, still grimacing from the kick between his legs. I hate doing this to him, but the shot is there to be taken, so I swing my foot back, then kick him square in the nuts again.

"Unbelievable!" Lord Luca hoots.

"He'll be a eunuch by the end of this," Vicky Wedge sniggers.

"It's bringing tears to my eyes," Dan-Dan squeals, crossing his hands in front of his groin.

One of the men tackles me from behind and locks his arms across my chest. The other man charges me from the front. I lift my legs, clasp them around his neck in a scissor motion and snap it. He groans and wheels away, tugging at his head, trying to set it straight.

The man behind me squeezes, but there's no air in my lungs, so he doesn't do much damage. While he's trying to suffocate me, I twist my body the way I was trained by Master Zhang and throw him over my shoulder. He lands heavily in front of me. I make a blade of my fingers and drive my right hand through the center of his forehead. He cries out, shudders, then falls still. I withdraw my hand and wipe it across his hair, cleaning my flesh of bits of the dead man's brain.

The woman slashes at me with the bones sticking out of her fingers. I block them with my own fingerbones, then jab at her eyes, forcing her back.

The boy lurches at me from the other side. He still hasn't properly protected his crown jewels, but I'm not able to find the angle to kick him a third time. He grabs me and digs his teeth into my left hip, tearing through my pants, into the flesh.

I wince and club the boy over the head. His skull snaps and some of the flesh tears open. I spot brain and swiftly dig in, finishing

him off. After the blows to his family jewels, I think death comes as a relative blessing.

The woman hurls herself at me, shrieking. For all I know, she was the boy's mother in life. Not that I think that factors into things now. She only wants to kill the beast who is threatening her. Zombies can't feel love, pity or affection. But they can feel fear. How unfair is that?

I shimmy out of the woman's way, slip in behind and get her in a stranglehold. She struggles furiously, but I was taught how to keep my grip tight. As she reels around the room with me on her back, I bare my fangs and bite into her skull. I chew loose a chunk of flesh and bone, and spit it out. I bite again. The woman mewls and shudders. After I tear away another chunk, there's enough space for me to jam in my chin, like a pig sticking its snout into a trough. I munch, rip and saw.

Seconds later the woman collapses beneath me and I push myself to my feet, spitting out brain. The brains of the undead do nothing for me. The taste is vile, nothing like the juicy, enticing brains of the living.

The only one left is the man with the broken neck. He doesn't provide much resistance. He's still trying to repair the damage to his spinal cord. I simply have to pad up behind him and crack his head open.

I step away from the last of the corpses and gaze at my handiwork.

Four dead zombies, in addition to the one Vicky killed. It probably didn't take me more than a couple of minutes to fell them.

The members of the Board are cheering warmly. I glance at them numbly, blood on my hands, brains dribbling from my lips. The Prince winks at me. Lord Luca gives me the thumbs up. Justin claps louder than the others and shouts over the noise, "Ladies and gentlemen, a gladiator is born!"

The nightmare begins for real.

SIXTEEN

It's been a week or more since I wound up in the clutches of the Board. A week of almost nonstop fighting, with rests only to allow my captors to sleep, eat and indulge in their other pastimes.

When I'm not needed, I'm kept in a room near the fore of the cruiser, in what used to be known as a mess. A few hammocks are slung across it. I lie in one of those when I'm relaxing, sometimes for hours without moving, staring at the ceiling with my unblinking eyes, trying to think of a way out of this horror show.

In an ideal world I'd kill the creeps of the Board, free the children and slip away into the night. Since I'm unlikely to score on all three fronts, I'd settle for murdering the manipulative monsters who think they're superior to the rest of us.

But there's not much chance of that. They keep themselves separate. I usually only see them in the converted dining hall when they want me to kill. And then they're always safe behind their wall of glass. Many of my opponents have tried to smash through that wall. I've even thrown a few of them at it with all my strength while fighting, to test it. Not so much as a crack. It's tough as steel.

The battles have drained me. Zombies are more resilient than humans, but we're not inexhaustible. We wear down. I've fought four or five times most days, usually against a handful of opponents, but sometimes as many as eight. I'm not stronger than those I've come up against, but I'm sharper. I can outwit and outmaneuver them.

Even so, I've suffered my share of injuries. I've broken several bones. My neck and chest have been slashed, chunks bitten out of my arms and legs. A couple of teeth were smashed from my gums—that *really* hurt and still does.

Justin spoke of keeping me on for months when I first arrived, but I'll be lucky to last a couple of weeks, maybe a bit longer if they reduce the number of daily bouts. I'm a short-term project for them.

I wasn't going to tell them that I need brains to function, that I'll regress if I don't eat. But they know that zombies need to feed to stay sharp, so they supplied me with brains without my having to ask for them, a couple of days after I'd fallen into their foul clutches. Coley delivered the first batch.

"Barnes and I rustled these up from corpses on the streets," he told me. "Not my idea of a good time, but anything to please our lords and ladies."

"What if I don't want to eat?" I said in a low voice.

Coley shrugged. "They'll see that as a sign of mutiny and give me the order to put you out of your misery. Which is fine by me, so go ahead and refuse."

I made a sighing noise and dug in. I wouldn't have been able to resist for long anyway, not once the brains had been set before me. I'd seen it in the zom heads when they were starved. As you approach the end of consciousness, you lose control. In a few days I'd have dug into the brains regardless.

"Dan-Dan didn't want us to go foraging for used brains," Coley said as I threw up the remains of the brains once I'd absorbed the nutrients from them. "He had a more novel idea. He wanted to put one of the guards in with you, make you kill him and eat his fresh brain. He's some piece of work, isn't he? Makes Barnes and me look like a pair of saints. You didn't know how lucky you were when we were the worst you had to deal with."

Coley got that much right. Dan-Dan is a real beauty, full of unpleasant ideas. He came to see me the day after my first fight. Six guards flanked him and he kept well back. He wanted me to wear a revealing leather outfit, the sort you used to find in seedy adult shops.

"Not a hope in hell," I told him.

"I'll kill one of my darlings if you don't wear it," he huffed.

"That threat won't work this time," I dismissed him. "I'll tell Justin and refuse to fight in protest. The others wouldn't like that, would they?"

"You're no fun," Dan-Dan pouted, then slunk away like the disgusting rat that he is.

Even given my functioning brain, I'd have come unstuck long before now if not for my training. Master Zhang taught me well. I zing around that room like a pinball, striking swiftly, slipping out of reach before my foes can counter. I'm improving all the time, learning new tricks, finding a whole string of ways to attack and defend. I'd be proud of how I've performed if I wasn't so sickened by what is being asked of me.

The living dead deserve better than this. I don't have a lot of sympathy for zombies. They're killers by nature. But they didn't ask for reanimation or the hunger that drives them. They're not responsible for their actions. The rest of us, on the other hand, are. And what we're doing here is disgraceful. Sure, I've killed reviveds before, like in the tunnel under Waterloo Station, but that was to prepare for a battle with evil. It wasn't for sport.

I tried wriggling off the hook a couple of days ago. I carefully dropped my guard while fighting, moved a bit slower than I could, let myself be pummeled. That's when I lost the teeth. I'd planned to lose a whole lot more, to let my opponents carve me up. But Vicky got wise to what I was plotting.

"You can do better than that, Miss Smith," she called out as I circled three undead guys, each double the size of me.

"Why don't you come in and try if you think it's that easy?" I snarled.

"That will not be necessary," she retaliated. "I can see what you're up to. The stench of treachery is thick in the air. You want out. Rest assured, if you are defeated today, every one of Dan-Dan's darlings will be executed within the hour. And it will not be swift or painless."

I cursed Vicky Wedge and the rest of them, but they had me by the short and curlies. There was nothing for it but to up my game and fight for real. I came out the undefeated champion, but the victory cost me dearly. I've been hobbling in pain ever since.

The door to my room opens and I raise myself, groaning, ready to fight again. But no guards enter this time. Instead it's Barnes. I haven't seen him since that day when I was first presented to the Board.

"Come to gloat?" I snarl, letting myself fall back into my hammock.

"No," he says, taking a seat. I'm not chained up, so I could attack him, but he doesn't look afraid. Either he's sure I'll leave him be out of fear of reprisal, or he's confident that he could draw his gun and open fire before I got my hands on him.

"Come to take my order then? Cool. I'll have my brains fried, sunny side up."

Barnes grins. "I'll pass your request on to Coley."

"Where is your trusty sidekick?" I ask.

"Taking it easy. Having some fun."

"I thought he might be cowering behind you again."

Barnes chuckles. "That wasn't his finest moment. I haven't brought it up with him yet, but I certainly plan to. I'm just waiting for the right time."

"This is all screwed," I mutter. "I don't care what these guys are doing for you, nothing can justify this. You've sided with a pack of demons. Dan-Dan torments and kills children. How can you live with yourself, serving a beast like that?"

"I don't have to explain my motives to the likes of you," Barnes grunts. "You killed plenty of kids yourself, I'm sure, when you turned."

"That's different. I couldn't control myself. I can now. You can too. But you choose not to."

"Our choices are sometimes limited," Barnes sighs, then shakes his head and squints at me. "Enough of the soul-baring. I'm here to offer you a deal."

"This should be interesting," I sneer.

"You've lost your sheen," Barnes says. "You're slowing up. The constant fighting has taken it out of you. You're slow to heal – if you heal at all – and your wounds are weakening you. Our lords and ladies have started to worry. They enjoy watching you in action. They don't want to lose their prize plaything."

"Tell them if they love me, they should set me free," I say sweetly.

Barnes laughs. "I like you, Becky, I truly do. You've got more balls than most of the guys I've ever known. I want to help you if I can."

I cock an eyebrow at the hunter. "If you're looking to break me out, I'm all ears."

Barnes smiles wryly. "I don't like you *that* much. But I've come up with a compromise that might work. The Board wants me to find other zombies like you, who can speak and think. They want to see you take on one of your own, someone who can mount a genuine challenge. They've instructed me to find a few of your friends, like the ones I saw you with in Leicester Square."

I flash my teeth at him. "I don't have any *friends*."

"Then you won't mind if I find some of the gang you were with, bring them back here and force you to fight them," he says calmly.

I glare at him and don't respond.

"*Or,*" Barnes says teasingly, "we can strike a deal."

"What's this deal you keep going on about?" I sniff.

"Simple," he says. "Tell me where your colleagues are. I'll round up the lot of them. Then we'll set you free."

I smother a laugh. "You expect me to believe you'd let me go?"

"I'm not a liar."

"But you're also not the main man here. Not even close. The lords and ladies of the Board would never sanction my release."

"They already have," Barnes says. "I took the offer to them

474

before I came to you. Said I didn't think you'd go for it, but that I wanted to know where they stood if you did. They voted four to two in your favor. I won't tell you who voted against you, as I'd hate to sour the special relationship you have with them."

"What makes you think they'd honor their pledge?" I ask.

"Easier to do that than betray me. They might not think much of me as a man, but they respect me as a soldier. Besides, I'm useful to them. There will be other ways I can help them farther down the line. You have my guarantee that we'll make good on our promise."

I don't really have to think about it, but I give myself a minute to mull it over, just to be absolutely sure of my answer. When I've decided, I smirk and rock in my hammock. "Sorry, Barnes. Couldn't help you even if I wanted. Like I told the Board, we moved around all the time. We don't have a base. I've no idea where they might be."

Barnes nods and stands. "I expected nothing more but felt I owed you the offer. I'll find them anyway. Hunting's what I excel at. I'll track them down, subdue them and drag their sorry asses back here."

"I hope those conscious zombies truly aren't your friends. Because soon you're going to have to face them in the arena and kill or be killed. And there's nothing worse than having to sacrifice someone you care about. Take it from one who knows."

On that enigmatic note he leaves and, as I carry on rocking, I reflect bitterly on the fact that my future, as short as it was already given my dire situation, probably just got a hell of a lot shorter.

SEVENTEEN

I'm marched down to see the children every day. They're being held on the deck beneath mine. They sleep in bunk beds. The boiler room is nearby and that's where they play and exercise. I usually view them there. They're pale from lack of sunlight and haggard-looking, but they seem to be enjoying their respite and have been a bit cheerier every day.

There are fifteen of them, mostly boys, but some girls too. I never get to spend a lot of time with them and we don't talk much. But at least I can see that they're alive and being taken care of. For however long I might last.

It's been nine or ten days since Barnes made his offer. Part of me wishes I'd accepted. I was telling the truth when

I said I didn't have any friends among the Angels. That was the advantage of keeping my distance. I could have sold them out, walked away a free girl, put this episode behind me and tried to forget about the Board and my treachery.

But, as bad as things get, I never really regret telling Barnes to get stuffed. I don't want to see out the rest of my days as a Judas, especially given the fact that I might live for a few thousand years. There are some things you can never forget or forgive yourself for.

Mind you, I won't have to worry about thousands of years in my current state. I've taken several severe hammerings over the last week. I'm getting sluggish. I can't move as swiftly as I did, or react as sharply as I could at my peak. I'm running on willpower alone these days. If it wasn't for the children, I'd give up the ghost. But I've got to buy them as much time as I can. A few days won't make any difference to me, but it might to them.

I watch the children running round the boiler room, smiling softly to myself as they play hide-and-seek. I wish the guards would leave me here for an hour or two, but they never allow me more than a few minutes, just enough time to do a head count and satisfy myself that they're all as well as they can be given the wretched circumstances.

"Aren't they wonderful?" someone murmurs behind me.

I glance over my shoulder and my smile disappears. It's Dan-Dan. He's wearing a fireman's outfit today. It doesn't fit him any better than his sailor's costume.

"Why don't you get clothes the right size?" I growl. "Nobody wants to look at your belly."

"*I* like looking at it," he giggles. "And I like my tight clothes. They feel much better when they're cutting into me."

He moves forward, careful not to get too close. My arms are tied behind my back and my ankles are shackled together, but I still pose a threat and Dan-Dan is all too aware of it. Keeping a safe distance, he stops at a railing and studies the children.

"I miss them so much," he sighs. "You have no idea how lonely and scared I get when I'm by myself. I never have nightmares when I torture and kill. And the nightmares are so terrifying..."

"Stop," I whimper. "You'll make me cry."

"I don't expect you to understand," he says. "Hardly anyone does. All I can tell you is that I bitterly regret the day I let you convince me to stop killing in order to watch you fight. The fighting bores me now."

"It doesn't bore the others," I note.

"Not yet," he concedes. "But their interest will wane soon, as mine has. They'll discard you like a dull blade once Barnes returns with fresh, intelligent zombies. Even if he can't find any, I don't think you'll enjoy their favor much longer. They're tired of your face. Nobody likes watching the same person triumph all the time. We only endure your victories because they'll make your ultimate defeat so much sweeter when it comes."

"Maybe I won't lose. Maybe I'll win every time, go on for years. What do you think of that, Fireman Dan?"

Dan-Dan shakes his head and smirks. "We can all see that you're close to the end. It's been fascinating, watching your energy ebb away. Educational too. We never knew a zombie could be worn down like one of the living. We've learned a lot by studying you. I think we'll push your replacements less strenuously, make them last longer."

Dan-Dan turns and stands with his back to the railing. "By the way, they won't let you die in the arena. When you reach the stage where you can't fight any longer, they're going to hand you over to me."

"What are you talking about?" I snap.

"I told them I couldn't bear it," he giggles. "Said I was going mad, not being able to kill. I demanded access to my darlings. To keep me quiet, they've offered you to me instead of the children. When you run out of steam, the guards will drag you out of there before you're killed. They'll tie you up neatly and deliver you to my personal quarters. I have so many things I want to share with you before the end."

"You won't get your filthy hands on me," I snarl. "I'll let the zombies kill me first."

"You think so?" Dan-Dan grins. "It won't be easy. If they could slit your throat open and finish you off that way, you might stand a chance. But they have to dig through your skull and tear out your brain, chunk by chunky chunk. That takes time. We'll shoot them before they rip you apart. Vicky and Luca will save you. For me."

Dan-Dan's grin fades and he takes a step closer. "You probably think you know pain intimately. But let me tell you, little girl, you don't. I'm going to put you through a whole new universe of torment before I grant you blessed release. I'm in no rush, and you can take so much more than any of my darlings. I might keep you writhing around on a leash for weeks. Imagine that, weeks of delirious suffering, where every moment is agony redefined and writ large."

"Screw you," I moan.

Dan-Dan smiles again. "No," he says breezily. "You're the one who's screwed. I'm looking forward to working with you more closely, Becky. You will be my masterpiece. The one to whom I reveal the true, unfathomable depths of my twisted fury. When I set to work on you, the results might shock even me.

"Cheerio, *mon cherie!*"

With a sick chuckle, he slides past and exits, leaving me in the boiler room with his darlings. Their excited cries as they search for each other don't sound quite so cheery now. In fact they sound eerily like the screams of the damned.

EIGHTEEN

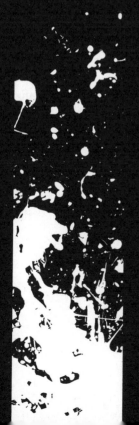

I'm led into the arena for another grueling bout. I keep hoping that the guards will grow careless. I've gone along with them meekly each time, acting as if my spirits have been crushed, obeying their every command, eager to please. Praying that they might stop regarding me as a threat. All I need is a small slip, a glimmer of a chance.

But so far they've followed their guidelines impeccably. They truss me up expertly, slip a collar round my neck and check the steel lead a few times before forcing me out of the mess. There are always extra guards around, guns cocked and aimed, ready to cut me down if I revolt.

"Here's our girl," Dan-Dan chortles as I'm guided in. He's back in his sailor's costume. The other zombies are already in place, still held captive by their guards. They always release us at the same time, so they can exit together.

"How have you been, my dear?" Lady Jemima asks, faking concern. "You were struck a nasty blow last time. We were worried about you."

"I'm fine," I mutter, trying to ignore the throbbing at the back of my head where I was clubbed in my previous fight.

"You don't look too lively," Justin says critically. "Perhaps you'd like to sit this one out? We can send you back to the mess if you'd prefer."

I'd love a good rest but I'm wary. I don't think I'll be returned to the mess if they judge me too weary to fight. Once they reckon I've run out of steam, I figure I'll be delivered straight to Dan-Dan's quarters.

"Nothing wrong with me," I sniff. "I'm all fired up and raring to go."

"Very well," Justin smiles. "Release the beasts."

Our handlers Taser us, set us free and retreat. Once I've recovered from the shock, I roll my arms around, limbering up, and check out my latest batch of opponents as they surge towards the glass and paw at the panels, trying to break through to the six smug humans on the other side.

There are seven zombies, five men and two women. Each

looks like they had plenty of experience fighting when they were alive. One of the women is wearing a karate outfit. She must have been training or taking part in a competition when she was attacked.

I've faced all sorts of opponents here, but most have been bruisers like this lot, especially in recent battles. The Board is pushing me to my limits, waiting for me to break.

"I bet she comes undone this time," Lady Jemima says as she studies the muscles on the two zombies closest to her.

"How much?" The Prince asks.

"This," she says, flashing a diamond ring at him.

"Nice," The Prince whistles. "If you throw in the rest of the rings on that hand, I'll wager my crown."

"Done," Lady Jemima smirks.

"I didn't think you would risk so treasured a possession," Vicky Wedge notes.

The Prince shrugs. "There will be plenty of crowns to choose from when the world is ours."

I decide to get things under way. I move forward wearily and make a nuisance of myself, angering the zombies, luring them away from the glass, focusing their attention on me.

We begin our waltz of death. Once they're riled up, I manipulate every last section of the arena, buzzing around like a fly, grabbing poles and whipping myself into the air, utilizing the walls and ceiling as much as the floor. I know this area inside out and I use that knowledge to my advantage.

I jump and grab hold of one of the overhead pipes as two of the men charge towards me. From that position I can lash out at both of them at the same time with my feet.

A couple of poles are set close together in one zone. I grab the woman in the karate outfit and propel her towards them, then angle her head down and ram it between the poles, jamming her in place. I leave her there, stuck, to finish off at the end when I'm done with the others.

I barge one of the men into a wall at a point that I've identified as a possible weak spot. The steel panel always shakes when someone is thrown against it. I keep hoping that it will tear loose completely one day, but no joy so far. Today it rattles as usual but holds.

The members of the Board keep up a running commentary. They're sipping champagne, casually discussing the battle, their plans for the future, what they fancy for dinner. They're a boring, self-obsessed lot. I'd rather total silence, but I can't tell them that or they'd talk all the louder just to spite me.

The other female zombie snags the hole in my chest with her fingerbones and tears five nasty channels through the flesh down towards my belly button.

"Yowzers!" Dan-Dan howls happily as I roar with pain.

"That's got to hurt," Lord Luca chuckles.

I kick the woman away and flee to the far side of the arena,

gritting my teeth. I quickly examine the wounds to make sure no guts are spilling out. Then I leap over the head of one of the onrushing men. But I don't get as much height as I thought I would. He clips my legs and drags me to the ground, then bellows and smashes a fist at my face. The bones jutting out of his fingers glint in the light. If he connects, it's game over and at least I won't have to worry about ending up in the clutches of Dan-Dan.

But it's impossible to lie still and let myself be killed. My defenses kick in automatically. I knock the man's hand aside and twist my head in the opposite direction. His fist slams into the floor and instead of breaking my skull, he breaks a few of the bones in his fingers.

I scramble to my feet and stagger away from the other reviveds, who are all closing in on me, except for the trapped woman. A long strip of ductwork runs the length of what was once the dining hall. I jump and haul myself up, wedging myself between the ducts and the ceiling. There's just enough space for me. I've squeezed in here before when I've needed a rest.

The zombies punch the base and sides of the ductwork, trying to grab hold and pull me down. But they can't get at me, except to scratch the sides of my arms and legs. If a few of them climbed up, the frame would come crashing to the floor, leaving me at the mercy of my foes. But thankfully they aren't smart enough to work that out.

"No fair," Dan-Dan shouts, slapping the glass. "I hate it when she does that. Why can't we take those ducts out of there?"

"Now now," Justin tuts. "We have to give her a reasonable chance. It's more fun this way. She can't stay up there forever."

I've tried crawling through the ducts at either end, but both exits have been sealed. Still, when I'm up here, I usually creep to one end or the other to hurl a few blows at the bolted-on steel plates, just in case there's any give.

I start pulling myself along like an injured snake. The zombies follow beneath me, scraping at the ductwork, gurgling furiously. I wonder if they hate me more than the humans, if they see me as a traitor to the undead cause.

As I'm mulling that over and trying to tune out Dan-Dan's jeers, the sound of gunfire echoes down from the deck above. Nobody takes any notice of it at first. The guards on the upper deck often fire at passing zombies, or even at corpses floating down the river, for practice. But this time it doesn't stop after a few seconds as it normally does. It's sustained. Then, moments later, mingled in with the gunfire, I hear what might just be the sweetest noise ever.

Human screams.

The lords and ladies of the Board have fallen silent. They're staring at the open doorway on their side of the glass divide, heads cocked, jaws slack. They don't look like the masters and mistresses of the universe anymore.

The zombies keep slapping at the duct, unaware of the change of play. I ignore them and stare at the doorway along with the living.

A guard spills into the narrow corridor, falls over, then clambers to his feet, His face is contorted with terror. "We're under attack!" he shouts.

"Who the hell dares attack us?" Justin barks, recovering his power of speech. "Is it the army?"

The guard shakes his head. "Zombies, I think. But we're not sure. They came from the river. They've swarmed the deck. I don't think we can hold for long."

Justin curses foully, then draws a gun and shoots the startled guard through the middle of his forehead.

"Why did you do that?" The Prince shrieks.

"I don't spare messengers when they bring bad news," Justin growls, then hops over the dead guard and into the corridor beyond.

The Prince stares at the corpse. There's another extended blast of gunfire overhead. He flinches, then hurries after Justin. Vicky, Lord Luca and Dan-Dan scramble after the first pair of deserters. Lady Jemima just sinks to the floor and covers her head with her hands. She starts moaning, "No, no, no. This wasn't part of the plan. It can't happen like this. I won't let it. This is *our* world."

Dan-Dan pauses in the doorway as the others flee. He looks back at me. I'm stunned to see him smirking. "Isn't this exciting?" he coos.

"Run, run as fast you can, fat boy," I snarl. "But it won't make any difference. You're history."

Dan-Dan snorts. "I think not, little girl. I have more lives than a cat. See you later, alligator."

"It'll be sooner than you'd like, crocodile."

Dan-Dan winks. "I'll be looking forward to the day."

He skips out, laughing, leaving me to fend off the zombies and wait for whoever or whatever is coming.

NINETEEN

My gut instinct is that Mr. Dowling and his mutants are orchestrating the attack. They set me free from prison once before when all seemed lost, and came to my rescue in Leicester Square when it looked like my goose was cooked. They're making a habit of saving my sorry neck from the chop. Long may it continue! I just hope they don't decide to kill me this time. Mr. Dowling has shown mercy previously for some unknowable reason, but there's no telling which way the demented clown will blow when the wind changes direction.

I hang tight to the duct and wait for the mutants or their master to find me. I'm hoping creepy Owl Man isn't with them. Then the door opens and a familiar figure bursts into the room and I realize my gut was just about as wrong as wrong can be.

"Rage!" I yell, for once with delight instead of contempt.

Rage squints at me. "What are you doing up there?"

"This is what I do for kicks," I growl. "Now quit gaping and help me, will you?"

"Wait a minute," Rage says, and steps outside. "She's here," he hollers, then returns and lays into the zombies.

As Rage shoves the zombies away from me and starts cracking their heads open, Dr. Oystein comes running into the room. "B!" he cries, hurrying to where I'm hanging. He offers me his hand and helps me down.

"Nice to see you, doc," I mutter.

"You too," he says politely, then embraces me with a surprisingly strong bear hug. "I thought we had lost you forever."

"You don't get rid of me that easily," I chuckle, and hug him in return, burying my face in his chest, wishing I could cry so that I could blink back tears.

The twins race into the room as Dr. Oystein releases me. They're dripping wet but they look ecstatic.

"We've taken control of the deck," Cian cheers.

"Some of the guards are still fighting, but we have them trapped," Awnya says.

"Master Zhang has started a sweep of the lower decks," Cian adds. "He says you should be cautious until he is certain the ship is ours."

"There are children on the deck below this," I tell the twins. "Make sure nobody hurts them. They were being held captive."

"We know all about the children," Dr. Oystein calms me. "We will take good care of them and escort them back to County Hall when we have concluded our business here."

"How did you find me?" I ask. "How did you board the ship? Where—"

A scream stops me short. I look up. An Angel has entered the viewing area on the other side of the glass. It's Ingrid, the Angel I went on my very first ever mission with. Lady Jemima is backing away from her, eyes wide, shaking her head wildly.

"Who's this?" Ingrid asks me.

"A bitch who needs putting down," I growl.

"Glad to be of service," Ingrid grunts, and closes in on the whimpering Lady Jemima. The human shuts her eyes and starts to pray, but why would God heed the prayers of a she-devil? Moments later it's all over as far as Lady J is concerned.

I push myself away from Dr. Oystein. "There were five others. They dressed differently from the guards. Have you seen them?"

"I saw one on the deck," Dr. Oystein replies. "He was dressed like a prince. He tried to make the gangway. He did not get very far."

"I spotted a few heading down the stairs," Rage says, pausing to address me over the heads of the zombies. "One was dressed like a sailor."

"Dan-Dan," I growl, and start for the door.

"B," Dr. Oystein calls me back. "There are plenty of us onboard. We can handle this. You look drained and battered. You should rest."

"I'll rest when those bastards are dead." I grimace and flash the doc an apologetic smile. "Sorry. I didn't mean to snap. But I need to do this. I want to make them pay for what they did to me."

"I understand," the doctor says, returning my smile. "Good luck, B."

"If you wait a minute, I can come with you," Rage says, knocking another of the zombies to the floor.

"It's okay," I tell him. "This is something I'd rather do by myself."

"Always the loner," Rage laughs, bashing the heads of two more zombies together.

I want to respond to that but there isn't time. I'm worried that Dan-Dan and the rest of them might slip the net. Waving briefly to the doc and Rage, I slide out of the arena, a free girl for the first time since I came to this stinking cruiser, and head off in search of my captors. The tables have turned and I plan to put them through a whole heap of hurt before I break their rotten necks and rid this world of their unholy, stinking presence.

TWENTY

I hurry to the nearest set of stairs and practically throw myself down to the deck beneath. I pause and sniff the air. I can smell the children but no one from the Board. Of course my nose isn't infallible. If they raced fore or aft, I wouldn't be able to sniff them out from here. But I'm guessing they delved farther into the bowels of the ship.

I carry on down to the next level. Gunfire starts afresh as I'm looking around. Screams. Master Zhang and his Angels must have found more guards. If the members of the Board are with them, they're finished. I just have to hope that they pressed on. If not, I'll find their corpses later and vomit over them to demonstrate my disgust.

Down another flight of stairs. The engine room is on this floor. I can't smell anything, but as I'm standing at the base of the stairs, weighing up my options, I hear a clanging noise. I move ahead cautiously, not getting my hopes up. There are all sorts of people on the old cruiser, crew members, guards, zombies, Angels. There's no guarantee that one of the louses of the Board made the noise.

More gunfire overhead helps mask the sound of my footsteps. I come to the engine room and let myself in. The place is filled with banks of dials and switches. I've no idea what any of them do and I don't care. All that matters to me is the smell in the air, familiar and sweeter the closer I draw.

I hear them before I see them. Lord Luca is muttering angrily. "I told you we should have stuck with Justin and Vicky. It was madness branching off on our own."

"They're the mad ones," Dan-Dan replies merrily, as if he hadn't a care in the world. "It was crazy, pushing on. We don't know how fast the zombies can move. I wouldn't want to get into a race with them. Better to get out of here as swiftly as we can."

"But how?" Lord Luca shouts. "I don't know which button we're supposed to press. I wasn't paying attention when they showed us. There were so many escape routes and options, I can't remember them all."

"You never did have the keenest attention span," Dan-Dan laughs.

"I don't see you doing any better, genius," Lord Luca snaps.

I round a bank of dials and come in view of the pair. Lord Luca is standing before a wall of switches, desperately flicking every one that he can. Dan-Dan is standing behind him, giggling.

"Having fun, boys?" I murmur.

Their heads snap round. Lord Luca yelps and throws switches faster than before. Dan-Dan tips his hat at me and says, "I didn't expect you to catch up with me this quickly."

"I don't believe in wasting time," I grin, taking a step towards them, savoring the moment, wanting to make it last.

"We can pay you!" Lord Luca shrieks. "We'll give you anything you want!"

"There's only one thing she wants," Dan-Dan chuckles, then grabs his brother by the arm and spins him towards me.

"No!" Lord Luca cries as he crashes to the floor in front of me. "What are you doing? Help me, fool!"

"You're the fool," Dan-Dan gurgles, rubbing his hairy belly, picking a crumb from it and placing it delicately on his outstretched tongue. "I never did like you, Luca. You were weak and scatter-brained like Mother. Father always said he only kept you around in case he ever needed an organ transplant. Poor Papa was always worried about his kidneys and heart."

Lord Luca gapes with disbelief at his grotesque brother, then gulps and stares up at me. His look of fear fades, to be replaced by one of calm resignation. "Is there any point begging for mercy?" he asks.

501

"No," I tell him, then grab the sides of his head and lower my mouth. I lick his forehead and rub my nose across it. He whimpers, fear creeping back across his expression again. Then I bite into his skull and gnaw through the bone into the brain beneath. I'd like to make it last longer, but I'm anxious to move on to Dan-Dan.

When Lord Luca stops moaning and struggling, I let his body drop and face Dan-Dan, wiping bits of his brother's brain from my lips. To my surprise, the child-killer is crying.

"It's silly, isn't it?" Dan-Dan weeps. "I cried when Mother died too, even though I threw her to the zombies, just as I've thrown Luca to you. I'm too soft for this cruel world."

"You won't have to worry about it for much longer," I chuckle grimly.

He squints at me. "You really are a beautifully fearsome creature. I'm sorry I didn't get a chance to go to work on you. There's so much more to you than any of my darlings. The sweet torments I could have put you through..."

"Sorry to disappoint you," I hiss.

"No need to apologize," he smiles. "You were simply doing what you had to. I don't hold it against you. I'm not one to bear a grudge."

"Well, the bad news is, I am." I flex my fingers and advance. "I'm gonna hurt you, Dan-Dan. It won't be quick like it was for Luca. You promised me a universe of pain. Well, you're gonna reap what you planned to sow. For what you did to me and the children, I'm going to make it long and slow and painful."

Dan-Dan shakes his head. "I don't think so. You might want to torture me but you haven't the stomach for it. Few people have. I'm gifted. Emotions never got between me and my desires. I've always had the power to do whatever I wished.

"I'm going to miss you, Becky," he says. "What I wouldn't give to pinch your clammy cheek and kiss you good night as I put you to sleep forever. That time will come, I'm sure, but the days will be long and lonely without you until then."

"Don't worry," I tell him. "You'll have plenty of company in Hell while you're waiting for me."

"Oh, I'm not going to Hell just yet," Dan-Dan says brightly. "My brother was feather-headed. I was toying with him before you arrived. I wanted him to sweat. I always loved to wind up Luca. But I have a very good memory and I pay attention to the smallest of details. So, without further ado..."

Dan-Dan reaches up and presses a switch. The wall behind him explodes. I cry out – with my sensitive hearing it's as if someone has struck a large bell with a hammer by the side of my head – and turn away instinctively. When the worst of the pain passes and I look again, Dan-Dan has leapt through a gaping hole in the side of the cruiser.

"Son of a bitch!" I roar, darting after him. I get to the hole, almost jump, but pull up short, not willing to throw myself into the great unknown. Instead, once I have control of myself again, I study the river beneath me.

504

Dan-Dan has landed in the water and is swimming towards a speedboat moored nearby. I think about jumping after him, but he has too great a lead on me. Reaching the boat, he climbs into it, starts the engine, waves nonchalantly at me, then powers away along the Thames, heading west.

"James bloody Bond," I snarl. Then I laugh with grudging admiration. I hate that child-killing monster, but I have to admit he knows how to make a cool getaway.

As I watch Dan-Dan disappear into the sunset (well, it's not long after midday, but he's earned a bit of poetic license), another chunk of the hull blows outwards and Justin Bazini and Vicky Wedge throw themselves into the river and make for a speedboat of their own. Now that I look closely, I realize there are several more tied to the ship. The lords and ladies of the Board had obviously planned for an invasion like this. I bet they never told the guards about the secret escape hatches. They wouldn't have considered their underlings worth saving.

Turning my back on the hole, I send a silent promise after Dan-Dan and the others. *We'll meet again, my wretched* darlings, *and you won't get away from me so easily next time.*

Then, still wincing from the noise of the explosion, I retrace my steps and head back up the stairs to see what's going on and discover how the Angels found me.

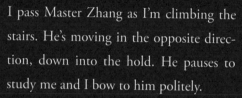

TWENTY-ONE

I pass Master Zhang as I'm climbing the stairs. He's moving in the opposite direction, down into the hold. He pauses to study me and I bow to him politely.

"You have been in the wars," he notes.

"They made me fight several times every day," I tell him.

He grunts. "The fact that you survived this long proves that you were concentrating during your lessons." Then he pushes on. I allow myself a wry chuckle. Master Zhang isn't a man to go wild with compliments.

I make my weary way to the arena. It's all quiet on the upper deck now. I want to run up there, get out of this prison as soon as I can. But Dr. Oystein is waiting for me in the old dining hall. Answers first, release later.

When I get to the arena, I see that the doctor isn't the only one waiting for me. All of the Angels from my room are present, Ashtat, Carl, Shane, Jakob. Rage and the twins have hung around. Plus there's one more addition, but this guy isn't so welcome.

"*Barnes!*" I bellow, charging towards him, fingers tightening, meaning to do all the things to him that I can't do to the departed Dan-Dan.

Carl and Shane slide together to block my path.

"Easy," Carl says.

"He's on our side," Shane says.

"Never," I bark. "He only looks out for himself."

I try to push through. Carl and Shane shove me back. I get ready to fight.

"It's true, B," Dr. Oystein says softly. "He came to us at County Hall, told us what was happening here, led us to you."

I stop struggling. If I could, I'd blink like an owl. Carl and Shane move apart. Barnes is standing directly ahead of me. He's taken the bullet from behind his ear and is tapping his front teeth with it. He raises an eyebrow when he spots my fingers clenching and unclenching.

"It's a real pisser when you don't know whether to thank a guy or spit in his eye, isn't it?" he smirks.

"I can't really spit these days," I growl, "but I'll never thank you either. What for—capturing me, enslaving me, bringing me here for Dan-Dan and the others to toy with?"

Barnes shrugs. "As I told you before, our choices are sometimes limited. I have a son, Stuart, who means everything to me. He survived the attacks and was staying in a compound in the countryside. He was relatively safe there, but the compounds are no guarantee of long-term security. Several have fallen and others will too. When you're landlocked, you're always open to attack.

"I carried on hunting after my first run-in with you," he continues. "I made sure the zombies I killed weren't conscious, but otherwise it was business as normal. The members of the Board heard about me. They invited me to come visit. I was curious, so I paid them a call. They wanted to employ me to find new gladiators for them. But they weren't interested in ordinary zombies. They'd heard rumors that I'd met one who could talk."

"How did they hear about that?" I sneer.

"I never discussed it with anyone," Barnes said, "but Coley and the others who were with us that day did. The stories intrigued the Board. They offered me a king's ransom to deliver you to them."

"And you jumped at the chance."

Barnes sniffs. "I never cared about money. I couldn't be bought that way. But every man has his price. Mine was the safety of my son." He sighs and sticks the bullet back behind his ear. "They offered Stuart a place on one of the islands that is free of zombies. I tried getting him onto one of those before, but it's virtually impossible to gain access. Justin and his cronies operate several islands. If I agreed to work for them, they promised to ship out Stuart. I didn't even have to think about it."

I glare at the hunter, still wanting to hate him, but finding myself thawing. If he's telling the truth, I understand. In his position I'd have done the same.

"So why the change of heart?" I scowl. "Why play the hero now after serving the scumbags for so long?"

"The children," Barnes says softly. "I didn't know about them until they let me in here to watch you fight. A zombie's one thing, even a conscious one like you. But a live child...As I said, my son means more to me than anything. But there are lines no man should ever allow himself to cross. I couldn't turn a blind eye to what Dan-Dan was doing to the children. As far as we've fallen, I don't ever want to fall that far."

"We will do all that we can to safeguard your son's future," Dr. Oystein says. "Zhang will scour every inch of this ship in search of the Board members. Two have already been dealt with. If the others are still alive, we will find them. They will not be able to harm your boy once we have dealt with them."

"Be careful what you promise, doc," I mutter. "I killed Lord Luca but the others got away. They had escape hatches in the hull that they were able to blow open. There were speedboats moored to the cruiser. Justin, Vicky and Dan-Dan all made it to freedom."

Barnes's face whitens. He starts to tremble, then stops himself. "I have to go," he tells Dr. Oystein.

"You can stay with us if you wish," Dr. Oystein says. "We can hunt for them together."

Barnes shakes his head. "I don't know where they'll go. But I know where my son is. I'll try to get to the island and rescue him before it occurs to them to order his execution. They might not even be aware of my treachery. They weren't on deck when we boarded. I might have time to play with."

"I wish you luck," the doctor says.

"Thanks." Barnes grimaces. "I'm going to need it." The hunter faces me and tries to think of something to say. In the end he simply shrugs. "Like I said to you once before, it won't mean anything, I'm sure, but I'm sorry."

"Me too," I mumble. "By the way" – I stop him before he leaves – "where's Coley?"

Barnes manages a weak grin. "He never would have gone for this. He didn't care about the children. I knocked him out and tied him up before I went to County Hall. I'll swing by and free him before setting off for the island. It's the end of our partnership, but I owe him that much."

"Was he the one you were talking about the last time you came to see me?" I ask. "When you said it was hard having to sacrifice someone you care about?"

"No," Barnes smiles, warmly this time. "I was talking about *you*."

As I stare at him, he flips me a quick salute, then hurries out of the arena and heads off to try to save the one person in the world he truly loves, the boy whose life he risked in order to do what was right.

Barnes did something heroic and noble today. But if his son is killed as a result, he'll feel like the most miserable man alive. Everyone knows this isn't a world of black and white, but it's not a world of gray either. It's a world of hellish, soul-tormenting red, and Barnes is adrift on that choppy, bloodstained sea the same as the rest of us. I hope the ex-soldier finds his son and enjoys a bit of peace before his number is called.

But I wouldn't bet on it.

TWENTY-TWO

"We should get you back home as soon as possible," Dr. Oystein says. "You need to spend a few weeks in a Groove Tube."

"I've been in there a lot recently," I sigh. "One mauling after another. I must be the most unfortunate girl in the world."

"Some might think otherwise," the doc murmurs. "If you had not been captured and forced to fight, and if you had not determined the conditions under which you would compete, how many children would Daniel Wood have killed? Some might say you are a hero."

I snort. "A zombie can't be a hero. We're monsters."

Dr. Oystein smiles. "Then all I can say is that I wish there were more monsters like you in the world."

We beam at each other. Then I shake my head before things get too mawkish. "So how did it go down? Barnes came to you, told you what was happening and led you here?"

"In a nutshell, yes. He spotted the twins while they were gathering supplies. He approached them, explained the situation and asked for their help. They escorted him back to County Hall."

"That's why Dr. Oystein let us come on this mission," Cian says proudly. He looks like the cat that not only got the cream but a mouse-flavored stick to stir it with. "If not for us, Barnes might never have found his way to County Hall, certainly not in time to save you."

"We begged the doctor and Master Zhang to let us tag along and they agreed in the end," Awnya says.

"I wouldn't say that we *begged*," Cian grumbles.

"Why are you guys soaked to the skin?" I ask.

"We were part of the river team," Awnya says.

"Most of us were," Carl adds.

Now that I look closely, I see that all of the Angels in the room are wet, except for Dr. Oystein and Rage.

"We could not attack from land," Ashtat explains. "The guards on deck had the surrounding area covered. They would have torn us to pieces with their rifles before we could close the gap."

"The doc and I came back with Barnes," Rage says. "He tied us up, loose knots that we could wriggle out of. Pretended to the guards that he'd captured us."

"We came at a time when he knew the Board would be watching you fight," Dr. Oystein says. "We hoped to swoop on them when they were together, for the sake of Barnes's son."

"While the guards were ogling the doctor and Rage," Carl says, "the rest of us scaled the far side of the cruiser. We'd swum here earlier in the day and were waiting just beneath the surface of the water."

"We plugged our ears and noses and kept our mouths shut," Cian says. "Bobbed about there for more than an hour. It was cool!"

"I spotted a couple of speedboats while we were climbing," Jakob says softly. "I thought that was how the humans got to and from the ship. If I'd guessed they were for getaways, I would have torn holes in their hulls and sunk them."

"How many of you came?" I ask.

"Most of the Angels," Ashtat says.

"Every single Angel volunteered," Shane says.

"I wasn't going to," Rage sniffs, "but I didn't want to be the odd one out. Would have looked bad."

"You're all heart," I grunt.

"We left some behind to take care of the place," Carl says. "Otherwise we're all here."

"For *you*," Dr. Oystein whispers.

I shrug. "What do you want me to do? Go round and thank everyone in person?"

"It wouldn't be a bad start," Rage growls.

"Well, don't worry," I laugh. "I was planning to do just that. I might even hug a few of you beautiful buggers while I'm at it."

"You see, B?" Dr. Oystein says with a justified smile. "You cannot be a true loner when you have so many people who love you."

"*Love?*" I ask, arching an eyebrow at Rage.

Dr. Oystein purses his lips. "Well, maybe that is not *quite* the right word."

"You don't have to hammer it home," I tell him. "I was wrong. I acted like an idiot. I'm sorry. I won't cut myself off from the rest of you again. I understand how lucky I am to have you guys on my side and I won't look to go it alone anymore. Now, high fives!"

And, like some overexcited kid after winning a cup final, I go around high-fiving everyone in the room, Dr. Oystein, the twins, Carl, Jakob, Ashtat, Shane, even a cynically grinning Rage. And I don't feel the least bit embarrassed, because I'm not in the company of roommates, colleagues or allies.

I'm with friends.

To be continued…

ONE

I'm in Timothy's gallery, the Old Truman Brewery, on Brick Lane. It's quiet and cool. Daylight filters through the cracks in the boards covering the windows.

The last thing Timothy asked, before he was killed by a mob of zombies, was that I take care of his paintings. He thought he had been given a commission by God, that it was his duty to record the downfall of London, so that future generations could study his pictures of this terrible time and learn from them.

Timothy was mad as a hatter but he was a nice guy. I feel like I owe him, since I was the one who set free the grisly baby who called the zombies down upon him, so I've come here several times since he died, to dump the food he had stocked up, wash the bloodstains from the floor and generally make sure that everything is in order.

There are hundreds of paintings stacked against the walls, spread throughout the various rooms. Some are hanging too. I rotate the pictures on display whenever I come, swapping them round, choosing new examples from the many on offer. I think Timothy would have liked that.

I'm holding one of the paintings, studying it critically, trying to decide whether or not it deserves a spot on the wall. It's a painting of a zombie tucking into the skull of a dead woman. It must have been dangerous for Timothy, getting that close, but he was always reckless. Anything to get a good angle.

A wildflower sprouts from a crack in the pavement close to the dead woman's head. It's more brightly colored than the corpse or the zombie, its petals painted in glorious yellows and pinks. The flower makes this painting stand out, but at the same time it makes it look a bit arty-farty. I'm sure the flower was real – Timothy only painted what he saw – but because of the way he's highlighted it, it doesn't *look* real.

I know I'm being silly, hesitating like this. Nobody's going to pass through here anytime soon. I'm Timothy's only audience, and probably will continue to be for many years to come. It makes no difference whether I give this pride of place on a wall or jam it behind a load of other paintings.

Still, it matters to me. I never paid much attention to art when I was alive, but I've been getting into it since I settled in at County Hall. I've spent much of my free time scouring galleries and reading about the history of art. It's become an interesting hobby, a way of keeping boredom at bay when I'm not training with the other Angels.

I've no artistic talent, but arranging Timothy's paintings is a way for me to creatively express myself. So I study the painting with the flower one last time, forehead creased as if I'm attempting to crack a difficult puzzle. Finally I snort and return it to the pile, at least for the time being. I might grant it wall space in the future, but not today.

As I'm carefully slotting the painting back into place, there's a loud thumping sound on the staircase behind me.

I whirl and adopt a defensive position. I flex my fingers, getting ready to slash with the bones sticking out of them if I'm attacked. I don't have a heart, not since it was ripped from my chest, but my mind remembers what anxiety was like when I was alive, and I imagine the sound of my quickening heartbeat inside my head.

I don't call out. I don't move. I just stand silently and wait.

There's another thumping noise, this time closer to the top of the stairs. I grit my teeth and suppress a shiver. Zombies don't scare me. Nor do the living. But this could be Mr. Dowling, Owl Man or that nightmarish baby. Maybe it sniffed me out and returned to finish the job. It let me go when it was here before. Maybe it changed its mind and came back to send me the way of poor Timothy.

Another thump, this one almost at the very top stair. I frown. By now I should be able to see whoever is making the noise. But there's no sign of anyone.

The silence stretches out. Then someone moans my name.

"Beckyyyyyy…"

I growl softly and relax. "You think you're clever, don't you?"

"I don't think it," comes the cheerful response. "I know it!"

Then Rage stands up from where he had been lying on the stairs and grins at me. I shoot him the finger and go back to appraising the paintings, trying to act as if the annoying hulk isn't here, hiding my relief, not wanting him to know that he really did spook me. Admit to being scared? Not in this unlife! And definitely not to a cynical, bullying piece of trash like Rage. I'd rather claw out my own eyes than give that creep the satisfaction of knowing how close he'd come to making a dead girl shiver.

TWO

"Aren't you surprised to see me?" Rage asks when I continue to ignore him.

"Nothing about you surprises me," I sniff.

"Don't you want to know how I found you?" he presses.

"I'm guessing you followed me from County Hall."

Rage chuckles and scratches the hole in his left cheek where he was bitten by a zombie when he was turned. Wisps of green moss sprout from it, like the world's worst designer beard.

"Don't flatter yourself," Rage says. "I wouldn't waste my time following the likes of you."

"Yet here you are..." I purr.

"I'm not alone," he says. "My partner wanted to check this place out."

"What poor sap is lonely and desperate enough to hang out with you?" I sneer as someone else comes up the stairs behind Rage. Then I spot who it is and wince. "Mr. Burke. I'm sorry. I didn't mean to insult you."

Billy Burke waves away my apology. "If I'd known you were here, I wouldn't have disturbed you. But we were passing and I remembered you telling me about this place. I was keen to see the paintings. We can leave if you'd prefer to be alone."

"No, that's OK, come in. I'll give you the grand tour."

Burke used to be my biology teacher. He was the best we had in our school, one of the few teachers I respected. He also saw the real me long before I did. He told me I was heading down the same racist path as my dad, warned me that I needed to change. I ignored him. Back then I thought I knew myself better than anybody else did.

I've often wondered how things might have turned out if I'd listened to him. Maybe I wouldn't have thrown poor Tyler Bayor to the zombies. Maybe I'd have survived the zombie apocalypse. Maybe I wouldn't be spending my nights staring at the ceiling, thinking about the blood I have on my hands, wishing I was truly dead.

Burke hooked up with Dr. Oystein after London fell and worked as a spy in the underground complex where I was being held when I recovered my senses. That's where we met again. He convinced the soldiers to feed me brains to keep my senses intact. I'd be a mindless killer zombie if not for his help. He saw something in me worth fighting for. Even though I thought I was worthless, he didn't agree, and he did all that he could to save me and steer me right.

In an ideal world, if we were able to choose our parents, I'd pick Billy Burke for my father without a second's hesitation. Not that I'll ever tell him that, or even hint at it. I don't want him thinking I'm a soppy bugger.

I show Burke round the gallery. He's fascinated by the paintings, though he finds some of them hard to look at—the living are far more sensitive about these things than the undead. Rage is less impressed and keeps yawning behind Burke's back, trying to wind me up. I treat him with the contempt he deserves and don't even reward him with another flash of my finger.

"There are so many," Burke murmurs after a while, shaking his head at the piles of paintings resting against the walls. "He must have painted like a machine."

"Yeah," I nod. "It was his entire life. He knew his time would probably be cut short, so he crammed in as much as he could."

"Have you looked at them all?" Burke asks.

"Most of them, though there are still a few buried away in places that I haven't got to yet."

"And did he arrange the paintings on the walls or have you hung them?"

I fight a proud smile. "He hung a lot of them, but I've been switching them and alternating the display."

"Are you looking to get a job as a curator?" Rage asks sweetly.

"Get stuffed," I snap.

Burke makes a shushing gesture. "This collection is quite something, B," he says. "Thank you for sharing it with us."

"Any time," I tell him happily. "But what were you doing out this way in the first place? And with Rage, of all people."

"What's wrong with me?" Rage barks, taking a step towards me, his beady eyes glinting in the dim light.

"Easy," Burke soothes him. "I'd have thought that the pair of you would have settled your differences by now."

"It's hard to settle your differences with a guy who pushes you off the London Eye," I snarl.

Rage cackles. "You're not still sore about that, are you?"

"I'll return the favor sometime," I jeer. "See how long it takes you to forget."

Rage fakes a sigh and makes a wounded expression. "See how she baits me, sir? Some people just can't find forgiveness within themselves."

"Grow up, Michael," Burke says witheringly, using Rage's real name to show his annoyance. Then he stares at me. "I thought you fell off the Eye."

I wince, remembering I hadn't told anyone what really happened up there. It's no big secret. I just didn't want people thinking I was a snitch. I can deal with my own problems.

"That's right," I mumble. "I did fall."

Burke frowns and starts to ask a question. Then he shakes his head. "Not my business," he says, and goes back down the stairs. Rage scowls at me, then trails after Burke. I follow.

There's a cart on the ground floor, stacked high with folders and files. Burke nods at them. "That's why we were passing. I've been researching something. The records I'm interested in don't seem to have ever been transferred to computer, so I've had to track down hard copies. I finally found them in a building north of here. It's a place where a secretive branch of the army used to keep their paperwork, one of a number of hiding-holes scattered around the city. I got the addresses when I was working for Josh Massoglia and I've been checking them out. Most of the buildings have been gutted, but this one seems to have been overlooked. I spent a few days gathering the documents I was after and asked Rage to help me transport them back to County Hall, so that I could go through them in my spare time."

"You should have asked me," I frown. "I'd have helped."

"I know," Burke smiles. "But the files are heavy. I needed a brute with lots of muscles."

"And they don't come more brute than me," Rage says, puffing himself up.

"What are you looking for?" I ask.

"Probably nothing important," Burke says. "I just have an itch I need to scratch. You know what it's like when something bugs you and you can't let it drop?"

529

"Yeah. Do you want a hand going through the files?"

"It's kind of you to offer, but no, I'd rather do it myself. As I said, I doubt it's important, so I don't want to waste anybody's time other than my own."

"It'll take you months to plow through that lot," I note.

"No," he says. "I know what I'm looking for. I'll be able to skim through the pages pretty quickly. But maybe you can help push the cart. Rage was starting to struggle."

"No I wasn't," Rage shouts, then catches Burke's grin and relaxes.

Burke turns to leave, then spots a painting hanging on a nearby wall and stalls. It's one of the most disturbing pictures in the gallery. I gave it a wall to itself, even though it's not a large canvas.

The crazed clown, Mr. Dowling, dominates the painting. Timothy captured him in all his finery, the *v*-shaped gouges cut through the flesh of his face from his eyes down to his mouth, the pinstripe suit, severed faces pinned to his shoulders, lengths of gut wound round his arms, clumps of hair stapled to his skull.

Owl Man is nearby, with his potbelly, white hair, pale skin and those incredibly large eyes. There are also several mutants, with their rotting skin and yellow eyes, wearing hoodies.

Burke edges closer to the painting as if mesmerized. Rage stumbles after him, looking every bit as somber. The pair stop in front of it and stare in silence.

"Is that Mr. Dowling?" Rage asks.

"No," I grunt. "It's Santa Claus."

"I've heard him described, but I never thought…" Rage falls silent again.

"Do you believe Dr. Oystein now?" Burke asks softly. "When he says that Mr. Dowling is an agent of universal evil?"

Rage shifts uncomfortably. "Do you?" He throws the question back.

Burke breathes out slowly. "I still find it hard to believe in a God or Devil who would get personally involved in our affairs. But when I look at that, I wonder."

"You've met this guy a couple of times?" Rage asks, turning towards me.

"Yeah. Underground in the complex, and when he brought down a helicopter in Trafalgar Square."

"Is he as creepy in the flesh?"

"Way more," I say shortly.

"What about the freak with the eyes?" Rage asks.

"I just know him as Owl Man. Dr. Oystein knows his real name, but he –"

"What makes you think that?" Burke interrupts.

"He told me."

"Did he tell you what it was?" Burke asks.

"No. He said he preferred the name Owl Man and would call him that from now on."

Burke grunts. "I must quiz him when I get back. *Owl Man* is one of the people I'm hoping to learn more about in the files."

"Why?" Rage asks. "Do you want to send him a birthday card?"

We all laugh and the mood lightens.

"It's some world we live in, isn't it?" Burke sighs.

"Imagine if you'd had to dissect something like Mr. Dowling in a biology class," I giggle.

"Maybe I'll get a chance yet," Burke says, turning back towards the cart. Then he pauses thoughtfully and looks around. "Would you mind if I did some of my research here?"

I shrug. "If you want."

"I wouldn't be in your way?"

"No. I was about done. I can go get you a chair."

"That's OK. I'm used to doing it on my feet."

Rage and I smirk at the unintended joke.

"Will he be safe here?" Rage asks me.

"Should be. Timothy got along fine until that bloody baby started screeching. The windows are boarded over – I replaced most of the planks that were broken – and I've made sure all the doors are properly barred. But what about getting back to County Hall?"

"Thank you for your concern, but I *am* able to look after myself," Burke says with a hint of irritation. "I managed to negotiate the streets of London for months without any help before you two came along to nanny me."

"But it wouldn't hurt to have one of us with you, would it?" I ask him.

Burke grimaces. "I'm not a child. Now get the hell out of here before I revive the custom of detention."

Rage and I laugh. "OK," I tell my old teacher. "The key's in the door. Lock up after yourself and leave it under the stone out front."

"If you're not back by sunset, should we come looking for you?" Rage asks.

"Give it until sunset tomorrow," Burke tells him, eyeing the tower of files and folders. "I'm going to be here a while with that lot. I'll work late into the night, sleep in, then hit the pile again when I wake up. If I can get through it all, it will save us having to push the cart any farther. I worry about getting attacked out on the streets, going slowly with a load like that."

"There's no food, but the taps work," I tell him. "Or they did the last time I checked. We could bring you some grub and bottled water."

"A bit of fasting will do me no harm," Burke says, and shoos us out. He's grinning when he waves us off, but I catch him staring at the painting of Mr. Dowling as he shuts the door. His smile disappears as the shadow of the closing door sweeps across him, and sorrow and fear eclipse him in one smooth, sliding motion.

DARREN SHAN is the bestselling author of the young adult series Cirque Du Freak, The Demonata, and the Saga of Larten Crepsley, as well as the stand-alone book *The Thin Executioner*. Shan's books are sold on every continent and in thirty-one languages, and have been bestsellers in countries including the US, Britain, Ireland, the Netherlands, Norway, Hungary, Japan, Taiwan and the UAE. In total, they have sold over 25 million copies worldwide. Shan divides his time between his homes in Ireland and London.

Darren invites you to visit his website at darrenshan.com.